TAKEN THE STARS

ROAD OF VENGEANCE

J. N. CHANEY
RICK PARTLOW

LAS VEGAS, NV

Copyrighted Material

Road of Vengeance Copyright © 2024 by Variant Publications

Book design and layout copyright © 2024 by JN Chaney

This novel is a work of fiction. Names, characters, places, and incidents are either products of the author's imagination or used fictitiously. Any resemblance to actual events, locales, or persons, living, dead, or undead, is entirely coincidental.

All rights reserved

No part of this publication can be reproduced or transmitted in any form or by any means, electronic or mechanical, without permission in writing.

1st Edition

CONNECT WITH J.N. CHANEY

Don't miss out on these exclusive perks:

- Instant access to free short stories from series like *Backyard Starship*, *Sentenced to War*, and more.
- Receive email updates for new releases and other news.
- Get notified when we run special deals on books and audiobooks.

So, what are you waiting for? Enter your email address at the link below to stay in the loop.

https://www.jnchaney.com/taken-to-the-stars-subscribe

CONNECT WITH RICK PARTLOW

Check out his website
https://rickpartlow.com

Connect on Facebook
https://www.facebook.com/DutyHonorPlanet

Follow him on Amazon
https://www.amazon.com/Rick-Partlow/e/B00B1GNL4E/

JOIN THE CONVERSATION

Join the conversation and get updates on new and upcoming releases in the awesomely active **Facebook group**, "JN Chaney's Renegade Readers."

This is a hotspot where readers come together and share their lives and interests, discuss the series, and speak directly to J.N. Chaney and his co-authors.

facebook.com/groups/jnchaneyreaders

CONTENTS

Chapter 1	1
Chapter 2	11
Chapter 3	25
Chapter 4	41
Chapter 5	53
Chapter 6	65
Chapter 7	75
Chapter 8	89
Chapter 9	99
Chapter 10	109
Chapter 11	121
Chapter 12	133
Chapter 13	145
Chapter 14	159
Chapter 15	169
Chapter 16	181
Chapter 17	193
Chapter 18	203
Chapter 19	217
Chapter 20	229
Chapter 21	241
Chapter 22	255
Chapter 23	269
Chapter 24	281
Chapter 25	291
Chapter 26	301
Chapter 27	311
Chapter 28	321
Chapter 29	329
Chapter 30	341

Chapter 31	351
Chapter 32	363
Chapter 33	377
Connect with J.N. Chaney	385
Connect with Rick Partlow	387
About the Authors	389

1

"Come on, you apes! You wanna live forever?"

Breaking cover from behind the Bradley Armored Personnel Carrier, I rolled off to one side and charged across forty yards of open ground. Way more open than I was used to—I'd been to the stars, to dozens of different planets, but this was the first time I'd ever been to Colorado. The air was thinner here than Florida or Ohio, and even thinner than most of those alien planets. Forty pounds of gear dragged me down, my bound to cover taking a lot longer than the three to five seconds I'd been taught was the maximum an infantry soldier should be up and exposed to enemy fire.

I knew it, and so did the squad of Army Rangers following me across that stretch of bare sand and rock, and I could feel their judging stares on my back, but the only alternative to the burnt-out remains of the M1 Abrams tank at the edge of the ridge was a low berm reinforced with tangled roots…and that wasn't a real option. I'd hit a seven count before I slid in beside it, and that had to mean that the rest of the squad was a second or two behind me.

One fire team used the cover of the tank while the other threw themselves against the earthen berm beside it, their pulse rifles coming up with just a hint of awkwardness at the unfamiliar weight and feel of the new weapons. I had no such hindrance, so when the first of the pop-up targets swung into place out of the brush a hundred meters in front of us, I fired first.

I understood their discomfort because I'd felt it myself, not that long ago. Pulse rifles didn't recoil, though there was a hint of vibration from the ignition chamber when the thermal cartridges detonated to create the scalar pulse, kind of like the little noisemakers in the toy automatic rifles I'd played with as a kid. It created an atmosphere of unreality to firing the weapon and that, in turn, made it harder for them to take it seriously and keep a good follow-through. I'd already seen it at the zero range, and it wasn't a surprise to see it here in the live-fire course, too. The sounds and sights of the guns were unfamiliar to them as well, and I tried to see it through their eyes, hear it through their ears.

Rather than the *bang-crack* of an M-16, or M-4, or whatever they called it nowadays, the pulse rifles made more of a *snap-crackle-pop*, a static discharge nearly drowning out the ignition of the detonator rounds, and in turn itself drowned out by the thunderclap of air rushing in to fill the vacuum burned by the energy pulses. Flashes of white with ruby-red at the center, a combination of the scalar pulse itself and the plasma tunnel it dug through the atmosphere. It was colorful and visually impressive, a horizontal fireworks show that tore up a hell of a lot of sagebrush and took some chunks out of the sides of the targets, but my shots were the ones that hit center-mass, the feel and aim of the pulse rifle as natural as breathing after two years of using the weapons.

They missed. I didn't. Ten targets had popped up once we'd hit cover, and I knocked down six of them while the Ranger squad, nine soldiers in all, took nearly a hundred shots to take out the other four. Their fire trailed off, one or two still popping away at silhouettes already blown to smithereens, ablaze on the dirt before a bellowing baritone cut through the crackling fires and stray shots.

"Cease fire! Cease fire! EndEx, EndEx, EndEx!"

End Exercise. A phrase I knew well from ROTC and the National Guard, and the tone was also one I knew well from that time—pissed off colonel.

"Safeties on, Rangers!" the squad leader, a squat, leather-faced sergeant named Booker snapped, and I took a moment to make sure my own was engaged before using the rifle butt to push myself to my feet.

It felt weird wearing Army gear, mostly because of how much it had changed since I'd left Earth the first time. No more LBEs, the suspender-like straps that held magazine pouches and canteens and such. Now they had vests that did the same thing, and I couldn't even remember the term they used for them. Even the Kevlar helmet had changed, becoming lighter and smaller, which was a definite improvement. It also felt weird wearing a helmet that lacked a visor or a neck yoke and didn't provide an emergency air supply.

The angry baritone approached on long, deliberate strides, dragging with it a tall, lanky frame and a stern, hawk-nosed expression. Lieutenant-Colonel Andrew Chapman, West Point, veteran of multiple combat deployments to Iraq, Afghanistan, and Syria, Purple Heart, Bronze Star, and not a fan of yours truly.

"*Colonel* Travers," he growled, whether angrier at the results of the aborted live fire or the fact that I technically outranked him, I couldn't tell, "could I have a word with you?"

"Of course," I said, nodding as I followed him away from the rest of the platoon. I'd thought it would take more effort to keep myself from adding *sir* to the end of the reply, but after all this time, it came rather naturally. "What can I do for you?" I asked as he spun to face me.

The chill of an early spring morning kept me from sweating even with the combat load, and certainly nothing Chapman could do would accomplish what the weather couldn't, despite his glare of disapproval and my history with colonels.

"This is a waste of time," he hissed, eyes darting over to his men, showing that he was, at least, thinking far ahead enough to understand that it would be unwise to criticize me or his orders in front of them. "My Rangers train to doctrine, and this is *not* doctrine!"

He was used to looming over people and tried to do it to me, leaning forward and looking down his nose like I was a brand-new second lieutenant fresh out of Officer's Basic Course.

"You're right about that, Chapman," I agreed, and his nostrils flared at the casual use of his last name. "Your doctrine's going to need to change. This"—I held up the modified pulse rifle, down-shipped from the *Liberator* and equipped with the latest in US military optics and a new fore-stock with all kinds of weird slots in it that apparently accepted lights and lasers and all kinds of extraneous shit—"is *not* an M-16. It's not an AK-47, either. Your definition of *cover* vs. concealment is going to have to change."

"And does our doctrine now include a colonel leading a squad yelling 'come on, you apes, you wanna live forever,' sir?"

I looked around at the wry question, offering a grin to the infantry major who'd snuck up behind us.

"It's a battle cry with a long and distinguished history, Major Barnaby," I assured him. "And since I'm the only one of them who has any experience with the new weapons, I felt like I should be up front, showing them the way."

He looked familiar, a mix between my college best friend and my college girlfriend…because that was exactly what he was. Chuck Barnaby was the son of my old—now older than me—friend George and Jill Beck, who'd just broken up with me about the same time that I'd been abducted by an alien robot. Once upon a time, I might have held it against George that he'd taken up with my ex-girlfriend, but the reason I didn't care walked up behind Chuck.

She was the only one not wearing Army field utilities or carrying a rifle, though she *did* have a heavy pulse pistol holstered at her hip…and a couple of long knives in sheaths at her back. Laranna looked better in the tight brown and green vest and leggings that were the traditional warrior garb of the Strada. She drew a lot of stares, and not just from me, both because she was smoking hot...and because she was green, of course. That part didn't garner much attention off Earth, but it sure did here.

"Colonel Chapman," she said, and the older man looked at her sharply as if he was surprised that she spoke English...or maybe just that she wasn't a hallucination, "I wonder if you watched the footage of the battle in your capital city a few months ago? I'm fairly certain it was on all of your news services."

"Of course," Chapman stuttered. "Who didn't?"

"And once you were assigned to this unit"—I took up the thread, seeing where she was going with this—"you must have received an after-action review of the battle. Including how effective your issue weapons were against the Anguilar personal armor?"

The colonel scowled like he'd bitten into something sour.

"I did. Nothing short of a .50 machine gun could penetrate."

"*This* will," I assured him, holding the pulse rifle at port arms in front of me so he could get a good look at it. "And that means, it'll also blow right through a couple feet of soil." I nodded toward the low berm that had been the only notional cover before the tank and the ridge. "That's barely concealment. Yeah, we were up too long, exposed to fire, but I'd rather be up and moving for a couple seconds too long than a sitting target."

"Sitting behind one of those flamethrowers," Chapman countered, making a face at the rifle, "you might as well just stand up and wear a neon sign that says *shoot me*."

I laughed in agreement and let the weapon hang off its patrol sling.

"Yeah, the thermal and visual signature is pretty gnarly. But until and unless the R&D types at DARPA come up with something better, it's all we have." I cocked an eyebrow at him. "Just like I'm all *you* have."

"Well, lucky us." Chapman barked a cynical laugh. "We have a Goddamned twenty-seven-year-old bird colonel who last saw service in ROTC almost forty years ago! How can we lose?"

My smile faded at the volume of his words, at the heads turning from thirty yards away or so as the sentiment carried to some of the Rangers in the platoon we'd been running through the live-fire training. I was about to launch into an ass-chewing, which would have been damned satisfying to deliver to someone of his rank, but Chuck Barnaby stepped between us, his face as hard as my thoughts.

"Sir, you've seen combat, right?"

"You are very aware I have, Major," Chapman shot back, glaring at the younger officer, too young to be a major really.

"Nine-month tours, right? Three of them altogether, if I recall correctly. Tell me something, sir—in those tours, how many actual firefights did you get into? With people actually shooting at you?"

Chapman's jaw worked like he was chewing bullets and getting ready to spit them at Chuck. He didn't answer.

"I bet it was two, if I read your medals right," Chuck went on as if he didn't notice the colonel's mood. "Eighteen months, two firefights. Charlie, tell Colonel Chapman how many firefights you've had the last two years."

"I've lost count," I admitted. "Twenty, maybe?"

"How many enemy have you personally killed?" he pressed.

It was my turn to glare at him and not answer.

"Charlie Travers," Laranna interjected, putting a hand on my arm, "is the finest warrior I have met outside the Strada. He has taken the lives of dozens of Anguilar…and that is not counting the enemy ship he's destroyed behind the controls of a Vanguard."

"He's killed more people than cancer, Colonel Chapman," Chuck concluded. "He's seen combat on a scale that no American has since World War Two, without much of a break. You know what that can do to soldiers. You've seen it. But not him. What do you think that says about Colonel Travers?"

"It takes more than being a killer to lead," Chapman said mulishly, arms crossed. At least he'd lowered his voice again.

"Then consider," Laranna suggested, "that when Charlie took over as leader of the resistance, we controlled one planet—and that only because the Empire doesn't know of its location—with barely four thousand in our lightly armed and barely trained militia. Now, we have four, including my own homeworld, which has pledged ten thousand warriors, as well as a wing of starfighters and the two cruisers we captured for your people."

My ears burned, and I finally stepped in, not out of anger but embarrassment.

"And if all of that isn't enough," I told him, "and even if you don't believe I've earned or deserve this bird"—I tapped the rank insignia on my collar—"it's still official, and you still have your orders. Now, tell me, Colonel, do you want to command the first American military unit to operate offworld? Or do you want to keep arguing with me until I have to ask the President to have you replaced?"

The man's face had shifted, and for a moment, I felt bad, like I'd taken out my frustrations with senior Army officers on this particular colonel unjustly. But on the other hand, it was better to nip this in the bud. If this guy couldn't work with me, there was no point in wasting time holding his hand. I sighed and spread my hands.

"I'll promise you one thing," I told him. "Maybe it's not kosher for a nominal colonel, but I won't send any of your Rangers anyplace I don't lead them personally. I've promised the same thing to the Strada, the Copperell, and everyone else who's fought alongside us. So, if I screw up bad, it's only gonna happen once."

Chapman regarded me with narrowed eyes as if trying to decide if he could trust me. Finally, though, he nodded.

"I guess it comes down to the fact that I know how to fight terrorists and Commies," he admitted, "but you know how to fight aliens."

"I know how to fight Anguilar," I corrected him, slipping my arm around Laranna. "Some of my best friends are aliens. Tell you what, let's get this platoon together and have a short refresher course on how to accurately fire a pulse rifle…then try this drill again."

"You heard the colonel, Lieutenant Pierce," Chapman called

to the platoon leader. "Gather in and listen to what the man has to say. And the next time through this drill, I expect to see *Rangers* hitting the majority of those targets, not a damned leg!"

I didn't bother correcting him, since I'd gone to Airborne School and was not, technically, a leg. We take our little victories where we can get them.

2

"This is stupid," Laranna murmured, pulling the door of the government SUV shut. "Why can't we just land the shuttle right at this Pentagon place?" She gestured out the window at the lander resting on the tarmac at the edge of the Joint Base Andrews airstrip, guarded at every corner by armed Air Force Security Police. "Surely there's enough room in the parking lot."

"We ready, sir?" the young enlisted woman in the driver's seat asked, twisting around to offer us both an expression reminiscent of a 1980s-era teenager getting to meet Van Halen in person.

"Yeah," I told her, motioning ahead of us. "Let's get going."

"Umm…" Her starstruck grin morphed into something more hesitant and embarrassed. "Not until you both put your seat belts on, sir. Sorry."

"Oh, jeez," I sighed, pulling the shoulder belt on. "I freaking hate the 21st Century already." I motioned at myself, cocking an eyebrow. "We good?"

"Yes, sir!" The driver sounded just as cheerful despite my grumpiness, but at least she started the car.

"It's what?" Laranna went on, not even bothering to complain about having to wear a seat belt. "Forty-five minutes from here to the Pentagon?"

"This time of day, ma'am?" the driver answered, apparently assuming the conversation was a general one. "Probably an hour, with traffic." The SUV weaved through security and emergency vehicles away from the landing field. "And that's after we get to the front gate, of course."

"Thank you, Specialist," I told her, hoping I'd put a firm enough finality into my tone for her to realize this was a private discussion. "They won't let us land at the Pentagon," I explained to Laranna, "because of security. Here, they have an entire military base to look out for the shuttle. And besides that, they probably don't want everybody knowing where we are. Remember what happened with the Russians."

She grunted skeptically.

"If they're so concerned about our security, why do they make us leave our weapons on the shuttle?"

I shrugged. She had me there, and while I knew their rationale, I didn't think much of it.

"Right now, I'm more worried about our friends than our enemies. I still don't know if Chapman trusts me."

"He's a man who respects his duty and the chain of

command," she said. "He'll follow orders. That should be enough."

"It's enough, but it's not ideal. You want your officers to trust you." Sagging in the seat, I rubbed at my eyes. I was running on not much sleep, and we'd lost two hours flying east. "At least they gave us a Ranger battalion. When this all started, I figured we'd be lucky to get a National Guard infantry platoon."

"The attack on the Capitol spooked them," she reminded me. "It wasn't even a full-scale invasion, and if we hadn't been there, the Anguilar would probably have taken out most of their government. You knew this wouldn't be easy, but at least they're trying."

I snorted.

"They're trying my patience. How many times are they going to drag us in front of Congress? Or worse, in front of another dumbass talking head reporter? We have real work to do, and God only knows how much time we have to get it done."

"They're making progress," Laranna insisted. "The crashed Anguilar ship is nearly repaired." She shrugged. "At least they're letting Mallarna and her engineers do their job and not getting in the way."

I scowled at her but couldn't keep it up, and the expression dissolved into a chuckle.

"When did you get to be the reasonable one all of a sudden? I thought that was my job. You were the one who wanted to charge off into battle headlong."

"That was a long time ago." Laranna grinned. "Okay, it was just a couple years ago. But a lot's happened since then." She sobered, eyes going out of focus as if seeing something light-years away. "*We've* changed since then. I didn't have anything or anyone to live for. I'd lost everyone I cared about in those thirty-five years in stasis. All I wanted was revenge."

"Do you still want it?" I asked her, forgetting the driver up front. Laranna's eyes snapped back to focus on me, looking a question. "Because I didn't originally. Teaming up with you and Gib and Brazzo was one of the best things that ever happened to me. I wasn't crazy about the whole people-trying-to-kill-me thing, but you guys weren't just my friends, you were my family. Brazzo..." I winced at the memory. "He died, but he did it on his own terms. He made the decision. But Dani was different. I know it's war, and people die in war, but it feels different somehow."

Laranna's shoulder pressed against mine as she leaned in to kiss me on the cheek.

"I know Dani was your friend. She was a connection to your home. But she made a decision, just like Brazzo. She could have stayed back in Ohio, stayed at her job as a police officer and never thought about any of this again. But that wasn't Dani. She wanted to do the right thing."

"It was my fault," I whispered, watching the driver's eyes in the rearview mirror. She wasn't looking at us, but that didn't mean she wasn't listening. "I left her there in the fighter. I should have taken her with me."

"You know you couldn't do that. The Vanguard was a combat asset. If things had gone badly on the cruiser, you would have needed her there. Even before I was kidnapped by Lenny and forced to confront the threat of the Anguilar, I knew that no matter how carefully you plan, how meticulously you train, the enemy always has a say and people die in wars. Even the people we love."

I sighed, but the tension wouldn't go out of my shoulders.

"Yeah. Maybe Chapman's right. Maybe I'm too young and inexperienced for this. Not because people won't follow me but because I can't let go when they get killed doing it."

"If you ever figure out how to do that," she told me, fingers stroking at my cheek, "don't tell me. Because I never want to learn."

I'd lost track of our drive during the whispered discussion, and when I returned my attention to the view out of the tinted windows, burned-out buildings and cratered streets caught my eye. We'd turned onto the path the Anguilar ground troops had taken when they'd advanced on the White House. No other traffic joined us, all entrances to the road still blocked off to civilians, but our driver weaved carefully between craters and cracked pavement.

"They haven't repaired much, have they?" Laranna said, nodding at the crumbled, charred façade of a burnt-out building.

"Good," I whispered. She shot me a questioning look, and I expounded. "See those drones?" I pointed upward at one of the half-dozen tiny quad-copters circling the area, their cameras and transmitters small enough that I couldn't see them from here, technology I would have expected from Lenny or the Anguilar. "Those are from the news agencies. They're putting out footage of this street twenty-four-seven. The longer people can see the effects of what happened, the more they'll understand the threat. No one should forget."

"You'd be surprised what people can forget, sir," the driver cut in as she brought the SUV to a halt in a nearly deserted parking lot. She turned back to us and gestured to the right. "We're here."

The Pentagon loomed over us, as impressive and intimidating as I suppose it was designed to be. This wasn't the first time I'd been here, yet every time I approached it, I still felt a chill like Frodo seeing Mordor for the first time.

"Thanks, Specialist," I told her, pushing open the door.

It was early evening, and I wondered how many people would be getting off work. I supposed that there had to be staff here around the clock, and I tried to imagine what it would be like to wander around the hallways of the massive labyrinth all night and leave at the break of dawn.

"I'll be waiting for you out here when you're done, sir," the woman assured me, stretching her legs out onto the bench seat of the SUV, her fingers interlaced behind her head. "Got nothing else to do."

I don't know why I felt naked walking through the doors into the Pentagon without my gun, yet I did. Maybe because it reminded me way too much of the Anguilar headquarters back on Copperell, or maybe because I knew that the senior officers who called this place home were every bit the bureaucrats that the Anguilar Empire functionaries in that giant alien complex had been.

The gauntlet of security at the entrance would have

precluded bringing in either my sidearm or Laranna's knives anyway...if we'd been forced to go through it. I might have been passed through with a brief swipe of the ID card I'd been issued, but no one was going to overlook Laranna.

A pair of Army MPs stepped forward, the senior of the two NCOs giving me a salute, which I returned with a little bemusement, not even sure if I was supposed to. I felt very much like a child playing dress-up as a soldier.

"Colonel Travers." Gaunt and pale, the sergeant could have been a barrow wight from D&D, cursed to haunt these halls for eternity. He glanced at Laranna, nodded to her as if unsure how to address her. "Umm...ma'am. I'm Sgt. Verde, and I'm supposed to take you to General Gavin's office."

I shared a look of amusement with Laranna.

"What? Does the general think we'd get lost on the way?"

"No, sir," Verde said, smiling apologetically. "But this place has a lot of rubberneckers, and well"—he spread his hands—"you two are hard to miss."

I STIFFENED to attention and delivered a salute as I entered the office.

"Sir, Colonel Travers reports." I couldn't *see* Laranna staring at me in amusement, but I felt it.

Gavin stood from his desk...and kept standing, unfolding like a praying mantis. The man was over six-four, I estimated, and built like an NBA point guard. A small, framed photo hanging on his "I love me" wall behind the desk showed him playing basketball at West Point, dunking on a hapless Navy midshipman. That was a long time ago, judging by the gray in his brown hair and the lines in his face. And the four stars on his lapels.

"At ease, Travers," General Ben Gavin, Chairman of the Joint Chiefs of Staff, told me, returning the salute without bothering to come to attention himself, which I suppose was one of the benefits of being the highest ranking military officer in the country. No one was going to chew him out for improper etiquette. "Have a seat."

Laranna pushed the door shut behind us, raising an eyebrow at me. She knew about our military procedures but still found the whole thing a bit ridiculous.

"You, too, ma'am." Gavin gestured to the two chairs on our side of the desk as he fell into his padded, leather office chair. I didn't know Gavin that well, but I had the impression that he enjoyed me having to salute and act subordinate to him after the way I'd charged in and thumbed my nose at the politicians and military when we first arrived. "So, tell me, Travers, how's the training?"

Of all the bullshit that my old nemesis, Colonel Danberg from college ROTC, had fed us poor cadets, one thing he'd said in passing had stuck with me. Senior officers never asked questions of subordinates that they didn't already know the answer to. Gavin had been getting regular reports from Chapman, I was sure. Which might have worried me if I'd had an intention of trying to lie to him.

"Slower than I'd like, sir," I confessed, hands clasped in my lap like I was back in high school and had been called into the principal's office. "The Rangers are taking longer to adjust to the new weapons than I thought. It's not just simple muscle-memory things like reacting to recoil and trigger pull, it's the realization that the enemy is going to have guns like these, too. But it'll come."

Gavin leaned back, the leather creaking under his weight, his brows nearly swallowing his dark eyes.

"Any complaints about Chapman?"

I wanted to laugh, and it was difficult keeping a sardonic grin off my face. The fact that he asked the question meant he knew there had been, and could mean that either Chapman had whined about me or he'd confessed he was being a dumbass. I hoped it was the latter, but something else Danberg had said came to mind.

Hope in one hand and shit in the other, and see which one fills up faster, Cadet Travers.

"Colonel Chapman is a good officer," I replied. "He has the best interest of his Rangers at heart, and I know he'll do his best to help get them ready for the mission."

And that was about as noncommittal a non-answer I could give without actually lying. Gavin's thin smile confirmed to me that he already knew what I'd say.

"I think," I pressed on, hoping to avoid any more leading questions, "that the training will go easier once we get the next shipment from Sanctuary. The *Liberator* is supposed to be bringing in the APCs and assault vehicles—basically tanks—from the weapons depot we seized a few months ago, along with those

Starblade fighters we promised. I think getting the full experience of a combined-arms task force will help everything come together." I shrugged. "Of course, using them is going to require training the drivers and pilots, but to be honest, if *I* can learn to fly a Starblade, then some Air Force fighter jock shouldn't have any trouble picking it up."

"Space Force," he corrected me. I couldn't help rolling my eyes, and Gavin chuckled. "Yes, I know, it's the hokiest damned name anyone could have thought up, but it's what we have. We'll recruit the pilots from the Air Force and Navy, but once they're assigned, they'll be Space Force, just like the crews for the starships."

"Yes, sir," was my only response, though I couldn't help but think the ship crews should come from the Navy. "Once the ships are both in service, our pilots can train yours in how to launch and land in their hangar bays. Unless you decide you'd rather keep the fighters land-based. They have a pretty long range for their size, pretty much anywhere in the inner Solar System, but they're limited more by the needs of the pilots."

"I wonder if we might try turning them into drone weapons," Gavin mused, rubbing at his chin.

"No, sir," I told him firmly, drawing a hard glare. "There's a reason no one out there uses remotely piloted vehicles. ECM is pretty high-level among the Anguilar…and anyone else with warships. That's why no one uses drones, and also why no one uses guided missiles."

"What about autonomous drones?" he asked immediately, a predator pouncing on his prey, as if he'd anticipated my objection. "We think we have adequate AI systems when put together with the fly-by-wire controls of the Starblade fighters to program them to operate without a pilot."

"That would not be accepted," Laranna snapped, her denunciation as fervent as any Bible Belt fundamentalist shooting down legalized prostitution.

"By *whom?*" Gavin demanded, glaring at her like she was a civilian intruding on the debate.

"By literally any other civilization or government off Earth," I told him, then sighed. "You know about Lenny, right?"

"The AI. Of course."

"Then you know he isn't allowed to wage war against any biological sentient," I pointed out.

"You told us that was Lenny's idea," Gavin objected. "He and his kind thought they'd screwed everything up and had themselves reprogrammed."

"It was." Though as many stories as Lenny had told us, it was hard to keep straight which one was true. If any of them were. "But that wasn't a one-off. They—Lenny and the other AI robots—pretty much created the societies that exist now, and they not only didn't want themselves being able to kill anyone, but they also wanted to make sure no artificial intelligence ever could. It's pretty much a religious belief at this point." I shrugged. "Now, I promised you the Starblades, and I wouldn't go back on that, but if you go through with making them unmanned, computer-controlled weapons…" I shook my head, and Laranna finished the thought for me.

"No one in the resistance would ever trust you again. They wouldn't work with you, wouldn't coordinate with your military."

"It doesn't matter anyway, sir," I assured him. "The main advantage of autonomous drones is that they can take more acceleration than a human, but the Starblades have inertial dampeners so a living pilot isn't really handicapped by that."

He grunted, not sounding convinced, but gears shifted behind his eyes, the change in subjects showing plainly on his face before he spoke.

"The training is going to take some time, both with the Starblades and the cruisers. Could be months before we have enough qualified personnel. I know you planned on withdrawing your Vanguard fighter wing once the second cruiser is able to lift to orbit, but I wondered if it might be a better idea to keep them around until the training is complete."

I closed my eyes for just a moment so that he wouldn't see them rolling. We'd had this conversation before, and it never ended well.

"The Vanguards are needed elsewhere," Laranna told him, not nearly as worried about pissing off a four-star general as I was. "They're our main advantage over the Anguilar, and by keeping them here, we're leaving the planets we've freed from the Empire vulnerable to being reconquered."

"We're currently taking up the slack by reallocating our Liberty ships," I put in, "but the problem with that is, doing it pretty much leaves Sanctuary unguarded. Sure, we don't *think* the Angular know the location of our secret base there, but that's a hell of a chance to take."

"You said that this General Zan-Tar is coming back," Gavin reminded me in a chiding tone.

"If we pull out the Vanguard wing, General," Laranna told him, "and the Anguilar return again to attack Earth, you'll suffer great losses, but you'll be able to hold them off long enough for help to arrive. You have over seven billion people and enough military might to keep any Anguilar invasion force busy for months, even without the cruisers and the fighters. With them… you might have enough to force them to regroup and reinforce. We'll be running patrols out here every few weeks anyway, and once you have the cruisers up and running, you can send out subspace comms. They're not instantaneous, but they travel faster than a ship."

"Of course," Gavin said. "I understand."

And I could believe that all I wanted, because he didn't look at all like a man who understood or accepted any of the arguments he'd just been given. He looked much like a dissatisfied general who was about to keep arguing until he got his way. Thankfully, the desk intercom interrupted him.

"General Gavin"—a nasal voice came over the invisible speakers—"there's a message for Colonel Travers."

"From whom?" Gavin asked, staring daggers at the speaker for interrupting him.

"From orbit, sir. The *Liberator* has returned to the system with the arms shipment."

Finally, there was *something* that could brighten Gavin's demeanor, and he smiled, probably at the thought of the armored vehicles and fighters aboard the ship.

"Excellent. Who's the message from? That robot, Lenny?"

"No, sir. It's from someone named Brandy. She wants to speak to Colonel Travers in person."

I exchanged a look with Laranna. Brandy was our equivalent of the head of the CIA, and for her to leave Sanctuary and come all the way to Earth…. Laranna put our shared thought into words.

"This can't be good news."

3

The *Liberator*, formerly one of the Kamerian Zoo Ships, formerly a warship of the Creators, was the biggest damned thing I'd ever seen. Well, okay, that's not exactly accurate. It was the largest artificial construct I'd seen floating in space, but that didn't sound nearly as impressive as the starship *felt* every time I approached her this way, in a lander heading for the hangar bay.

She was bigger than the Empire State Building, as big as a New York City block, formed from clusters of gleaming silver in mind-bending curves and spirals, the product of a non-human mind from hundreds of thousands of years ago. How, I wondered, had anyone ever thought that these things were built to collect zoological specimens?

"Feels like we haven't seen the old girl in years," I sighed, settling back into the lander's acceleration couch. Laranna flew her this time, which had become a rare thing for me since I'd started piloting the Vanguards. I didn't trust anyone except Gib or Laranna to fly if I wasn't at the controls.

"That's because you're just as tired of dealing with politics and"—she frowned, glanced away from the controls for a moment—"what do you call it? *Red tape.* Yes, you're as tired of red tape as I am, and the last few weeks have felt like years."

A chuckle bubbled up despite the misgivings I had about the meeting Brandy had called.

"What? You mean you *don't* enjoy listening to overstuffed generals and politicians tell us why they know better than we do how the assets we've volunteered to protect them with should be used?" I rolled my eyes, tugged at the collar of my field utilities. "I should never have accepted the damn commission in the Army. If I was just a civilian, I could have punched Gavin in the nose for being such a dick, and I wouldn't have to worry about winding up in a stockade."

"*I* could punch him for you," Laranna volunteered, her lip curling as her fingers danced across the controls until a green line flashed on the navigation screen, indicating that the ship's docking systems had taken over and would guide us in. "They might *try* to throw me in a stockade, but they'd regret it quickly."

"So much for you being the reasonable one," I said with a chuckle.

"I didn't say we should abandon our efforts to enlist your world in the struggle against the Anguilar," she pointed out. "Just that I would be happy to inflict minor damage on General Gavin."

"Minor damage," I repeated. "Maybe you *are* turning reasonable after all."

The lander passed through the airlock field of the hangar bay, and a shudder went through me, a chill I'd been assured was psychosomatic rather than physical, or at least that was what Lenny had told me. I wasn't so sure. Any energy barrier that could hold in air had to do something to the human body. I was used to the hangar of the *Liberator* being filled with the brawny, broad-shouldered curves of the Vanguard wing, but the starfighters were out on patrol, their temporary base the captured Anguilar cruiser where Gib and a dozen or so Copperell techs were in the process of training an international crew to run her.

Instead, the hangar was awash with Starblade fighters. Slender, sharp-edged daggers compared to the war clubs that were the Vanguards, the Starblades were maneuverable and versatile, cheap to produce, and, particularly advantageous for us, easy to steal. The Anguilar had enough problems guarding their shipyards without trying to devote their thinly stretched resources to adequately protect every tiny weapons depot where the spacefighters were stored.

The main problem for the US… I sighed, having trouble taking the designation seriously. The main problem for the US *Space Force* was going to be keeping the things stocked with ammunition. The Starblades were too small to carry a particle beam weapon, thus their primary armament was a pair of rotary pulse cannons, and those went through ammo like a congressman through tax money. I hoped Val and Lenny had brought a shitload of spare rounds for those cannons.

There wasn't much room left between the multiple rows of space-fighters, but the automated system set us down gently right next to the only other lander on the hangar deck. Its hatch opened just as we touched on our landing treads and Giblet stepped out of the shuttle, shoulders sagging, eyes focused downward, as if it would have been too much trouble to lift them up.

"Shit," I murmured, unstrapping from my seat.

"You should talk to him," Laranna urged. "He's been off by himself for too long." She stood and yanked open the hatch. "I'll go on ahead to the operations center."

I let her head out ahead of me, heard her quiet greeting to Gib and his mumbled response before I sucked in a deep breath, squared my shoulders, and stepped down the boarding ladder. It took only a few seconds to catch up with Giblet because he wasn't walking so much as shuffling, and I had the feeling he wouldn't have bothered to transfer over to the *Liberator* from the cruiser at all if Brandy and Val hadn't insisted.

"Hey, Gib," I said, matching his pace. "How you doing, man?"

He didn't look up, barely stepped aside as a hoard of Copperell techs streamed from one end of the line of Starblades to the next.

"Fine."

He didn't *look* fine. Giblet's people, the Varnell, had…well, not *evolved* from because it hadn't happened naturally, but Lenny's Creators had engineered them using DNA from birds combined with that of humans, or at least anthropoid apes. The result wasn't exactly a bird-man, not in the sense of the old Flash

Gordon comic strips, but of a humanoid with some avian features, including red-blond hair that was more like feathers and covered most of his body. If you can imagine what your hair feels and smells like when you haven't washed it in a while, imagine how that would be magnified a hundred times if it covered your arms, back, and chest. I didn't gag, but it took some effort.

"I left a couple messages for you the last few weeks. I guess you didn't see them, huh?"

Gib's only answer was a shrug, but at least he walked faster, maybe trying to get away from me. I gritted my teeth and kept apace with him, wishing he'd at least look at me.

"Gib, come on, talk to me. You shouldn't have to go through this by yourself. I'm your friend."

He stopped so abruptly I nearly ran into him, his eyes dark and cloudy, the only emotion in them irritation.

"I know you mean well, Charlie, but I don't *want* to deal with it. I just want to work." Gib laughed, as bleak and humorless a sound as I could ever put that word to. "That's what she would have wanted, don't you think? For me to keep working, to keep doing what she thought was the right thing? I mean, that's what she *died* for, isn't it? For the right thing? For something bigger than her…bigger than *us*?" He blinked, a muscle in his cheek twitching. "I gotta keep telling myself that. That it was worth it. Because if it wasn't, then…"

He spun around and kept walking toward the bridge, his step brisk, almost a run, and I had to jog to keep up. Getting tired of this shit, I grabbed his arm and spun him around, then barely got my other hand up in time to block the punch he aimed at my head. I shoved him away with a hard push in the chest and stabbed a finger toward where I'd pushed.

"Goddammit, Gib!" I blurted, not caring whether any of the Copperell, Peboktan, or Strada passing by heard me. "She did *not* die for nothing! She believed in what she was doing or she wouldn't have stayed with us! She believed in *you*, and what she would want is for you not to give up on yourself!"

Which was a shitload more than I'd *meant* to say, and sure as hell a lot more than I *should* have said, particularly in public, but he'd pissed me off, and there it was. Giblet squared off like he meant to come at me again, and I noticed a couple of the Strada warriors in the passageway staring at us, concerned, like they were considering whether or not they should intervene. I didn't back off, just glared at him, daring him to disagree with me.

"You don't know what she would have wanted," he finally said, and the words weren't the accusatory shout I'd expected. Instead, they were hopeless, listless, the passion and anger of a moment ago drained away. "Neither do I. Neither of us got the chance to know her well enough for that."

"You knew her well enough to love her," I reminded him. "And she loved you. I knew her well enough to know that."

Gib's shoulders sagged, and I thought he hadn't agreed so much as given up on trying to argue with me.

"Look, man," I said, putting a hand on his shoulder, "after we have this meeting, why don't you and I go have a drink? I sure as hell need one after fighting with generals and politicians for a couple months." I tried not to sound like I was pleading with him, though that was clearly what I was doing.

Gib nodded.

"Okay, we'll do that. Come on." He motioned for me to follow. "Let's get to this stupid meeting and find out why Brandy decided to grace us with her presence. I can't even remember the last time she left Sanctuary." Giblet sighed. "It's gotta be bad news."

I nodded, though he'd already turned away.

"That seems to be the general consensus."

VALENTINE MCKEE WASN'T much of a hugger, and neither was I, but I gave him one anyway, and he didn't seem to mind.

"It's been too long, brother," he said, clapping me on the arm.

Val was a tall, lanky drink of water who still looked very much like the 19th-century frontier lawman he'd once been before Lenny had snatched him out of the plains of Texas and put him to sleep for almost 120 years. He'd woken up on a tiny outpost world once colonized by the Copperell but long since taken over by the Anguilar…the home of Brandine and her young son, Maxx.

Brandine McKee—Brandy to Val and the rest of us—was a petite woman who might have passed for one of my elementary school teachers if it hadn't been for a skin tone a darker, golden tan than any race of Earth could have duplicated. She dressed like a schoolmarm from the old west, which matched her husband's style of homespun wool and linen and leather riding boots. It was camouflage, though…she was every bit as deadly as

Val McKee, except she was more inclined to using her brain than her trigger finger.

"Hello, Charlie," she said, kissing me on the cheek before doing the same to Laranna. "And you, too! Are you ever going to come back to Sanctuary? Everyone needs some time off every now and then!"

"Charlie has this strange idea," Laranna stage-whispered to Brandy, "that the entire resistance would fall apart if he took a vacation. Sometimes, I wonder how he fits that head inside a helmet." I made a face at her, but she ignored me. "How's Maxx doing?"

"That child is growing like a weed!" Val put in, raising his palm up past his shoulder. "Gonna be taller than me pretty soon."

"He's back on Sanctuary," Brandy replied. "Doing well in his classes and I'm sure enjoying not having his parents around looking over his shoulder, but we miss him terribly. And honestly, I'm worried leaving him at Sanctuary without any of the Liberator ships defending it."

Brandy didn't try to comfort Gib, probably because she'd barely known Dani, and probably just as well. Gib didn't seem to be in the mood to be comforted. She just put a hand over his and squeezed before letting go.

The others crowded into the ship's operations center were just as familiar to me, though I'd also seen them more recently. Nareena, the commanding officer of the Strada warriors who'd accompanied us on this mission, had been back and forth to

Sanctuary with the *Liberator*, but she'd been around for the battle at the Capitol and we simply shared a nod.

The other humanoid at the table was a Peboktan, insectoid, the least human of all the species that the Creators had produced when they started messing around with Earth DNA. Yet she still wasn't so insect as humanoid, and I'd long since gotten over the *ick* factor with the Peboktan. Brazzo, one of their number who'd also been a cyborg, had been a close friend, and the only one of our original four who we'd lost.

I would have hugged her, but it wasn't a thing among her people, and I settled for nodding.

The last to enter the compartment wasn't human, wasn't humanoid, and definitely hadn't been engineered from Earth DNA or *any* genetic material. Lenny had once been biological, or at least that was the story he'd told us, but nothing remained from that earlier incarnation apart from his brain patterns, now read into the arcane inner workings of the computer at the core of this ship. That was something else about Lenny that I found hard to accept, that the thing that made him…well, *him* wasn't actually inside his body. I could blow that shining metal carcass to bits, and not only would Lenny still exist in the heart of the *Liberator*, but he'd also still be around as separate but functionally identical consciousnesses in the other four Liberator ships.

Just the knowledge of that made it harder to look at the robot body as anything except a puppet, for all that Lenny *tried* very hard to get people to look at the body. It was seven feet tall and twice as broad as an adult humanoid, for one thing, its base a metal skirt covering caster-like wheels. It narrowed as it reached the waist, becoming more humanoid…except for the multiple arms. Never the same number, though. He seemed to grow them when he needed extra.

The face wasn't just humanoid in appearance, it also had moving plates that shifted as if mimicking the emotions and expressions of a living being. Not just *any* living being, either. It had to be a coincidence, since Lenny had been around in the same form at least as far back as the 1870s, when he'd abducted Val, but the first time I'd gotten a look at the robot's face, I'd been sure he'd used the actor Michael Keaton as a model. Not the Michael Keaton of the 2020s, who I'd seen in a few movies since I'd returned to Earth the first time, but the one who'd starred in "Mr. Mom" and "Johnny Dangerously." And "Beetlejuice," of course, though I hadn't seen that one until recently since it came out the year after I'd been taken.

"Greetings, Charlie Travers," he said, his tones rich and resonant even though they weren't passing through a set of living lungs or diaphragm. "Laranna, Giblet. I trust you are all well."

"Hey, Lenny." I nodded to him but didn't give the others time to comment on whether they were well because I was frankly afraid of how Gib would reply to that. "Did you bring a good load of ammo for the Starblade pulse cannons? Until we get fabricators set up for them to make their own, they're going to have to get their resupply from us."

Gib sprawled in one of the chairs around the table, showing no interest in the conversation, so I probably needn't have worried.

"We were able to procure close to a million rounds for the

initial shipment," Lenny reported. "It's going to take several shuttle trips to bring it all down, and I hope your country has the equipment to offload it."

"I'm sure they have enough forklifts for all of it," I assured him. "But we're going to need to bring in more with the next shipment, if we can get it."

"How proceeds the training?" Brandy asked, sitting at the head of the table, and as if her question marked the official commencement of the meeting, we all took our seats as well. Except Lenny, of course, who sort of just hovered behind Brandy's shoulder.

"Slower than I'd like," I told her. "But they're professionals, they'll adjust. I think the biggest adaptation is going to be to the fighters. They're used to depending on guided missiles as the primary weapons in their atmospheric fighters, and I think most of their pilots haven't even trained much in guns."

"If they wish," Lenny put in, "the Starblades *do* have external hardpoints that can be used to mount missiles, and the internal targeting systems can adapt to it, as long as they understand how little use the weapons will be against Anguilar spacecraft."

"What about the cruisers?" Brandy pressed. "Have the Americans and their allies learned their systems?" She speared Gib with a hard look, but he just shrugged.

"They're primitives. They still expect to get plastered against the back wall whenever the ship accelerates, and they don't have a clue about using the hyperdrive to bleed off momentum. Hell, we've barely gotten into the operation of the hyperdrive at all. Too busy getting them familiarized with the propulsion and weapons systems. I think about the time that Mallarna gets that wrecked cruiser off the ground, they might be ready for their first short-range hyperspace jump."

Brandy sniffed in obvious dissatisfaction but turned to the Peboktan engineer.

"And when *will* the second ship be ready to lift off?"

"Possibly two weeks," she said, her multijointed fingers folded atop the table. "The repairs have gone well, and the Americans have provided all the supplies we've required. The only holdup has been reinforcing key structural areas against the initial liftoff burn. All the weapons systems are operational, and we have the power junctions fully repaired."

"Excellent work," Brandy told her, offering a thin smile.

"Remind me," I murmured into Laranna's ear, "who's the commander of this operation again?"

"She's been here longer than you," Laranna reasoned with a barely perceptible shrug. "She feels a sense of ownership."

Fair enough, I supposed, but I was only going to let this whole proprietary thing go so far.

"Brandy," I interrupted, "you haven't told us why you came all the way out here. I know it wasn't just to get a progress report, not when you had to leave Maxx at home. What's so sensitive that you couldn't send a message?"

Only the tightness around Brandy's eyes betrayed the annoyance she no doubt felt at my acceleration of her intended pace of revelation, but she was a pro and only allowed herself an exasperated sigh before answering the question.

"As per Charlie's instructions in a message he sent after the battle you fought against the Anguilar, I've had my intelligence sources searching for information as to the whereabouts of General Zan-Tar."

Gib's head snapped around, and he sat up straight, staring intently at Brandy like a starving man staring through a restaurant window at a steak dinner.

"What did they find out?" he demanded, his voice a hoarse rasp.

"I've received indications from a source on Wraith Anchorage that Zan-Tar arrived at the Anguilar construction dock there two weeks ago."

"Damn," Laranna murmured, sitting back in her chair like someone had slapped her in the face. "Wraith Anchorage."

"Exactly," Brandy agreed, her tone and expression grim.

I looked between the two of them, frowning in confusion.

"What's a *Wraith Anchorage*?" I asked, wishing for the outer-space equivalent of a road atlas.

"A shithole," Giblet replied, his expression thoughtful. "One of the biggest, most dangerous shitholes in the galaxy, and that was almost forty years ago when there were no Anguilar there."

I guess I shouldn't have been surprised that Gib had spent time in the biggest shithole in the galaxy, but that didn't exactly answer my question, and I made a pleading gesture at Brandy.

"It's a long story," she warned me, and I wondered if I imagined the look of satisfaction on her face at me being forced to ask her for help after rushing her explanation before. "Wraith Anchorage predates not just the Anguilar Empire but even the Kamerian Alliance. It was built by the

Gan-Shi in an attempt to create the base for an interstellar civilization."

"The Gan-Shi?" I repeated, shaking my head.

"They were among the first of our creations," Lenny provided. "We were…experimenting. The Gan-Shi were a physical species, engineered from herd beasts, large and strong but good-natured. We chose them for their gentle character, hoping that they would make good use of the technological gifts we gave them. Unfortunately, their good nature proved to be their undoing."

"The Gan-Shi built what they called the Convergence," Brandy went on, "at the center of a system with the largest asteroid belt in the galaxy, the failed remains of what might have been a dozen planets orbiting a white dwarf star. They used the place as a construction yard to pass on their technology to other peoples, to build starships and reactors, to mine raw materials from the asteroids and eventually, extract exotic matter from the star. They had grand plans, but as Lenny said, they were gentle and unprepared for confrontation with those who wanted what they had."

"The Kamerians?" I guessed.

"They never made it that far. The Krin beat them to it." Brandy's lip twisted in distaste. "How do you think they garnered their reputation? They took the station and turned it into a center for everything banned from civilized worlds. Slavery, drugs, gladiatorial combat, weapons smuggling. That's when it got its new name. Wraith Anchorage. A place for ghosts, for phantoms, criminals who didn't officially exist."

Brandy pulled a squeeze-bulb of water from a cabinet built into the bulkhead and took a sip, then followed it with a deep breath, as if the presentation had drained her.

"The Kamerians took it from the Krin and used it as a military base, and once they fell, the Anguilar moved in. It's one of the first places the Anguilar took over since it gives them a fallback place to manufacture ships and fighters, though it's not ideal because it's farther from their governing worlds. They would have destroyed it if not for that, because while they control it nominally, they don't have enough troops to get rid of the crime and intrigue going on in the place. It's still a hive for everything illicit, which shouldn't bother the Anguilar." Brandy sneered. "I think it's the fact that other people are making money off of it and they aren't in charge that rubs them the wrong way. But they do run the ship construction facilities for themselves as a backup to their own shipyards. They haven't produced much in the last few years, but with the pressure we've been putting on their conventional yards, the word I'm getting is that Zan-Tar has been put in charge of producing a new fleet specifically to deal with us. With you and Earth."

"Well by the Feathered God!" Gib exploded, bursting out of his seat with energy I hadn't seen from him in weeks. "You know what we have to do! We have to go there and kill that bastard!"

4

"That's probably exactly what they want us to do," Brandy warned, interrupting Gib's rant.

"What the hell are you talking about?" Giblet demanded, squaring off with the Copperell spy, hands clenched into fists.

Brandy sighed and leaned heavily against the table, her eyes closing for a moment as she collected her thoughts.

"I have *one* source for this intelligence, and it's not one I fully trust. There is the very real possibility that this is a trap. General Zan-Tar is a far more intelligent and far more dangerous leader than the Anguilar have had before."

I nodded, remembering something that Master-Sergeant Redd had told me in college ROTC.

"Military Darwinism." Every eye turned toward me, and my face warmed slightly as I realized the phrase hadn't translated very well. "Survival of the fittest. When a country gets into a shooting war, the ones in charge are going to be basically aristocracy, either actual or metaphorical. Senior officers who got their positions by following the rules and kissing the right asses. People who don't know how to fight a war, they just know how to play politics." I shrugged. "Then, once the real bullets start flying and casualties start piling up, the *real* fighters start moving into positions of authority, and things get a lot harder for the other side. I think maybe this Zan-Tar asshole is the reward we get for beating the Anguilar over and over."

"Then it's simple," Giblet insisted, spreading his hands like a Bible-thumping preacher inviting the flock to come to God. "We go to Wraith Anchorage and kill the son of a bitch, and then they don't *have* this hyper-competent prick to lead them. What's there to think about?"

"Because it's a trap," Laranna said, beating me to it. "It's *obviously* a trap. Wraith Anchorage is weeks away, far from our logistical support. They want us to attack with everything we have to draw us out and either ambush us there in that system or go behind our backs and strike us here, or at Strada."

"I'm afraid I agree with Laranna," Brandy told him, then looked at the rest of us. "I have grave doubts that someone as important and notable as General Zan-Tar would isolate himself far off in such a place if it wasn't to lure us in." She placed her hands flat on the table as if grounding herself. "That's why I came in person. I was concerned, given the heightened feelings after what happened, that if I simply sent a message, it might not adequately convey my feelings on this matter. My opinion is, under no circumstances should we consider sending a force to Wraith Anchorage."

Gib made a sound that was half a choked scream and half a groan of utter frustration. He spun away from Brandy and fixed me with a glare.

"Tell me you're not buying into this," he begged. "We have one chance at the guy, and this is it."

And the thing was, I *really* wanted to agree with him. Not that I didn't trust Brandy, not that I couldn't see her point, but as bad as Giblet wanted Zan-Tar, I might have wanted him worse. Gib had loved Dani, but I was the one who'd gotten her killed. I nodded to Val.

"We've heard Brandy. I want everyone's input here. Val, what do you think?"

"Oh, like he's gonna go against Brandy," Gib scoffed, but I held up a hand to quiet him down.

Val took a half-step forward like he was going to take a swing at Giblet, but I tilted my head his way with a warning look.

"I ain't no general," he said finally, "but I served under some competent ones during the war." A chill went up my spine at the knowledge that he meant the *Civil War* when he said that. "Wasn't a one of them that would have let the enemy know where he was gonna be unless it suited him. You gotta think with your head, not your heart, especially when whatever decision we make could mean life or death, freedom or slavery, for *billions* of people."

Gib sighed theatrically, but I moved on to the next one in line. "Mallarna?"

The Peboktan didn't respond immediately, her big eyes lost in thought, her long fingers tapping rhythmically against the glass-like surface of the table.

"The Anguilar destroyed my world," she ventured slowly, carefully, "and I'm loath to pass up any chance to make them pay for it. Which is why I force myself to carefully examine my judgment in these matters. I'm an engineer, and I must look at things from the point of view of what we have and what we can build. We can't build cruisers, we can only steal them. We can't build Vanguard starfighters, and there are no more to be had. We can't replace them when we lose them. These Liberator ships—if we lose one, she's gone. We'll never see another built in our lifetime. If we're to risk losing assets we can't replace, it should be for an operation that will be a step toward ending this war. Not for revenge."

Gib's jaw clenched, but he didn't say anything, and I knew him well enough that I figured that was because he didn't consider Mallarna one of the inner council, the people whose opinions mattered the most to me. Fair enough, she wasn't. I trusted her ability as an engineer, but she wasn't a soldier, wasn't a warrior. The next one at the table was.

"Nareena?"

The Strada female hadn't said a word during the argument and looked reluctant to do so now, but hers was one of the opinions that interested me the most. She was an outsider, charged with the safety and proper use of her own warriors, with no personal stake in our actions. But Nareena was also from a world that had been conquered by the Anguilar, and she'd seen great personal loss to their predations.

"I'm a simple warrior," she told me, pulling a short dagger out of the sheath on her forearm as if to illustrate her words. Casually flipping the blade between her fingers, she continued. "You point me at the enemy, and I'll do my best to kill them. And perhaps I'm more…aggressive in my strategy now after being forced into a conservative path back on Strada during the occupation. It may indeed be that this is a trap, yet it also may be a trap that General Zan-Tar has baited with himself. You are the commander, Charlie. You must make this decision, and I don't envy you the responsibility. I think that, were it me, I might charge in headlong and damn the consequences. But if I held the fate of entire planets in my hand as you do, perhaps my thinking would be different."

I didn't audibly curse, but I thought it hard enough that any telepaths around would have blushed. That hadn't been the definitive answer I'd been looking for.

"Laranna?" I had a good idea what she'd say, and unfortunately, I knew Gib wouldn't accept her opinion any more than he'd accepted Val's. But she deserved the chance to state it just the same.

"I'm not *totally* against the idea," she said, shocking me. My surprise must have shown on my face because she shrugged apologetically. "It *is* a trap, that much is obvious, but I'm also aware that traps work both ways. We can't just charge in, but perhaps there's something we could do that they wouldn't expect. What we can't do is leave Earth and all our other protected worlds unguarded." She rubbed at her chin, eyes slightly unfocused in thought. "Perhaps we could make some use of the

American troops we've been training. If we could smuggle the entire battalion onto Wraith Anchorage, we might be able to take the station from the inside and make up for our lack of warships."

Giblet's eyes lit up, and the frustration turned abruptly to hope as he wagged a finger at Laranna.

"I *like* that!" he insisted. "That could work! We could find out what ships are coming in and hijack a freighter or a transport, smuggle your buddies on board. Along with us. We get in there and blow through whatever security those Krin have, and the Anguilar probably wouldn't even manage a full battalion of their own on the station. We take the whole place and hunt Zan-Tar down and gut him like an animal."

Gib's bloodthirsty intensity brought up the hackles on my neck, but I guess I understood, and I nodded slowly.

"Okay, that's workable. But I can't make this decision on my own. I need to run it by Gavin and the President. It's their troops, after all. But I'll need something to sell them on the risk. Something more tangible than revenge." I eyed Gib sidelong. "And it might be intelligence they want. Which would mean taking Zan-Tar alive for interrogation. You gonna be okay with that?"

His lip twisted in a sneer, but he harumphed surrender.

"As long as when they decide to kill him, I'm the one who gets to do it."

"Okay, I'll make an appointment to talk to Gavin tomorrow…" I began, but Gib was already shaking his head.

"What is this? You think you're back in the horse and buggy

days with Valentine? We have videoconferencing. Get your ass on the phone and call them now."

"Fair enough," I admitted, pushing up from the table. "I'll go to the comm room and call it in. But I can't promise I'll get an answer back immediately. This *is* the government we're talking about."

NOT THIS TIME, though. This time, the government was depressingly efficient.

"Not a chance in hell," General Gavin declared, unblinking.

A muscle in my cheek twitched, the price I paid for controlling my temper, though if I had to do it too many more times, I was afraid I might rupture something. I was suddenly grateful that I'd made the call in the privacy of the ship's comm center rather than doing it in front of everyone else in the operations room. Partially because I knew how Gib would have reacted, and mostly, I think, because I would have been embarrassed for them to see him talking to me in that tone of voice.

The communications compartment was tiny compared to the rest of the ship, designed mostly for recording messages intended for transmission through the subspace transmitter. Those conversations were, by the restrictions of hyperdimensional physics, one way, and usually took several attempts to get just right, so if the message was the only one you could send, the guy on the other side wouldn't misunderstand it.

Taking a deep breath, I tried again.

"Sir, you *do* understand that this is the Anguilar commanding general, the same one who ordered the attack on the Capitol and pledged to return and take over the planet? Pretty much the only competent leader they have left?"

Gavin interrupted me with a slash of his knife hand downward through the view of the camera.

"I understand very clearly, Travers. But this isn't a James Bond movie. You're talking about some half-assed plan to sneak an entire *battalion* of Rangers onto an enemy base in a situation that you admit is probably a trap."

"Yes, sir," I acknowledged, speaking quickly to avoid him cutting me off again. "But the thing is, the fact that we know it's likely a trap means that we can spring it in a way they won't be expecting. We think they'll be waiting for an attack from our warships."

"You just said that this Zan-Tar is the smartest, most competent officer you've run into on their side, right?" Gavin interrupted again, not interested in what I had to say. At my reluctant nod, he went on. "Then why are you so damn sure that he won't be ready for the Ranger battalion and this hairbrained hijacking idea?"

My mouth snapped shut on the answer I'd been about to give instinctively. It wasn't a bad question.

"I can't be sure, sir," I admitted. "I'm just going on the experience I have with the Anguilar in the past couple years." The last couple years of kicking their ass, I didn't add because I thought it would have sounded insubordinate.

Gavin seemed to pick up on the unspoken intimation though,

and for a wonder, he didn't get angry. Instead, he sighed and rubbed at his cheek, as if debating whether he needed a shave.

"Look, Travers, I'll pass this up the chain to the National Security Advisor and the President. They need to know the intelligence update anyway. It'll be in President Louis's hands, but I wouldn't hold my breath. I'm giving him the recommendation I just gave you, and as for Parker Donovan, well…" Gavin snorted a laugh. "You know *him* all too well."

I sure as hell did. When we'd first come here to offer help, he'd had us black-bagged, drugged, and interrogated, and had been ready to send Gib off to be dissected. I had no illusions but that he'd advise the President to do the opposite of whatever I suggested.

"Yes, sir." I managed not to sound whiney or miserable, but it wasn't easy.

"I'll let you know what they say, but unless I tell you different, taking the battalion on this mission is a no-go." He shrugged, his intense eyes going thoughtful. "Bear in mind, son, that your position in our chain of command only applies to the *American* forces under your authority. If you decide to send your"—Gavin frowned, hunting for a word—"*allied* troops on such a mission, that's entirely your call. I'd suggest finding someone you trust and sending them on a scouting mission to feel things out, but as long as you aren't using American troops—and that includes *yourself*, by the way, in case you get any ideas—or any of your people that are necessary for the continued training, then that's not my problem." He sniffed. "Gavin out."

He hung up, which seemed pretty rude, but generals didn't

have to say polite goodbyes to colonels. I didn't leave immediately—not because I expected further clarification soon but because stepping out of the comm center would mean I would have to deal with Gib…and he wasn't going to like what I had to say. But there was no use putting off the inevitable any longer.

A touch of my palm on the security plate unlocked the door and a moment later, it slid open automatically at my presence. Giblet stood on the other side of it, arms folded.

"What the hell did they say?" he wanted to know. "Did they give you an answer yet?"

He looked, if anything, more ragged and threadbare than when I'd seen him get off the shuttle, as if the last couple hours had aged him years. He unfolded his arms and stuffed his hands in his jacket pockets as if unsure what to do with them. I didn't want to answer, but he'd know what that meant and get even angrier with me for not being honest with him.

"I did," I confessed. "It's a no-go. They're not willing to use their troops when we basically know it's an ambush. Plus, they're not willing to send *anyone* out on a mission before the training is complete, and that includes the people doing the training. Which means me and you."

"Those primitive, short-sighted, hairless apes," he snarled, hands coming out of his pockets and curling like talons. "Don't they understand this is our one chance to get Zan-Tar?" He slapped a palm against the wall hard enough for the impact to echo up and down the corridor, though there were no other crewmembers in this passage to hear it. The impact seemed to drain his stores of nervous energy, and he leaned against the bulkhead as if he might collapse to the floor. "You know what I'm talking about, Charlie. You know how dangerous this guy is. We have to take him out." He blinked and stood up straight again, a manic smile spreading across his face. "I know. We could send just a small team. Me, Nareena, and a few of her Strada…we could infiltrate the place. He wouldn't be expecting that. Get close, take him out."

It was my turn to feel exhausted, though I refrained from leaning against the doorframe or rubbing at my temples, as much as I wanted to. This was going to require at least the appearance of strength, even if I didn't feel it.

"You know as well as I do that there aren't any Strada criminals or mercenaries. You take Nareena and her people along, you'll get all kinds of attention you don't need. And that's not even mentioning *you*." I motioned toward him. "You're a Varnell, dude. The Anguilar shoot guys like you on sight. One look at you or the Strada, and you're all dead."

"I don't give a damn!" he insisted. "I'll go alone if I have to!" He slapped his palm against his chest. "No one else at risk, just me. Send *me*, Charlie." Gib's voice was pleading. "I want to go. I don't care if I die."

"But I *do*," I told him. "You're my best friend, Gib. I've already lost Brazzo and Dani…I can't lose you, too." I shook my head. "But that's just me being selfish. You can't go because the resistance needs you. You're our best pilot, and our best trainer, too, since you can talk those Space Force nerds into doing everything your way."

Gib's lip curled, his expression showing no sign of him having been won over by my argument.

"I could talk *you* into doing this my way," he pointed out, maybe half a threat. "You'd never even know."

"But you won't," I said softly. "Any more than you would have with Dani. Because I'm your friend."

Pointed teeth bared like he was about to sink them into my carotid.

"If you were my friend," he raged, "you'd let me go. If it was Laranna, you know sure as hell you'd have already left. And I'd go right alongside you."

I started to reply, but he'd already spun on his heel and headed off down the passage. I didn't go after him. He'd cool down, I was sure of it.

Eventually.

5

I HADN'T BEEN MUCH of a drinker in college, which was probably a good thing.

Not because it had meant better grades and perfect attendance and maximum scores on the physical fitness tests in ROTC, but because that meant I couldn't tell if the swill the *Liberator*'s food fabs turned out tasted anything like top-drawer tequila.

I lifted the shot glass, knocked back three fingers in one gulp, and hissed out a breath. It gave me a nice buzz quickly, which was good enough. After slapping the glass on the surface of the bar, what felt like real wood but probably wasn't, I gestured to the service bot.

"Another."

The thing stared at me with as much judgment as a faceless collection of insect-like arms and clawed hands could muster, but it pulled out the metallic feed line from behind the bar again and refilled my glass.

The *Liberator* hadn't had a bar before we'd come aboard her, of course. It was one of the first additions we made to her, with Lenny's help. He'd actually played bartender himself for a while, before he repurposed a maintenance 'bot to handle the duties for him. Though, I considered, since the 'bot was controlled by the ship's systems and Lenny's brain was *in* the ship's systems, I supposed Lenny was *still* the bartender. Maybe he was the one looking at me judgmentally.

"Go to hell," I told him with feeling, though if Lenny knew I was talking to him through the service 'bot, he gave no sign.

"Since when do *you* drink alone?"

I'd left the lights turned down low to give my body the idea it was nighttime, which it was back in the United States, just so my circadian rhythms wouldn't be too screwed up when I decided to rouse myself from my self-pity and head back to Ft. Carson and the training course. It was dark enough that the tall, lean figure was barely a silhouette against the light from the passageway streaming through the open door, but I already knew who it was.

I raised a toast to Valentine McKee and downed another shot. Warmth spread out from my gut in all directions, along with a general feeling of well-being that was so much nicer than what I *had* been feeling.

"Since Laranna had to go down to the cruiser that's being repaired," I explained, "to supervise the launch. And Chuck is covering for me at the training ground in Colorado, where I should really be right now if I wasn't hiding. And since Gib took off back to the cruiser and is making a point not to return my messages these last two days, that leaves…well, *you*. Want a drink? It's on me." I waved at the robot. "Or on Lenny, anyway."

"Sure, why not?"

Val pulled out one of the metal stools and slid in beside me.

"Give Mr. McKee a tequila shot," I said to the robot. "In a clean glass."

The robot eyed me askance as if mortified that I'd suggest it didn't clean its glasses, but it grabbed another and poured a shot for him, then refilled mine without being asked.

"How many is that for you?" Val wondered.

"Four, I think," I said, then frowned. "Or maybe five. But I think four because every time I've had five, I've passed out, and I don't feel close to passing out."

"Maybe you should pass on this one," he suggested, taking a sip, which I thought was an incredibly disgusting way to drink tequila. "At some point, you're going to have to go back to work, and the more you have of this shit, the harder that's going to be."

"Maybe if I drink enough," I suggested, "I just won't go back at all. Maybe I'll just say the hell with it and fly away from here so I don't have to deal with any of this shit anymore."

"Son, if you could do that, you would have bowed out of all this a long, long time ago." Val laughed and took another sip. I scowled and took the shot the way God intended, then rocked back at the multicolored lights exploding in my head.

"Oh, yeah, that was definitely the fourth," I said, concentrating to make sure I put the shot glass all the way onto the bar. I doubted it would break since Lenny had probably used something unbreakable to make them, but I also knew that if I dropped it, I'd have to bend down and pick it up, which might get messy at the moment.

"You worried about Gib?" Val asked. "Because I am."

"He'll be okay," I insisted. "I know he'll be okay. He's a survivor. He's lived through worse than this."

"Has he?" He shrugged. "Because I don't know that he's ever loved anyone before. I don't know that he's had the chance before he met Dani. You tell me. You're a man in love. Would you be okay?"

If I hadn't been drunk, I might have lied. Not because I didn't want to be honest with Val but because I didn't want to admit it to myself.

"No. I wouldn't be. I'd be out there killing Anguilar until my damn arms fell off, until they killed me. I'd never stop."

"Yeah, I think I'd be the same," Val admitted. "In fact, that's why I came to find you." He looked down at the empty glass, staring at it as if the answers were in the dregs. "I'm past my expiration date for this kind of thing, Charlie."

Squinting at him, I considered his words and wondered if I understood them right.

"What do you mean this kind of thing?" I asked.

"I mean the whole being out in the field, getting shot at thing. I've done it enough. Went through the war, hunted down outlaws for a living, and now, these last few years, I've been dodging bullets of a different kind." He chuckled. "The shiny, red kind that'll blow a hole clean through you. I've been talking about it with Brandy, and I'm going back to Sanctuary full-time to train our militia there."

I wasn't aware my mouth had dropped open until I closed it.

"Damn, Val," I blurted. "I'm gonna miss you, man, but if that's what you feel like you have to do…"

"We're gonna have a baby," he said, grinning with a hint of guilt, like he knew it wasn't a good time for it but couldn't help himself. "We had Lenny do that genetic thing he was talking about, and we're gonna have a little boy. He's due in six months."

"Oh, my God!" If my mouth had dropped open in shock before, now it did so in amazement. "Congratulations!" I grabbed his hand and shook it warmly until it just didn't feel adequate, and I pulled him into a hug. "Holy shit! You're gonna be a dad!"

"I've been a dad since I married Brandy and adopted Maxx," he reminded me in gentle reproach. "But yeah, we're gonna have another."

I pulled away, embarrassed that I'd slighted Maxx, delighted at the fact they were having a baby, and yet still sad that we were losing Val as one of the team. I was rarely speechless, but I couldn't find anything to say for a solid ten seconds and just shook my head, patting him on the arm until it got awkward and I stepped away.

"What made you decide to do it now?" I asked, which was a stupid question but the best I could do under the influence.

"I've wasted a lot of time in my life, Charlie," he said, not seeming offended at my nonplussed state. "I could have had four good years with Betsy, but I went off to war instead. That was a whole life wasted. I'm not wasting any more time, not with Brandy. I want to make a life with her, and running around trying to get myself killed isn't any kind of life." He grabbed my shoulder and stared me straight in the eye, as if he wanted to make sure the message got through. "Time ain't something any of us should waste. I know you're young and it won't mean as much to you now as it should, but I want you to remember that."

I nodded, a bit numb but sensing this was important.

"For sure," I agreed. "I get you, totally."

I was not as drunk as I had been a moment ago, and I wasn't sure if that was a good or bad thing, since sobriety helped me to understand exactly what he was talking about. Laranna and me. I didn't want to think about that right now.

Luckily, I didn't have to think about it for very long.

"Charlie." Brandy's voice echoed through the bar and through my head. "Turn your damned comm on!" Oh yeah, I'd forgotten about that. I'd turned the notification sounds off two drinks in because I'd been determined to get a massive drunk on and hadn't wanted to be cut off by a well-meaning Lenny.

"Sorry," I told her, not meaning it and not bothering to use the comm to answer. "What's going on?"

"Meet me on the bridge. We have a big problem."

"Giblet is gone," Brandy declared, her expression bleak.

"What the hell do you mean he's *gone*?" I demanded, then winced, realizing I'd said that too loud on the crowded bridge of the *Liberator*…and that I shouldn't be that harsh with a pregnant woman. Part of me that was still thinking clearly—a very *small* part at this point in time—wondered why Lenny wasn't on the bridge with everyone else.

"I mean, he told the training crew on the cruiser that he had to fly back to the *Liberator*," she said with the cadence of an elementary school teacher lecturing a student. "But instead of hopping on one of the shuttles and heading over here, he boarded the interstellar transport still docked with the cruiser and jumped into hyperspace."

"The transports are still here?" I asked inanely, because of course they were since he'd taken one.

The transports were the smallest hyperspace-capable ships we had aside from the Vanguard fighters, the smallest anyone could build currently since the technology for the starfighters had been lost. They weren't warships and couldn't be turned into them, which meant the Anguilar didn't attempt to regulate them, and they could go basically anywhere without anyone giving them a second look. We'd had two of them dropped off the last time the *Liberator* had made a cargo run just as a contingency in case the Anguilar had launched an attack and we'd needed to run and get help.

"They were scheduled to be loaded on the *Liberator* before we headed back to Sanctuary," Brandy explained, banging her fist lightly against the sensor display housing, perhaps in anger at Giblet or perhaps frustration at my stupid questions. "But we haven't offloaded all the Starblades yet because nearly half of them are scheduled to be stored in the second cruiser, and it hasn't launched yet."

"No one tried to stop him?" Val asked, and thank God he was there to ask the question because if he hadn't, I would have, and if Brandy had been angry before, it was nothing compared to her reaction to him.

"No, my dear husband," she growled. "No one thought to stop our most senior pilot and training officer and one of our commander's closest and most trusted companions from taking whatever transport he wanted, because no one knew they had a *reason* to." She glared between the two of us. "Maybe one of you should have thought to *tell* them there was a reason to."

It was taking my life into my hands to ask anything further, but there was just enough left of the tequila buzz to give me courage.

"He didn't leave any message?" I wanted to know. "He didn't tell us where he was going?"

She didn't fly off the handle at that one, though. Instead, she acted as if that was the first intelligent question I'd asked.

"In fact, he did. He sent a brief transmission just before he jumped out of the system."

Brandy touched a control on her comm, and a small section of the main display switched to a close-up shot of Giblet's face in the shadows of a darkened cockpit, lit only by the controls in front of him.

"I'm sorry we couldn't do this face-to-face," he said glumly. "I couldn't take the chance that you'd try to stop me." Gib shrugged. "You said you were being selfish, and so am I, I guess. I tried to be a better man for her, tried to be something maybe I'm not. Maybe something I can't be. That Anguilar son of a bitch stole it from me, stole any chance Dani and I had at a life together. Now I'm going to make sure he doesn't get the chance to steal anything else from the rest of us. Don't come after me. Don't try to stop me. I have to do this, and you have to let me." He tried to smile, but it couldn't quite make it to his eyes. "Goodbye."

"Goddammit," I murmured, turning from them and running toward the bridge exit.

The walls blurred on either side of me, and so did my thoughts. Gib was heading right into the belly of the beast, into what we were all one hundred percent sure was a trap, and all I could think of was that I'd driven him to this, that I'd made a huge mistake accepting a commission and tying myself to another authority who could tell me what to do. I'd told everyone I'd done it because we needed the manpower, but maybe the truth was, I just didn't want to be the final arbiter of life or death for millions of people.

And I'd let it get in the way of what I knew I had to do.

I ran, heading for the cargo bay. I'd take a lander to the cruiser, have a Vanguard meet me there—we had four of them orbiting the Moon, the rest in the outer system on patrol, but they docked with the cruiser or landed at Andrews every twenty-four hours for rest and a shower in shifts. I'd grab one and load it up with provisions from the cruiser. The trip would suck, but I'd get there before him thanks to the Vanguard's advanced hyperdrive.

I'd need some guns, too. They had some rifles on the cruiser.

I'd grab one, some armor, some ammo. Ten minutes in and out. I'd leave a message for Laranna before I left, and that would piss her off but...

"Goddammit, Charlie, hold up!"

The strong grip might not have stopped me most of the time, but between the panic and the tequila, I wasn't as steady on my feet as usual, and the push threw me up against the wall. The air went out of me, and I collapsed to the floor, looking up at Valentine, who was breathing harder than I was, hands on his knees. Cursing, I tried to push myself up, but he held up a hand to stop me.

"For God's sake, Charlie, I can't run that fast anymore. Just sit there for a second and listen. You can't do this."

"I can't *not* do it!" I yelled back at him, jumping to my feet. "I can't let Gib do this alone! He's gonna get himself killed!"

"Gib did this *knowing* he was gonna get himself killed!" Val yelled back. "He did it knowing it was stupid, knowing he was being selfish, because he loved Dani and he couldn't live without her. *You* don't get the luxury of being selfish! You don't get the luxury of revenge! You're our commander. You hold all our lives in your hands, and you don't get to throw all that away because you're worried about your friend. It's natural." He shrugged. "It's what any of us would do, but you gave up that right when you took the job. Gib screwed up, and I wish like hell I'd caught him before he did, but that doesn't mean you get to make his screw-up even bigger by becoming part of it."

"I can't let him do this," I told Val, pushing him away from me. "I'm going after him, and there's not a damned thing you can say that'll stop me."

"If you go," Val said, "then Laranna's going after you."

That stopped me, and I blinked, then stared at him.

"You know it's true," he went on. "You'll head out and do what? Start blasting shit with your fighter? Until you either get killed or run away? And then what? Laranna is going to come in after you and get herself killed too? If you want to do this, you make it an order, and you make it a military operation, and to hell with what the American government says. I follow your orders, not theirs. I haven't been in the Army since 1865, and it ain't likely I'll be going back. But you can't just head off headlong like some stupid kid. Because if you do, then you don't belong here, and I've been wrong about you for the last couple years. But I don't think I am."

"Damn it," I hissed, slumping back against the wall. "Why the hell do you have to be right?"

Val put a hand on my shoulder and sighed.

"Because it's my job."

6

THE FARM LOOKED different during the day, and particularly different from the air. The last time I'd been to this little corner of rural Virginia, we'd snuck in at night and snuck out the same way, with most of the federal government on our trail, which hadn't left excess time for sightseeing.

It wasn't much of a farm, not in the traditional sense, because they didn't grow anything there except trees, grass, and wildflowers, but it sure was pretty. And it had a lot of flat ground for me to land the shuttle. I was sure there was a lot of chatter on the radio from the Air Force and various air traffic controllers, and probably comms from the *Liberator* and the American cruiser, but I'd shut down my transceiver before I left orbit. I didn't want to hear from anyone right now, except the one person on this farm, the one I'd come to see.

He knew I was coming. He was the one call I'd made before I

turned off the radio, and he stood in the driveway, arms folded, watching me land the shuttle as I watched him. The stocky figure, shorter now than when I'd known him in college just from natural shrinkage with age, disappeared completely behind the cloud of dust and debris as the landing jets set the small, oval lander down gently in the side yard of the farmhouse.

The dust had settled by the time I opened the hatch and jumped down the steps, and George Barnaby, former Assistant National Security Advisor, former Army general, former ROTC cadet at the University of South Florida, and still my friend, walked up to meet me. He'd grown a beard since I'd last seen him, shot with gray, and I smiled thinly at his denim overalls and work shirt.

"You're looking very Green Acres there, George," I told him, offering a hand.

George threw back his head and guffawed before he ignored my hand and gave me a hug instead. He smelled like sweat and horseshit, which told me what he'd been doing before I'd called.

"You know, Charlie, about nine people out of ten wouldn't even get that reference," he warned, letting me free of his agrarian embrace. "Hell, I haven't seen that show since I was a little kid, and even then, it was on reruns on syndication." He laughed again, though this one was shorter and sharper, with a hint of bitterness. "Not that *reruns* or *syndication* even mean anything nowadays."

"I haven't had the chance to watch much TV," I admitted. "But farm life seems to be agreeing with you."

"It's not like I actually have any crops to tend," he admitted.

"I just have to take care of the horses and chickens and goats, and look after the place, and in exchange, I get free room and board. You want to go inside?" George motioned at the house. "Can I offer you something to drink? Water? A beer?"

"I'm cooped inside a spaceship most of the time," I replied, taking a deep breath, enjoying the aroma of damp grass and dandelions. "Why don't we take a walk so I can enjoy some fresh air for a change?"

"Sure, I can give you the nickel tour of the place," he offered, waving for me to follow him. Before we rounded the edge of the house, George gave a nod back at the lander. "Still blows my mind how much like a flying saucer that thing looks."

"That's exactly what I thought the first time I saw it," I agreed. "Coming down on top of me in the woods across the street from DeLuca's Pizza in Brandon in '87. You're lucky I didn't use the same immobilization beam on you that Lenny used on me."

"Immobilization beam?" he repeated, eyes going wide. "That's actually a thing? Why haven't you handed that one over to the Department of Defense, along with the pulse guns and particle cannons?"

"Because it's useless against anyone wearing armor, and you have to be insanely close for it to work. It's been two years, and I still haven't a chance to try it out yet. Unless you think I should go scoop up some poor schlub on a farm across the border in West Virginia just for shits and giggles."

"I have to admit, that *would* be entertaining," George told me as we passed by a storage shed. One of the doors hung open, revealing the riding mower within, and I wondered if that was what he'd been doing before mucking out the horse stalls. "But I've been talking to Chuck, and he tells me you should be busier than a one-legged man at an ass-kicking contest. I'm happy to see you, but I can't believe you landed your alien spaceship on the farm just to say hi. What's going on?"

And there was the biggest difference between the twenty-five-year-old George Barnaby who I'd left behind that fateful night in 1987 and this version. Not so much as a chuckle at the idea of buzzing rednecks in a flying saucer, but he'd laughed hard at a reference to an old TV show. Was that what middle age was going to be like? Wading through nostalgia, reminiscing about the good old days? A shudder went through me, the thought nearly enough to make me wish for a death in battle before I got old and decrepit.

"Yeah, we're all pretty busy. I'm supposed to be in Utah right now, actually, supervising the relaunch of the Anguilar cruiser that crashed there. But I made a slight detour."

Which was probably going to get me yelled at by General Gavin, though at this point, I couldn't give a shit less.

"I need someone to talk to," I confessed, watching a lithe calico cat cleaning herself on the open windowsill of the barn. A horse whinnied in reproach as we passed by. George said nothing, just eyed me sidelong, the patience of his years tempering natural curiosity. "Someone who knows who I used to be," I clarified.

"I thought you were all about moving past the old Charlie." He stepped over a pile of poop, and I followed his path gingerly, more used to wearing my old Nikes than the issue combat boots that went with my field utilities. I hadn't had the opportunity to wear my Chicago concert T and blue jeans in months now. "Stepping into your new role as *el jefe supreme* and all that."

"That's what I want to talk to you about." We'd made it to the back of the barn, and I paused there, staring through the large double doors at the Appaloosa chomping hay in one of the stalls inside. "It's Gib."

George swatted at a mosquito absently as I related the gist of what had happened yesterday, and I might have thought him disinterested if I hadn't known the man since he was a teenager. When I'd finished, he nodded thoughtfully, hands stuffed in the pockets of his overalls.

"Giblet always did strike me as the impulsive type. Not that I can blame him. I never understood the relationship he had with Dani, but then, according to Jill, I wasn't much good at understanding plain old human relationships, either." He smacked at another bug and cursed. "Only thing I hate about spring is all the damned skeeters. Let's keep walking and try to find a breeze." George glanced back at me curiously. "Are there skeeters on other planets?"

"Unfortunately," I sighed. "I asked Lenny why they bothered to bring the pests along when they rearranged the ecologies on all those worlds, and his explanation was something about how they were important for the amphibians and the fish, and us humanoids would just have to deal with it."

"Well, that kind of sucks. Lenny sounds a lot like God."

I barked a laugh.

"Yeah, he thinks about himself that way sometimes. I wish he could give me all the answers like the real God because I could use that right about now."

"You want to go after your friend," George assumed. There was no judgment in the words, just a matter-of-factness like we were discussing the weather. "You want to drop everything and go rescue him."

"Yeah, and everyone keeps telling me that's the wrong thing to do." I walked ahead of him so he wouldn't see the grimace I couldn't keep off my face. "That it would be irresponsible and reckless, and I'd be abandoning everyone who was counting on me."

"And you don't agree?" he assumed.

"I do. I mean," I corrected myself, "I *think* I do. But part of me just doesn't care, and what I can't figure out is whether that part of me is the part that's the real me, the one you knew from 1987. Because it feels a lot like I'm not being myself, that I'm letting all this change me into something I'm not."

A glance back over my shoulder showed me George's nod.

"I understand that more than you know. I've been thinking about that a lot lately. Who I am and what I became. Particularly since Jill died. I retreated into my job after that. By the time you showed up, I'm not sure if the man I was at twenty-five would have recognized the man I'd become at sixty."

"People grow," I allowed with a shrug. "They change. That's not a bad thing, right? We couldn't stay twenty-five our whole lives."

"True. But the thing is, Charlie, I had thirty-five years to adjust to that change. You've just had the last two. Everything kind of rushed up at you all at once. There's no way for you to adjust to it, which is probably why you're running into this now. Twenty-five-year-old Charlie would have dropped everything to go bail a friend out of trouble."

I was about to object that I wasn't that much different than twenty-five-year-old Charlie, but I realized that was exactly what he'd been trying to say.

"What should I do, George?" I asked him, spreading my hands helplessly. "What do *you* think I should do?"

"If you're asking me what you would have done before, I can tell you that you would have left already. If you're asking me what the right thing to do is…well, that's more complicated. I was a general, Charlie. I followed orders. The mission, the men, and then me. Which meant the mission came first."

I nodded, remembering the saying very well.

"The thing is, though," he went on as we made it to the edge of the trees and turned to follow the line of the irrigation ditch, "it's not just because it's your duty. It's also because Giblet made a choice, and he asked you to respect it, even if you think it's the wrong one."

I snorted in derision.

"People make bad choices all the time. Should I just let him get himself killed?"

"I was in Iraq over twenty years ago," George said, apropos of nothing, and I just stared at him, waiting for him to continue. "I was a battalion commander and never fired a shot in anger, but I had a friend from my Advanced Course and Ranger school, Simon Park, who was a staff officer of the transportation unit attached to us." He chuckled, though the humor in the soft laugh was tempered with sadness. "I always gave him shit about that, about him being in Transportation now and not a grunt anymore. But you know, the thing is, my battalion didn't have a single KIA the whole time, but his Transportation unit…IEDs, ambushes, snipers, they'd all go for the truck drivers. He lost over a dozen soldiers in a nine-month tour. And he couldn't handle it. We got back, and I tried to stay in touch with him, but he pushed me away. Fell into alcohol and prescription drugs and wound up out of the Army, and only a good lawyer helped him avoid a court-martial. He wound up divorced, wife took their kids and moved away, and he got one DUI after another, almost wound up in jail."

George's pace slowed, and he stared at the grass at this feet.

"I did everything I could, tried to get him into AA, tried to get him back in touch with his family. He didn't want help. He told me that this was what he deserved. He died of a heart attack at fifty years old, alone in a one-room apartment."

The story left a lead weight in my stomach, and not just because it was depressing as shit.

"You're saying I can't help him?" I demanded. "That he won't want me to save him so I should just let him die?"

"I'm saying that you can't save someone who doesn't want to be saved. You'll wind up losing them anyway, being forced to watch them die and not being able to do anything about it. Or dying yourself, right alongside them."

George didn't look or sound like my old friend anymore. Instead, he sounded more like my father…or rather, the father I'd wished I had. Comforting in some ways, definitely uncomfortable in others. Uncomfortable enough that I changed the subject.

"Are you getting along okay here, George?" I asked, turning to keep walking, back around the property toward the house. "I mean, do you need anything?"

"Not as long as Larry's willing to let me have a place here." George smiled as he looked around at the rolling fields, the trees, the wildflowers. "Honestly, I'm happier now than I have been since Jill died. And I still have the money from selling the house, gathering interest. If I find a place I like, I'll make an offer…or, well, I was thinking I might see what Larry would take for this place."

"If you need a job," I told him, "I have a lot of connections now. Not just the government, but all kinds of defense contractors we've had to deal with getting the cruiser up and running. They're all bending over backward to ingratiate themselves to the Peboktan so they can get all the engineering secrets. They'd hire Kermit the Frog if I asked them to."

"That's very flattering," George said with a snort. "And I do appreciate the thought, but I think I've spent enough time dealing with the defense industry from one side to ever have interest in dealing with it from the other." He grinned churlishly. "Besides, if I get hard up enough for money, I have multiple offers for book deals and exclusive interviews…hell, one streaming service offered me a limited series about our time in college together. I've resisted the temptation so far, but if the bills start to pile up…"

I laughed softly. We were almost back to the lander.

"You go right ahead," I told him. "Just make sure you tell the whole story and let them know that I was an academic prodigy, a PT god, and a hit with all the college girls. Gotta have some journalistic integrity."

"Yeah, well…one out of three ain't bad. You *did* max out the Army PT test."

I paused at the hatch and shot him a bird.

"You sure you don't want to come with me?" I offered. "It may be your one chance to watch a full-sized cruiser lift off from a planet. Because I'm sure the EPA, the FAA, NASA, and the St. George, Utah Chamber of Commerce won't let it happen again."

"Naw, I get airsick." His smile faded, eyes growing serious. "What are you gonna do, Charlie?"

I didn't look back, didn't want him to see my expression if it matched the dead feeling in my chest.

"I've got no choice. I'm going to let him go."

7

"Where the hell have you been?" Laranna asked softly, grabbing my arm before I'd taken the last step off the lander. She kept her expression placid, but there was an undercurrent of tension in her voice. "I've been trying to get you on the comm for an hour."

She walked me past a single row of Starblades, and I blinked at the sight.

"How did *they* get here?" I asked her, ignoring her question for now. I'd explain later, when I was sure no one would overhear. "I thought the plan was to hold the complement of fighters for this ship until we got her in the air." I stopped and turned to her, frowning. "Have they come up with a name for the thing, yet?

"The USS *Victory*," she told me, one eyebrow shooting up. "Which seems hopeful, if presumptuous. The other one is being christened the *Endeavor*."

"Not bad," I reckoned with a shrug, then turned and headed back for the bridge. "What about the Starblades though?" I motioned back at my lander. "I mean, it was tough enough squeezing the shuttle in with half the hangar bay entrance blocked off by rock and dirt."

"The *Liberator* needed the space for the Vanguards to rotate back for rest breaks, and the *Endeavor*'s hangar deck is already full. They off-loaded a single squadron to the *Victory*, but the rest will ship over once we're in orbit." She scowled at me. "Now do you want to tell me where you ran off to and why you weren't answering your radio?"

The ramp upward to the bridge rang under the boots of Space Force…

What are they called again? Not airmen. Not soldiers. I couldn't remember. *Spacemen?* Probably not.

The Space Force troops rushed past us, hurrying to get to their stations before the launch, and none of them spared either of us a look. That had to be a product of working for weeks with the Peboktan, because otherwise, none of them would have passed by a green-skinned warrior woman without even a glance.

Either way, they weren't paying attention to either of us.

"I went to see George," I told her quietly.

Laranna didn't respond for a moment, though I saw the twitch of a muscle in her cheek.

"There's nothing you can do about Gib," she said, finally. "You know that, right?"

"That's what George told me." The thump of footsteps faded behind us as the crew reached their destinations. Everyone else had to be in place already, including the Peboktan and Copperell assisting in the engine room. "I'm not so sure. If it had been you instead of Dani, he'd have come with me without a second thought." I shook my head. "Hell, it *was* you back on Strada."

"I was alive," she reminded me. "There was still hope. And back then, you weren't responsible for anyone except the four of us and Lenny. Things are different now."

"Different doesn't always mean better."

I didn't remember ever seeing a starship bridge as crowded as the one on the *Victory* that afternoon. I could understand it, of course. It was a historic event, and simultaneously, a risky maneuver that had the potential to blow the whole ship up and destroy a good-sized city if things went really wrong. The American crew had to be there, of course, and so did the Copperell trainers who were supervising their every move. The others were observers, so I'd been told, nearly an entire second crew of them, and from the patches on their uniforms, they'd been brought in from the UK, France, Australia, and…I squinted at the flag trying to place it. Red and white with an eagle…Poland? We were allies now, and they were part of NATO, so it was possible.

"Colonel Travers," the commander of the ship said, nodding to me as he rose from his seat at the center of the bridge. "I expected you an hour ago."

Which was a little rude for someone who was, theoretically, the same rank as I was, but I suppose the fact that he was in his mid-forties and I was, by appearance anyway, not even thirty, had something to do with his brusqueness. Not that I was going to indulge it.

"Well, I expected you guys to have flying cars and robot maids when I got back, Colonel Whistler, but we all have to deal with disappointment."

Colonel Simon Whistler's brow furled in anger at the slight, but that was just something else he was going to have to deal with. He was used to being in command, and with good reason if he'd been put in charge of one of only two starships in possession of the entire planet, but it had been made very clear to him and every other senior officer assigned either to the cruisers, the fighters, or the Ranger battalion that I was not subordinate to any of them.

"I'm here now," I continued, "so, what's our status? Everything on schedule?"

"Yes, we've all been doing our jobs," he shot back. "The launch is still scheduled for 1700 local time." Whistler glanced aside at the main screen and the countdown display in the corner. "Thirty-five mikes." Mikes was the military phonetic shorthand for *minutes*, but it was mostly used for radio communications and seemed pretentious for a Space Force officer. "We have acceleration couches for you, if you want to get strapped in."

That was another slight. The seats he nodded toward were at the rear of the bridge, fold-down spares for unimportant guests, while the foreign observers had been given the ones closer to the center.

"That's okay, Colonel Whistler," I told him with a casual wave. "The gravity resist should make it a pretty smooth ride. I'll just stand."

Whistler tucked his chin into his chest like he was getting

ready to wade into a fistfight, the overhead lights gleaming off his hairless skull. From the faint shadow, his hair had begun to desert him long before he'd banished the rest to exile with its fellows.

"That's against safety regulations…" he began.

"This ship has been in the possession of the United States government for about three months," I reminded him. "Knowing how slowly the big green machine works, I find it hard to believe that there even *are* any safety regulations that apply to this ship."

The man began to sputter, and Laranna surreptitiously kicked me in the ankle, a subtle warning not to needlessly antagonize the man. I turned away from him and examined the view of the ship from camera drones surrounding her. I'd seen it on the way in, but I'd been preoccupied with the tricky approach to the landing bay and hadn't taken the time to absorb the surreality of the scene.

It could have been a backdrop for a classic John Ford western, with the buttes and hoodoos of the desert southwest spread out in an epic tableau around us, stained red by the evening sunset. Beautiful like nothing I'd seen before, and I wished for the time off to go hiking through the sandstone vistas.

And then there was the ship. She'd been half-buried in the dirt when they first sent a reaction force out to investigate her, though a good deal of that had been cleared away by heavy machinery in the intervening weeks. She'd also had at least a few remnants of the Anguilar crew, though I'd been assured all of them had died rather than surrender. I could believe that as much as I wanted, but if they had a handful of Krin or Anguilar stuck in a blacksite somewhere, trying to sweat information out of them, all I could say was, more power to them.

The ship was a fair-sized office building plucked out of a city skyline, turned on her side, and tossed into the desert like trash discarded from a passing car. She glistened crimson under the pink and purple sunset sky, a relic from a science fiction flick accidentally mislocated on that John Ford western set, or perhaps left over from the filming of one of the more recent movies Dani had convinced me to watch. No sand worms rising up to devour the intruder, but the resemblances were there.

The newly christened *USS Victory* was, at least, more level than she'd been after the crash. That had taken weeks on its own as braces were put in place beneath her to keep her on an even keel while Mallarna and her engineering crew had repaired the drives. And in just a few minutes, she'd rise above this fairy-tale desert highland and not stop until she was among the stars.

"Any complications?" I asked, not caring who answered the question. "Anything that might delay us?"

"Security concerns."

I turned at the unfamiliar voice, saw the female captain behind it. She was as sharp and crisp as a brand-new twenty-dollar bill, every crease in her uniform screaming professionalism and perfectionism. Her dark, curly hair was cut short, just a couple inches off her scalp, and her eyes pierced me with judgment that actually seemed to matter, where Whistler's rolled off my back like water off a duck.

"And you are?" I asked.

"Captain Emma Quesada, Office of Strategic Intelligence," she told me.

"The OSI?" I repeated, grinning at a childhood memory. "Do you work for Oscar Goldman?"

Quesada stared back at me blankly, and not one single person on the entire bridge got the joke, which was just sad.

"Never mind," I said, gesturing to her to go ahead. "Security concerns?"

"What we're doing is hardly a secret," the intelligence officer expounded. "Even the timing couldn't be kept purely compartmentalized, not with so many different nations involved." She did *not* look at the international observers on the bridge, and it was obvious to me that she deliberately didn't look at them. I liked her already. "We have the airspace and ground approaches carefully guarded," she went on, "and once we reach high orbit, no other nation has anything that can reach us. That leaves a window of vulnerability, however." Quesada shrugged. "I'm not a technician nor a physicist, so I can't make any assumptions about the ship's defenses…"

"I can," Whistler interrupted, scowling. He might have been scowling at my interruption of his bridge activities or, more likely, at Quesada for actually attempting to answer my question. "We have no actionable intelligence of any threats, and even if they exist, what would any of the possible aggressors have that could touch this vessel? *Colonel* Travers?"

"I'm quite aware of the capabilities of this ship's defenses," I told him, "as is my second-in-command." I motioned to Laranna. "And the Copperell and Peboktan advisors right here on the bridge, of course. What none of us know as well are the current weapons systems of the Russians, the Chinese, and whoever else you might consider a threat at the moment. I could tell you that the defense shields on the"—I struggled not to sneer—"the *Victory* are potent enough to turn aside a few hits from a particle cannon and pretty much all but an overwhelming volley from pulse guns. I can tell you that it usually takes me three or four good barrages from multiple main guns to take down her shields. But *you* tell *me*, Colonel…what's the worst that our enemies could throw at us?"

Now I had no trouble at all divining the source of his irritation, but to his credit, he was a professional and answered the question.

"ICBMs, SLBMs, nuclear-tipped cruise missiles. Any of which they'd be nuts to try since it would start World War Three."

"Yeah," I said, casting a long glance around the compartment at the high tech and the aliens and the views of the starship. "Because there's absolutely nothing nuts about this entire situation. No reason at all to think the leaders of Russia or China or Iran might do something desperate."

"Are you suggesting we should abort the launch, then?" Whistler demanded.

"Hell, no," I said. "The whole point behind this is to show everyone that the threat from without is a lot scarier than the ones from here on Earth. Nothing short of the end of the world is stopping this launch."

The colonel smiled thinly.

"Finally, something we agree on completely."

WE DID wind up strapping in, but only once two of the observers, the Polish major and a British *leftenant*-colonel, volunteered to switch seats with us.

"Are we sure," Colonel Jeffcoat, the agreeable Brit, asked as the countdown reached thirty seconds, "that there won't be harmful radiation from the drives?"

"The majority of the lift," Mallarna replied, back up on the bridge for the launch to monitor things from the engineering station, leaving the nuts-and-bolts to her assistants back in the bowels of the ship, "will come from the gravity-resist. Not all of it, but enough that the ionizing radiation from the plasma drives should be negligible. By the time we're at a distance where the gravitational pull ceases to interact with the graviton field, the atmosphere will be thin enough that fallout won't be a concern."

Jeffcoat's jaw clenched, the muscles around his eyes tightening in what I took to be a concerted effort to control his expression, to *not* make a horrified face at the sight of the Peboktan. The American bridge crew kept their eyes averted from her with practiced ease, but it wasn't hard to tell they hadn't gotten used to the buglike aliens either.

"Thanks very much, Ms. Mallarna," Jeffcoat said with stereotypical British reserve. "I'm surprised that your government gave the okay for this, Colonel Whistler."

"The only other choice was leaving a starship sitting in the Utah desert," the ship's commander said with a cynical grunt. "The President declared a state of emergency for the city of St.

George, Washington County, and the entire state of Utah, and basically dared the Congress to stop him from getting this ship off the ground."

"I must say, I don't seem to understand how your government works, sir."

"It doesn't, most of the time," Whistler admitted with a rueful chuckle, "but then you have something like this happen, and they all get off their asses. Hopefully. Engineering, do we have a clean feed from the power cells?"

The American engineering officer, a female major with the classic thick glasses of a math nerd, shot a look at Mallarna as if seeking her approval, the only one of the Americans or our allies who'd managed to face her eye to eye. She nodded.

"Green across the board, sir," the younger officer confirmed. "Ready for gravity-resist."

"Helm," Whistler snapped. "Full power to the gravity-resist field."

The Copperell technician assigned to monitor the helm station shifted his balance to the balls of his feet as he watched the American officer carefully, as if anticipating a leap to take over the controls in an emergency. If the helm officer noticed, he didn't show it, simply pushing the controls upward. My balance shifted just barely enough for me to notice it, not enough to throw me off my feet if I'd been reckless enough to go through with my threat to ride out the launch standing on the deck like a surfer.

On the main screen, the view from the drones told the real story. Sand and dirt poured off the edges of the massive cruiser like water off the conning tower of a submarine as it surfaced.

She lifted what didn't look like a great distance on the screen but had to be at least fifty feet, and none of us felt a thing. The entire length of the ship gleamed in the sunlight, the powerful curves reminiscent of the barding of a medieval warhorse in a tournament, ready to charge down the lists.

"Maneuvering thrusters," Whistler ordered. "Bring our nose up thirty degrees and give us twenty percent power to the main drive."

If rising from the dirt with no sense of lift in a ship this size had been weird, the view from the nose cameras tilted upward into the darkening sky without so much as a rollercoaster-ride stomach twist was downright unnatural. Even the Vanguards didn't have that kind of gravity control, despite their sophistication, because the cruiser had more power to play with. When the main drive kicked in, though, I felt it.

Even at twenty percent of max output, the rumble of the plasma shook the superstructure, and the feed from the drones whited out from the thermal bloom out of the drive bells at the rear of the cruiser. I suddenly had my doubts about Mallarna's assurances that there wouldn't be significant radiation from the takeoff, but that was someone else's problem—maybe the President's, maybe the residents, but surely not mine.

Pressure about the force of a single-handed push, nothing like the acceleration would have been without the inertial dampeners, just enough to press me back into my seat.

"Altitude one thousand meters," Captain Lombard announced from the helm station, "and climbing."

The closest drones had fallen behind, and the blinding flare of the plasma drives still dazzled their cameras, but not enough to totally drown out the much smaller shape of our cruiser at the top of the candle flame. The climb was slow at first, but the *Victory* picked up speed with altitude, and soon, we were nothing but a dazzling star high in the sky to the drones, stuck back around 5,000 feet up.

"Ten thousand meters," Lombard said. "Passing Mach Three."

"Vampire! Vampire! Vampire!"

Every head snapped around at the announcement from the Tactical station, a baby-faced major named Ramirez. Including mine, though I had no clue what the hell the call meant. He explained it immediately, thankfully.

"We have three inbound missiles traveling at Mach 10! ETA thirty seconds!"

"Hypersonics," Jeffcoat said, his voice unbelievably calm. "Must be the Russians."

"Anyone want to bet that they're nuclear tipped?" I put in. "I can't promise the shields will stop them in the atmosphere. Generally, cruisers don't engage in combat in the atmosphere, and if the warheads are large enough…" I shrugged. "We need to climb, get to orbit. We can outrun them."

"I have strict orders," Whistler said tautly, not meeting my eyes, "not to go over thirty percent drive output until we're out of the atmosphere."

"Well, that's Goddamned stupid!" I snapped back at him. "I'd call the White House and get those orders reversed before we're nothing but confetti."

"Too late," Ramirez said, shaking his head. "I'm activating the point-defense system!"

That was something new, something the Anguilar hadn't bothered with, but apparently, the US defense establishment couldn't bear not to add their own accoutrements to the design. The point-defense turrets the cruiser had come with were pulse guns designed to take on fighters, but most of those had been burned away by the damage that had caused the ship to crash in the first place. They'd been replaced by CWIS turrets from Navy ships…and the automated target acquisition system to go with them.

The cruiser was huge, the turrets small, but they were also incredibly numerous, squeezed into every nook and cranny where they would fit, and when half of them fired at once, the vibration rattled my teeth. Tracers whipped across the dark sky in the optical camera view, sawing back and forth, seeking out the missiles. A flash way too close. Another.

"Two down," Ramirez announced, and I realized my fingers were numb from digging into the armrests of the acceleration couch. "Last one is still incoming…ten seconds until estimated detonation."

One last flash of white, and the guns fell silent, the only sound the distant rumble of the drives and the hiss of two dozen sighs as everyone relaxed on the bridge.

"That's it," Ramirez said. "Though I can't promise they won't launch more."

"Can you trace them back to their origin?" I asked, yanking loose my seat restraints and hopping to my feet. Laranna must have intuited what I had in mind because she was right behind me.

"Yeah," the Tactical officer said, staring at me in confusion. "They were…"

"Send the coordinates to our fighters," I told him.

"What the hell do you intend to do, Travers?" Whistler demanded, though this time less in anger than fear.

"Far as I can tell, that was just an act of war," I told him over my shoulder as I jogged off the bridge. "I'm gonna go show them that they can't get away with it."

8

"Echo One, Echo One, this is X-Ray Base, over."

I frowned, racking my brain for what the hell the code meant. I'd tried to get our pilots to use call signs and proper radio etiquette when we'd begun training in the Vanguard fighters, but it had been a waste of time. Most of them had been from a culture with no military tradition, and the Kamerian pilots we'd recruited as trainers thought the whole idea was ridiculous since there was no chance that the transmissions could be intercepted.

Then I recalled—*I* was Echo One, since the Starblade squadron on the *Victory* was Echo Squadron and since I was the highest-ranking officer currently flying a Starblade, that made me Echo One. As for X-Ray Base, that was the designation for whatever the highest command level was for a particular mission. In this case, that would be the Pentagon, and the man in charge there would be Gavin.

"X-Ray Base," I replied, counting on the helmet mic to key itself automatically. "This is Echo One. I read you, over."

"Echo One, what the hell are you doing? Over." *That* was Gavin. I'd recognize the voice anywhere.

It was a stupid question, I reflected, glancing around the cockpit. He'd obviously talked to Whistler and knew I was inside a Starblade fighter, jetting east at hypersonic speeds right next to Laranna in what I supposed would be designated Echo Two.

"X-Ray Base, I'm tracking down the launchers for those hypersonic missiles, and I intend to destroy them." *Obviously.* "Over."

"You do *not* have orders for that!" Gavin was pissed enough that he'd forgotten transmission protocols himself. "You're talking about attacking the damned Russians!"

"No," I snapped back at him. "I'm talking about the Russians launching *nuclear freaking missiles* at an American vessel, which is, last time I checked, an act of war."

The hell with it. If he wanted to lose his cool and talk in the clear, I could do that, too.

"The way I see it, General, you're either going to ignore this and pretend it didn't happen or launch a retaliatory strike that may or may not hit anything or anyone that had a hand in the attack. If you want to make a point, if you want to teach the Russians that they can't get away with this shit, the two of us can do it. You send the cruiser to do it, the Russians can play the victim and say that was exactly why they launched those missiles. You send conventional military forces to do it, you're going to get our pilots and soldiers killed. Or you can let the two of us show them what a waste of time it is to screw with the United States with minimal collateral damage and minimal casualties. Your call." I sucked in a breath and calmed myself down. "Over."

Silence for a moment. A long moment, maybe long enough to pass the whole thing up the chain. Not that far to pass, just one man. I imagined the conversation with President Louis and laughed to myself.

"Echo One, this is X-Ray Base." Gavin was calmer now, though probably still angry. "You're cleared to proceed. Targets are limited to strategic missile launchers and antiair assets. Are we clear? Over."

The corner of my mouth twisted upward, part in amusement, part in fierce joy. I'd been looking forward to some payback ever since the damned Russians had sent their mercenaries after us in DC.

"X-Ray Base, this is Echo One. I read you loud and clear. Wilco. Over."

"X-Ray Base, out."

At least he'd had the courtesy to sign off instead of leaving me hanging.

"What was that about?" Laranna asked. The Starblades all shared the same Resistance security codes, and she shared mine, which was the highest clearance, which meant she'd been listening in on the conversation.

"We were both just trying to make sure we weren't about to start World War Three," I explained.

"Great gods," she murmured. "Isn't it bad enough that your people had *two* world wars to begin with?"

"It wasn't my idea. Keep your eyes open, though. The Starblades aren't going to get picked up by radar, but the Russians have satellites, and they might see us on optical or thermal."

"And what if they do?" she sneered. "Do they have anything that can touch us?"

"Same thing I told him," I warned her. "We haven't tried it before."

I'd expected darkness below us, would have welcomed the embrace of the night, but we were outracing the dusk, and paradoxically, the farther east we flew, the lighter it got. I felt exposed, a bug on a plate, alone in the gaudy blue of the afternoon sky, hanging over the open ocean. I'd never appreciated the sheer speed of the Starblades before, not when the planets I'd been soaring above were unfamiliar, the distances unknown.

But I knew exactly how far it was from the Utah desert to the Pacific coast, how far from the coast to northern Japan. To the Sakhalin Islands, where those launchers had fired from. I had a vague idea where the Sakhalins were thanks to a vaguely remembered news story from my high school days. A Korean airliner, KAL-007, had been shot down by the Soviets over the Sakhalins in 1983, supposedly by accident because they'd thought it was a spy plane. Some American congressman had been aboard, and it had been a big shitstorm.

I wondered how big *this* shitstorm would be.

We hadn't received any radio challenges from the US military bases in Hawaii or Guam, and I didn't expect any from Japan. The White House would have alerted them to our overflight, and that might mean the Russians would have prior warning we were coming. Not that I thought the Japanese were trying to screw us over, but the more hands a message passed through, the likelier that the wrong eyes would read it.

The outlines of the islands of Japan were unmistakable on the Starblade's nav sensors, and once we'd cleared the northernmost of them, I shoved the stick forward, the black-tinged blue turning to turquoise as the ocean spread out to welcome our sudden dive.

"Follow my lead," I told Laranna, grunting the words past the *g*-forces that the inertial dampeners couldn't quite overcome. "We're going in one hundred feet up and we're gonna follow the missile trace straight in."

Pulling up just over the waves, I couldn't help but sneak a glance at the rear camera view just to get a glimpse of the Mach shock wave kicking up sprays of water at the back of the Starblade. I'd seen video of fighter jets flying close to the ocean in the past and never once thought I'd be in the cockpit of one. I sure as hell never thought I'd be flying an alien space-fighter into Russian airspace to attack their missile launchers.

"You know what's gonna scare them?" I asked Laranna, my hands riding gently on the stick, keeping the Starblade steady against the bucking thermals this close to the waves. Ahead of us, the rocky shores and the green mountains beyond them grew with alarming speed in the cockpit canopy, threatening me with the prospect of slamming straight into them if I didn't cut the throttle.

"Us blowing the crap out of their military facilities?" she guessed, not showing a bit of the stress or strain either of the attack or the nap-of-the-earth flight.

"No. The fact that we were able to trace them back here like it was nothing. I bet they transported the launchers way out here right near Japan hoping that they'd be able to deny they launched the missiles in the first place, blame it on someone else."

"That's your plan, then?" Laranna wondered. "Intimidate them? Let them know we can find them no matter how carefully they try to hide?"

"Yeah, that…and blow the crap out of their military facilities."

No more words. Talking distracted us, and the mountains required our complete attention. Young and petulant, challenging us with their sharp edges and jagged peaks, trying to intimidate us into pulling up and avoiding them entirely. I took the dare and hugged the passes on the way through them instead. Green and gray and black on three sides of me, the inviting blue up top, comforting with the thought that if worse came to worst, I could just blast straight up into the open sky.

The track led over the mountains to the edge of a town. Not a city, really not even that much of a town, it reminded me of the little resorts in New England that had once been fishing towns. It wasn't surprising that they'd based the launchers near the civilian populace, probably hoping that the possibility of collateral damage would keep the US from striking back at them, if we found the launch sites at all. Not that they weren't *prepared* for a counterstrike.

"Missiles!" Laranna warned almost simultaneously with the flashing red lights and warning buzzer from the Starblade's sensor screen.

Smoke trails streaked upward, seeking both of us out, way too close and way too fast to outrun even in the hypersonic fighters. Except we didn't need to. I'd told General Gavin that advanced Electronic Counter Measures was the reason that no one out in the wider galaxy used remotely piloted vehicles, but ECM was also the reason no one used missiles. Not just the basic signal jammers that militaries had been using for decades, since I'd been a freshman in ROTC, but active scramblers that could throw off any sort of guidance, from heat-seeking to laser-guided.

Half a dozen missiles arced toward us...and then spiraled away, out of control. I hoped they'd miss the town, but there was nothing I could do about that, except make sure no more of the things got fired to begin with.

"Get the SAM launchers," I said, cutting the throttle and yanking the stick to the left, pushing the left pedal simultaneously.

The Starblade banked into a tight roll, the nose angling downward, and even though I hadn't been any sort of pilot before being taken, I was pretty sure the response from an Earth-manufactured fighter to that maneuver would have been for the wings to fall off. That was the great thing about the Starblades—and the Vanguards even more so. The materials technology behind them was decades ahead of our own, maybe centuries, and so was the computer control, which allowed a novice like me to fly like I was a Top Gun pilot with twenty years in the cockpit.

The targeting reticle appeared on the screen when my thumb pressed the control, and it only took another nudge of the stick to bring a mobile Surface-to-Air-Missile launcher into the center of it. Had to watch the length of my bursts. These Starblades didn't have a particle cannon that could fire over and over until the power cells drained, it had a souped-up pulse gun that fed consumable ammo. Just a half-second squeeze of the trigger and a hundred or so crimson streaks connected me to the SAM launcher.

Long enough. The ungainly vehicle showered sparks until I hit one of the unfired missiles, and that was it. The blast spread outward in a concussion wave that shook the SAM launcher beside it, though the crew inside it wouldn't have time to panic. A long burst from Laranna's fighter made sure of that, and in another moment, there was nothing left of either vehicle except flaming debris and a smoking crater.

I didn't bother banking for another pass. It wasn't necessary. The Starblades had directed thrust nozzles like a Harrier, and with nothing else they could shoot at us that worried me, I put the bird into a hover and surveyed the scene below us.

The hypersonic missile launchers were portable in the sense that they'd been brought here on a ship and hauled to the clearing outside town on huge trailers towed by massive tractors, but they weren't running away from us anytime soon. The troops who'd been manning them did, scattering like cockroaches from the light. Good. I wouldn't cry for the Russians who'd tried to kill us, but fewer human deaths on my conscience wasn't a bad thing.

It wasn't hard to target the things because they were huge, four launch pods, each larger than a semi-trailer, tilted upward, each with one missile gone and the second ready to go, though to where, I wasn't sure because the *Victory* was already in orbit. I suppose it didn't matter since they wouldn't get the chance.

Slewing the fighter left to right, I held the trigger down probably longer than I needed to, hosing two of the launchers with a storm of scalar energy. If the fuel explosion from the SAMs had been spectacular, the eruption of the hypersonic missile propellant tanks was apocalyptic.

I was 200 feet up and maybe 300 yards away from the launchers when they went up in an explosion. I thought for a brief, panicked moment that, against everything I knew about them, the nuclear warheads on the missiles had detonated. Then I didn't have the luxury of thinking because the shock wave from the blast slammed into the Starblade, and it was all I could do to keep the fighter from tumbling out of control. I didn't recall making a conscious decision to thrust away from the concussion wave, or to pop the fighter up on its tail and feed power to the rear thrusters, but when my vision cleared, my Starblade was over a mile away from the ascending cloud of dust and debris.

"Laranna, you okay?" I asked, blinking my eyes free of floaters and trying to read the sensors.

"Barely," she said, and I sighed in relief. "Next time you're going to blow up tanks full of rocket fuel, give a girl a heads-up."

She'd stabilized even farther away than I had, a dot almost

two miles south of the clearing, hovering over the town. Smoke rose from the closest buildings, their wood smoldering with the heat of the distant blast.

"Gonna be a shitload of broken windows over there," I mused, then glanced back at the black clouds rising hundreds of feet into the afternoon sky, so close to mushrooms in shape but not quite. "But it could have been worse."

It could have been *so* much worse.

9

THE FACE on the TV screen had the look of an aging mafia enforcer, his eyes dark and dead, free from conscience. Looking at him, listening to him speak even in a language I couldn't understand, all I could think of was Hannah Arendt's quote about the banality of evil.

"This unprovoked attack on sovereign Russian territory will not go unpunished," the translator intoned, his clinical precision not capturing the hostility in the Russian phrases spoken a moment before by the older, balding man. "We will seek justice for the destruction of our defensive missile batteries and the deaths of our soldiers, as well as the damage to civilian structures and the injuries of innocent people."

The drooping, cold-eyed face vanished, replaced by heavily edited video footage of the Starblades taking out the missile launchers. From the angle, I guessed that the video had been taken from somewhere in the town, and the main thing that struck me about the replay, other than whoever edited it leaving out the SAMs trying to shoot us down, was just how badass the Starblades looked in action. I'd always thought of them as second-class weapons systems, good for ground support and not much else, but the Russian video impressed me with just how formidable they were to 21st-century Earth technology.

Back to the dead-eyed Russian, his head inclined forward as if trying to intimidate the camera.

"The Americans have already violated international law by involving us in this military conflict without our assent, without even an opportunity to even examine whether this war is justified. They did this to acquire advanced alien weaponry, and now they've used that weaponry against us. The threat is implicit. If the rest of the world doesn't fall in line with their demands, they'll use it against them, as well. Russia will not sit still for this. We are the masters of our own fate and will never put our destiny in the hands of another nation."

The recording ended, and the screen went black, though I wasn't sure who had turned it off.

"So, are we in trouble?" Chuck asked.

I eyed him sidelong, wanting to ask him what he meant by *we*. Chuck Barnaby hadn't been within 10,000 miles of the Sakhalin Islands, because I'd left him in charge of training the Rangers back at Ft. Carson. But I suppose I appreciated the show of solidarity with Laranna and me, particularly considering that we were standing under the not-very-friendly glare of the Chairman of the Joint Chiefs of Staff, the National Security Advisor, the Secretary of State, and the President.

President Louis was sitting behind the desk in the Oval Office, elbows resting on its surface, hands clasped with his fingers steepled just under his mouth, the pads of his forefingers tapping together rhythmically. Madison Barrett, the short, almost elfin Secretary of State, had taken a seat on the other side of the huge desk, while Gavin stood like a statue off to the side, his arms crossed, face fixed in stolid unhappiness.

Parker Donovan paced like a lion on the opposite end of the desk, seemingly unable to calm down enough to stand still, his hands working like he wished he were grasping a weapon. I knew the feeling.

"No," President Louis decided finally. "Given the provocation the Russians were willing to risk, they came off light."

"And diplomatically," the Secretary of State put in, more relaxed than the others, "we came out of this just about as well as we possibly could." She waved dismissively. "Oh, the Russian president is filing a formal complaint with the UN that we've broken the Outer Space treaty and a bunch of other agreements that no one has honored for the last twenty years, but everyone saw what they did, and no one is taking their side in this, not even the Chinese."

"I think that's a fairly rosy picture of our current situation," Donovan snapped, glaring at us and then at Barrett. "The Russians launched *nuclear weapons* at an American ship. That's a declaration of *war*, Mr. President. What the hell are they thinking?"

"That's pretty obvious," Gavin told him. "They're thinking that not only has the United States involved Earth in an interstellar war without so much as a by-your-leave, but we also came out of it with a pair of huge starships with weapons that could level any nation on Earth. They're desperate because we've just made them and every nation on Earth who's not allied with us irrelevant. Desperate enough to risk annihilation to undo the whole thing."

"They shot their wad," Louis declared. "They know they won't have the chance again, and if they launched a nuclear strike against us now, the *Victory* and the *Endeavor* could take them out in the launch phase. Even submarine-launched weapons."

"I wish I had your optimism, Mr. President," Donovan fumed, stopping in his tracks, hands spread. "If an open nuclear strike is out of the question, they could smuggle weapons into the country, or give them to terrorists and let them do the dirty work." He looked me in the eye and sighed, as if unwilling to speak the words. "Your decision was a smart one, Travers. If we'd launched a cruise-missile strike against the launchers, there's a very real chance they would have panicked and sent those last four missiles at DC or Los Angeles. Or New York. The fighter attack caught them with their pants down."

"Yes, agreed," Louis told us. "Though I wish this was going to be as easy to sell to Congress. It's been bad enough getting them to absorb this whole business with the Anguilar, and one of the ways we pitched it to them was that this mutual threat to the entire human race would unite the warring nations of the world, give them a common opponent. The idea that we'll be fighting a war in space and another here on Earth is going to bring about calls for my impeachment."

"There's one thing we could do," Donovan suggested. "Take out the Russian nuclear capabilities now, before they get the chance to try another attack."

"And how would you suggest we do *that*, Parker?" Gavin demanded, his temper apparently getting short with the man.

"With the Starblades!" the National Security Advisor suggested. "Travers already proved the Russians can't intercept them."

"We don't have enough trained pilots. And even if we did, nothing they can mount or fire is going to be able to take out Russian ballistic missile submarines."

Donovan's mouth worked soundlessly for a moment, as if he was revving it up, gaining momentum.

"The Vanguards," he finally suggested, pointing a finger at me. "Those particle cannon things they carry could penetrate the water far enough to disable a sub."

"No." Laranna's declaration was as final and firm as the one from July 4, 1776, her eyes flaring in anger at Donovan's presumption. "Our pilots are not going to fight your internecine family conflicts. Our purpose is to fight the Anguilar, to free the worlds they've enslaved. That is the oath we've taken, the reason our people fight. Killing your Russian enemies is not part of that."

"Does she speak for you, *Colonel?*" Donovan asked, bristling like a dog thrown into the fighting ring.

"You're Goddamned right she does," I told him, squaring my

shoulders, ready to take a swing at the man who'd had us kidnapped.

"That's insubordination!" Donovan barked, taking a step closer to me, almost to the line I wasn't going to let him cross, the one that would take him to the point where I'd lay him out. "I could have you arrested."

"You could *try*," Laranna warned him, her voice a low growl.

"Ladies and gentlemen," President Louis said, coming to his feet, eyes flaring in anger, "there'll be no fighting in here."

"This is the *war* room," Barrett murmured, and I laughed unwillingly at the reference. Louis glared at the joke, but Barrett rolled her eyes. She hadn't stood from her chair. "It's a stupid idea," she insisted. "Right now, you have the perfect opportunity to do exactly what you promised Congress, Mr. President…to bring everyone together."

Louis towered above her, disapproval in his downward stare.

"And how the hell would you suggest I do that?"

"Give them what they want," Chuck blurted, then seemed to shrink in on himself as everyone stared at him. But he visibly gathered his resolve and went on. "Mr. President, Russia is desperate, panicking because they think they're being cut out of history, that America and our allies are going to leave her behind. We just need to make sure they know we're not doing that."

"Exactly," Barrett agreed, pointing a finger at the Army major. "Chuck here is brighter than he looks. We're going to need troops, right? We're going to need warm bodies, and I've already heard the worries that we don't have enough."

"It's simple," Chuck suggested. "Tell the Russians—hell, tell the Chinese, too—that if they contribute ground troops to the cause, they get to share in the spoils. Lenny's going to teach us how to build fusion reactors, so tell them we'll build them one." He shrugged. "Eventually. Tell them we'll help them set up their own space industries, bases on the Moon, whatever. Anything that doesn't involve giving them any of our ships or even putting their officers in positions of authority over our people."

Donovan made a face like Chuck had suggested he wipe his ass with the flag.

"That's brilliant, Major Barnaby. The bastards just tried to *nuke* us and you want to reward them for it! What kind of lesson do you think that's going to teach them? What message is that going to send to our enemies?"

"Parker," President Louis said, "I need you to calm down."

"Sir, don't tell me you're actually considering this?"

"If I am, it's my business, Parker." Louis sighed. "If the alternative is nuclear war, then leading the Russian government along with promises of a seat at the table might be preferable."

"Or just doing it," Laranna suggested. "Telling the truth, honoring your word, and actually trying to unite your world against the real enemy." She glared at Donovan. "Or is that too much to ask from a man with no honor?"

"Enough," Louis snapped. "We're not doing this again. Parker, you're my National Security Advisor, which means I count on you to make recommendations regarding policy I intend to implement. If you disagree with that policy so vehemently, I won't stop you from following your conscience. As much as I'll miss your counsel, I *will* accept your resignation."

Donovan blinked as if the President had slapped him across the face.

"Sir, are you saying…"

"I'm saying," Louis interrupted, "that if you find you can't do your job, then I will find someone who can. You need to make up your mind. And I'd prefer if you go do that somewhere else at the moment." He jerked a thumb toward the door. "I'll discuss this with you later."

Donovan said nothing, though I could tell he wanted to, and from the venomous look he shot at Laranna, I knew who he wanted to say it to. Instead, he stalked out the door and ignored the polite nods from the Secret Service agent stationed there as he closed the door behind them.

I sighed and dropped into one of the other chairs, feeling about half the tension leak out of the room.

"I think," President Louis said, "that it might be best if you two keep a low profile for a while, until the fallout from this attack has died down." He winced. "No pun intended. But no more interviews, no more testifying before Congress. The cruisers are out of sight, out of mind, and once the only news of them are the reports we give, we can start controlling the narrative on this." He nodded to me. "We're sending the *Endeavor* on her shakedown cruise with your trainers in a couple days. I want you on it. All three of you."

"But the Rangers…" Chuck started to object, but Louis cut him off.

"Put some of your Strada warriors on it," Gavin said, less a suggestion than an order. "The different methods and points of view will be a plus for an experienced officer like Whistler. Remember, the point of the training isn't to get the Rangers to fight just like you do but to develop a fighting style that fits their doctrine and their existing patterns."

Which was fair and perhaps something I hadn't considered. For all that General Gavin was a pain in the ass, at least he knew his shit. I wanted to say he was better than Donovan, but that seemed like damning with faint praise.

"I'll notify Nareena," Laranna offered. "But wouldn't it be better if Chuck…that is, Major Barnaby, accompanied her, to familiarize her with American military protocols?"

"Theoretically," Gavin acknowledged. "But we still have that, uh…Master Sgt. Harden that you worked with during the capture of the *Endeavor*."

"Master Sgt. Harden?" I repeated, shaking my head. The name didn't ring a bell.

"He called himself Gray," Chuck supplied.

I nodded. Gray had been the leader of the Delta Force team that had accompanied me on that operation, and I suppose I shouldn't have been surprised that he didn't share his real name with some civilian kid who'd dropped out of the sky in a flying saucer.

"Harden has experience both with you people," Gavin went on, "and with the new weapons. He can be the go-between for" —he scowled—"Ms. Nareena. God, I wish this resistance of yours could come up with a coherent rank structure."

Something else he might be right about. It hadn't been as

important when our ground forces had been mostly Strada, but now that we were growing…

"Pardon me, sir," Chuck said, "but why is it more important that I go with Colonel Travers aboard the *Endeavor* than stay with the Rangers?"

Any warm and fuzzy feelings I had about being fair to Gavin disappeared when his glare settled on me.

"Because it seems that our Colonel Travers requires someone to remind him that he accepted a commission in the United States Army…and whether he likes it or not, he damned well needs to remember that."

I kept silent because I had the sense that anything I said would just make things worse. But he was right about one thing. I didn't like it at all.

10

IT SHOULD HAVE MEANT MORE to me, being one of the first human beings to orbit Mars, yet it didn't. I'd been to dozens of planets in star systems all over the galaxy, which made the red ball of dust and rock beneath us pale by comparison. It wasn't habitable, didn't even have any vital resources that the United States or the Earth in general needed.

Oh, if they'd reached all this on their own, using conventional drives, I could see Mars being a way station or a rest-and-recreation base for people prospecting for minerals in the asteroid belt, but now, thanks to us, none of that was going to happen. Beyond the military usefulness of the cruisers, they could also give Earth an almost-instant commercial space enterprise system, bringing asteroids in for mining, transporting equipment from Earth to the Jovian moons in hours instead of months or years. And that wasn't even counting the fusion-drive spaceships we'd promised to help them build.

"What's wrong?" Chuck asked, following my gaze to the image of Mars floating in the holographic display of the main viewer. "Not a big Mars fan?"

I realized I must have allowed some of the misgivings I felt to show through to my face. If Laranna had been on the bridge instead of down in the hangar bays, checking on the Starblade squadron, she would have been the one asking me…probably would have asked before the scowl had made it all the way to my face. Not that I was the only one with a sour expression.

Colonel Voight, the commander of the *Endeavor*, had been giving me the side-eye ever since we'd emerged from hyperspace and I'd left my seat and its safety restraints to pace the bridge. The rest of her crew had been ordered to stay strapped in unless they were required to move around to carry out their responsibilities, sort of like the passengers on an airliner, because this was the military and every single move had to be controlled to allow for the most reckless and brainless action possible from the fevered imagination of the most junior enlisted present.

But I *wasn't* a junior enlisted man, and I also wasn't in her chain of command, and I felt like standing. I'd half expected Chuck to scold me for ignoring the safety guidelines, but I think he enjoyed the autonomy being part of my entourage conferred to him, and he'd taken advantage of it to the fullest, leaning against the back of his acceleration couch like the chillest warrant officer.

"Never given much thought to my comparative favorites

among the planets of our Solar System," I replied, then glanced over my shoulder to see if Voight was listening to me. She was deep in conversation at the moment, going over the details of our recent jump and the plans for the next one, and there was no danger she'd overhear, but I still leaned closer to Chuck before I spoke again. "I'm just worried they're not ready for this."

"The crew?" he asked, frowning in confusion. "They've been trained well enough, or at least that's what your chief bridge officer said." He nodded at the Copperell advisor. "What's his name again?"

"Tenera," I supplied. "But that's not what I mean. I mean they're not ready for"—I made an expansive gesture—"*all* of this. For what's going to happen."

"You mean because of the thing with the Russians?" he guessed, taking a careful look back over his shoulder at Voight before he continued. "I mean, it's the *Russians*. You were around in the seventies and eighties. They haven't changed that much since then, even though they don't call themselves the Soviet Union anymore."

"No, I expect the Russians to act like…Russians," I admitted, shrugging. "I'm talking about Donovan."

"Donovan's an asshole," Chuck agreed. "But you already knew *that*, too. From when he tried to dissect Giblet."

Of all the things I didn't want to think about at the moment, Gib was right at the top.

"You think it's *just* him?" I challenged. "God's sake, Chuck, I've just read about the politics these days—you've *lived* through them. Can you stand here and honestly tell me that they're not going to screw this up?"

"Oh hell, no," he admitted, loud enough that Voight glanced over from her command station, scowling at him. He turned back to me, looking abashed. "Charlie, you've read about the modern problems we have, but have you read about the shit that happened back in your day? Because bad stuff happened back then, too, but no one knew about it for years afterward because there wasn't any internet, any social media, and frankly, people didn't feel the need to tell everyone in the world everything that was going on. Corruption didn't stop after Watergate, man, politicians just got better at covering it up." He cocked an eyebrow at me. "You're telling me it's any different out there? That all the governments and politicians are perfect?"

I sighed, not wanting to agree with him but too damned honest not to.

"No. They're not. I guess I just had higher hopes for America."

"That's because you left when you were a kid," he told me. "It's only been two years, but you're not a kid anymore. It's like coming back home after you're grown up with your own family and realizing your parents weren't as perfect or in control as you always thought they were."

I closed my eyes, jaw clenching. Oh good, my parents, the one subject I wanted to avoid just as much as Gib. Chuck was batting a thousand today. Maybe I should talk to Voight.

"Yeah, I get it," I said instead. "Who knows? All this could bring everyone together after all. Hating us."

"Come on." He nudged my arm. "It's Mars down there. *Mars*. I know you've seen a bunch of different alien planets, but this is Mars. That's gotta do *something* to you."

I shrugged, turned back to Voight.

"Colonel," I said, "are you planning on launching a lander?"

The woman's already scrunched-up face contracted even more in a frown as she looked away from Tenera.

"It wasn't on the schedule, Colonel Travers."

It sure would have been nice if at least one of the senior officers I worked with could say that rank without putting a sneer in the middle of it.

"As my aide de camp here has pointed out," I said, gesturing at Chuck, "this is *Mars*. And you have the chance, with a slight change of schedule that is certainly within the scope of your authority, to launch a lander and decide who is going to be the first human being to land on Mars."

She looked as if she was about to snap an instinctive denial but paused with her mouth open, eyes going wide as if she'd just thought about it.

"How long would it take?"

"Less than half an hour," Tenera supplied. "Not counting getting suited up, of course."

"Hour round trip," I said, raising my hands palms out. "Maybe an hour to…look around? Two hours added to the entire operation. The only question is, are you going downstairs yourself? Might be cool if the first man on Mars is a woman."

That made her eyes light up.

"I couldn't…" she stuttered. "I'm the commander."

"Captain Kirk did it all the time. Do you trust your second-in-command? And do you have a spacesuit that fits?"

Colonel Voight did something I never expected from her. She smiled. Leaning over the control panel, she touched the intercom control.

"Major Prentice," she said, "report to the bridge."

"Be right there, ma'am," the XO replied. As per the new regulations, when the ship was in realspace, the XO would stay in the auxiliary control room just in case the bridge took a hit. I hadn't the heart to tell them that if the bridge got skragged, the entire ship was pretty much toast.

Voight eyed me carefully, as if judging what my answer would be to a question she hadn't asked.

"What about you, Colonel Travers? Do you want to come along?"

"No, Colonel Voight," I told her, shaking my head, not even considering it. "I've been on enough planets to fill an astronomy textbook." I grinned, clapping Chuck on the back. "But you might want to take Major Barnaby along. I think he always wanted to be an astronaut."

"Where," Laranna wondered, staring at the image from the nose camera of the lander, "did she get an American flag?"

I shook my head, trying not to laugh in front of the bridge crew as Colonel Elsa Voight hammered the flagpole into the Martian surface. Not that I was laughing at the flag, or at the idea of her being the first human on the world. But I couldn't get her first words upon stepping out of the lander out of my mind.

"Today," she'd said in what had to have been a statement she'd thought up in the last hour, "humanity takes its next giant leap in the vast expanse of the cosmos."

It was so self-consciously momentous, which might have been less ridiculous if she'd arrived in some lowest-bidder piece of aluminum slapped together by NASA on a shoestring budget after a voyage that had taken months, instead of an hour-long flight in an alien starship.

Not that the general sense of manufactured drama seemed to register on the bridge crew. Their eyes were fixed on the screen, their faces transfixed with awe or perhaps envy. Every one of them wanted to be on that shuttle, wanted to be shuffling across the Martian dust of Elysium Planiti. It wasn't a particularly interesting place to land, just a nice, flat area, and I was sure Voight had chosen it because of that fact, because there wouldn't be any complications or navigation hazards. And because it was daylight on that side of the planet. Wouldn't want to land in the dark where the cameras couldn't see it.

"What's your situation down there, Mars lander?" Jack Prentice asked into the audio pickup at the command chair. Him, I couldn't quite figure. He was putting up a suitably awestruck, serious exterior, but I caught a twinkle in his eyes as he made the transmission.

"Just taking the lay of the land, Jack," Voight replied after a moment, her words clear and free of static, relayed from her suit to the lander. "God knows if I'll ever be back."

She'd taken only five other people with her in the lander. Pilot, copilot, herself, Chuck Dixon, and two Space Force security troops, the final three all armed just in case. That was the only way I could tell them apart, since they all wore identical blue pressure suits and helmets with mirrored visors. They shuffled in the dust carefully, not seeming to want to get too far from the lander, just scanning the horizon.

Except Chuck. I knew it was him because before he'd left, while he was suiting up, he'd told me he was gonna John Carter it. And he did, taking a series of long, loping steps that carried him ten yards with each bound in the low gravity. All that was missing were a few four-armed Tharks and scantily clad Martian princesses.

"Damn," I murmured. "Now I kinda wish I'd gone down with them."

"It's not a particularly pleasant world," Laranna pointed out. "If it were, I'm sure Lenny's Creators would have terraformed it."

I glanced aside at her, eyes narrowing. Anyone else might have missed the note of bitter cynicism in the remark, but I knew her better than that. I stepped closer, slipped an arm around her, and put my mouth next to her ear.

"Having doubts?"

She didn't turn away from the screen, but I felt the stiffening of her shoulders.

"Aren't you?" she answered my question with a question.

I'd told her about my conversation with Lenny in the ship's gym after the battle. He hadn't confessed to arranging the

Anguilar attack on DC in order to convince the American government to cooperate with us, but he hadn't *not* confessed to it, either. I'd tried not to think about that too much, partly because I had too much else on my plate these last couple months but partly because I didn't *want* to. If it was true, Lenny was just as culpable for Dani's death as Zan-Tar...maybe even more, since he was supposed to be our friend.

"I don't know," I confessed. "I have doubts about so much of this shit. I doubt I should be here."

"You wish you had gone after Giblet."

"No, not really." I shook my head. "I wish he'd come to me first and told me he was going. I wish he'd asked me to come with him."

She looked up at me, her dark eyes curious.

"Would you have done it?"

"Probably," I admitted. "I know all the arguments, what everybody's said about my duty and responsibility and how badly I was needed here, how it's a trap and we'd probably just get ourselves killed. But if he'd asked me, I can't honestly say I would have thought about any of that."

"Maybe," she suggested, her hand resting on my arm, "that's why he didn't ask you."

"He's there by now," I said bleakly. "He's at this Wraith Anchorage. Whatever's going to happen has already happened. One by one, we're getting picked off, and I wonder if there'll be any of us left when it's all over."

"We knew it could happen when we decided to fight this war," Laranna reminded me, her touch on my arm comforting while her words did the opposite. "Dani knew it, too. The very first time she met us, she nearly died. She was a brave woman, intent on serving the greater good, for all that she liked to play the cynic."

"I guess now I know how it felt for my parents when I disappeared." My gaze flickered away from the view of the Martian surface to the starscape on the opposite side of the cruiser, the vasty deep. "They never found out what happened to me. I wonder if we'll ever find out what happened to Gib."

"If I know Giblet, he won't go quietly. One way or another, we'll hear."

I grunted doubtfully, checked the time on the display. It was set for Greenwich Mean Time, though I couldn't remember how that related to Eastern or Central, the only time zones I'd ever lived in. What it did tell me was that the landing party had been on the ground for over an hour.

I pulled my comm off my belt and tapped the control to tie it into the ship's network.

"Colonel," I transmitted, "you wanted to know when it had been an hour. Time to head back up."

"Oh, come on, Charlie," Chuck Barnaby said, laughing, so caught up in the moment that he forgot about my notional rank and transmission protocols. "It's Mars...we could bend the rules a little bit."

I wanted to snap at him, but that was just me being upset about Gib, and there was no point in taking it out on Chuck. I forced my tone to something casual, almost cheerful.

"Sure, Major Barnaby," I agreed. "We could. If Mars is as far as you want to go. We're scheduled to jump to hyperspace and travel to a whole 'nother star, where you all can be the very first humans to pilot their own starship all the way out of the Solar System." Except *me*, of course, but I strategically didn't point that out. "But if you want to stay and play around a little more in the low gravity…"

"No, Colonel Travers," Voight cut in. "We're heading back up. Major Prentice, get the crew ready to break orbit as soon as we dock." I couldn't see her face, but I could hear the grin in the words. "We've had our fun. Time to get back to work."

11

"I would have thought," Chuck said, staring at the star map hanging in the main viewscreen's projection, "that Proxima Centauri would be the closest system to jump to."

"It doesn't work that way," I told him, giving into the flashing warning lights and securing my safety harness. "Jumping through hyperspace ain't like dusting crops, boy."

Chuck turned and gave me a confused frown.

"Sorry, classical reference. The way I've had it explained to me…"

"Over and over," Laranna added from beside me, rolling her eyes.

I gave her a dirty look, but her annoyance was probably justified. I'd bugged the hell out of Brazzo when he was alive about how all this stuff worked, kept bugging Lenny and Mallarna to explain it, even though I still wasn't sure I got it.

"…is that the connections there aren't straight lines. I mean, hell, the connections here in realspace aren't *actually* straight lines because spacetime is curved. But there's some kind of gravit… gravito-inertial connection between stars that has nothing to do with how close they are through realspace and more to do with some hyperdimensional math shit that I couldn't hope to understand. How long it takes to get from one star to the other in hyperspace depends on how strong that…umm, let's just call it *G.I.* connection is." I pointed at the map. "Getting from Earth to Proxima Centauri is like getting to the other side of a mountain. The fastest way is to take the road around it. And it still takes like a week to get there, even though you can reach systems that are hundreds of light-years away in a couple days."

"Perhaps that's why we never detected any signals from all these civilizations out there," Voight mused, chin resting on the heel of her hand, eyes fixed on the map. "The ones with a big enough EM signature to be seen from interstellar distances are too far away."

"That, and they don't exactly use radio waves," I added. I'd asked about that, too, and understood more of the explanation. "From what Lenny told me, it wouldn't have been much longer before the orbital observatories you've launched picked up something."

"Good timing on your part, then," she said.

Laranna's eyes narrowed, and I knew she was thinking the same thing I was. Perhaps the timing had been a little *too* convenient. Another one of Lenny's machinations.

"Ten seconds to hyperspace exit," Captain Lombard announced with a hint of irritation behind the force of the words, as if he resented us talking over his periodic updates. "All hands secure for hyperspace exit."

"What's the name of this star again?" Chuck wondered.

"Doesn't have one, Major," Voight informed him. "Just a number."

"Doesn't *need* a name," Laranna interjected. "It's got no habitable planets, just a couple gas giants and a few asteroid fields from failed planetary formation."

She thought we were wasting time making such a short jump, just a few hours in hyperspace, and her recommendation had been to hit the nearest inhabited system, but that would have taken a couple weeks, and I didn't want to be away from Earth that long, particularly since the *Liberator* had left for Sanctuary. The only defenses left in place were the Vanguards and the *Victory*, and her crew wasn't yet tested or fully trained.

Not to mention that I didn't know how the independent colony in that system would react to what looked a hell of a lot like an Anguilar cruiser hopping out of hyperspace.

"Emergence," Lombard announced, though the topsy-turvy feeling in my gut told the story better than he could have, even using the fancy new military term for a hyperspace jump.

A rainbow spray of stars streaked by on every side, elongated and distorted, before shrinking back to their natural pinpoints of light.

"We have what looks like a K-class star," Captain Denholm

announced, pointing to the distant orange glow on the main viewscreen. She was what the Space Force had decided to call the astrophysics specialist. She had been a civilian a couple months ago. I'd asked why they didn't call her the science officer, but no one else had got the joke. "I'm picking up a couple gas giants, one about the mass of Jupiter at three AU out, another that I think is the size of Uranus at six or seven."

I couldn't control the amused snort at her pronunciation of the planet, but I tried to turn it into a cough, though I don't know how believable it was. Denholm either didn't notice or pretended not to, continuing her scan of the system, sounding like a kid with a new toy with the Anguilar-tech sensor suite.

"There's the asteroid belt, out between the two of them." As if the main screen was following her description—and maybe it was—the view changed from a close-up simulation of the gas giants to an endless cloud of glittering, tumbling bits of rock. "God, it's huge, like three times the size of ours."

"Might it be worthwhile to mine?" Colonel Jeffcoat wondered. Dutifully strapped into the acceleration couch at the back of the bridge, he'd somehow managed to cross his legs casually as if he were in the officer's club back in England. "I know we'd have to haul the ore back in the cruisers, but it's only a few hours round-trip—what?"

"It *might* be worthwhile," Laranna allowed with a dismissive sniff, "if the field weren't mostly carbonaceous chondrites. This system is known for one thing—causing prospectors to go bust and have to sell their mining ships."

"Well, that's disappointing," Jeffcoat murmured with a tsk. "I thought perhaps I had my retirement all figured out."

Which caused a smattering of chuckles among the foreign observers, and even I had to grin. The Brit was cool as a cucumber and not stupid either.

"Orders, ma'am?" Lombard asked, hands hovering over the helm controls. "We're at a virtual stop relative to this system thanks to the hyperdrive emergence absorbing our momentum. Do you want us to look around a little?"

"Once around the park?" Jeffcoat asked dryly.

"It's surprisingly…bleak," Voight said, eyebrow shooting up at the images on the screen.

"It's not much of a system," Laranna agreed. "Which is why we shouldn't have bothered coming here."

"Baby steps," I reminded her. "When you're teaching Strada kids how to knife fight, don't you start out with wooden blades?"

She offered me a challenging grin.

"I was given my first knife at age six…and I cut myself approximately one hour later. It's important to know that weapons are dangerous."

Colonel Jeffcoat barked a laugh.

"Oh, Ms. Laranna, I shudder to think how a Strada would go over with the current government of the United Kingdom. We don't even allow people to have points on their steak knives."

Outrage sparked behind Laranna's eyes, and I thought I was going to have to interrupt a tirade about soft Earth people, but Ramirez interrupted…or at least the warning buzzer on his tactical board did.

"We have company," the Tactical Officer snapped, fingers flying over his controls, his voice urgent.

"There shouldn't be anything out here!" Laranna said, yanking her safety harness loose and rushing over to the tactical station. "There's no reason for anything to be out here!"

I hit the quick-release for my restraints and followed her, not that I could read the sensors any better than she could, since neither of us had been trained to handle a cruiser. The Copperell advisors, though, knew exactly what they were looking at, and they looked worried. Which worried me.

"That's an Anguilar cruiser," Tenera announced, leaning over Ramirez's shoulder. "A single ship, on a patrol course across minimum jump distance. She's a scout."

"Shit," I murmured. "Has she seen us?"

"We're getting a transmission from the cruiser," the younger officer, whose name I hadn't caught, announced from the communications console. "It's registering on the original Anguilar recognition systems as an IFF challenge. They want to know who we are."

"We should still be sending the same transponder signal as when this thing was under the previous ownership," I said, hoping I was right. "Won't they think this is…whatever the Empire called her before?"

"Theoretically," Tenera agreed. "But the Anguilar *know* this ship was taken. If they receive that IFF, they'll know immediately that we're the enemy…which is why I disabled it."

"Can we tell them something?" Colonel Voight asked, her

eyes gone wide. "Maybe convince them that we're one of their ships? Do you have the codes for that?"

"No," Tenera told her, shaking his head. "They change those codes frequently, particularly since this one"—he gestured at me—"stole one of their security code generators right out from under their noses on Copperell. They've caught on. We have about two minutes before they figure out we're not on their side."

"And then they're either going to attack, or run," Laranna said. "And tell their bosses that their missing cruiser is under enemy control."

"We have to hit them first," I told Voight. "Lombard, can you jump us right on top of them? Do you remember how to micro-jump?"

"Uh, I *think* so," the helmsman stuttered, glancing between Voight and me. "It's been a couple weeks, but…"

"We don't have time for I *think* so," I snapped at him. "Tenera, you do it. Get us as close as you can, and then you target their drives, Ramirez."

"I'm not sure about this, Travers," Voight said, and I heard in her voice the one thing I didn't really want to hear in the voice of the commander of our ship—doubt. "If they're going to run, maybe we should let them. They might already know the ship is in our hands…"

This was bad. The look in her eyes wasn't panic, but it also wasn't certainty, and while I technically outranked her, being the commander of this ship made it tricky for me to push that. I sucked in a breath, grabbed the arm of her command chair, and leaned in close.

"Colonel Voight," I said, softly but urgently, hoping no one else would overhear it, "that ship is the enemy, and they're about to deliver vital intelligence to the Anguilar Empire. You need to take them out before they do. I understand if you don't think you're ready for this yet…and if you don't think you can handle it, then let me take care of it, because we can't let that Anguilar ship get away."

She was a deer in the headlights, mouth working but nothing coming out.

Goddamnit.

"Tenera, micro-jump, close as you can." I gave the order to the Copperell, but I kept my eyes locked on Voight's, challenging her to counteract the order. "Ramirez, can you handle the weapons?"

"You bet your ass I can," he said, grinning in anticipation.

I was about to give the order when Voight snapped out of her fugue and grabbed my shoulder.

"I've got this," she told me. It was a risk believing her, but a bigger risk having her in charge of this ship if I didn't. I nodded and got out of the way. "Tom," she said to Lombard, "micro-jump us in. Minimum safe distance. Do it now."

Tenera glanced at me, and I gave the Copperell a nod. He backed away from the controls, and Lombard wiped sweat off his forehead and tapped in a quick command, then shot Voight a thumbs-up.

"Ready, ma'am."

"Do it," she ordered.

He didn't bother with the dramatic announcement this time,

and I barely had a chance to grab the back of Voight's chair before the *Endeavor* snapped into and out of hyperspace in less than a second. Reality stretched taut and snapped back like a rubber band, taking me with it, my teeth clacking together, only my hold on the chair keeping me from tumbling forward, not from any physical force but just from the psychic jolt.

We'd been far out from anything, away from the sun, away from the gas giants, but with this jump, something the size of Jupiter snapped into being close enough that I could count the orange and white stripes across its surface and see the black dots that were its moons passing over the forever storms.

Yet all of that was dwarfed by the bulk of the Anguilar cruiser looming just ahead of us, so close I could have reached through the screen and touched her, a mirror image of our own vessel. But pointed the wrong way to fire her main guns at us.

"Helm control to tactical," Voight ordered without hesitation.

"Firing!" Ramirez snapped, not waiting for the order.

The raw, unbridled fury of the particle cannons lashed out across kilometers of open space and speared into the Anguilar ship just ahead of her plasma engines, finding the hyperdrive and ripping through it like a Zoology student pithing a frog before the dissection. Her shields flared white, painful to look at even through the filter of the cameras, and I wasn't sure if we'd penetrated them until a fountain of white energy blossomed out of the rear of the craft and she listed to one side in reaction to the impromptu propulsive force.

Spinning her nose toward us, and if she had the juice for return fire…

"They're signaling us," the communications officer said, looking younger than me as confusion screwed his face into almost a pout. "I can't…"

But it was too late for that. The cannons had already recycled, and Ramirez cut loose with both barrels. The first shot had crippled the enemy ship, overloaded her shields, but this one was the *coup de grace*, coring her like an apple almost straight on, stem to stern. She wasn't carrying chemical fuel, but she had a shitload of power cells, just like we did, and while they were the handiest thing since sliced bread, making FTL travel and particle cannons and all that other cool stuff possible, they also stored a whole bunch of energy.

When you shot them with high-energy weapons, they had a nasty tendency to let it all loose at once. The Anguilar cruiser erupted like a supernova, and our own shields glowed as if basking in the radiance of the victory, though I knew they were actually saving us from a flood of deadly radiation. When the cloud of burning gas cleared, all that was left of the cruiser were scattered chunks of debris, curved support ribs tumbling away in every direction while bits of hull armor spun like the last sparks from an elaborate firework.

"Yes!" Ramirez exulted, pumping a fist, and he wasn't alone. The entire bridge cheered, even the reserved and very English Colonel Jeffcoat. Voight didn't actually cheer, but she allowed herself a relieved sigh.

I was neither cheerful nor relieved and, from the look on her face, neither was Laranna.

"That was too easy," she said softly next to my ear. "Something's off here."

"Sir," the comms officer said, having to raise his voice to be heard over the chatter on the bridge. "Ma'am? The Anguilar ship…before we blew her up, she sent a message. To us." The young officer looked at me. "In point of fact, to *you*, sir." He shook his head. "I think you need to listen to this."

12

"I knew it was too easy," Laranna declared, staring at the screen, arms crossed.

We'd taken the recording to the ship's operations center, not too different than the one on the *Liberator*, and for the same reason: humans had designed it. Lenny had even loaned some of his Bob the Builder 'bots to come aboard and rearrange what had once been a luxury cabin for the ship's captain into the nerve center for the cruiser.

We'd jumped into hyperspace immediately after the battle and headed back for Earth, and I'd waited until we were insulated from possible threats before deciding to watch the message. I'd chosen to watch it alone not because I didn't trust the crew, but because of the foreign observers. They might all be stand-up guys and gals, but their primary loyalty was to a foreign government, and they'd share whatever they saw with that government.

It was just Laranna, Chuck, and me, and I knew that probably pissed off Colonel Voight, but the message hadn't been addressed to her, either. Chuck sprawled in one of the chairs around the operations center table, staring at the screen in stunned silence.

General Zan-Tar's face stared back.

My hand shook as I touched the control to play the recording again.

"Charlie Travers," Zan-Tar said, smiling broadly. "I trust you and your crew of Americans are finished celebrating your glorious victory against the enemy cruiser you encountered." He shrugged. "Unless you attempted to board her, in which case, there won't remain anyone alive to receive this transmission, which will be just as rewarding. But I doubt you're that foolish. You wouldn't have survived this long if you were. So, either you were there personally for the bait, or your American allies took care of it and you're getting this message shortly after. Either way is sufficient."

The background behind Zan-Tar was a featureless gray blur, and I figured he'd recorded the message in an office somewhere, but when he made a motion at the camera, it followed him. One of his subordinates must have been filming it with a portable camera…their equivalent of a cell phone, maybe.

"I was disappointed when you didn't show up yourself," Zan-Tar went on as he strode through the passageways of… somewhere.

Not a cruiser—the corridors were too wide. And there were others around besides Anguilar troopers. Civilians, not wearing uniforms, not Anguilar. Krin, a few Copperell, and something else, a species I'd seen before but not often. Tall, incredibly wide across the shoulders, with a massive chest and a broad, open face with wide-set eyes. And the horns, of course. Vestigial rather than useful, barely poking out of their lined foreheads, surrounded by shaggy, dark hair.

They were Gan-Shi. That must mean he was still on Wraith Anchorage.

"Perhaps I laid things on too thickly," Zan-Tar admitted, turning back toward the camera for a moment to offer a shrug of apology. "But they say the best lie is spiced with the truth, and I *am* going to be staying here in this wretched accretion of the worst this pitiful galaxy has to offer for the foreseeable future. And for the reasons your intelligence sources have given you. You've made it necessary for us to produce more ships. You think by arming your homeworld, you can turn the tide in this war, but you neglect the reality that we can produce ships, and you are forced to steal them. It's not winnable, though I wouldn't expect you to admit this. It's not in your nature to surrender, or you would have done so already."

The corridor twisted through some sort of Anguilar military facility, the civilians gone now, replaced by troopers in armor and functionaries in their dress uniforms.

"Which is why I resorted to this elaborate ruse, of course," Zan-Tar continued, still walking. "In the hopes that I could lure you here to avenge your friend's death. Not out of any overt malice to you, Charlie." He shook his head. "No, I wasn't lying when we spoke before. I admire you as an opponent. But wars are destructive, and this one more than most since…" Zan-Tar rolled his eyes. "Well, if I may be brutally frank, the leadership in the Bloodline Council has been less than circumspect in their prosecution of these hostilities. I fully acknowledge that my people are cursed with a certain racial egotism that may not be warranted given our history, but it might have been wiser to cultivate allies among the subject peoples rather than simply apply brute force to every situation."

Zan-Tar affected a beleaguered expression and laid his fingers on his chest.

"I have and am attempting to ameliorate this situation, but to do so, I require a certain"—he waved demonstratively—"reputation for success. So, please bear in mind that what I'm doing, I'm doing with the best of intentions and not out of any personal grudge against you."

Wherever he was going, he'd arrived, the camera and him both stopping in front of a thick, metal door guarded by motionless armored soldiers, their visors dark enough that they could have been statues left by some ancient civilization. Zan-Tar passed between them as if they *were* terracotta figures and slapped his palm against a security panel set in the wall to the side of the door.

The thick, gray metal slid aside to reveal a jail cell as dreary and sterile as any I'd imagined in a 1960s-era Eastern Bloc concentration camp. Sitting on a fold-down cot at the center of the claustrophobic room, ragged and bruised, a trickle of blood staining the feathers at his temple, a thick, silver collar fastened around his neck, was Giblet.

It was my second viewing of the video, yet the sight still kicked me in the gut, and my fingers tightened into a fist as I searched for something to punch.

"I want to assure you," Zan-Tar told me, "that the injuries your friend sustained were in the course of his capture and not due to any mistreatment by us. I've made sure that he not be touched. I would even have had his injuries seen to if he hadn't insisted on resisting every attempt to treat him."

Giblet stirred, eyes flickering toward Zan-Tar, rage kindling behind them. He tried to surge out of his seat, but the collar around his neck crackled, and he arched, mouth opened in a silent scream, until the charge released. Gib slumped back onto the cot, breathing heavily.

"Go to hell, you glorified pigeon," he muttered at Zan-Tar. "I've seen smarter birds on a damned plate with mashed potatoes."

Zan-Tar frowned, shook his head.

"I'm sure that means something to him...or perhaps to you. I'm sorry for the gruesome display, but as I said, your friend has been extraordinarily uncooperative, and the control collar had to be put in place to protect our soldiers from assault."

Giblet grimaced, sucked in a breath, and managed a yell that echoed through the hallways.

"Charlie! Don't give them anything! Leave me! I was an idiot!"

Zan-Tar smiled and touched the control to close the door.

"You have my word that Giblet will not be harmed in any way...as long as you surrender yourself to me here, at Wraith

Anchorage, within thirty days." He shrugged. "Your Earth-style days just to simplify matters for you. Within thirty days of the destruction of the ship that sent this message." His faux geniality drained away abruptly, revealing the cutthroat ruthlessness beneath. "If you do *not* surrender yourself, Charlie Travers, then I'm afraid I'll have no choice but to adhere to the strict Anguilar policy of executing any captured Varnell without hearing or recourse. And the prescribed method of execution isn't a pleasant one, I'm afraid. I'll spare you the details for now, but trust me when I tell you, I wouldn't wish it on my worst enemy."

The aura of bonhomie returned, though Zan-Tar's smile didn't make it all the way to his eyes.

"If you do surrender yourself, you have my word that I will release Giblet. On a primitive world, with no shipping in or out, but he'll live." He spread his hands helplessly. "Yes, I'm afraid you'll be paraded past our conquered peoples as an example, then taken to one of the Imperial headquarters worlds and executed by the Emperor himself, but it *will* be quick and relatively painless. It's the best offer I can make you."

Zan-Tar leaned against the wall, frowning thoughtfully.

"I'm sorry it's come to this, but after the debacle with Seraph Nix and her bounty hunters, I discovered something about you. Your primary weakness is your loyalty to your friends. And I'd be a fool to let that weakness go unexploited."

One final nod, a regretful sigh.

"The choice is yours."

It ended. Again. And this time, I didn't replay it. I'd seen what I needed to.

"Oh, this is some real bullshit," Chuck murmured, rubbing at his eyes. Just a few hours ago, he'd been about as happy as he'd ever been in his life, if I read the man right, gallivanting across the surface of Mars. And now… His head snapped up, eyes wide as he stared at me. "You *can't* go."

"Of course I'm going," I told him. There was no point in denying it. Chuck was smart enough to know. "You think I'm going to let them kill him?"

"Charlie, what the hell has changed?" He burst out of his seat looking like he wanted to tackle me to the floor. "You didn't go after him before because you knew it was a stupid thing to do, that it might be a trap. Why would you do it now, after you know for sure it's a setup?"

"Because now we know that Gib will die if he doesn't," Laranna said, and I looked at her sharply, surprised. She sighed, offering me a gentle smile. "I know you're going, and you know you're going. If you stayed here and let him sacrifice himself, you wouldn't be the man I married. Hectoring and shaming won't change that, so we'll skip it and go directly to the part where I convince you that I'm going with you."

My mouth hung open, and I closed it, trying not to look like a fish ready for the hook.

"You know it's suicide," Chuck said, pacing beside the table, his glare swinging from one of us to the other alternatively. "You do this, not only are you both dead, but the resistance is also dead right alongside you."

"What's the old saying, Chuck?" I asked him mildly, giving Laranna a smile of implicit surrender. "If I'm irreplaceable, I'm not doing my job. Look at it this way, worst case scenario, neither of us makes it back. You still have two star cruisers and a whole flight of short-range fighters. Not to mention all those Peboktan engineers building you fusion reactors and superconductor fabricators. And Lenny, of course." The smile faded. "He always plays the long game. I wouldn't be surprised if he already had my successor squirreled away somewhere in stasis. After all, we humanoids have a nasty habit of dying, and I doubt that AI is ready to put all his eggs in one basket." I laughed softly and nodded to Chuck. "Hell, it might be *you*."

"No, it's not," he snapped, pounding his fist on the table, jaw clenched in frustration.

"How can you be so sure?"

"Because *I'm* not going to be the one who has to stay behind and tell the Goddamned *President* that the two of you took off without authorization to get yourselves killed." He jabbed a thumb at his chest. "I'm going with you. And if you get any ideas about telling me no, remember that I can get you both thrown in a stockade for the duration if I don't keep my mouth shut."

"I don't know if you're thinking this through, man," I told him, deciding that just telling him no probably wouldn't accomplish anything. "If we die, you die, but what if we don't? Best-case, we all get back and you're facing a court-martial." I shrugged. "I mean, I am too, but I don't give a shit. I can tell them to stick their commission where the sun don't shine and go back to doing things the way I want without checking with the White House first. This is your career we're talking about here."

"Hey, man, I'm just a major," he said, raising his hands.

"You're a full bird colonel *and* my direct superior officer. If you order me to go with you, I'm just going to assume you have clearance for this mission because why wouldn't I? All I need is a direct order."

I stared at him, speechless. Of all the things I hadn't expected, including Laranna immediately agreeing to this and wanting to come along, Chuck asking me to *order* him to go on the mission was among the least probable.

"Are you serious?" I wondered.

"Bro, I'm coming along either way. At least this way, you salve your conscience because, in the unlikely event we survive, you can take all the blame." Chuck smirked. "I've been around you long enough to know that's your thing, that no matter what happens, you're gonna feel responsible for it. Since you're gonna feel guilty anyway, you might as well deserve it."

That…was disturbingly accurate. And if I *did* give him an order, he'd have a reasonable defense. It probably wouldn't work, since General Gavin wasn't an idiot and knew Chuck wasn't one, either. But it was a chance, and if I couldn't keep him from going with us, it might be the best I could do. Plus, the object of this entire thing was to get Giblet out of there alive. Chuck could help pull that off.

"All right," I sighed, burying my face in my hands for a moment. I rose from the chair and faced him with my hands clasped behind my back, my stance a copy of my least favorite person, Colonel Danberg. "Major Charles Barnaby, I, Colonel Charles Travers, your commanding officer, do hereby order you to accompany Laranna and myself on a rescue mission to Wraith

Anchorage." I eyed him suspiciously. "This is a strictly compartmentalized, need-to-know operation straight from the office of the President, and you will not share the details of it with anyone. Are we clear?"

Chuck stiffened to attention and saluted.

"Crystal, sir."

I rolled my eyes and returned the salute.

"Are we taking Vanguard fighters?" he asked, eyes lighting up like a little kid at Christmas at the thought of flying in one of the things. Which just showed he hadn't ever tried long-distance travel in one of the things, because it was like a week-long road trip in a VW Beetle, except you couldn't pull over to use a gas station bathroom.

"No. We fly anywhere near this place in a Vanguard fighter, they'd be all over us before we could get close enough to dock. There's still a transport on the ground at Andrews, just like the one Gib stole. The *Liberator* left it there in case we needed to call for help."

"Aren't they gonna notice that it's just the same as the ship Gib just flew in on?" Chuck asked.

"They're very common ships," Laranna informed him. "The smallest FTL ships other than the Vanguards. And the resistance keeps their registration clean, constantly changing them with ID transponders purchased on the black market. We...*may* be able to get aboard without being recognized."

"Are we bringing a squad of your Strada warriors along?" Chuck didn't sound as excited about this possibility as he had about going in the Vanguard fighters, but at least he was a little hopeful.

"No," I said, "there's an entire army of Anguilar in this place. Three of us or thirteen, it's not going to make much difference if we get into a straight-up fight. We're going in undercover and on our own."

"Not quite on our own," Laranna said. "Brandy has a source on board. She gave me the contact information before the *Liberator* headed back to Sanctuary."

"Didn't she tell us she wasn't very confident about that source?" I asked her, the question going up at the end before I could bring it under control.

"As your people like to say, beggars can't be choosers."

Chuck frowned, leaning against his chair.

"I think I've made a big mistake."

"Not too late," I assured him. "We could always use someone to stay here and keep everything running while we're gone."

"No," he sighed, then chuckled softly. "I have my orders."

13

"I wanted to thank you," Colonel Voight said quietly from the seat beside me on the lander.

I blinked, realizing I'd been ignoring her—and everything else, of course. The *Endeavor* had taken seven long hours to reach Earth orbit from the nameless system, and with each passing minute, I had less time to get to Wraith Anchorage before Gib was executed. I'd been hoping that Laranna, Chuck, and I would get called down for a debrief on our own, which would give us a better chance to slip away to the transport, particularly if we'd flown the lander ourself, but the orders that had come through had requested Voight to come along. Which meant that one of her pilots flew the shuttle, and getting away from them would be even harder.

"For what?" I asked her, realizing that had sounded a little short and dismissive and trying to force myself to be more civil. "What did I do?" I tried again, making the question more convivial.

"You forced me to do the right thing," she explained, her face reddening at the whispered admission. "Back in that other system...when we encountered the enemy ship. I froze up. You got me going, and you did it without embarrassing me. I appreciate that."

I looked at her again, this time trying to be objective and less inclined to resent her for her rank and her earlier attitude toward me. Voight was about forty, a fighter pilot before she'd transferred to the Space Force, and everything about her had screamed competence and confidence prior to that moment on the *Endeavor*. I put myself in her shoes and wondered how someone like that would react to what was probably their first instance of on-the-job doubt.

"It's not the same as anything you've gone through before," I allowed. "I've got some experience in fighters now, and space battles in capital ships are nothing like that. No offense meant against either the Space Force or the Air Force, but I think maybe they should have considered recruiting Navy captains to run the ships."

Her expression turned from embarrassment to irritation in the blink of an eye.

"Offense accepted, boy! There's not a damned thing that those swabbies can do that the Space Force can't! We just need a little more stick time."

I couldn't help but laugh at the phrase, drawing curious

glances from Laranna and Chuck, who were in the row of seats ahead of us. They both seemed as tense and keyed up as I was, and I guessed they had to be wondering what could possibly be so funny under the circumstances.

"That," I told Voight, "sounds just like something a fighter pilot would say."

She tried to maintain a harsh glare, but the expression cracked and shattered in a laugh of her own.

"Seriously, though, Travers…" She hesitated, pursed her lips, and tried again. "…*Colonel* Travers, if you ever need anything, if there's ever anything I can do to help, please let me know."

"I might just take you up on that," I warned her. Maybe she could be a character witness at my court-martial.

"I'm sorry about your friend," she added, and the hackles went up on the back of my neck. I didn't reply immediately, but she must have noticed my questioning look. "The message came through my ship's communications officer…she showed it to me. That has to be rough, knowing your friend is in trouble and not being able to do anything to help him."

"Yeah," was all I managed to say, which was better than the alternative, which was to yell at her for reading someone else's letter.

She surprised me by patting my hand in a motherly gesture.

"I know you'll figure something out. You seem to have a gift for it."

"We're touching down," the pilot announced from the cockpit of the lander, interrupting the conversation and shaking me free of the sense of surreality.

I wondered how many people down below us lost their shit at the sight of what looked a lot like a flying saucer touching down at and taking off from Andrews multiple times a day. I couldn't see their reactions, nor could I see the ground below us because the stupid little shuttles didn't have shit for windows in the back, which was why I always sat in the cockpit when I could get away with it. The only way I knew when we landed was the slight jolt of the landing struts on the tarmac…that, and the Space Force captain who'd been our driver powering back his seat and cutting loose his restraints.

"All right," he said cheerfully, "everyone out, sirs and ma'ams. Next flight up is in six hours, and I plan on getting myself a nice nap in the meantime, so if you'll excuse me…"

Tamping down a nearly irresistible urge to rush for the door, I let the pilot open it for us instead, then motioned to Voight to step out ahead of me. Light rushed in, too bright after most of a day on the cruiser, and I flinched away from the glare.

"What time is it, anyway?" I asked the pilot as Voight clambered down the steps. I could have checked the cell phone I'd been issued by Gavin's office, but I had it turned off for a reason.

"Eleven in the morning Eastern," he informed me, stifling a yawn. "And I haven't slept for two days." He grinned apologetically. "I probably shouldn't have been flying. Too bad for you guys, no rest in the forecast. White House sent a car for you. Apparently, President Louis is anxious to talk to you all about that Anguilar ship we blew up." He sketched a salute and hopped out the side, not bothering with the steps. "Better you than me!"

Laranna paused in the door, looking back at me.

"Do we know where it is?" she asked, hand hovering over the hatch control.

"Pretty close," I said, raising an eyebrow. "The lander?"

"Faster than walking," she said, yanking the control to fold up the stairs and shut the hatch.

Outside, alarmed shouting faded out as the soundproof material sealed itself into the side of the shuttle, but I didn't wait to watch the final strip of light turn gray behind the hatch—I was already scrambling up into the cockpit. The pilot had locked down the controls because that was standard procedure, but I had the override codes for every piece of equipment we'd given to the US military because I wasn't stupid.

I punched it in, and the control panel lit up in greeting like I was a long-lost friend.

"Should be over by the hangar where they tried to kidnap us," I said, feeding power to gravity resist and the belly thrusters.

At least I could see this time, and the view as the little spacecraft leapt into the air was stomach-twisting, the first drop on a rollercoaster. Below us, Voight and the pilot still waved and yelled, though I couldn't hear what they said. I imagined the younger officer was complaining that he'd signed this bird out, and if we didn't bring it back, he was going to be up shit creek.

"Sorry, man," I murmured. "Guess you won't be getting that nap, after all."

No other flights were taking off at the moment, thankfully, which was one less thing I had to worry about. I paused the lander at a few hundred feet up and got my bearings, finding the corner of the Joint Base Andrews airfield where the old hangar squatted seemingly abandoned. At least that's how it had looked when we'd been snatched by Parker Donovan's goons, taken into holding cells, drugged, and interrogated. I'd never actually forgiven Donovan for that, and the fact they'd stored our interstellar transport there was sort of like rubbing salt in the wound.

"They fixed the place up some, didn't they?" Chuck asked from behind my seat. Neither he nor Laranna had bothered to strap in, knowing that we'd need to get out quick.

He was right. The hangar didn't have to pretend to be neglected and disused anymore, and they'd given the thing a facelift, turning it into one of the coordination centers for space activity at the base. Which was why the transport was *really* there, if I was being honest, not just to stick the whole thing in my craw.

The transports were ugly, utilitarian things, lacking the otherworldly charm of the landers or the streamlined deadliness of the fighters. The things brought to mind a paper towel tube flanked with half-used rolls of toilet paper, a jumble of cylinders, and fat, rounded ends. No weapons and only the shielding that was a side-benefit of having a hyperdrive, enough to absorb the normal radiation of space flight but not nearly powerful enough to stop a pulse gun, much less a particle cannon. The thing was a bus, plain and simple, but it was all we had.

And it wasn't alone. Space Force techs scrambled in every direction as the lander touched down where they'd been standing a second before, and Laranna had the door open before the belly jets shut down. I locked the control panel by instinct, then followed them out.

More shouting, this time by outraged enlisted men wondering

what the hell we were doing, but Laranna ignored them and sprinted the twenty yards between the two spaceships, then tapped her own code into the security lock at the utility airlock.

"Sorry, guys," Chuck Barnaby told the Space Force crew, hands raised in a quelling motion. "It's an emergency. I'll buy you all a beer when we get back, I promise."

And thank God he was here because I just would have told them to stop whining and get the hell out of the way.

"Sir, hold on a minute."

Laranna had the door open and clambered up into the transport cockpit, leaving Chuck and me to talk to the Air Force Security Police NCO running over from the hangar, one hand on his holstered service pistol.

"Sir, what are you doing with that aircraft?" he asked, a quaver in his voice but the determination of a man doing his job on his face.

"Major Barnaby just told you," I said, keeping my tone even and authoritative, even though the sergeant was older than me. "We have an emergency, and we're taking this ship."

"Sir, I've been instructed that no one is to board this craft without written orders from the White House."

Concern and doubt vanished in a flare of righteous indignation, and I took a step toward the man, shoulders squaring.

"*Have* you?" I snarled. "That's just freaking amazing to me, Sergeant, when this vessel doesn't actually belong to the United States government. It's a Resistance transport left here for our people to use when we need it and was never authorized for use by the military. In fact, the only reason it's even *on* this base was at the suggestion of the Defense Department in order to prevent civilians from endangering themselves by screwing around with it."

My vehemence took the military policeman back a step, but he wasn't giving up that easy.

"Be that as it may, sir, I have my orders…"

"Then get your superior on the phone, Sergeant," Chuck told him, pointing back at the hangar, "and tell him this ship is taking off. Because it is, your orders be damned."

The sergeant made a mistake, then. He *should* have called for help, should have called his superior to assess the situation. Instead, he went for his gun. Chuck flinched, hand going to his own sidearm, but I couldn't let him get in trouble for this any more than he already was. I saw the movement of the SP's shoulder, his fingers wrapping around the grip of the SIG, then I grabbed his wrist and moved in from that side.

His left hand came up instinctively, but I beat him to the punch, smacking a ridge-hand into his throat. Not hard. It didn't *have* to be hard. I'd found that out the painful way by accident during sparring. The SP's hands went to his throat as he gagged, and I yanked the pistol out of his belt before push-kicking him backward. He wasn't choking, just gagging, but it was enough to keep him occupied while I ran up the steps into the transport. Chuck stared dumbly at the stunned SP until I reached down and grabbed him by the shoulder.

"Get in if you're coming," I snapped and he nodded, shaking free of the shock and following me up.

I hit the control to close the hatch the second he was inside and waited there with the SIG in my hand to make sure no one else tried to stop us. It clunked into place with a metallic finality, and I breathed a sigh of relief. Maybe it wouldn't stand up to a Starblade's pulse cannon, but nothing else they had handy could touch it.

"Might want to strap in," Laranna advised from the pilot's seat. "We're boosting straight out of orbit, and the inertial dampeners on this thing aren't that great."

"Why the hurry?" Chuck asked, though he did as she said even as the transport lurched off the cracked pavement. "It's not as if they can send an F-35 after us."

"They can send Starblades," I reminded him, sliding into the copilot's seat and fastening the harness. "Or one of the cruisers."

Chuck's face went white as if he hadn't thought about the possibility.

"Shit. Do you think they will? I mean, it's going to take some time for them to figure out what you're doing…"

"Some," I agreed, a small portion of my thoughts not totally engulfed in the current crisis reflecting that the process of becoming a Vanguard pilot had changed me. A couple years ago, the steep ascent through the noonday skies would have left me with an empty pit in my stomach and my fingers would have ached from clenching the armrests of my chair. Now, I watched the clouds fall away on either side with the same equanimity I would have experienced on a Sunday drive. "Maybe ten minutes for them to get the word. But we have to get to minimum safe jump distance, and that's going to take nearly an hour."

"We have a head start," Laranna said. "It should be enough even if they order an intercept, but I'm not taking any chances."

With her flying and nothing else to do but wait for the inevitable call ordering us to land, I took a second to check out the inside of the transport. It was small, just the cockpit, a utility bay with equipment lockers, a table that doubled as a galley with food storage cabinets above it, a john, and two tiny cabins. Thank God there were two, or else we would have had to sleep in shifts, which would have made it real inconvenient for someone when we arrived at our destination after they'd already been up for sixteen hours.

It was gonna be bad enough eating ship rations for over a week. I'd made it policy for every starship to be stocked with rations, weapons, and ammo for emergencies, but the food was freeze-dried camping-style crap, and it got old, fast. Or maybe I was just spoiled by the giant freezers on the *Liberator* that we kept filled with the produce and meat from Sanctuary.

Of course, that was all getting ahead of myself. First, we had to make it out of orbit.

"Resistance Transport Two-Zero Bravo, this is Houston Control, do you copy?"

Maybe it had been habit or maybe tradition, but the consensus had been to maintain the traffic control for all space-flights at the space center at Houston. I kinda liked it, since at least it meant I wouldn't have to talk to the Pentagon every time. Sighing, I hit the transmit key at my station.

"Roger, Houston Control," I replied. "We read you."

"Two-Zero Bravo, you are not cleared for orbital flight. We

need you to turn around and head back to Joint Base Andrews." Well, the messenger might have been different than if it had come from the Pentagon, but the message was the same.

"That's a negative, Houston Control," I told the man. I imagined him as some relic of the space race, sitting behind a console with mechanical switches and dials, wearing a short-sleeved dress shirt and clip-on tie and smoking a cigarette. "There's been an emergency that requires immediate response. I'll contact you as soon as possible."

"Ah, Two-Zero Bravo, I've been instructed to inform you that this is an order and that it will be enforced if you disregard it."

It was hard to keep from grinding my teeth at the ungrateful bastards. I wanted to bite the guy's head off, but this wasn't his fault. Hell, I was pretty sure who was passing those orders on to him, and his initials were Parker Donovan.

"Houston Control," I said, "do me a big favor and remind whoever it is that's instructing you that you wouldn't have anything to enforce *with* if I hadn't brought it to you. Hell, you wouldn't have a pot to piss in. I have an emergency that I need to attend to, and whether or not I or *anyone* else from the resistance comes back when I'm done with it depends entirely on what you guys do next."

"Laying it on a little thick, aren't you?" Chuck asked softly, eyebrow tilting.

"I mean every word," I assured him.

No response came for nearly five minutes, and by then, the blue had shifted to star-filled black, and we were on the other side of the planet. Was Russia listening in on this? China? Or our allies? I hoped not. It wasn't going to sound much like a united front between the resistance and America. Maybe that sad-faced contract killer who ran this new version of the Soviet Union would talk about it in front of the UN Security Council.

"Charlie, you hear me?"

Damn. It wasn't Donovan, who I wouldn't have minded telling off. It was General Gavin, who I more or less respected.

"I hear you, sir."

"Tell me what's going on," he urged.

"Ask Colonel Voight," I suggested. "She knows why I have to leave."

His sigh was a rasp of static on the speakers.

"I listened to that message. I was afraid you were going to say that. Charlie, *please* tell me you're not going to trade yourself for Giblet."

"Well, it isn't Plan A, sir. But I'm going after him anyway."

"You could be throwing away everything we've been working for, son," he warned me.

"I could be," I agreed. "But I'm not abandoning my friend. I hope I get to talk to you again in a couple weeks, sir. But if not, it was a pleasure working with you."

"You know, you would have made a shitty soldier, Travers," Gavin said, his voice a gruff rumble. "You don't like following orders, and you always think you know better than your commanding officers. But you're a hell of a leader, and I know why your people trust you. Good luck."

The transmission cut off, and Laranna looked at me, wide-eyed.

"The cruisers haven't changed orbit. No fighters launched. They're not coming after us."

"They're letting us go," Chuck sighed, sounding as if he'd been holding his breath. "I can't believe it."

"I believe it," I told him, unable to keep a grim note out of my voice. "It means they don't think we're coming back."

14

"I feel weird doing this with Chuck in the next room," I admitted, still breathing hard, Laranna's hair teasing at my cheek.

She purred and curled beside me, though it reminded me more of a leopard than a housecat.

"That didn't seem to affect your enthusiasm," she observed, the words a hot breath in my ear. "Don't worry, the bulkheads are soundproofed."

Warmth flooded my face, though I couldn't be sure if that was from the exertion, and I wondered if we could turn up the air conditioning in just this compartment.

"That's not what I meant. It just feels…impolite somehow."

Laranna propped herself up on an elbow, and I caught her tilted eyebrow from the dim light of the compartment's comm panel on the wall by the door.

"Well, I don't know how you do things on Earth, but I am *not* okay with inviting him in."

I rolled my eyes, though I wasn't sure if she could see it.

"What's really bugging you is that you let him come along in the first place," she intuited, and I didn't bother to deny it. She'd always been good at reading my moods.

"I already owe George a lot," I admitted, resting my head back against the pillow and staring into the dim shadows of the ceiling. "He gave up his career to save me. Now I'm taking his son somewhere he could get himself killed."

"His son was an Army Ranger," Laranna reminded me. "George had to know he would be in danger at times."

"It's one thing to know that in your head, another when it actually happens. It feels like I'm risking one friend's life to save another."

"Then we'll just have to make sure we all come back alive, won't we?" she said, yanking on my chest hair hard enough to make me yelp.

"Careful!" I told her, putting a hand over my chest. "I don't have that many!"

To make up for it, she rubbed at the spot, and the rubbing turned into something else as she leaned in for a kiss. I returned it, but something of the thoughts still ruminating in my head must have shown through because she paused, frowning at me.

"What is it?"

"Did you know that Val and Brandy are gonna have a kid together?" I asked her. "That Val is going to stay on Sanctuary from now on, be a full-time trainer for the militia?"

Laranna blinked, sat up straight in bed.

"No, I hadn't heard that. I'm surprised Brandy didn't tell me."

"She's got a lot going on right now. But it's got me thinking…" I went quiet, trying to figure out how to put it into words.

"You want to have a child," she said, and this wasn't as surprising as when she'd read my discomfort at having Chuck on the mission. We'd talked about it before.

"I do," I agreed. "And yet, here we are, throwing ourselves into yet another impossible situation. I don't know how we can think about a family when we're both constantly doing shit like this. But Val told me something that I can't stop thinking about. You only get so much time, and it's never a good idea to waste it."

"You know I would love to make a child with you, Charlie," she said, putting a hand on my cheek. "But you also know that means one of us has to leave the fight. Not just for nine months, but for *years*. I'm not having a child just to turn around and orphan them." Laranna shrugged. "You *can't* abandon the resistance any more than you could abandon Gib. And I can't abandon you. What solution is there other than to simply wait until the war is over?"

"I can only think of one," I admitted. "To end it now."

Laranna frowned and tapped the lamp on the wall beside the bed as if she needed to see my face clearly to ask the next question.

"What do you mean?"

"I mean," I replied, not flinching away from either the light or the question, "that if we pull this off, if we bring Gib back and live through it, that's it. We're going to take what we have, all our forces, everything that the US and her allies will give us, and we're going on the offensive." The idea seemed to gain momentum along with the explanation, and I sat up, talking faster. "The Anguilar are on the edge. I can tell from the way Zan-Tar talks about them. They're close to the breaking point. Politically, I mean. They turned to him because they lost faith in the rest of their leadership. That's bad for us because he's competent, but if we can force him into a couple more failures, big ones, he'll be out, too. And at some point, they're going to start thinking they should move on. They've done it before, stripped a galaxy bare and left. If we can convince them this place is a case of diminishing returns, they'll do it again."

She nodded slowly.

"I like the idea in principle. Do you have anything concrete yet?"

"No," I said. "Not yet. If—*when* we get back, I'll come up with an operational plan to propose to everyone. But I swear to you, I'm gonna do it. I'm going back to Copperell and ending this damned war."

"Because you want us to have a family?" she asked, seeming bemused at the passion and conviction in my voice.

"No," I said, fierce, angry but not at her. Thinking of the teenage gangsters back on Copperell, orphans forced to prey on each other to survive. "Because everyone deserves to."

"JESUS CHRIST," Chuck moaned, tossing down the plastic spoon, "I never thought I'd *miss* MRE's, but somehow you guys have managed to pull it off."

"What's an MRE?" Laranna asked, shoveling down her freeze-dried, reconstituted mystery meat without complaint.

"Meal Ready to Eat," I explained, secretly agreeing with Chuck's assessment of the food quality but determined not to whine about it since this had been my idea in the first place. "They're the pre-packaged, preserved food that the US military uses out in the field." I shrugged. "They're famous for tasting horrible."

Laranna eyed Chuck balefully.

"How spoiled do you have to be to expect home-cooked meals during a combat mission?"

"I don't expect home-cooked meals," Chuck insisted, then took a drink from the water bulb, sloshed the liquid around, and swallowed it, as if to get the taste of the food out of his mouth. "But when you're out in the field, you're usually humping a ruck and digging holes and sweating your ass off and you're so hungry, almost anything would taste good." He waved around at the tiny galley and the rest of the cramped quarters inside the transport. "There's barely room in here to do calisthenics, and it's been almost *ten days*. I've watched every movie and listened to every song on my phone twice now, and if I'd *known* ahead of time that we were going to run off on some secret mission, I would have downloaded some more books to my e-reader because I've already read them all."

"There's a saying that Charlie has taught me," Laranna said

as she scraped the last remnants of her meal out of its container, "that would seem to apply to this situation." She swallowed the bite theatrically, then dropped her spoon into the disposable plate and rubbed the thumb and forefinger of her left hand together. "This is the world's smallest violin, and it's playing My Heart Bleeds For You."

I couldn't help it. I burst out laughing hard enough that I actually spit some of the noodles and desiccated meat out onto the plate, then laughed even harder. Laranna chuckled, though whether at her own joke or my reaction, I wasn't sure. Chuck's mouth dropped open as he stared between the two of us.

"That's not fair," he said plaintively. "I mean, at least you two have each other and a private cabin. If I could have brought along a girlfriend…"

"Wouldn't that require you to *have* a girlfriend?" I pointed out.

"Hey now! I've been busy with my career! Not all of us are lucky enough to stumble across the perfect woman in an alien zoo ship."

"Would it make you feel better if we engaged in celibacy during the trip," Laranna teased him, "so that we might better share in your misery?"

Chuck made a face at her.

"Sure, you offer that *now* when there's only another day left in hyperspace." He shook his head. "Hyperspace. I can't believe I'm actually using that word in a sentence that isn't a review of a science fiction movie."

"It's not an exact translation," I told him. "It's just closest to what we've heard before. I think if we'd injected a theoretical physicist with the translation goo, he'd hear it as something more exact and detailed."

"Would he also hear the term *translation goo*? Because that just sounds as scientific as all hell." He rubbed at his ear. "I can't believe I let you guys talk me into getting that shit put inside my head. If it hadn't been for the direct orders from the President himself…"

"You do bring up a good point, though," I said, raising a finger. "We're going to be coming out of hyperspace in just over twenty-four hours, and we need to go over a few things with you."

"First of all," Laranna said, unable to conceal a grin, "*don't* go falling for the first good-looking female you meet just because she has green skin. Not all green-skinned humanoids are Strada, and some of them have *very* sharp teeth."

"Oh, you're just hilarious," Chuck told her.

"Seriously," I interrupted, "there're going to be a shitload of different species on that station, and you can't afford to be rubbernecking like a tourist. You'll give yourself away in five minutes. You see something that looks like a minotaur on steroids? That's a Gan-Shi, and they're going to be all over the place. You see ill-tempered, sadistic snake people? Krin. Don't stare at them, don't talk to them, don't get in their way. Most of them work for the Empire, and the ones who don't are probably gangsters."

"Everyone else is going to be either working for or subjugated by the Anguilar, and even the ones who've been subjugated will sell you out because they have no choice."

"You haven't dealt with Anguilar except to shoot at them," I added, "and this time, we likely won't have that option until after we find Gib. Here's what you need to know about the Anguilar. They're full of themselves and think their shit doesn't stink. Imagine a Parisian mixed with a hardcore Soviet Communist Party member." I shrugged. "Mixed with a mafioso from the fifties. Your best bet is to avoid eye contact, don't be in the way, don't do anything to attract attention to yourself. If you don't annoy them, they won't notice you at all, not because they're sloppy or careless, though that is sometimes true as well, but because you're not *worth* noticing in their view."

"Real sweethearts," Chuck murmured. "Got it, keep my mouth shut and my head down." He sneered at Laranna. "And don't fall in love with the sharp-teethed chicks."

I winced, remembering my first experience with aliens on the pirate planet.

"Maybe you should stay in the car."

"Don't worry," he assured me with a wry chuckle. "I'm just giving you shit. I'll follow your lead. You're the alien experts. Just tell me when to shoot something."

"That's the other problem," Laranna told him. "According to Brandy, the Anguilar don't allow guns on Wraith Anchorage."

"No weapons?" Chuck exclaimed, crestfallen. "Well, that sucks! Maybe I should wait in the car after all."

"I didn't say no weapons," Laranna corrected him, sliding a dagger out of a sheath inside her boot and flipping it through her fingers with a dexterity trained from childhood. "I said no *guns*."

"Shit," he sighed. "And me without my bayonet."

"I hope you've been paying attention in your knife-fighting

classes, Chuck," I said, then slipped an arm around Laranna's shoulder. "Because I sure have. It helps when you get to sleep with the instructor."

"Teacher's pet," he accused, then held out a hand. "Where's mine? All I got is a lockblade pocket knife."

"Check the equipment locker," I suggested. "It's supposed to be fully stocked. But that brings up the last point. Money." I jerked a thumb back toward the utility bay and the aforementioned equipment locker. "These ships also come stocked with a supply of tradenotes. They're the universal currency out here for people who aren't part of the Empire, backed by independent accounts maintained basically by organized crime." He squinted at my explanation, and I shrugged. "Yeah, I know, it's screwed up, but the last home-grown galaxy-wide civilization fell to a civil war, and then the Anguilar moved in, so there's no organization that could back the currency other than the mob. In practice, that means this place is partly controlled by the Anguilar and partly controlled by the mob. The Anguilar are only going to take Imperial Credits, and the rest of the station is only going to take tradenotes, which means we can only use our money with the mob-controlled parts of the station. So don't offer anyone a bribe unless they'll take tradenotes."

"This all sounds complicated. Why don't you guys handle that part, and I'll just look menacing? I'm a Ranger…breaking things and blowing shit up is our strong suit, not diplomacy."

"Since you're a Ranger," I countered, "you should know that everyone down to the lowest private should know the whole plan and be able to carry it out in case everyone who outranks them gets killed."

"Since that would be us," Laranna said, indicating her and me, "I'm hoping it doesn't come to that, personally."

"Yeah, me too," I agreed. "But if it does, well…you can't just let Gib get killed because we screwed up."

"You mean because *you* screwed up," Laranna corrected me. "*I* don't screw up."

"Except for that whole thing where you got yourself captured by the Anguilar and I had to rescue you," I said, looking at the ceiling.

"You must not enjoy sleeping with your knife-fighting instructor all that much, Charlie Travers," she warned, punching my arm.

We laughed, but somewhere deep inside, in a place I didn't want to visit right now, I was very aware that the part about the two of us getting killed was no joke. In fact, it was the likeliest scenario. I took a drink of my water bulb and reflected that I wasn't that good of a logistician.

While I'd been busy arranging for food, water, guns, and ammo…I'd totally forgotten to stock the transports with tequila or vodka. I really needed a drink.

15

"Whoa," I breathed. "That's pretty damned big."

"That's what she said," Chuck muttered, though I could tell by the expression on his face that he was just as impressed as I was.

Wraith Anchorage. The name conveyed mystery, sounded exotic and vaguely malevolent, promised danger and adventure… and was totally inadequate to describe what I saw in the main viewscreen as we exited hyperspace.

"It's the size of a moon," Laranna said, nodding, eyes wide.

I consider it a statement on my maturation as an individual that I didn't respond with *that's no moon, it's a space station*. But I really, really wanted to.

She was right, though. Wraith Anchorage had been built out of the riches of a vast asteroid belt, as big as the one we'd encountered in the nearest system on the jump-lines to Earth but not littered with worthless carbonaceous chondrites. This one held the wealth of the ages, apparently, because they'd felt confident enough in its bounty to melt down three of the largest rocks in the system and make this place.

That was what Brandy's intelligence briefing had told us, but it hadn't given a true impression of the sheer size. It was bigger than either of the moons of Mars, which I'd gotten the opportunity to see close up, and looked bigger still because it wasn't a simple spheroid. The builders had used artificial gravity to its full advantage, creating what was the equivalent of a city in space—towering spires, massive hemispherical domes, pyramids that would have put Giza to shame, at least twenty-five miles across at the widest, nearly that in length and extending in both polar directions for at least ten miles.

I suck at math, but I figured that was a shitload of surface area and interior volume.

"According to the files Brandy gave us," Laranna said, "the city is big enough to hold over a hundred million people comfortably. It never got that sort of population before the Krin took it over, though."

The city itself was mind-blowing, awe-inspiring. The rest of it, though, inspired something darker. A web of metal expanded outward from the main structures of Wraith Anchorage, and touching strands of the web like flies caught and cocooned for future nourishment, were starships under construction. Angular cruisers. At least a dozen of them in different stages of construction, from the barest skeleton to one that looked to be nearly complete.

Those were worrisome, but in the long term, not as much of an immediate problem as the cruisers berthed at the needle-like docking cylinders sticking out from the south polar region of the station. And the Starblades patrolling the traffic lanes.

"I'm transmitting our registration," Laranna said, tapping the control like she was knocking on wood for luck.

If there was any comfort to be had, it was the sheer number of spacecraft waiting to dock with the station—the *city*. Hundreds, maybe thousands, dotting space with all manner of starships, cargo haulers, personal transports, and shuttles, some of them coming in from larger vessels hanging out hundreds of thousands of miles away. Probably looking to avoid being inspected by the Anguilar garrison.

Not that I could see *all* of that on the optical cameras, but the one extra that the otherwise innocuous transport came equipped with was military-class sensors. They weren't something that could be picked up by a casual inspection, but they were worth their weight in gold. If gold were worth anything to most planets.

"Transport Indigo 23A out of…Caranova?" Indifference and apathy weighed down the officious voice that came over the cockpit speakers, a functionary who'd been forced to ask the same questions hundreds of times a day and resented the hell out of both the superiors who'd stuck him with this job and the travelers who forced him to perform it. Probably a Krin or one of the other subjugated peoples, since I didn't see an Anguilar doing this job. "This is Wraith Anchorage Traffic Control. What's your lading?"

"No cargo, Wraith Control," Laranna said. "Passengers only."

"And what's your business here?" Annoyance piled on apathy as he was forced to ask even more questions he didn't want the answers to. I crossed my fingers, mentally at least.

We're nobody, just another ship. Ignore us.

"Arranging a shipping arrangement with a local concern," Laranna told him. "His name is Janus."

A pause and I just knew the traffic control officer had to be cursing as he ran through the records to check our story.

"Fine. You're cleared to dock in hangar eighteen. You're fourth in line. Slave your controls to the beacon, and don't deviate unless you want to have a Starblade fighter up your ass."

"Will do, Wraith Control," she assured him, then cut off the mic and sagged into the seat with a relieved breath. "Well, we have to wait out here about fifteen minutes, but that could have gone a lot worse."

"Thank God," I murmured.

"Is that it?" Chuck asked, looking between the two of us. "Now we just dock and we're good?"

"There'll be security once we're inside," I told him. "But this is the first hurdle. And maybe the biggest, because there's gotta be millions of people in and out of this place every month, so they can't spot everyone who might be a threat. Also, we kind of all look alike to the Anguilar. The only chance they might spot us is if they have those face-reading things, the computers?"

"Biometrics," Chuck supplied. "And why wouldn't they? We've had them for years now. We can pick out a single face from all the people passing through a subway station as long as the cameras saw them. With the technology the Anguilar have, they should be able to spot you from just the files that big, ugly bounty hunter had on you, right?"

"If this were America or Europe or China, sure," I agreed. "But just because the Anguilar have better tech than us for spaceflight and weapons doesn't mean *everything* they have is more advanced. The way they use computers is different from us...not just the Anguilar but almost everyone out here except for Lenny. It might have been in reaction to Lenny and his Creators for all I know, or they might have arranged it that way themselves and he just hasn't bothered to tell us about it, but computers here are mostly kind of like the fly-by-wire systems in Starblades or Vanguards. They run in the background and take care of their operations without being noticed. I read up on those AI programs you guys are working on...those wouldn't be put up with out here. They don't want computers that think, they just want computers that *do*. The most sentient shit they have are construction and maintenance 'bots and the Anguilar don't even bother with those, since slaves are cheaper."

"That's kind of short-sighted, isn't it?" he mused, rubbing at his chin. Neither of us had bothered to shave on the trip out since being scruffy kind of fit with the cover we were using, and he was already developing a short beard and mustache. Not me. After a week and a half, all I had was a five-o'clock shadow. "I mean, they're basically space Nazis. You'd think they'd want as much security as possible with all those slaves."

"That's another part of their ego problem," Laranna chipped in. "They consider themselves so far above the rest of us that they're only concerned with physical security, and they farm most of that out to the Krin—they think it's beneath them. Since Charlie took over the resistance, they're discovering the weaknesses in that system. And maybe this Zan-Tar will try to change it, but we just have to hope he hasn't gotten around to reforming it enough for Wraith Anchorage to have that biometric security you're talking about."

"Hope?" Chuck asked, looking a little aghast at the idea.

"Well, the only other alternative is to not come," I pointed out. "And that ship has sailed. Literally."

"You could wear a disguise. Fake beard maybe, since you can't seem to grow one yourself."

Chuck grinned, and I returned it with a middle finger.

"I can't change my genetics," I told him. "At least you can use Viagra."

"Oh, you're a riot, Travers," he sneered, returning the one-finger salute. "Now I know why my dad and you got along so well. You have the same sense of humor."

A *thump-thump-thump* from the maneuvering jets startled him in mid-winge, and he grabbed at his armrests and looked around in alarm.

"The station traffic control beacon has the conn," I explained. "It's guiding us to our approach vector."

"We're on our way in," Laranna added. "Faster than I thought. Maybe that's a good sign."

"I'm not worried about how fast we get in," Chuck said, settling back down in his chair. "Just about how fast we can get out."

CUSTOMS WAS…WELL, a joke. I thought it might be, but it was good to see that I'd called it right. Weapons detectors and a few Imperial armored troopers standing guard in desultory boredom was the extent of the security on the other side of the hangar bay, and we passed through it without so much as a sidelong glance.

Not that I blamed them for their disinterest. We were in more danger of being trampled going through those weapons detectors than being deemed a risk by the Anguilar. I hadn't seen so many people in one place since my one and only visit to Manhattan, except this crowd was even more self-involved and impolite than the New *Yawk*ers. And even more diverse. I didn't notice any other humans, but there were Copperell, and there was Krin galore, plus a few other species whose names I couldn't even remember and even a few Kamerians. My chest constricted at the sight of them, both because every one of them I'd ever come across had been mean, competent, and deadly, and because the sight brought Dani back to mind.

I'd been trying not to think about her. I'd been pretty successful at it, mostly because the worry about a living—I *hoped* —Giblet trumped the guilt over a dead friend. But now it flooded back as if it had never left, a distraction I didn't need at the moment, and I wondered if it would ever stop, if I'd ever not feel like it was my fault. Maybe this was just, as Sgt. Redd had called it way back when, the burden of leadership. And maybe that meant that, no matter what Lenny thought, I wasn't cut out for it.

Later. Think about this shit later.

I felt inside my jacket for the knife I'd sheathed on my belt, crossdraw style—not because I thought I'd need it immediately, but more to make sure none of the crowd pressing in on all sides of us stole it from me. My other hand was on Laranna's arm, keeping track of her so we didn't get separated. Chuck's hand rested on my shoulder for the same reason. Or at least I hoped it was Chuck's hand, because I didn't want any of these other assholes touching me.

A babble of sound crashed over me like a wave, overwhelming, deafening, but worse than that was the stench. Not that aliens all smelled bad, but every single one of them smelled *wrong*, not like people, or at least not like any people I'd ever met. I couldn't put words to the smell, couldn't compare it to a weed or a chemical or an animal, I just knew it was wrong, and it was overpowering.

The combination of the crushing crowd, the sounds, and the smells triggered a wave of claustrophobia, like I was about to be buried under a wave of flesh, suffocated by the weight of them. I tried to keep my breathing under control, tried to force myself to calm down, but the only thing restraining the panic was the movement forward, and it was all I could do not to push Laranna forward through the press. She must have sensed my mood because her elbows flashed, and people darted away on either side of us under the onslaught.

Then we were through, past the thickest part of them and huddled against the far wall, and I sucked in air with desperate relief. I hadn't been able to see much of our surroundings through the crowd before, but now the entire scene came into focus. The hangar bays were past the row of huge doors we'd just exited, large enough to allow cargo through or the thousands of travelers who'd exited all at once before everything was filtered through the weapons detectors.

Those were the bottleneck, and the Anguilar didn't care enough about the criminals and smugglers and lowlifes who visited Wraith Anchorage to bother with any sort of traffic control to make sure no one got hurt squeezing through the metal arches. The only thing that concerned those guards was when the detectors went off.

The blaring klaxon sent my hand seeking out the knife again, but it wasn't for us. I don't know how the guards knew which of the dozens of people passing through the arches had set off the alarm, but they transformed in an instant, from zero to wolf pack in one second. The guilty party must have made the same mistake I did, thinking there was no way they could track him down before he could get away, because he broke through the crowd, making a dash for the train station at the end of the corridor.

It reminded me of the monorail at the airport, and one of the cars had arrived a moment before, disgorging hundreds of passengers, and the Copperell runner made a beeline for the center of them, trying to get lost in the throng, maybe get onto the train and un-ass the area. It wasn't a bad plan, but he'd made one mistake: he thought the Imperial soldiers gave a damn about all the other people in the crowd.

"Get down or get shot!" one of the soldiers bellowed, his voice amplified by the speakers on the exterior of his helmet, and he gave everyone about three seconds to comply.

Some of them—a *lot* of them—must have been experienced hands at the inner workings of Wraith Anchorage, because they wasted no time throwing themselves to the floor. Still, they barely made it before the Anguilar Imperial soldiers opened fire. No setting phasers for stun or any of the other nonsense I'd seen on science fiction TV and movies, either. Pulse guns didn't work that way. You couldn't set one for stun any more than you could set a Colt .45 for stun.

There was no stunning involved in what happened to the poor sons of bitches who didn't duck fast enough. Crimson threads of scalar energy sliced through them, cutting down at least a dozen people before they converged on that Copperell moron who thought he could smuggle a gun through the detectors. People spun and dropped and screamed, their clothes smoldering, yelling for help that wasn't coming, but the smuggler didn't make a sound. He was dead before he could.

The Imperial soldiers didn't let up until his body stopped jerking at the rounds still impacting him, until he caught flame and billowed smoke. When the firing stopped, everything fell into an eerie silence, broken only by the crackling of burning clothes and the moaning of the wounded.

I hadn't moved. The entire thing had unfolded in front of us, away from us, and I hadn't even thought to duck. I'd just stood there, back against the wall, and watched like an idiot who'd never seen anyone get shot before. Beside me on the right, Laranna's jaw clenched, anger flashing in her eyes at the display of reckless slaughter. On the left, Chuck stared at the scene in wide-eyed disbelief. We'd told him how bloodthirsty the Empire could be, but it's one thing to be told, another to see it for yourself.

The troops advanced, and I thought for just a moment that they might intend to treat the wounded, to evaluate them and call for help. Instead, one of them, with a rank insignia I recognized as their equivalent of a senior NCO, knelt down over the dead Copperell and patted at his body until he came up with a pulse pistol. He nodded to the others, whatever he said to them lost inside the confines of his helmet, and they went back to their guard stations, leaving the dead and wounded behind.

"Jesus Christ," Chuck hissed, staring at the wounded. "Should…should we help them?"

"Here?" Laranna said with a humorless snort. "There's no better way to draw attention to ourselves on Wraith Anchorage than to act like a decent person." She gestured to the tram station. "Come on, we need to get on one of those trains. Our contact is nearly ten miles from here."

"Charlie, come on," Chuck pleaded, glancing between me and the carnage. "Are we just gonna ignore them?"

"Chuck," I told him, sounding so much calmer and logical than I was, "look at the wounded. You see them? They're dressed well, wearing expensive clothes, jewelry, and they looked pretty self-important before the shooting started. There are two kinds of people who're rich on a place like this—criminals and people who deal with the Anguilar. If there are innocent people in this city, you're not gonna find them here. Come on," I said, stepping away from the perceived safety of the wall with what felt like a monumental effort. "We came to rescue Gib, and he's the only one here I'm interested in helping."

And God help me, I believe I meant it.

16

"Are you sure this is the place?" I said, looking askance at Laranna.

"This is what Brandy told me," she confirmed, shaking her head, lip curling in disgust.

We'd taken the train for what felt like half an hour, and got off in what was announced as level B-85, exiting into what might have been an entirely different station than the one we'd entered at the hangar bay. Gone were the powerful people in fancy clothes, gone were the Anguilar soldiers, and gone was the bright, overhead lighting that had turned the hangar bay and train station into a sunny noonday in Florida.

B-85 was more like a fall evening in Seattle. If there'd ever been glaring overhead lights here, they'd long since fallen into disrepair, leaving the narrow walkways and battered buildings in a perpetual twilight that seemed to suit the patrons of this part of

Wraith Anchorage. Creatures of the shadows crept through the streets, hugging the walls, glancing aside with a paranoia that might have been justified or staggered along at the center of the walk, eyes unfocused, lost in a haze of alcohol or drugs, or both.

There were others besides the frightened and the inebriated. Not many of them, and they stayed in the shadows, not wanting to be seen, but I noticed them nonetheless. Predators. I'd seen their like everywhere the Anguilar ruled, those who'd given into the temptation to attack the weak and the poor, to take what little they had from them in order to carve out their own sort of power. They wouldn't bother us. We projected an alert readiness, a strength that wouldn't interest them. Risk-benefit ratio. They were too likely to get hurt if they came after us. Easier targets out there.

The businesses that catered to the scared and the high and the dangerous alike were about what I expected from a place like this. Casinos came first, offering every sort of game of chance including bare-handed fighting and racing wild animals, and some of them looked large enough to host the Kentucky Derby all indoors, bigger than any of the largest Vegas had to offer but not as fancy. Everything here looked thrown together with whatever material that they'd had to hand, the walls bare metal covered in ugly welds or blocks made from the original asteroid material and cemented in place. No wood, of course, because even if they grew trees or plant life in the city, there wouldn't be enough to spare to use for building materials. No plastic because oil required a biological ecosystem. Just rock and metal.

Bars, of course, though the ones here advertised not only

intoxicants but hallucinogens and other harder drugs, most of them regulated or outlawed on more civilized worlds. Some of the places specialized in the hard stuff and offered rooms to enjoy the trip or sleep it off for a hefty charge.

That was one way to step out of an unpleasant reality. The other was just as ancient and just as predictable. Brothels, that was a safe name for them. The 21st Century had so many euphemisms and forbidden words, I'd gotten into trouble a few times referring to various controversial subjects with the terms I'd learned in the 1980s, but I *think* brothel was still an acceptable way of referring to these places. We'd seen as many of those as we had bars, though they advertised more aggressively, with males *and* females of various species out front, wearing next to nothing except for a sleazy grin and making catcalls at passersby, daring them to come in and promising what they'd do for them if they did.

Maybe I'd led a sheltered life, but my face went warm as we walked between the rows of shabby buildings, and I couldn't look at Laranna.

Then more casinos, only these were full-service—hotels, bars, brothels, and casinos all in one. No race tracks or boxing matches, but they were as large as the ones that had them and perhaps more subtle about their flesh-peddling since the people who intended to stay here for a long-term debauch needed a room and these were the best around. They depended on the broad front windows that gave a view of the entire first floor, flashing lights and dance floors and writhing bodies.

It worked. More of the streams of people diverted into the

sluiceways of the casino-bar-hotel-brothel-dance club combinations than had strayed at the temptation of any of the more singular pursuits. At that point, I relaxed, thinking the worst was behind us and wondering if Laranna actually knew where we were going, since there didn't seem to be much left of this section of the city. The bigger structures tailed off, giving way to buildings little more than lean-tos constructed using the interior walls of the section to cut costs.

They barely bothered with signs, as if everyone should know what they were, some with just hand-painted descriptions on the outside wall. *Food. Clothes. Knives.* That last one I gave a second look, curious as to what everyone else might be carrying as a weapon, but Laranna had assured me it was cheap junk, not nearly as well made as the Ka-Bar I'd brought along, much less the Strada blades she carried. She'd packed her collapsable staff as well, and while I'd trained with it some, Laranna had told me with some regret that I wasn't good enough with the weapon yet to try to use it in a fight for my life.

And then.

Past the little shops were the places people who couldn't afford biological *companionship* or couldn't deal with a living being seeing them at their neediest and most pitiful came for some release. I'd seen it before, but not recently, and I certainly hadn't expected to find our contact here.

Robot pleasure dolls. They swayed provocatively on specially built stands outside the windowless walls of the bunker-like shops, looking *almost* like living men and women but not quite. Dani had told me about something called the *uncanny valley*, which was a reaction to early attempts at creating human faces with computer graphics. I wondered if non-humans shared that trait, because the pleasure dolls engaging in their perpetual-motion dance outside the self-proclaimed "House of Desire" sure triggered that valley in my head. Far from turning me on, the blank look in their eyes and the cold mechanism behind them inspired me to turn and sprint away from there as fast as possible.

Laranna must have felt something similar, unless it was just the moral and ethical issues that brought the sneer to her face. Chuck stared at the things with incomprehension for a minute until the truth of them finally sank in and his expression turned into a mirror of Laranna's.

"That's kind of…" He trailed off, shaking his head. "I mean, at least they're not exploiting real people, but it's just…sad."

"They *are* exploiting real people," Laranna told him, pushing past us to head for the entrance. "They're exploiting the poor, lonely beings who are desperate enough for contact that they'd come here."

Which I couldn't argue with, though I was sure there was some ethical argument to be made about choice and free will. Not now, though. I trailed behind her by less than an arm's length, unsure what I'd find inside.

It was less a house of ill repute, I thought, and more a showroom for appliances. The various models, patterned after Copperell, Strada, Anguilar, Kamerian, and even a couple humans—though where they'd attained the specs for that one, I wasn't sure—stood at regular intervals inside the well-lit foyer, all of them scantily dressed but not naked, as if the tease of the brief garments could distract from their subtly robotic movements.

Ahead of us in line at the main counter, a male Krin negotiated with the Copperell at the counter, pointing at, to my shock, the Kamerian male robot, which brought up all sorts of imagery about the towering, powerful conqueror robot and the slimy, scaley snake-man that I would rather not have had inside my head. Brain bleach wouldn't do it, I'd have to take a pot scrubber to my neurons.

I tried to keep myself occupied watching for threats and finally found them in the back corner of the showroom, where a pair of huge, broad-shouldered figures loomed. At first, I'd thought they were robots themselves, but there was something about their movements that spoke of biology rather than cybernetics, and I recognized their silhouettes from the others of their species who I'd seen on Sanctuary.

Not many. Not many of the things were found anywhere, from what I understood. They reminded me of minotaurs, though only in the abstract. They didn't have hooves either for feet or hands, nor did they have a long, squared-off snout nor fully curled bull horns. But their features were distinctly bovine, the faces flattened, ears set high up and folded over at the tip. Not to mention the vestigial remains of horns. They were Gan-Shi, and I guessed they were the muscle, making sure no one damaged the merchandise or got mouthy with the clerk when the time came to pay.

The Krin finally reached an accommodation and headed into a side room with his own private Kamerian, leaving us next up at the counter. The Copperell looked us over with a leer and spread his hands.

"Just so you know," he told us, "the charge is per person, not per group, even if you only use one of the 'bots."

Chuck frowned and advanced a step on the little man, but I caught his arm, and Laranna stepped between him and the counter.

"We're not here for the 'bots," she told the Copperell, ignoring his innuendo. "We're here to see Janus. Tell him some friends of Brandy have stopped by and we'd like to catch up "

"Janus is busy," the clerk told her flatly, leaving no room for discussion. "He doesn't see customers."

"We just established we're not customers," I put in. "We're old friends, and he'll want to talk to us."

A flare of irritation sparked behind the clerk's bland, tan-colored eyes, and he leaned forward, apparently unimpressed by our confidence.

"Mr. Janus doesn't entertain *friends* at his business. And if you're not customers, then you need to get the hell out of here and stop wasting my time."

The Gan-Shi stepped out of the shadows, apparently drawn by the tone of the clerk's voice, and advanced on us, appearing even larger than I'd judged initially as they came closer.

"Shit," I murmured, my Ka-Bar suddenly feeling very inadequate. Each of the two had to be the height and weight of an NFL offensive lineman but without the gut, and all three of us together couldn't have taken down one of the Gan-Shi, much less two.

"I'm sure we can come to some sort of agreement," Laranna soothed, pulling a stack of tradenotes out of her jacket pocket. "Mr. Janus *is* going to want to talk to us. He won't be angry with you—and as a bonus, you get a little spending money."

The clerk's face screwed up into a thoughtful frown, and he snatched the cash from her hand, counted it, then took a scanner out of a drawer beneath the counter and ran it over the money like he was worried it was fake.

"All right," he said, tucking the wad of cash into a pocket with one hand, waving the Gan-Shi away with the other. "Shindo," he snapped at one of the minotaurs. "Take these people in to see Mr. Janus. I'll call ahead and tell him to expect you."

I very carefully didn't sigh in relief because it would have looked like weakness, but I couldn't keep my shoulders from sagging at the reprieve from a potentially fatal running of the bulls. The bigger of the two Gan-Shi motioned to us, whatever his reaction to the cancellation of hostilities a mystery behind the cow-placid expression.

I shot a look at Laranna, and she shrugged.

"There's a reason we brought the money along," she told me quietly once we were out of earshot of the desk, heading into a narrow hallway behind the counter. "Sometimes a bribe is as potent a weapon as a pulse gun."

"It's sure as hell more potent than this damned knife," I agreed.

"Those things look like they could ram right through a brick wall," Chuck whispered from my other side, still staring at the

Gan-Shi. "How the hell did they ever lose control of this station if they used to own it?"

Laranna shushed him, but the Gan-Shi didn't show any indication he'd heard the comment. The hallway was long and grew darker with each step until I thought I might run directly into the back of the minotaur, but finally, a thin sliver of light shone from beneath a door at the very end of the passage. The Gan-Shi known as Shindo paused and knocked on the door with surprising gentleness.

"Sir," Shindo growled in a thunderous rumble of a voice that came from somewhere deep inside that massive chest. "They're here."

"Open the damned door then, you gigantic moron!" a harsh, nasally voice snapped from the other side of the door. "I don't have all day!"

I wasn't sure how the hell anyone could tell night from day here, or ever call the dank shadowy, perpetual twilight "day," nor was I sure why anyone would talk that way to a creature that could break them in half. Again, though, Shindo surprised me by not reacting, simply pulling open the door and motioning for the three of us to precede him into the office.

There was only one man inside the room and he was a Copperell. That shouldn't have surprised me, given that he was Brandy's contact and most of her contacts were Copperell, but it did. Because of where he was and what he was doing. Most Copperell I'd met over the last couple years had been victims, a very few heroes determined to free their people, but this one was different. I could see it in the set of his eyes, in the way his mouth seemed perpetually constricted in a sneer, the way he attempted to disguise his thinning hairline with a pitiful combover. And he was fat. Not that being fat made anyone evil, but he wasn't human, he was Copperell, and I'd yet to meet a fat Copperell, until now. I'd asked Brandy about it, and she'd told me it was part of their ethic as a society dating way back before the Kamerians had taken over, almost a religious precept.

Not for this guy. He wore a tunic of what I recognized as genetically engineered silk, hanging loose over his ample belly and he made no move to rise to greet us. He didn't have a desk, which was not unusual. Desks were a human thing. This guy sat on a cross between a couch and a beanbag chair that molded to the curves of his body and looked very comfortable, so maybe I didn't blame him for not getting up.

"Close the door, Shindo," he barked, and the Gan-Shi did as he was told, blocking the entrance with his considerable bulk. "All right, you said you're friends of Brandy. What does the nasty bitch want?"

"We should talk alone, Mr. Janus," Laranna said, eyeing the Gan-Shi significantly.

"Oh, don't worry about Shindo." Janus waved the thought away with a swollen hand. "He's just like the rest of the cows on this hunk of metal—too stupid to understand what's going on, and even if he weren't as dumb as a side of beef, who would he tell? The Anguilar certainly aren't going to listen to one of his kind. They consider them to be little more than animals. Now out with it! I owe that conniving harpy, but that doesn't mean I plan on sitting here playing guessing games!"

He had a nasally, high-pitched voice that exacerbated the whiny nature of his demands, but I figured people didn't get into a position to be an intelligence source on a place like this by being an upstanding citizen. I didn't trust him, but the shitty part was that I had to.

I looked to Laranna, and she nodded, though I could sense her reluctance.

"We need information about the Anguilar," I told him. "Particularly about their commander, a general named Zan-Tar. I want to know his whereabouts on Wraith Anchorage, where he keeps his offices, his military headquarters. And I want to know about one of his prisoners." The words didn't want to come out because I was scared shitless he'd tell me that Gib had already been executed, or transferred out of here, taken back to one of the Anguilar Imperial headquarters. "I need to find out where he's holding a Varnell. Location, security around him, everything you can find out."

"I don't know anything about any Varnell prisoner," Janus declared. I met his petulance with a cold, harsh stare, and eventually, he sighed, scowling at the idea that he'd have to actually put some work into answering the question. "Fine. Shindo, help me up."

The Gan-Shi didn't offer his boss a hand, and I got the distinct impression it was because Janus wouldn't have wanted Shindo to touch him skin-to-skin. Instead, Shindo leaned over and placed a thick-fingered hand at the small of Janus's back and pushed him up from the chair.

"All right, enough," Janus told him, slapping away the big creature's hand once he was on his feet.

The back of the Gan-Shi's hand was covered with the same sort of coarse, wiry hair as the rest of his body, the same length everywhere, including his head. And I could see too much, since the minotaur wore no shirt or shoes, his only garment a pair of baggy, knee-length shorts. Maybe that was why Janus didn't want to touch the Gan-Shi.

"I'll have to go make some calls," Janus said, waddling across the office to another exit, this one partitioned off with a hanging curtain. "In private, as the people I have to talk to won't take kindly to being overheard. You three have a seat." He motioned to hard benches against the far wall, looking so much less comfortable than his personal beanbag. "Shindo will stay with you, just in case you get any ideas about going through my files or helping yourself to the contents of my bar."

Which I hadn't noticed either until just then. The files I could have cared less about, but the bar was another story. After the last couple hours, I badly needed a drink. Before I could ask Janus for a special dispensation about the whole bar thing, the Copperell passed through the curtain and was gone.

17

Chuck watched the corpulent Copperell go, then turned back to me and rolled his eyes.

"What a charmer," he said, slumping down onto the bench.

"We work with what we have," Laranna said with a shrug, then sat down beside him.

I didn't feel like sitting, but Gan-Shi eyed me suspiciously until I did it anyway, just to reassure him that I wasn't planning on ransacking the office in his boss' absence. I stared back at him for a moment even after that, questions nagging at me that it was probably a mistake to ask. Yet I couldn't keep them suppressed.

"Why the hell do you let him treat you like that, Shindo?" I wondered.

The Gan-Shi didn't answer, his gaze shifting away from me as if he couldn't meet my eyes anymore.

"Seriously," I insisted. "You could break that bastard's neck with one hand. Why do you let him get away with that?"

"I have no alternative," the Gan-Shi replied after a long moment, shocking me with his honesty. "None of us do. We take what work we can because the only other choice is the arena."

"Arena?" Chuck asked him, shaking his head. "*What* arena?"

Shindo regarded the Ranger officer in a like manner as someone from America might have stared at a foreigner who'd admitted they'd never heard of Elvis Presley. Or whoever the 21st Century equivalent of Elvis might be.

"You truly know so little about this place?" he wondered, and if it had been mind-bending to have a humanoid bull talking to us at all, having one sound disappointed in us was even stranger. "This section is only one of many entertainment districts on Wraith Anchorage. The largest by far is the arena, and the betting facilities that service it." I had very little experience with the Gan-Shi and couldn't be sure of my interpretation of his expression, but I guessed it was one of disgust. "Nearly the entire city wagers on the arena, and those who can't afford to attend in person pay to watch on closed-circuit screens in betting parlors across Wraith Anchorage. Even the Anguilar, who loathe everything about this place, take advantage of their position to claim front-row seats at the arena."

"Is this arena anything like the bare-knuckle fighting we saw at some of the casinos?" I wondered, picturing something like the MMA that Dani and Chuck had told me about except without referees and rules. Brutal but not outlandish, not even something I couldn't imagine happening on Earth.

"No," Shindo snorted in derision, making a sweeping gesture with his massive arm that came just inches from my face even though he hadn't moved away from where he stood beside the door. "The amateur brawling at the casinos is playtime for children. Serious injuries are rare, and patrons are encouraged to enter the matches. The arena…" The Gan-Shi's chin went down to touch his chest in grim contemplation. "The rewards for winning the brawls are trifles. A free room, a free night with a companion, living or robot. A free dinner. The rewards for the arena are enough to make a life outside the Below possible for such as ourselves, and with such a great reward, the risk is much higher. All fights in the arena are to the death. I am unable to number how many of my people have lost their lives in the endless search for a sustainable existence."

"It's bad for you Gan-Shi here, then?" Chuck asked, stumbling and hesitant, no doubt just getting used to the idea of talking to a humanoid bull. "I thought you guys built this place."

Shindo's nostrils flared, eyes narrowing, and I thought maybe Chuck had gone too far, gotten too personal with the Gan-Shi. But Shindo seemed to relax.

"The Gan-Shi built the Convergence," he said with an air of righteous indignation, "a paradise that would have united all the species of the galaxy under one purpose, would have provided all the resources needed to forge a technological civilization across the realms of Strada, Copperell, Varnell, Kamerian…even the Krin." He spat aside, not just a spray of saliva but a honking big lugie, and I grimaced as it hit the floor. "We might have been strong enough, free enough to present a united front against the

Anguilar when they came to our doorstep. The Kamerians might never have attempted to conquer the rest of us, sparking the civil war that devastated this entire galaxy and left us as a wounded animal for the scavengers to pounce on."

Shindo's head wagged like a hellfire-and-brimstone preacher lamenting the failings of the ancient Israelites in the Old Testament.

"But my people were naïve. We were gullible. And when the Krin came and offered us a partnership, offered to help make our dream a reality, we believed them. In months, they'd taken over, brought in armed soldiers, and herded us into the lower levels, the ghettos…the Below. Where we've been ever since. The only work available to us is this"—he motioned down at himself—"security for the criminals who turned our paradise into hell. Or as brute labor. Any of us who cause trouble are sent to the arena, unprepared, untrained, to die. As my father was."

Shindo sighed, and his shoulders slumped.

"My mother was ill, and her medical treatment cost more than I could earn as a laborer. I tried to make up the difference by stealing from Mr. Janus, and he offered me the choice of the arena or working for him." His eyes closed. "She died of her illness. And now I have no one and no choice."

"There's always a choice," Laranna told him, standing, putting a hand on his arm.

I tensed up, sure the big brute would take a swing at her and prepared to shove the knife straight into his throat if he did, but instead, Shindo looked at her hand in wonder, as if it was the very first time anyone had touched him.

"We may not see it at the time," she went on. "We may think it will cost us everything. But the choice is always there. It's the reason we do what we do."

Shindo regarded her with a narrow, suspicious look.

"You're with the resistance."

"Shit," Chuck said softly, then winced an apology when I glared at him.

"Why do you say that?" I asked the Gan-Shi, trying to keep my tone neutral.

Shindo eyed me with an undisguised smile. The bull-headed bastard was a lot smarter than Janus gave him credit for.

"Because Mr. Janus speaks of the resistance often, in the privacy of his office here, when no one else is around. He complains constantly to his closest confidantes and business partners that the resistance is to blame for the Anguilar increasing their presence here, for the Empire exerting more control and collecting higher taxes from Wraith Anchorage." His dark, deep-set eyes flickered toward me. "And how he was forced to aid them because of a bargain he made long ago."

"Sounds like Mr. Janus needs to drink a big, fat cup of shut the hell up," Chuck growled with the fierce conviction of a military officer.

"I don't know," Laranna reasoned. "I'd almost rather he helped us from obligation rather than out of the goodness of his heart." I goggled at her, horrified that she'd admit to the fact we were resistance right in front of the Gan-Shi, but she shrugged, and in her eyes I read her thoughts—she was acting on her gut and daring me to disagree, given how often I'd done it.

"I can assure you," Shindo told her, "that he has no goodness left in his heart to offer." The flat, bovine face twisted into a sneer that didn't fit it well. "Mr. Janus barely has a heart at all." He shrugged. "But yes, you're likely correct. A man like him would be unable to make a deal with the Anguilar to betray you, even if he were so inclined. They despise him and the others who sell the pleasures of the flesh."

"The Anguilar are remarkably uptight about that sort of thing," Laranna agreed.

"That's a relief, I guess," I said, though I couldn't confirm that as it wasn't something I'd ever been interested in finding out about them. "We don't have to worry about the Anguilar because they're uptight prigs."

"You're with the resistance," Shindo repeated, his features set stubbornly, arms crossed over his chest. He was intent on making his original point despite the intervening discussion.

"No one's admitting that," Chuck insisted, winking at me. "But why do you want to know?"

"Your cause is hopeless," he declared. "That is what Mr. Janus believes, what his business associates believe. They discuss how they might best profit from your victory or your defeat, and not one of them is willing to risk money on the chances of you winning. Why do you keep fighting when you know you can't win?"

Laranna was about to answer, I could see it in her eyes, and I gave her a quelling gesture. *Let me handle this one.*

"You ever consider," I asked Shindo, choosing my words cautiously, "that the perceptions of the resistance and their chances that your boss and his friends have might be colored by the fact that they're living under Anguilar domination? That they might think there's no way the Anguilar can be beat because *they* can't figure out how to defeat them?"

The Gan-Shi's expression clouded with thought as he considered the notion.

"Yet you've seen their shipyards here," he countered. "You know what they can do, what they can build. Do *you* have shipyards?"

"Does the resistance *need* shipyards?" I tried to keep things vague, though I wasn't sure how much good those sorts of plausible deniability type statements were going to do. "Or do they just need to destroy the Anguilar shipyards? Do they just need to make holding worlds and keeping people subjugated too expensive in lives and ships and resources for them to stay here?"

I don't know why, but I felt a compelling need to convince him we had a chance…even without admitting *I* was part of *we*. It was stupid, and I should have just shut the entire conversation down, even if there was no hope of making believe we weren't with the resistance after Chuck's slip. But I couldn't. This big ox was an avatar of the doubts I'd been having, of the doubts we'd all been having about whether this war was winnable, and it was suddenly crucial that we make him believe.

"That sounds like a long war," Shindo said after a moment's silence. "One that you might not live through. None of you."

Yeah. There *was* that. Was that the real issue I had trouble with? Not the idea that the war was unwinnable but that it wouldn't be survivable for me and the people I loved?

"Maybe not," I admitted. "But that's what wins wars, Shindo. Men and women who realize the cause they're fighting for is bigger than their lives." Swallowing hard, I shared a bleak look with Laranna. "Maybe it means you don't get your happy ending so a lot of other innocent people can have theirs."

"That is"—Shindo hesitated, as if searching for the words—"depressing."

"Yeah, it is," I agreed. "But war is a depressing business." A quote came to my mind, something I'd read in my military history class. It was long, far too long for me to reasonably recall the whole thing, yet as I said the first few words, it all came back to me. "War is an ugly thing, but not the ugliest of things: the decayed and degraded state of moral and patriotic feeling which thinks that nothing is worth a war, is much worse. A war to protect other human beings against tyrannical injustice; a war to give victory to their own ideas of right and good, and which is their own war, carried on for an honest purpose by their free choice—is often the means of their regeneration. A man who has nothing which he is willing to fight for, nothing which he cares more about than he does about his personal safety, is a miserable creature who has no chance of being free, unless made and kept so by the exertions of better men than himself. As long as justice and injustice have not terminated their ever-renewing fight for ascendancy in the affairs of mankind, human beings must be willing, when need is, to do battle for the one against the other."

Chuck nodded, a smile of recollection passing across his face.

"John Stuart Mill."

"Pretty words," Shindo grumbled deep in his chest, looking

away from us as if unwilling to meet our eyes. "But not words spoken by someone who'd lived their life as a slave."

"No," I admitted. "But here're some that were spoken by someone who had." This took a deeper dive into the memory pool, but it had struck me at the time, way back in high school, and it hadn't completely slipped away. "I had reasoned this out in my mind; there was one of two things I had a right to, liberty, or death; if I could not have one, I would have the other."

Chuck shot me a questioning glance, apparently unable to place that one.

"Harriet Tubman," I supplied, then turned back to Shindo. "A woman born a slave who, once free, devoted her life to freeing others."

"And did she give her life in that war?" he asked me, and I laughed softly.

"No, she lived a long life and died a natural death. But she was willing to die. For the right cause. For her people."

Shindo harrumphed, looked away, and said nothing. The conversation ended definitively, which was just as well since I think I'd used up every argument I had. Tilting my head back against the wall behind the bench, I frowned.

"How much longer is Janus gonna be? I thought he had to make a couple calls." I peered up at Shindo and jerked a thumb toward the curtain. "Is there another way out of that room?"

"There is. A door that leads into a secret passage out to the rear entrance of the House of Desire. Mr. Janus never enters a room unless there are at least two ways out of it."

Laranna's eyes narrowed, and she pulled the collapsible staff out from the sheath between her shoulders as she stood and headed for the curtain. Shindo took a step away from the door, raising a hand, alarm on his bovine face.

"You're not allowed back there…"

My attention divided between Laranna and Shindo, I didn't catch the exact moment that the door to the office burst open, but the sound drew my eyes in that direction quickly enough to see the first of the Krin come through, a stun wand raised high.

18

I MIGHT HAVE BEEN CAUGHT with my pants down, but Laranna was *not*. Already grasped in her right hand, her staff extended with a flick of her wrist, and one end of it smacked the lead Krin right between the eyes. That had to have hurt, but more importantly, it startled the snake-like humanoid, sending him into an out-of-control stumble, the stun wand flying out of his hands.

I didn't try to catch it, instead ducking out of the way as it crackled through the air only a few inches from my head. Basically a three-foot-long cattle prod, it didn't turn off automatically when pressure was let off a switch, just stayed on until it was switched off on purpose, and I didn't want to get a handful of the non-insulated end. I finally drew that Ka-Bar.

My heartbeat thumped in my ears, a harsh, red tinge covering everything as time slipped into slow motion. Betrayal. That was the word that echoed in my head, my thoughts racing a hundred miles an hour. But these weren't Imperial soldiers in armor with pulse guns, they were Krin enforcers carrying knives, stun wands, and clubs, all weapons a civilian could get on Wraith Anchorage, which meant things were more complicated than Janus selling us out to the Anguilar.

Not that it mattered in the moment. In the moment, this was a fight, and if I'd built up the reflexes for anything since that fateful night in 1987 in central Florida, it was for a fight. The Krin Laranna had nailed between the eyes stumbled out of the range of her staff and, even if he hadn't, she'd moved onto the next scaley bastard coming through the door.

The guy was stunned and unarmed and not an enemy combatant, technically, and I couldn't bring myself to bury the Ka-Bar blade in his gut, so I buried a fist there instead. He folded around it, and I slammed an elbow into the side of his head. That was, in its way, nearly as dangerous as the knife to the stomach, and if his brain had been shaken up badly enough by the two blows to the head, it might leave him just as dead, but hey, nobody's perfect.

He went down and didn't get up, and that's what I'd wanted him to do, so I moved on.

Laranna took the next of the Krin in the solar plexus with a jab of the end of the staff, then followed through with a swinging blow to the side of the neck, and the heavy club the snake-man had been midway through swinging at her head clattered to the floor at my feet. The snake-man who'd been swinging it crashed not too far from the one I'd put down, and I kicked him in the back of the head to make sure he stayed there at least for a while.

Three more crowded through the door, pushing together, rushing us to make up for the fact that they were facing a deadly Strada warrior. Time for us Earth boys to take up some of the slack. Chuck threw himself forward off the bench, catching the Krin in the middle just below his waist in a classic takedown, and if there'd been room, the scaley-skinned alien would have wound up flat on his back on the floor. There wasn't, and the Krin smacked the back of his head into the wall with a shocking, hollow *clunk*.

I couldn't afford to watch how the rest of that fight went, having one of my own to start. Two Krin left, and with Chuck tied up, that left Laranna and me. I didn't have to make a split-second choice about which one I wanted to tangle with because one of them made the choice for me, launching himself across the room at Laranna, trying to get inside her guard with a crescent-moon shaped blade. Maybe I should have played the worried husband, tried to shield her from him, but I had more faith in Laranna's ability in a fight than anyone else I knew, so I did the right thing and concentrated on my own opponent.

He was short and squat, shoulders broad, neck thick, and unlike the first two through the door, he wasn't carrying a club or a stun wand or anything potentially nonlethal. The blade was a cross between a khopesh and a Gurka kukri, curved and deadly and about fourteen inches long, and if he knew what he was doing with the knife, he could have gutted me like a fish.

That's the thing, though...it's easy to swing a knife around and act like a badass, but very few badasses have actually trained with the weapon. It's a huge commitment of time and effort, as I'd found out the hard way when Laranna started giving me lessons. They say you should never have a loved one try to teach you anything because there's too much opportunity for hard feelings. That's an even bigger issue when the thing being taught is knife-fighting, trust me.

The hurt feelings and hours of being notionally eviscerated paid off in this one instant, though. The thing that most wannabe knife fighters don't count on is someone going after their weapon hand. This guy sure didn't, and when I sliced right through his thumb tendon, he screamed like a tweenage girl at a Justin Bieber concert—at least, that's what Dani had told me—and dropped the curved blade. This time, I didn't hold back. He'd been trying to kill me, and there was a limit to how much forbearance I was prepared to show. I buried the Ka-Bar up to the hilt in his throat, and when I pulled it out, I ripped sideways and, as Laranna had cautioned me, quickly jumped back.

You wanted to jump back because the alternative was getting a faceful of arterial spray. The wall took the brunt of that instead, and I imagined Janus wasn't going to be happy about the way I'd repainted his office. One of the Krin I'd stunned was already trying to get up, but the dying knife-fighter collapsed on top of him and pinned them both to the floor. I turned to see if Chuck or Laranna needed help, but they didn't. Laranna gave the coup de grace to the knife-wielding Krin she'd been facing, swinging the weighted end of her staff behind his ear hard enough that he wouldn't be getting up from it. Ever.

Chuck still had a front mount on his opponent and delivered a flurry of hammer-fists that penetrated the Krin gangster's faltering defenses and slammed into his jaw. The Krin slumped, eyes rolling back in his head, and for the first time, I looked up at Shindo. He hadn't moved since the moment the door had opened, and even now, he simply watched, impassive.

"Anyone hurt?" I asked quickly. I didn't think they were, but there was a lot of blood splattered around, and I couldn't be sure all of it belonged to the bad guys.

"I'm uninjured," Laranna said, not even sounding out of breath. I wish I could breathe so easily, but the post-fight adrenaline withdrawals were hitting me hard in a way they wouldn't have been in a gunfight.

"Yeah, I'm okay," Chuck said, panting just a little, like he'd just got done with a hard workout. Of course, he hadn't killed anyone. The guy he'd battered was conscious again, though still lolling, hands grasping his head.

"They're not Empire," Laranna observed. "Local mob?"

"They work for Mr. Janus's connection in the Krin Syndicate," Shindo informed us. "The Syndicate runs everything on Wraith Anchorage that the Anguilar don't. If Mr. Janus sent them, he's planning on having the Syndicate make an arrangement with the Empire to turn you over for a large reward."

"So much for us being able to trust him because he couldn't afford to betray us to the Anguilar," Chuck muttered. He'd jumped to his feet and had his own Ka-Bar drawn, but then he stashed it back in its sheath and grabbed the crowbar-like club one of the Krin had been carrying, and he smacked its weighted end into his palm.

"What about you, Shindo?" I asked the Gan-Shi. "Are you going to try to capture us for your boss?"

"I have no orders to do so," he said. "And I am certainly not viewed as intelligent enough to do such a thing on my own initiative."

I nodded. It wasn't as much as I'd hoped for, but perhaps more than I had a right to expect.

"Let's get the hell out of here," I said, motioning toward the door.

"Not that way," Shindo warned. "These"—he motioned to the dead or unconscious Krin—"will have friends waiting back at the front entrance. Come with me, and I will lead you out the back way."

He ducked through the curtain door, and I was happy to let him go first, not knowing for sure what was on the other side. No commotion or sounds of violence met his entrance, so I slid through behind him, careful to disturb the curtain as little as possible so as not to let whoever might be lying in wait know I was coming.

No one was, though. The small chamber had the look of a spare bedroom, likely for those times that Janus decided to sleep at the office, but I only paid attention to the furnishings enough to make sure that no one could be hiding among them in ambush. There wasn't space to hide anything bigger than a facehugger, and these were the wrong sort of aliens for that. I motioned for the others to follow as Shindo pulled aside a set of shelves and pushed open the door concealed behind it.

Claustrophobic darkness loomed on the other side of the

hidden door, but beggars couldn't be choosers, and if the broad-shouldered bull man could make it through the passage, I surely could. Behind me, Laranna collapsed her staff, tucked it away, and retrieved her knives instead for better deployment in the cramped space, though I suppose Chuck was going to have to figure out how to fight with that club, if there was a fight to be had.

I hoped we could avoid one, hoped that Shindo wouldn't turn on us the way his boss had. I don't know why I trusted him, yet for some reason, I did. The hallway was long, and it would be since it was supposed to go all the way to the back of the shop, the walls so close together that Shindo's shoulders scraped against the sides even with his upper torso turned partway to give himself more room. It wasn't *quite* that bad for the rest of us, but a constricted chokepoint wasn't the ideal place to run when the bad guys were after you, and all I could think was that I hoped we didn't get trapped inside this hallway.

That thought had barely bounced from one side of my brain to the other when shouting started from the way we'd come, from the door to Janus's office. One voice stepped on another to the point that I couldn't pick out any of the words except a demand that we stop. He had to be one of the stupidest of the pack unless that somehow worked on aliens better than it did on humans, but at least his stupidity had given us warning.

Shindo increased his pace, and finally the door at the opposite end became visible in the gloom, an outline of the dim light outside only showing through because it was even gloomier in this hallway. The Gan-Shi pushed it open with a creek of untended hinges, and the light flooded the corridor...but not uninterrupted. Motion in the shadows, silhouettes outside, and they might just be customers or indigents, but I didn't think we were that lucky.

"It's the Gan-Shi," a Krin voice hissed. "What are you doing here?"

The question ended in a grunt of pain, and as I slipped through the open door, a Krin enforcer slammed into the wall just to the side of the door, his face a mask of blood. He slid to the ground, groaning incoherently, but I had other things to concentrate on—like the half dozen other mob thugs clustered in the alleyway, waiting for us.

This time, Shindo didn't sit back and watch...and this time, he didn't need any of us to intervene. Fists the size of cured hams swung with surprising speed, and the Krin gangsters flew away from the blows like my old action figures scattering from the superhero fights I'd put them through when I was seven. Unlike Spider-Man and Batman, though, these guys didn't jump back up without a mark in their plastic, and what Shindo crunched *stayed* crunched.

In the middle of pounding the last of them into the pavement, the big Gan-Shi didn't notice another Krin racing through the doorway behind us, aiming what looked like a miniature crossbow the size of a pistol at his back. We were all too far away to reach the Krin before he fired, but one of the things Laranna had taught me was how to throw a knife. She hadn't recommended it except as a last resort, since it left you without a weapon in your hand, but I didn't see any other choice.

Throwing a knife the size of a Ka-Bar was different than the little throwing blades you could pick up in the back of martial arts magazines back in the 80s, though. The best way to do it accurately was to palm the unsharpened part of the blade and let loose just as your hand hit parallel to the ground. I'd gotten good enough at it to sink my knife into the trees on Sanctuary every single time, and if this guy wasn't a tree, well…he made almost as good a knife stop.

Staring at the Ka-Bar buried hilt-deep in his chest, the Krin let the crossbow sag, and the bolt fired harmlessly into the ground, joined a moment later by the man who'd pulled the trigger. Laranna took the next one out of the door with the end of her staff and Chuck slammed the door shut with a press-kick while I pulled free my Ka-Bar.

The Krin gasped his last as I did, and I gritted my teeth at his death rattle. This was *very* different from a gunfight, and even though dead was dead, I very much wished I had a pulse pistol and that I never had to fight with a knife again.

"They know I helped you," Shindo said, staring down at the gangsters writhing on the ground—or just knocked out cold. "Janus will have me killed if I stay."

"Looks like we all have to run," I told him, scanning up and down the alley. Someone tried to push the door into the shop open again, and Chuck slammed it shut with his shoulder, a squawk from the other side evidence that the other guy hadn't been careful enough to stand back from it. "Got any suggestions?"

Shindo eyed me from beneath ridged brows, his gaze shrouded in shadow, then he nodded.

"All right," he said. "Follow me."

Chuck shook his head, doubt obvious in his expression, but we had no alternatives, and I took off after Shindo, counting on the others to do the same. No more Krin blocked our way, which didn't surprise me. There had to have been two-dozen of them inside the robot sex parlor, and even the mob didn't have unlimited manpower—not on Earth and not here, either. They'd be coming after us, but the Gan-Shi ate up ground with long, deliberate steps, like stampeding cattle.

I struggled to keep up, not from lack of stamina—I'd actually gotten more miles in running the last couple months in the states than I ever had in the same period on the *Liberator* or back on Sanctuary. But adrenaline bumps only lasted so long, and mine was in mid-crash, leaving me with a hollow in my gut, breath coming hard, heart beating out of my chest. My only advantage was how many times I'd experienced it already, the knowledge of what to expect.

Chuck lagged behind a few steps, and maybe that was because to my knowledge, he'd only been involved in a couple fights before this, and neither of them had involved much hand to hand. Laranna, I wasn't worried about, except that I was still a faster runner than her and Shindo was faster than me, and if I hung back for either of them, the Gan-Shi would lose me and we'd be helplessly turned around in the damp, dimly lit outer-space Seattle that was level B-85.

It was a maze of debauchery, and while we were hardly the

weirdest people in those crowded streets, we were the only ones running, and that was bound to attract attention.

"You there!" The voice was too clear and piercing to be a Krin and not arrogant or mechanical enough to be an Anguilar soldier's loudspeaker. "Stop! Station security! Stop!"

A Copperell, dressed in a dark green uniform, soft body armor, and a helmet with no visor, carrying something that looked like a cross between a pump shotgun and a 40 mm grenade launcher. This had been part of the briefing package on Wraith Anchorage, though not one Brandy had considered a significant threat. Station security were sad sacks hired by the larger business ventures to keep some kind of order in sections where the Anguilar wouldn't go, wouldn't be held responsible for maintaining any sort of order.

If the Anguilar were the alpha dogs and the Krin were the betas, then Station Security sat in the corner waiting for scraps that fell from their jaws. At the moment, that was us. Shindo made no move to stop, not even any attempt to evade, and I didn't question his wisdom in the matter, just lagged back a step to make sure Chuck kept up with us.

I glanced back at Chuck, which meant I was looking in the direction of the uniformed security officer when he raised the weapon to his shoulder and fired. A deep *thump* echoed off the facades of more robot sex doll shops and various other houses of ill repute, and hot on the heels of the sound came something moving fast but not as fast as a bullet or a pulse-gun round. White and amorphous, it splatted against one of the support columns of a business I couldn't even identify except that its advertising involved frightened bunnies running away from a ravening wolf. Where the round hit, foam fizzled up and solidified in the space of a second, forming a strait jacket of something like foam rubber around the thick, metal pole, a demonstration of what we had to look forward to if it hit one of us.

"In here!" Shindo called, squeezing through the narrow alley between that business and the next.

A drunk lay in the middle of the alley, passed out lengthwise, snoring softly, and for a horrific moment, I thought Shindo would trample him underfoot like a bull in a China shop. But he defied my expectations, his stereotype, *and* gravity by leaping the entire length of the sleeping boozer in one bound.

Able to leap tall lushes in a single bound! It's a bull, it's a man, it's super-Gan Shi!

Me, I took a couple bounds, hugging the edge of the wall, and I think Chuck actually stepped on the guy, but we all got to the end of the alley. And a metal hatchway secured with a wheel like the pressure door on a World War Two submarine. I blinked, wondering what the hell the door was doing there, but Shindo apparently had no time for an existential crisis and immediately put his back into turning the wheel.

I thought about offering to help, but given the strength of the Gan-Shi, I didn't think I'd be able to contribute much to the effort, so I just turned to keep watch on the other end of the alley. Just in time for that damned rent-a-cop to catch up with us. He swung around the barrel of the glue gun, but Laranna knocked it aside with her staff, and Chuck grabbed it before the Copperell could bring it back in line with us.

The Copperell wasn't a small man, but he also hadn't been trained by the best the US Army had to offer and then done more unarmed combat training on his own dime like Chuck Barnaby. The Ranger twisted the less-than-lethal weapon out of the security guard's hands and slammed the buttstock into the Copperell's face, knocking him to the ground. The rent-a-cop tried to roll back to his feet, but Chuck turned the barrel and pulled the trigger.

Thump, Splat!

The glue gun encased the security guard's upper torso in a solid plastic marshmallow, and the Copperell screamed in frustration.

"You can't do this to me!" he bellowed. "I'm an official security officer of the Wraith Anchorage Chamber of Commerce! You'll be prosecuted in the Chamber Court and banned from this station for life! Fined a minimum of three thousand tradenotes each!"

"Gotta admire a man that dedicated to his job," Chuck commented, dropping the glue launcher with a clatter of metal on pavement.

The hatchway opened with a reluctant, metallic grumble, and Shindo pointed inside. If the secret passage in the robot sex shop had been dimly lit, this one was jet black, a deep forest track on a moonless night.

"Come with me," Shindo said urgently. "If you want to live."

19

"Where the hell is this taking us?" I asked, instantly regretting my choice of words.

Because for all I knew, the downward spiral of the staircase *was* leading us straight into the bowels of hell, or at least the closest thing this station had to offer. We'd certainly been descending long enough to reach the underworld. It was eerie, preternatural, a set of steps cut right out of the original stone of the asteroid this place had once been. No handrails, no signs, and the only light came from thin strips of some sort of luminescent material running like racing stripes along the wall and around the edges of every door we passed.

We'd passed a *lot* of doors. Shindo had shown no indication of interest in any of them, just kept leading us downward.

"This will lead you to the home of the Gan-Shi," was the extent of his explanation, and I half thought he meant we were walking all the way to their planet of origin, as long as the journey had dragged on. But then I thought about what I'd been told, that the Gan-Shi lived in ghettos in the depths of Wraith Anchorage, and I figured that was more likely.

"What about the Syndicate?" Laranna asked, projecting her voice to be heard past me, the words bouncing off the rock walls. "Won't they look for us down here?"

"No one comes down here," Shindo assured her. "No one other than the Gan-Shi. Those who try are often never seen or heard from again."

"And they don't get pissed off about that?" Chuck wondered. "They don't send their people in to clean things out?"

"If they did," Shindo told him flatly, his tone neutral though underlain with bitterness, "who would they get to work for them? Who would carry their cargo from one dock to another? Who would fight for them in their arena?"

My legs ached, and my big toes were on fire from being jammed into the front of my boots on the Empire-State-Building-sized descent. Actually, that might be an underestimation. This was starting to feel more like hiking down into the Grand Canyon, and if we didn't stop soon, it would transition into Valles Marineris territory.

We did stop. But only because the damned staircase ended.

"This is as far down as you can go in the depths of the city," Shindo informed us, one hand on the wheel lock for the door. "This is our home. When I open this door, you three will be the only non-Gan-Shi in the Below. You must stay with me and do as I tell you. If anyone thinks you are there without invitation…"

Shindo snorted and tossed his head. "Well, you will not have to worry about the Syndicate *or* the Anguilar."

I nodded, and he turned the wheel. This one worked smoother than the first, and I had an intuition that was because it saw more use. The door swung open with a hard tug that took more muscle from Shindo than the three of us could have managed together, and light flooded in, bright enough that I had to look away and shield my eyes until they adjusted. Shindo held the door patiently, waiting for us to move through, and I blinked away afterimages and stepped over the high threshold, rock turning to metal underfoot.

I moved aside to make room for the others, the tableau unfolding before me as my eyes cleared. Gan-Shi weren't insect-based, I knew that already…but if I hadn't, if I hadn't seen them, knew nothing about them and could only judge by the architecture laid out before me, I might have guessed they'd been engineered from some hive-builder bug. Because that was what the Below was—a hive.

One housing bloc piled atop another like a child's construction playset, crude and simple and worked by hand, not by machines. From ceiling to floor, two hundred feet up and stretching as far as I could see in any direction, the buildings told a story of a people who were once advanced enough to forge Wraith Anchorage out of bare rock. A people who'd been forced out of their homes and out of their positions of power, who'd been stripped of their resources and pushed down into a cave with hand tools. They'd carved all this themselves, while working like slaves for the food to survive.

External stairs went from the ground floor to walkways around the outsides of each story, all the way up to the top. No elevators, and I wondered how the hell the poor people who lived up there managed the stairs every day…unless there were more entrances to the passages upward somewhere in the featureless rock above. I couldn't say for sure because the glare of the overhead lighting blinded me whenever I tried to focus on the ceiling.

"Did you guys install those damned lights, or did the Krin?" I asked. An inane question, but if the Krin had done it, that would seem like psychological torture. Shindo peered at me curiously, as if I'd asked him why the sky was blue.

"Of course. We would not live in the dark like the Krin. It is not the way any decent being would choose to exist."

Different strokes for different folks, I suppose. None of the Gan-Shi seemed to be bothered by the bright illumination, though. They moved in large groups from one place to another like, well…cattle, if I'm being honest. The females were obvious, their mammaries as numerous and pronounced as any other bovine and not covered, either. They wore even less than their male counterparts, and I found the sight disturbing, enough that I had to fight an urge to look away. Younger children were carried, often feeding in the process, while others walked close beside their mothers, though I saw none past early adolescence.

The females walked in clusters, each dedicated to carrying small cargo containers from a communal stack of the things at the center of this particular neighborhood. It couldn't be the only one, otherwise the entire population of the Below would have to walk miles upon miles to retrieve whatever supplies had been delivered in those metal boxes. Food most likely, I guessed. They certainly didn't need clothes, they obviously weren't allowed sophisticated tools, so that left food.

All of it brought in from outside, all of it earned, I thought, by the adult and adolescent males and whichever females weren't here, taking care of the children. No males among the caregivers. Not very progressive of them. If they tried that shit back on Earth, they'd get canceled for sexism, but it fit with the herd animals they'd been engineered from. I'd read about the bison in Yellowstone, and the rutting season was the only time females intermingled with adult males.

Not that there were *no* adult males around. They wandered solitary paths through the Below, eyes flickering side to side, never stopping. Guards? Probably, though they reminded me more of the homeless people I'd seen wandering around Cleveland back in the day, constantly on the move and desperate for purpose. One close enough to us to have a view of the hatchway stopped in his pacing and homed in on us, turning like a drill team soldier practicing the column right maneuver for a parade.

Shindo didn't attempt to evade the male, just planted his feet and stood his ground, waiting. I didn't reach for my knife, and neither Laranna nor Chuck made an aggressive move, though I noticed their grips tighten on their impact weapons. Not that they would have done any good against this guy. He was, as unbelievable as it sounded, even bigger than Shindo, as well as appearing older, with gray noticeable in his wiry hair.

"Shindo, why have you brought these outsiders?" the older Gan-Shi demanded, fists clenched at his side, shoulders hunched and ready for violence. "Why are you here at all? You sold your soul to that Syndicate pawn, Janus. How dare you show your face in our home?"

Shindo said nothing for a moment, meeting the other Gan-Shi's eyes, not looking away. The bigger male didn't exactly blink, but there was the slightest shift in his expression, a give to the harsh mask.

"Warrin," Shindo rumbled, "I have turned against Janus and the Syndicate. They will kill me should they find me, just as they would kill these strangers." He motioned toward us. "They are enemies of the Anguilar and came to Janus for help. Instead, he and the Syndicate conspired to capture them and turn them over to the Anguilar for the hope of a reward. I have brought them with me for their safety, and they are under my protection."

A good question might have been why that would mean anything to this meathead, and I expected Warrin to ask it, but he just blew out a long breath through his flattened nose as if in exasperation.

"Very well. I will bring you before the Mothers, and the decision will be theirs. But remember," Warrin went on, jabbing a finger toward Shindo, "that if they rule against you, I will carry out their judgment myself."

A CHILD LOOKED up at me with the bright, coltish expression of a youngster of any humanoid species and smiled.

"You're small," he confided, bouncing a ball against the door of the crude, rough-surfaced building. It ricocheted with a heavy thud, then bounced off the pavement and back to his hand. "You all look tiny."

"You're not that big yourself," I told him with a laugh, sharing an amused look with Laranna. "How old are you?"

"Ten and a half," he told me, straightening indignantly. "I'm tall for my age! I'll be as big as my uncles when I grow up!"

I looked around, but the child's mother wasn't around. We'd been standing here by the door of what we'd been told was the Council of Mothers for what felt like at least an hour while Shindo and Warrin went in to speak to the older females, and I'd expected them to leave a guard. Instead, we'd been left alone until the kid had walked up without introduction and started staring at us.

It was interesting that the kid had mentioned his uncles rather than his father. That fit with the thoughts I'd had about their society and the way the females separated from the males. He probably had no sort of relationship at all with his biological father and the male role models in his family were his mother's brothers.

"What's your name?" I asked him, kneeling beside the kid. He barely had the nubs of his horns peeking out from his forehead, and aside from the dusting of curly hair all over his body, he could have been a human child.

"My child-name is Bonoano," he explained, bouncing the ball off the sidewalk. "But when I grow up, I'll pick my own name. I think I'll call myself Tomin."

"Tomin's a good name," I agreed. "Let me tell you a secret,

Bonoano," I confided in a stage whisper. "Even if you don't get as big as your uncles, you can still be strong. I'm not *that* big even for my people, but I've beaten people a lot bigger than me. It has more to do with how big the fight is in you, not how big you are."

Bonoano's expression was openly skeptical as he looked me over.

"*You?*" he asked. "You couldn't beat a Gan-Shi in a fight! Not even my mother, and she's kind of old now."

"Maybe not," I admitted. "But there's one fight you can never win, and that's the one that you already gave up on."

Laranna smiled gently, regarding the child with a wistful gaze. Chuck, though, spoiled the mood with a derisive snort.

"You sound like a damn fortune cookie," he told me. His fingers flexed open and closed, like he missed the feel of the club he'd stolen. We'd been disarmed by Warrin, and none of us had been too happy about it, but this place was the only shelter we had. "What's next, you gonna tell little Joey here that he can be anything he wants if he just sets his mind to it?"

Sighing, I straightened and offered him a glare.

"You do know the people inside there are deciding whether we live or die, right?" I cocked my head to the side. "They're gonna call us in eventually. I hope you're gonna be a little less… sarcastic with them."

"I can modulate my sarcasm," Chuck assured me, "but it's a coefficient to my stress level, so no promises."

I took a closer look at him, noted his ragged breathing, the trickle of sweat running off his brow. It wasn't particularly warm here in the Below, not over sixty degrees, which I suppose made sense when most of the inhabitants weighed north of three hundred pounds, so there was no good reason for him to be sweating.

"Rougher than you expected?" I asked him, voice low, casual. He glanced up sharply, lips peeling back in a scowl.

"I'm fine," Chuck insisted. "I just...I guess I'm not used to being this far behind enemy lines."

"Oh, you get used to it," I told him. "Out here, there's no fire support, no relief, no quick-reaction force. The only help you get is the help you recruit."

"If I wanted to deal with shit like that," he murmured, "I would have gone Special Forces instead of Rangers."

"What's the difference?" Laranna wondered.

"Rangers come in hard and fast," I supplied, "get in and get out."

"That's what she said," Chuck said in a stage whisper, and I rolled my eyes. I'd watched the show with him, and it was funny, but not nearly as funny as he thought it was.

"They raid enemy airfields and other installations," I went on, determined to ignore him. "Take them, clear the way for regular infantry to come in and hold them. Special Forces go behind enemy lines and interact with foreign nationals—usually some kind of ethnic or religious minority with a grudge against the enemy. They give them medical treatment, set up schools, whatever they can, and recruit them to fight against the enemy. They train them, arm them, and sometimes lead them into battle."

"And sometimes get themselves killed doing that," Chuck added.

"And what about that other group," Laranna asked, ever curious about the arcane military organization of my world. "The one that was guarding us with you in charge, Chuck?"

"Delta Force," I told her. "Or sometimes CAG—Combat Applications Group. Or ACE, which I forget what that's supposed to stand for."

"I don't even remember," Chuck admitted. "They're like the top, top-secret operators. They're mainly supposed to be for hostage rescue and assassinating or black-bagging high-value targets in enemy territory, but they wind up getting used for shit like executive protection and other various missions that are too secret-squirrel for regular joes." He snorted a laugh. "Except when DevGru manages to steal the glory missions for themselves."

"DevGru is another name for SEAL Team Six," I interjected, and Laranna shook her head.

"I'm never going to keep them all straight. Why do your people need so many different special operations groups?"

"It's a long story. Once upon a time, they all had their own individual uses in certain specific situations, but once we stopped having big, all-out wars and started with things like counterinsurgency and guerilla warfare, the spec-ops guys started getting more attention from the politicians."

"And more money," Chuck added. "And when *that* happened, each of the services had to make sure they had a piece of that funding pie. But the Rangers are the OG special operators. We were around before the country even existed."

"Yeah, there is that," I admitted, remembering the Ranger

Handbook with the rules set down by Roger's Rangers in the French and Indian War, back when the US had been a colony of Great Britain.

The French and Indians always attack at dawn.

"We Strada just have warriors," Laranna said with a sniff that showed what she thought of the tangled TO&E of the US military.

The door opened and Shindo stepped out, his face grim. I thought. His face *always* looked grim the entire time I'd known him, so I couldn't be sure.

"The Mothers," he told us, "wish to talk to you. To one of you. One of you must plead your case to the Elder, and she and the rest of the council will decide whether you're to be aided, expelled from the Below, or…" He shrugged, leaving the final possibility to our imaginations. "Who do you wish to speak for you?" Shindo looked between the three of us and I sighed.

"I guess that would be me.",

20

If someone had told me as a teenager that I'd ever be forced to stand before a circle of mostly naked females and talk politics, I would have wondered if this was some fever dream. If they'd told me they'd be cow-women, I would have been sure of it.

There were some alien females who were attractive from the point of view of a human—like Laranna and the other Strada—and others who were just too different, at least for me, like Mallarna, the Peboktan engineer and her people. The Gan-Shi Council of Mothers definitely drifted into the too-different category, but the pendulous mammaries drooping from each of them without so much as a bovine bra distracted the hell out of me.

Particularly when the rest of the chamber was nearly featureless. No table, no chairs, not so much as a beanbag. Just a circle painted on the floor of the windowless room, like an actor's mark to line them up. Everyone stood. Even outside, watching the other Gan-Shi go about their business, not a single one had sat down other than children. And when the children sat, they folded their legs beneath them and sat on their heels rather than using a log or a rock. I was pretty sure they didn't *sleep* standing up, but it was clear they did most everything else that way.

All I could think standing before them was that my feet hurt. And I wished they'd all put shirts on.

"Tell us who you are, outsider," the oldest of the females instructed. Her hair had gone gray on her head and shoulders, and I wondered if she was Bonoano's mother.

I considered the question and what my answer should be. This wasn't like a movie where I could tell them that I was *Bond, James Bond,* and somehow no one would know that I was a British secret agent. The Anguilar were very familiar with my name, and telling these Gan-Shi who I was set us up for yet another betrayal if they didn't like what I had to say.

But it didn't feel right lying. Lying was something guilty people did, people who had something to hide, and yes, I knew that was ludicrous. I was acting as a spy at the moment, and spies lied. Real spies, not movie spies. I could just tell them that we were agents of the resistance trying to help one of our own. But the talk about Special Forces had gotten me to thinking. The work they did was covert, but they weren't spies. Their purpose was to build relationships with potential allies, and lying was a horrible way to do that.

The internal debate took all of a second, and, as usual, I went with what my gut told me was right.

"My name is Charlie Travers. I'm the military commander of the resistance against the Anguilar."

The eyes of the Mothers went wide, and a low murmur went through their circle, disbelief, worry, fear. But not the Elder, the old female who'd asked the question. Her eyes were fixed on me, a keen intelligence somewhere behind their placid brown.

"Silence," she hissed, and the chatter in the circle ceased as abruptly as it had begun. Her eyes never left me, judging, taking my measure. "Even here we have heard of Charlie Travers. It is said that he is of a people rare in the rest of the galaxy, humans, and that may be true, although you all look alike to me. It would be pure foolishness for such an important leader of the resistance to come to Wraith Anchorage, surely one of the Anguilar's foremost strongholds in this part of the galaxy."

"It probably is," I admitted. "At least that's what all my allies told me. But one of my closest friends was captured here by General Zan-Tar. The general told me if I didn't surrender myself to him here within the next week, he'd have my friend executed."

"So, you came to here to give yourself over to the Empire to save your friend." She smiled thinly. "Very admirable."

"Not exactly." I shrugged. "I came here to rescue my friend, not trade myself for him. And to do that, I need intelligence."

The Elder snorted a laugh.

"I'd agree. And you are, apparently, sorely lacking in that area if you went to Janus for help."

"He's been an asset of our intelligence chief for two years," I confessed. "But apparently, he's more loyal to the Syndicate than he is to us. I need help finding General Zan-Tar and a Varnell he's holding here."

"And why would the Council of Mothers be inclined to help you in this?" the Elder asked, an eyebrow shooting up. "Not that I wouldn't cheer anything that hurt the Anguilar, but they aren't the first oppressors over we Gan-Shi, merely the latest. The Krin Syndicate would have us under their heel whether they ran this city or the Anguilar. Or you and your resistance."

"The Krin Syndicate is trying to hand us over to the Anguilar," I told her. "They're no friends of ours, and the Krin in general have been no friends to the civilized worlds of the galaxy. They were among the first to declare themselves allies of the empire, and their numbers fill the ranks of the Anguilar infantry."

"Your enemies should be our enemies, then?" she demanded. "Is that what you think?"

"I'm not asking you to fight anyone," I countered. "I'm just asking if you can find out where my friend is being held. That's it. You tell me where to go, and I break my friend out…or get killed doing it. Either way, it's on me. Nothing comes back to you."

"I hate to sound uncaring, but what is in this for the Gan-Shi? Why should we take this risk, even if you claim it's slight? You ask for our help, but what do you offer?"

"We're not in this for ourselves. I didn't join the resistance because my people or my world were at risk. Hell, they didn't even know any of this existed until a few months ago. I agreed to lead them, I put my life on the line, because I couldn't sit by and watch what the Anguilar were doing to the Strada, the Copperell.

And I won't sit by and watch what the Krin are doing to you and your people, either. We're going to take down the Empire, and when we do, the management of this place is going to change. And if you haven't noticed, the Anguilar are the only ones with guns in this place…and when they're gone, it's just you and the Krin."

Her eyes lit up at that, like I thought they might. From what I understood, the Krin had come down with a pretty heavy hand when they'd taken Wraith Anchorage over from the Gan-Shi and slaughtered thousands of them.

"We are pacifists," she demurred, as if reminding herself of it. "We do not touch weapons. It's part of our way of life, our devotion to our Creator."

"Does that mean you're going to sit back and let the Krin run things?" I wondered. "Does that mean you're going to keep sending your males into the arena to kill and be killed? Is *that* part of your way of life?"

"The males go their own way," the Elder said with a shrug. "They follow their own faith, such as it is. If they choose to defile the sacredness of life, it's not our responsibility. We teach them as best we can before they leave us, their mothers. Once they go, their life is theirs."

"Then you don't care if the Krin remain in power over you?" I pressed her. "Or are you just saying you want *someone* else to take care of the problem for you?"

Maybe that was going too far, given that we were counting on these people to conceal us from the Anguilar, and I knew Laranna would be kicking me in the shin right about then, but she was pissing me off. I had the greatest respect for true pacifists, like the guys who volunteered to be unarmed medics during World War Two, but this sounded more like someone who wanted other people to fight their battles for them.

"You require our help," the Elder pointed out. "We may be isolated from the rest of the galaxy here, but I think that means we set the terms."

"What do you want?" I asked, shifting my weight. I knew what I wanted. I wanted a damned chair. "I'm here to get my friend out, not take down the Anguilar. I only have the three of us."

"As I said," the Elder arched an eyebrow, "if the males choose the way of violence, there is nothing we can do to turn them aside from it. But we could put one in charge who would be inclined to follow your…advice. As long as you agree to guide them in the proper direction."

I remembered cartoons from when I was a kid, where the characters would get so angry that steam would come out of her ears, and in that moment, I could have sworn that the pressure valve inside my head was about to burst. All that shit about religion and pacifism and what she *really* wanted was for me to lead her expendable male in an impromptu revolution. I'd been raised never to hit a female, and in this case, it would have felt like animal abuse, but I searched the room for anything softer to punch than the brick wall and had to settle for clenching my fists so hard that my fingernails dug into my palms.

"Fine." The word came out as close to a growl as any I'd ever said, and just about as reluctantly. "But we get Giblet out first.

You find out where he's being held, and we get him out, and *then* we see if your males are…morally flexible."

The Elder said nothing and looked away from me, searching the faces of each of the other females on the Council, asking a question with her eyes. Each of them nodded, and she turned back to me.

"Very well. We will send people out to get your information. You and your friends will stay here until then."

She started to turn away, but I raised a hand to stop her.

"One other thing I'm going to need if we're staying here," I told her, "is a damn place to sit down. Three of them."

"We agreed to *what*?" Chuck asked, eyes going wide as he stepped away from the wall where he'd been leaning.

"Oh, great creator," Laranna sighed, rubbing her temples. "Charlie, we did *not* come here to take the station. It's not possible, not even if we had every one of those Gan-Shi on our side. All we'll accomplish is getting them killed."

I glanced around, trying to make sure none of the bovine aliens were around to hear that. We didn't need to start a panic. But not even the kid was still around. The whole bunch of them had left us alone since the meeting with the Council, including Warrin and Shindo, as if we were bad luck, unclean. Which was a hell of a way to treat someone who'd just made a deal to free them, but it was just as well for now.

"What did you want me to do?" I said with a shrug, taking

Chuck's place against the wall. "These people are our only chance to get Gib out. I would have promised them to turn this place into a party disco if it meant they'd help us."

"What's a party disco?" Chuck and Laranna asked almost at once.

"What I want to know is how they're going to find Gib or Zan-Tar?" Chuck asked, pacing back and forth. "They don't exactly blend in."

"That's where you're wrong," Shindo said, and I nearly jumped out of my skin. For a 300 pound, seven-foot-tall bull man, he was surprisingly stealthy and had snuck up on us around the corner of the Council building. "We're everywhere. Working in the corners, hauling cargo, cleaning, repairing walls and doors. Bodyguarding for the Syndicate. No one pays attention to us, no one restrains themselves from talking in front of us."

"You're going to be the spy, then?" I asked him, looking him up and down, and for a wonder, he laughed.

"No. The younger males do most of the grunt work. The older of us wind up either working for the Syndicate or fighting in the arena. The workers will report back to us as soon as they have word of where your General Zan-Tar is…or your friend." He motioned for us to follow. "Come. The Elder has instructed me to take you get you some food and find you a place to rest in the meantime."

The route was circuitous through the hand-built canyons, yet also strangely empty. The crowds of women and children we'd seen earlier were gone, the only faces staring at us individual males, standing like statues.

"No offense, Shindo," I told him as we walked, "but this whole place creeps the hell out of me. Where is everyone?"

"They've gone to the sleep chambers," he explained. "It is well into the night for those of us who still maintain a schedule based on our old ways."

"You mean the ways from before the Krin," Laranna guessed, and Shindo nodded.

"Not for such as me…or for any of the males who find work outside the Below. Our sleep is based on our shifts."

"Your Elder, whatever her name actually is," I ventured as we passed through the maze of buildings, one looking much like another, "said that you males have a different religion than the Mothers. That they're pacifists while you males are not. Is that the truth? Or was she just trying to tell us what she wanted us to hear?"

He didn't turn around and didn't answer right away, and I thought maybe he hadn't heard me, but after a few moments, he nodded.

"The way of the Mothers is the way of peace," he said, and it sounded as if he was quoting a scripture verse. "The Mothers follow the path of the gods of the green hill, of the open plain, the old gods of our home." A sigh that was half a snort. "We're taught that Gan-Shin, our homeworld, still exists, but I doubt it sometimes. If this place, meant to be our paradise, was so easily lost, then what hope did Gan-Shin have?" His massive shoulders shrugged. "The Mothers *will* fight, but only in defense of themselves or their young, and only if attacked. Other than that, they'll shield their families with their own bodies to keep them from harm, but they will not attack. This is why they were so easily herded into the Below once the Krin took over. Most of the older males, the ones already apart from their families, were slaughtered. Once, the adult males would have been led by our own priests and taught the gods of our fathers, but none survived."

"Then why don't you just worship the gods of the Mothers?" Laranna asked him. "They raised you. Wouldn't they have taught you their ways?"

"That is not the tradition of our kind," Shindo insisted, stopping in his tracks and turning on Laranna as if she'd insulted him and his entire species. "The males must walk a different path. Anything else would be an affront to hundreds of generations of my people." His natural expression seemed to be a frown, but now it deepened. "Yet without the guidance of the ages, there's nothing to lead us on the old paths, and we must make our own. Some of us, like Warrin, have found purpose only in the duty to guard the herd."

"What about you?" I asked him. "What purpose do you find? You told us you tried to steal to save your mother…yet the other males don't seem much concerned with them, according to you."

"I was considered unnatural for trying to maintain my ties to her and my sisters," he admitted, turning away as if in embarrassment, continuing the trek toward food and comfort. "And Mother was shunned for continuing to allow me within her house. None would care for her but me."

"The Mothers won't touch weapons," I said, repeating what the Elder had told me. "Will the males? Because I'll tell you right now, you're not going to kick the Anguilar off this place with your bare hands."

"Some of us will do whatever it takes to win our freedom," he said. "Others…"

He didn't speak again for a few seconds, stopping in front of a smaller building, not reaching all the way to the ceiling the way the others did, only rising a few stories. No stair-climbing, for which I was grateful. He just waved us through the open doorway into a storage room packed with the small cargo containers. Some of them were stacked at a convenient height for using as chairs, and I settled atop a tower of three of them, sighing as the weight finally came off my feet.

"I do not share the confidence of the Mothers," Shindo went on once we were alone in the shadowy confines of the first-floor room, away from any possible listeners, "that this will work. They dream of a simple solution, either one that sees you and the males ridding us of the burden of the Krin and the Anguilar…or one which rids them of the inconvenience of the males. We're expendable, after all. They can always have more, and a missed generation would only mean fewer mouths to feed."

He pulled open a cargo container, retrieved small loaves of some kind of dark bread, and handed one to each of us. I tore a small chunk out of one of the loaves and bit into it experimentally. It tasted like rye bread, which I wasn't a huge fan of, and it was gritty enough that I expected a steady diet of the stuff would wear my teeth down to nubs, but I ate it for the moment because I was starving. Laranna and Chuck did as well, though Chuck made a face at the taste of the stuff.

"You think it will be suicide," Laranna said, more a statement than a question.

"I would not think the less of you," Shindo told us, "if you went back on your bargain with the Elder and simply left this place once you found your friend."

And wasn't that a kick in the head? Because I'd certainly thought of it. But...

"Let's worry about finding Gib first," I decided. "After that, we'll see what the situation is. But I promise you one thing, Shindo. Whether we can free this place or not, if we get out alive, you can come with us. We'll take you out of here and get you back to Gan-Shin if it still exists."

It was an easy promise to make. The odds were, we'd all be dead well before then.

21

I BLINKED awake to Laranna shaking my shoulder, and I wondered through the haze just when I'd fallen asleep. The floor of the storage room was neither clean nor particularly comfortable, and my wadded-up jacket made a shitty pillow, but I must have been exhausted enough after the fighting and running to doze off. And not just me. Off by the wall, Chuck snored softly.

But not Laranna. I think there was something about the Strada warrior culture and the way they supported their soldiers when they returned from battle, but she handled the whole post-traumatic thing a lot better than the rest of us.

"What is it?" I murmured, rubbing sleep out of my eyes as I sat up. "Am I late for breakfast?"

"They found him," she told me, and I jumped to my feet, instantly alert.

"Where?"

"Shindo's outside," Laranna said, kicking at Chuck's boot. His eyes popped open, his knife in his hand as he glanced around. "Shindo's outside," she repeated. "Time to go."

Chuck looked at the knife in his hand as if he'd forgotten it was there and awkwardly stuck it back into the sheath under his jacket. I offered him a hand. He took it and scrabbled up with my help, shaking his head to clear it.

"Damn, I've slept in some messed-up places," he mumbled, "but this has to top them all." He pulled the edge of his jacket up and sniffed at it. "I smell like a stockyard."

"The whole place smells like a stockyard," I agreed. "Let's see if we can get out of here and leave the stench behind us."

Holding a hand up to shield my eyes against the glare, I stepped out and waited for them to adjust before Shindo's imposing form came into focus. Beside him stood a smaller, skinnier male. He walked up hesitantly, eyes downcast as if he were scared to talk to us. He was still taller than me and outweighed me by thirty pounds at least, yet he somehow seemed intimidated by us.

"This is Mayak," Shindo introduced us. "He works for the Krin Syndicate transporting food supplies to the Anguilar headquarters. I showed him the photos you had of Zan-Tar and Giblet and sent him to search for them." He patted the younger male's arm. "Tell them what you found out."

"I made an excuse," Mayak said before his voice broke and he cleared his throat, trying again. He was barely past adolescence, I realized, probably just recently kicked out of his Mother's house. "I made an excuse to get to the command offices of the

Anguilar...took the place of one of the other workers. That Anguilar general was there, talking to a Krin Syndicate head. I couldn't hear about what. It might have been something about you people because he mentioned the resistance and I think a deadline?"

"The deadline we're running up against," I guessed, spitting out a quiet curse. "What about Giblet? Did you see a Varnell there?"

"I didn't see him," he confessed, "but I heard the Anguilar mention the Varnell. They said he was in a holding cell in Block Four. I don't know where that one is, but their holding cells are on the lowest level of the Anguilar headquarters section."

"Thank God," I murmured. "That means he has to still be alive."

"How do we get there?" Laranna asked, the question directed at Shindo rather than the kid.

"The tunnels," Shindo told her. "The same ones that we took to get here from Janus's pleasure doll shop. They remain from when our people constructed the city, work tunnels used to complete the finishing touches on the interior. They extend to every section of the city built during the original digging. Only the annexes the Krin added near the shipyards aren't connected. There's a tunnel exit that will take you inside the Anguilar headquarters, to their storage section. It won't get you into the holding cells, but it should be close enough."

"You're not coming with us?" Chuck asked.

"I can take you to the correct exit," Shindo offered. "Not past there. I've been instructed by the Mothers to gather the males and wait for you to return with your friend. We are not to act until then."

"Plausible deniability," Chuck said, snorting derisively. "If we don't succeed, they don't get any retaliation from the Krin or the Anguilar. We're cut loose, and they go back to the status quo." He nodded at Shindo. "Except *you*, of course. You got seen helping us, so they'll have to serve you up as a sacrificial lamb to the Krin. Dead, of course, because then they can't interrogate you."

"Chuck," Laranna admonished, but the Ranger officer shrugged.

"What? If he doesn't know already, he *should*."

I was about to tell Chuck to stop, that it was none of our business, but my mouth snapped closed on the realization that he was exactly right.

"That's what they're going to do," I agreed, eyes locked with Shindo's. The big Gan-Shi's face was impassive, as if the idea meant nothing to him. "Are you okay with that?" I pressed.

"My existence only has meaning," he said dully, "if it serves the herd."

"Well, isn't *that* all communist?" Chuck muttered.

"Does it serve the herd," I asked him, "or does it serve the Mothers?"

That finally got a rise out of him. Shindo speared me with a glare, and I was suddenly glad those horns were vestigial.

"One is the same as the other," he rumbled. "Without the Mothers, we are nothing but aimless vagabonds, roaming without a home, without connection except at the breeding time. If we have no purpose, then the Krin should have killed us off entirely."

"Maybe it's time," Laranna suggested, "that you start determining your *own* purpose instead of letting someone else decide it for you." She surprised me by speaking up since she'd seemed determined a few moments ago to keep from upsetting the Gan-Shi.

"It is time," Shindo said, "that we set out. If you would have us fight beside you, then you must retrieve your friend. We will not accomplish that by talking."

Unable to argue with that, I shrugged and waved for him to lead on.

Time to take the bull by the horns.

I TRIED to picture in my head where we were, but the tunnels were a rabbit warren, and the only thing I could tell was that we were going up. And up. And up. If miles heading downward had been painful, climbing out of the Grand Canyon was even harder.

"These damned tunnels are stuffy as hell," Chuck complained, wiping sweat off his brow and shaking it off his hand. "What good are those vents?" he asked, gesturing at the concentric circles of the ventilation system that we were passing. "I sure don't feel any breeze. Are we even getting enough oxygen in here?"

"My ancestors built this city to last for eternity," Shindo said, not looking back at Chuck. "These tunnels are sturdier and safer than any other part of the city."

He was probably telling the truth, but I had to empathize with Chuck. My shirt was already soaked through, my quadriceps burned with each step, and breathing wasn't easy, though I didn't blame it on lack of oxygen or CO_2 buildup. Exertion was a lot more likely and less paranoid.

"How much farther?" Chuck asked. At least he managed not to make it sound like a whine. "Because if we have a lot longer to go, I need to take a break." He shrugged apologetically. "I mean, I'm a Ranger and all, but I've been watching other people train for months now and not doing much of it myself."

"Less than a mile," Shindo assured him.

Chuck grunted and rolled his eyes.

"I can manage another mile. I guess."

"Hydrate, soldier," I advised, taking a swig from the water bottle the Gan-Shi had given me—given each of us—before we left the storehouse.

That, and the use of Shindo as a guide was all they were going to give us. I'd asked for guns, but those were too hard to get on this station, and even if they weren't, they were against the religion of the Mothers. Somehow, that meant that *we* couldn't get them, either, though I wasn't sure if that would hold up to close scrutiny by religious scholars.

I wished for a gun, but more than that, I wished for a cruiser, or a *fleet* of cruisers. A fleet of cruisers to take this entire place out and blow up the whole shipyard. A whole fleet of cruisers would have solved a lot of problems. Hell, even one more cruiser would have made things easier. Might have meant this entire thing wouldn't have been necessary.

"This is it," Shindo said, and I realized I'd been staring down at the steps instead of watching for the door. It had snuck up on me, and I felt foolish for allowing my attention to wander, but not as relieved as my legs felt that we'd arrived.

"The storage area is on the other side of this door?" Laranna asked, pulling her staff out of its sheath and extending it with a flick of her wrist.

"You'll emerge behind a row of shelving filled with cargo containers of food," Shindo said, one hand resting on the wheel for the hatch. "From there, you should follow that wall until just after it curves to the left. You'll come to an intersection, and to the left will be the Anguilar headquarters section. According to Mayak, there's no security before the holding cells."

Chuck nodded impatiently, making a "move-along" gesture.

"You told us all this back in the Below," he reminded the Gan-Shi. "Could you just open the damned door? Unless you've changed your mind and decided to go inside with us."

Gan-Shi didn't respond except to turn the lock, the muscles bunching in his shoulders at the effort. I winced at the grinding metal, hoping it was louder in the tunnel than it had been on the other side. The knife felt totally inadequate in my hand, but it was all I had. I held it in front of me as Shindo pulled open the hatch just enough for me to slip through.

Gloom and shadow gripped the other side, though no darker than the tunnels, and I didn't have to wait for my eyes to adapt to move forward. Nothing opposed my entrance, the dull gray of cargo containers greeting me in silent disinterest. The hatch opened up deep in a corner behind the intersection of two shelving units, hidden from view and, I saw as I risked a look back, camouflaged with the same bare stone facing as the rest of the wall.

Mayak and Shindo had been right about the storage room and its lack of guards, though that was no surprise. The Krin Syndicate, as ruthless as it was, wouldn't risk selling the Anguilar food only to turn around and steal it back, and nothing else of value would be stored here. Weapons and armor were locked away in the armory, components for the ships under construction in the shipyard kept in a hard vacuum, safe from anyone without a spaceship that could stand against the Anguilar cruisers guarding the station.

No reason for guards, no need for video security. The Anguilar weren't big on automated security systems or motion detectors anyway. Not that I'd even known what those were until I'd gotten a taste of 21st-century Earth, with cameras everywhere, facial recognition software, gunshot locators, thermal, infrared, motion sensors… It was hard to see how anyone went unobserved anywhere, but it didn't seem to solve violent crime for them. Maybe the Anguilar were smarter than we were because they didn't bother with it, preferring actual, living soldiers that were expendable, easily replaceable, and didn't require machinery that needed repair, and trained techs to maintain it.

I stalked down to the curve in the wall and confirmed we were alone before jogging back and motioning for the others to follow.

"I will wait here as long as I am able," Shindo told me, still on the other side of the hatch. "If you can get your friend back here, we can seal the hatch. It would take the Anguilar hours to breach it, and they'd still never be able to locate us in time."

I waved acknowledgement and led the others up around the corner. We'd gone over that part, too, before we left. Possible exit strategies included the obvious, back the way we'd come, then through the tunnels to the Below. Plan B was to attempt to fight through to the Anguilar docking bay at the edge of the shipyards, and from there to steal one of their ships. Plan C was the escape pods on this level and hope to hell we could guide them back to the main hangar bay to get to the transport we'd come in on. That one was the least likely of all, which was why it was also last. The final two did have the added bonus of getting us off the station without having to lead the Gan-Shi on a suicidal revolt against the Anguilar. Not that I intended to backstab them, but I didn't think much of the plan the Council of Mothers had come up with.

Around the curve in the wall, no change in the scenery of row upon row of shelving, stack upon stack of food stores grown in the city's hydroponic farms, tended by Gan-Shi...sweatshop labor, barely above the level of a serf. Or a slave.

The scenery was the same, but the illumination changed, more light leaking through from the sections of the facility still ahead. Not much, not above a twilight gloom, which was fine since it gave us a psychological comfort, a sense of concealment if not a real advantage. Anguilar techs and officers in garrison uniforms wouldn't spot us, but the enhanced vision in one of their combat helmets would pick us out as if it was noonday in the Sahara.

Laranna tapped me on the shoulder and pointed ahead, but I already saw the intersection looming, the light growing stronger on either side of it. That was where the stacks of supplies ended, their termination marked by a half a dozen motorized cargo sleds, reminding me of pallet jacks in a warehouse back home. Just past that intersection, and we'd have to watch out for…

I moved before the noise registered as footsteps on the stone floor and ducked behind one of the last shelving units, Laranna and Chuck right behind me. A shadow stretched out from the left-hand side of the T-junction, impossibly tall and lanky, multiple legs and arms moving in brisk efficiency.

Go back, I urged silently, projecting the thought at whatever insect-like creature threw the shadow. *Turn around.*

It wasn't some giant, multilegged bug, though, not even a Peboktan. It was three Anguilar in field uniforms, walking together from the brighter illumination of the hallways off to the left into the gloom of the storage section. Retrieving food, I guessed, and eager to get it done as quickly as possible.

No, I realized as they moved into the open, I was wrong. Not three Anguilar in the sense that they were the hawk-faced aliens. These three were Imperial troops of the subject peoples, two Copperell and a Krin. But they wore the uniforms, and most importantly for my concerns, all three carried sidearms.

I tapped Chuck on the arm to get his attention, knowing Laranna would catch the motion. Gesturing with exaggerated movements meant to be seen in the dim light, I silently relayed the plan. Three Imperial troops in uniform, three of us. Three handguns. Finally, I tucked my knife away, signaling that it had to be bloodless. No problem for either of them since Laranna had her staff and Chuck still held onto the metal club, but a pain in the ass for me.

Oh well. I moved to the edge of the row, watching the trio try to pull out one of the cargo sleds, griping the whole time, their voices echoing off the stone ceilings.

"Why the hell do *we* have to move this shit?" the Krin demanded, a sibilant hiss to his voice. "Isn't that what those ignorant herd animals are for? I didn't join the Imperial army to stock the cafeteria."

"Why *did* you join the army, Sgt. Silmallon?" one of the Copperell wondered. "I mean, it sure wasn't to get laid!"

The other two laughed in a universal instinct of soldiers. All three were males. The Krin were like the Anguilar, the sexes segregated, their females kept on their homeworlds to breed, but the Imperial military enforced that standard on the other peoples under their sway as well. No Copperell females in the Anguilar uniform under arms, and I figured that had to get pretty lonely for the males.

Distracted, engrossed with getting their unpleasant tasks finished as quickly as possible, they weren't expecting anyone to come out of the storage shelves, definitely weren't ready for an attack. One Copperell bent over the front end of the cargo sled, cursing loudly and yanking at a chock beneath the wheels, trying to free it, while the other touched a control to start the wheel motors. The Krin just stood there, hands on hips, intent on being a supervisor. His back open and inviting.

Two long steps, holding my breath, heart pounding, before I jumped. Krin were tough, their skin thick and scaley, their skulls hard enough to make stunning one with a blow to the head an iffy proposition. But they still had to breathe. I wrapped an arm around the snake-man's throat before he had the chance to react, locking in the chokehold just as I'd been taught, first by Laranna in the style of her people, then by Chuck as part of the Brazilian Jujitsu he'd trained in.

Sinking in the hooks, Chuck called it, and if a Krin had stronger neck muscles than a human, air still had to reach their lungs, blood their brain.

If you prick us, do we not bleed? If you cut off the blood supply to our brain, do we not pass out?

Shakespeare had said that, or I imagined he would have if they'd had BJJ back at Stratford on Avon. I didn't think this Krin was a fan of the bard, but after two seconds of thrashing, he finally spun me around, my feet smacking off the side of the cargo jack, and attracted an audience, the two Copperell looking up, their faces mirror image of shock, mouths dropping open, eyes wide. In about half a second, they were both going to raise the alarm, and I wondered what the hell was taking Laranna and Chuck so long.

The scene blurred on either side of me, the Krin's head blocking most of my vision, his breathless choking and my own desperate grunting drowning out any other sound. Planting my feet flat on the floor, I twisted his neck around as hard as I could, a sudden jerk that threw his weight to one side while his head stayed on the other. A sharp, crackling pop, a noise I'd never forget, and a sudden give to the Krin's neck, and he slumped, no more struggle left in him.

I'd broken his neck, what doctors called—or so Chuck had told me during training—a traumatic dislocation of the cervical spinal cord. I let him fall, dead weight, and turned to face the other two soldiers, but neither of them would be a problem. I'd been too occupied to notice, but Laranna stood over one of the Copperell, watching with her staff raised for a follow-up blow as he choked, clutching at his shattered hyoid and trachea. Chuck added a finishing strike to the back of the head of the Copperell soldier he straddled, and the man gave a final shudder before slipping out of consciousness.

A pang of regret ached in my chest at the two dead Copperell. Unlike the Krin, who'd embraced the Empire and all it stood for with open, scaley arms, the Copperell had been conquered twice over, once by the Kamerians, then again by the Anguilar. Generations of subjugation and the only way out was joining the military. But to free entire worlds of Copperell, I'd have to sacrifice the ones who'd gone turncoat, no matter how much I wished it didn't have to be that way.

"Get their uniforms," I told the others. "We just got our way in."

22

THERE ARE few things less comfortable than wearing the clothes of a dead man. Even a dead Krin, and bear in mind that, while I'd never thought of myself as a bigot, I never, ever liked Krin. I'd met Kamerians I trusted and admired, even Anguilar who I could understand and somewhat identify with, making allowances for their differing culture, but I'd yet to run into a Krin who didn't deserve a punch in the face.

That still didn't change how creepy it felt, how the Anguilar field uniform abraded my neck and wrists. The uniform came with a cap, nothing like the Army brimmed cap, though. More like a watch cap, what everyone not in the military variously called a knit cap, a took, or a stocking cap. I *really* didn't want to wear that, not knowing what various mites or lice Krin might carry, but we were running smack-on into the undeniable fact that the Anguilar had no humans or Strada in their ranks, and while they weren't the most observant species in the galaxy, someone might notice that. Which meant we all pulled our caps down as far as we could and kept our heads down as we pushed the cargo cart ahead of us.

"This isn't going to work," Chuck hissed from beside me.

"Why didn't you say that before?" I shot back softly.

"I *did* say so before," he insisted.

"Shut up, you two," Laranna chided.

She was right. The storage area had fallen away behind us, and as we advanced through the administration areas, uniformed Imperial troops passed by on either side of us, some with their noses buried in handheld tablets like modern-day teenagers with their smart phones, some glancing at us in apathetic indifference. But all it would take was one looking a little bit more closely at our faces or our skin tones beneath our caps, and we'd be well and truly screwed.

I tried to get an idea of where we were, but I didn't dare raise my eyes far enough for a good look. Doors lined the hallway, yet I couldn't have sworn to what was through them, whether offices or living quarters or cleaning closets. All I had to go on were the directions we'd been given by Mayak and Shindo, and that meant we just kept going until we reached the end of the admin section.

If there was any comfort at all, it was the weight of the pulse pistol on my belt. It seemed years since I'd had a real weapon even though it had only been a day, and it wasn't so much the idea that one handgun would get me out of this alive as it was the idea of holding my fate in my hands. A psychological comfort, just like the darkness, but I'd take any I could get at the moment.

More uniform shoes, and here and there, armored boots striding past us or standing guard outside what had to be important control rooms or maybe armories, yet no one had challenged us yet.

"Just keep moving," I whispered to Chuck.

We looked like a typical exercise in military efficiency, three of us doing the job of one person, with Laranna operating the controls in front, the motorized hubs doing all the work, and yet Chuck and I pushed at the load of supply cannisters like we were the ones propelling it. I was being overly cynical, I knew. Three people would be needed to unload the food once we arrived at… wherever the hell we were supposed to be going.

I prayed to the gods of bureaucratic inertia that no one would notice, no one would care. We were just an NCO and a couple junior enlisted making a food delivery. No reason to pay any attention to us…we were someone else's problem. Finally, I decided I had to risk a look up at our surroundings, just to make sure that we hadn't gone too far, that we were still bound for the holding cells.

It was bad timing. Just as I looked up, we passed by a broad, open doorway, guarded on either side by armored infantry soldiers, their pulse rifles held at rest across their chests. Some kind of master control room, the nerve center of this facility, I guessed from the number of officers moving purposefully from one station to another, giving orders to the techs actually monitoring whatever the instruments were, trying very hard to look too important to get rid of.

I'd seen the look before, and it was actually good for us since it meant they'd be too busy trying to impress the boss to notice a food run passing by outside in the hall. Unfortunately, that boss was General Zan-Tar, and he was looking straight at me. My initial impulse was to glance away and pretend I hadn't seen him, but there was no mistaking the look of recognition in his eyes, the alarm in his expression.

I went with my second impulse instead, the Han Solo impulse. The Anguilar holster wasn't built for an Old West fast draw, but I'd worked on it in my spare time with an unloaded pulse pistol in a mirror just because there wasn't much else to do in hyperspace. The sidearm leapt into my hand, and I tried what Chuck liked to call point-shooting, not using the sights, just aiming by instinct at less than twenty yards away.

It was a good shot. I knew it before I pulled the trigger, sensed it as if my consciousness rode the bolt of scalar energy like Slim Pickens riding the H-bomb down into the Soviet Union in "Dr. Strangelove." It was perfect, except for the dumbass brownnose Anguilar staff officer who chose that exact moment to try to put himself in the general's field of view to make sure he got noticed.

What the junior staff officer got instead was a burst of pulse pistol fire right through the chest. Zan-Tar spun away, clutching at his arm, yelling an alarm as everything slipped into slow-motion inside my head, slow enough that I could tell the movement of his lips didn't match the words the translation goo put into my brain.

"Travers!" he yelped, throwing himself to the floor. "Kill him!"

And then, of course, it all went to hell.

The guards were the most immediate threat, and to his credit, Chuck saw that. This was a gunfight, much more in his wheelhouse than the sneaking around and hitting gangsters with clubs, and if anything, he reacted faster than I had once the first shots were fired. The compact pulse pistols that we'd appropriated wouldn't penetrate the Anguilar armor, and Chuck knew it, had been trained often enough in it by Laranna and Val and me. The target on these guys was the narrow visor, a concession to the limits of technology.

Theoretically, it would have been possible for the Anguilar to make the helmet entirely enclosed in armor just as thick as the stuff over their torsos, to project a video feed of everything onto the inside of the helmet from cameras on the outside. But combat was a chaotic thing, and electronics failed. Even the Anguilar knew that. Besides which, the more technology they crammed into their armor, the more maintenance it would require, the more factories they'd have to build, and the more of their highly valued Anguilar they'd have to train as techs.

I couldn't fault the logic, but it did leave a three-inch high, eight-inch wide Achilles' Heel right in the center of their faces. Hitting something that small on a moving target was tough, even at just a few yards away, but if Chuck hadn't been a good soldier, the Army wouldn't have picked him to be a Ranger company commander.

The armored trooper stiffened and toppled, but before he hit the ground, Laranna took out the second of the guards and bought us a few seconds. Not much time, but enough. The crew in the station control room were staff officers and technicians, issued sidearms but not that good with them in my experience. It would take them a good five seconds to figure out that the enemy had infiltrated their base and was shooting at them.

There wasn't much behind us, a few offices, maybe three or four armored infantry soldiers, and I wasn't even sure they had rifles. The major threat was ahead, which also happened to be the direction we had to go to get Giblet. That was where the infantry troops would be concentrated, and we only had about thirty seconds to get there before surprise as a force multiplier ran out and left us sitting in the middle of an enemy stronghold with our thumbs up our asses.

"Take the cart forward!" I yelled to Laranna as I holstered my handgun and scooped up one of the rifles the dead troopers had dropped. "Get behind it! We'll use it for cover!"

Chuck took the hint and grabbed one of the other rifles, and Laranna hopped onto the small platform at the front of the machine and started us forward again, this time giving the cargo cart all the juice the motors had to offer. It wasn't a Formula One car, but opened up to the stops, it moved at a fair running pace, about as fast as we could move.

A plan drew itself in my head. Get into the holding area, blitz the armored guards, break Giblet out of his cell, and then head back the way we'd come, where the enemy was their weakest. As plans sketched out on the fly while under fire, it wasn't bad. It lasted about ten seconds.

We made it past the command center, with Chuck watching our back and me covering the front, and maybe I should have switched that, but I figured the biggest threat was from the front, that the brass in the control room wouldn't expose themselves to our fire. I forgot who I was dealing with.

Motion from the rear caught my eye, and I turned just in time to catch Chuck opening fire on a pair of deadweight staff officers who'd stumbled out of the room as if they'd been pushed, pistols filling their hands but not nearly pointed in the right direction. Chuck shot them down in a long burst—too long, but he wasn't as accustomed to the rate of fire on the pulse rifles as I was. It was one thing to fire the things in training, another in combat. That meant he was still shooting the two staff clowns when Zan-Tar ducked out from around the cover of the doorway and emptied his pistol in our direction.

Chuck threw himself down, though not quickly enough. A pained grunt and a clutch at his arm was demonstration enough of that, though he retained enough presence of mind not to drop his rifle. The cargo sled slowed to a crawl, and what little concentration I could give that fact led me to the conclusion that Laranna had stopped it to let Chuck get to cover. I had bigger concerns.

With a shouted curse that still couldn't have been heard over the *snap-crack-bang* of pulse-gun rounds, I laid down a hail of fire at Zan-Tar, hoping I could rob this beast of its head and cause enough chaos to ensure a successful escape. I could never be that lucky, and Zan-Tar had too great of a sense of self-preservation. He ducked back inside the millisecond his pistol mag was empty, and the sporadic fire from the other doorways in the corridor petered out with his absence.

"You okay, Chuck?" I asked, backing around the other side of the cart to check on him, still watching the doorway.

"Forget me," he bit off, nodding to the rear. "Laranna…"

My blood ran cold, and I forgot all about the Anguilar, Zan-Tar, and even Giblet in that instant of terror. I didn't bother running around the side of the cart, instead vaulting the top of it…and finding Laranna sprawled at the front of the machine, a pool of blood around her head.

Biting back a scream, I knelt beside her and lifted her up… and she moaned, hands going to her head, and I nearly sobbed in relief. She had a nasty burn on the side of her head, and a gash to go with it where she'd smacked her brow against the cargo cart on the way down. Her eyes fluttered and she was out of it, unable to hold up her head…but she was alive.

"Chuck, get the hell over here!" I bellowed at him.

I lifted Laranna up as if she were weightless, her 120 pounds of lean muscle feeling like nothing compared to the fear and fury coursing through my veins. Her blood stained the arm of my stolen uniform as I set her in the narrow gap between the cargo cannisters and laid her head down as gently as I could before I jumped back off the machine.

"Take this this thing back to the storage section," I told Chuck. His hands froze on the controls, and he blinked as if he thought the pain in his arm had made him hallucinate. "Now!" I yelled at him, then grabbed his rifle away and tucked it under my other arm. "You're both wounded and she's incapacitated and we've lost surprise." And that was all the explanation I had time for. "Get going!"

He jumped up onto the platform and gunned the engine, at least moving faster than either of them could have run at the moment. I backed up behind them, knowing what was coming, both rifles pointed down the corridor toward the holding cells, toward the armored troopers I knew were on their way. More than anything, I wanted to run into that operations room and chop Zan-Tar to pieces, put an end to the misery he'd caused us, and I almost did it…before the first of the infantry soldiers charged around the curve from the holding area, firing blindly, not caring what he hit.

Must have been a Krin. I walked double bursts from both rifles onto him, sliced through his armor in a shower of sparks, then the one behind him, and would have kept going if the cart hadn't been about to outrun me. I couldn't leave a gap between me and the cart. That would allow any of the Anguilar we'd passed along the way to get between us, to put a round in my back before they killed Chuck and captured Laranna.

I wasn't thinking far enough ahead to go past that. Get to the storage area, get to the hatch, get through it. Get back to the Below and get Laranna help and then worry about regrouping, figuring out what to do next. One step at a time.

Intersecting threads of pulse fire interrupted even those thoughts, blind shots from around the corner, coming nowhere close to me but a few impacting storage cannisters at the edges of the cart, blowing them apart in sprays of powdered, burning grain.

I ignored it, ignored the flare of heat and the sting on the back of my neck from the flaming bits of wheat or barley or whatever it was, concentrating on the curve in the wall where I knew they'd come from. Someone had to be first. There. Just a flash of gray and black but enough to make a target. I blew the helmet apart, and the head inside it, and a suit of armor suddenly bereft of control from the soldier inside it clattered to the floor. The others pulled back, still confused, giving us an opening.

"Faster!" I yelled at Chuck, punctuating the order with a blast of crimson energy through the nearest open door. Inside, someone cried out either in pain or alarm, and no one approached the doorway, which had been the idea.

Chuck twisted the throttle on the cart, and the battered, scorched machine surged forward, fast enough that I had to jog to keep up with it and couldn't keep up the backward walk. Run three steps, spin around, fire a burst at any open door and another back at the end of the hall to let the armored troops know I remembered them, lather, rinse, repeat. It wouldn't last long, but I didn't *need* long. Just back to that intersection, just get one more corner between us and the infantry.

Just one more corner, and we'd be okay. The idea was a brass ring hanging ahead of me, the only goal I could allow myself.

"Faster!" I yelled again, as if there was anything else Chuck could have done.

Impatience surged in my veins, a companion drug to the adrenaline, simultaneously slowing everything down and making that slowed-down perception infuriating. Seconds turned into hours inside my head, and with the illusion of tachypsychia came the conviction that this was one of those nightmares where I was being chased by some monster down an impossibly long hallway, racing for the door to safety except the door kept getting farther away with each step.

One more turn to the rear, another burst to keep the Anguilar back, and when I turned around again, we were there, at the intersection.

"Right turn," I snapped at Chuck.

"I *know*," he yelled back. "I just came from here!"

Which was true and irrelevant. Stress, combat, the wound could all combine to cloud his thoughts, and I'd seen soldiers turn the wrong way and blunder right into enemy guns in a fight...on our side *and* theirs. Chuck twisted the steering T-bar, and the cart went up on two wheels. A handful of cannisters tumbled off the side and clanged against the pavement like a church bell.

I hopped to the left to avoid the crashing food containers, and a barrage of pulse fire exploded against the wall where my head had been just a moment before. A wash of light and heat rolled over me, sending me stumbling backward just before Hank Aaron swung at a home run ball and connected with the side of my head.

I was on the ground and didn't know how I'd gotten there except that it hurt. Wetness dripped down my face, and the wall behind me had cratered like a meteor had smashed into it. Dimly, from a distance, I understood that debris from the wall had hit me in the side of the head, but that knowledge hovered out of reach of my conscious thoughts, esoteric and unimportant. What was important was who had fired those shots, and even rolling on the ground, my head throbbing and my vision blurred, I knew they'd come from the column of Anguilar troopers advancing up from the opposite arm of the intersection.

Chuck turned back, slowed the cart, and took a step to jump off of it, but I waved at him to keep going.

"Get Laranna out of here!" I yelled at him, grabbing one of the two rifles, the one close enough for me to reach. "Go!"

I didn't try picking up the weapon, didn't attempt to get to my feet, just got the muzzle pointed in the right direction and jammed down the trigger. Shooting low was something they probably hadn't expected, and surprise, as always, was a force multiplier. I was concussed, though, and somehow, I found the sight of half a dozen Imperial infantry cascading off their feet with smoking leg wounds hilarious. Laughing, I rolled onto my other side, swinging the barrel of the rifle around to the group still pursuing us from the detention area.

The maneuver brought with it a wave of nausea, and I clenched my teeth to keep the weird bread I'd eaten earlier from making a return appearance. No time for puking, had shooting to do. The rifle was getting hot, I realized, but I didn't care if I burned my hand. It wouldn't bother me much longer. The first couple rounds I fired went into the floor, which annoyed the hell out of me, and I stopped laughing, concentrating on getting the barrel lifted up enough to hit the target.

More Anguilar went down—or whatever they were, whatever poor sons of bitches had gotten themselves shanghaied or volunteered into the infantry armor. Or had decided that they just liked being the oppressor rather than the oppressed. That had happened before, on Earth, so many times that I could have taught a class on it. I would have felt guilty about killing them if they hadn't been intent on killing me, and if that event hadn't been so clearly imminent.

Three of them tumbled backward, another two pitched forward and the rest wised up and moved to the sides, pinning me down with a fusillade against the wall just above me. More debris, hot this time, and I had to pat out a fire smoldering on the back of my leg, grateful that the Anguilar at least made their uniforms heat resistant.

Had to move again, and I rolled toward the other rifle but found that it had already taken the hit I, miraculously, had not. The ammo drum had exploded and taken the trigger mechanism with it. No joy. I snugged the stock of the one I'd been firing against my shoulder instead.

That's okay, baby, I still have you.

Lining up on the right side of the corridor, I pulled the trigger and walked a long burst through two of the troopers there before red lights flashed in the sights and the trigger froze.

Out of ammo.

You faithless little trollop.

Oh well. It was gonna happen at some point. Drop the rifle, roll off that position, and draw my pistol. Going down in a blaze of glory with a pistol in my hand like an Old West outlaw. It wasn't the worst way to go, at least not if the whole dying of old age surrounded by my great-grandchildren thing was out the window.

When the shot came, it felt different than I'd thought it would be. I'd expected a sharp, burning pain the same as the times I'd been wounded, but instead, the impact was dull, cushioned. My eyes stung and my vision went blurry and I couldn't move…but I wasn't paralyzed. Something had me restrained, like an opponent in high school wrestling pinning me to the mat.

I blinked my eyes clear and found myself looking up at General Zan-Tar. His hands were full of something that looked like a cross between a pump shotgun and a grenade launcher, something I'd seen before. I could move my head, and when I looked down, I saw the white foam encasing my body from the chest down. Zan-Tar smiled down at me.

"Welcome to Wraith Anchorage. We've been expecting you."

23

I was alive, but I wasn't sure why.

Zan-Tar hadn't been about to tell me. After he'd shot me with the glue gun, he'd tossed it to one of the armored troopers, snapped an order to take me to the cell, and stalked off. I hadn't been too talkative myself, not with the Anguilar soldiers looming over me, seven or eight pulse rifle muzzles pointed directly at my face while they pried the pistol out of my hand. The one with the glue gun pulled a spray can out of the stock and hosed the hardened foam down with it until the gunk began to melt and run. The rifle muzzles pressed closer then, and when the glue had melted completely away, one of the troopers rolled me over and slapped restraints over my wrists.

The concussion I'd suffered from the debris hitting me in the head faded, its absence filled by a blinding ache and a lingering nausea, which meant I couldn't have resisted the troops when they pulled to my feet even if I'd been so inclined.

"Move," one of them snapped, pushing at my shoulder. I almost fell but caught myself and started walking.

These guys didn't sound or look happy that I was still alive after so many of their compatriots had been killed, and I didn't want to give them an excuse to see how badly they could hurt me while still making it look like an accident. *They* certainly had no issue with killing me, which meant Zan-Tar did, and it wasn't hard to imagine why. Me dying here was a personal coup for him, but me dying publicly, in front of their emperor, was a triumph of propaganda that would kill the resistance. *After* they'd interrogated me for a few weeks or months, most likely.

A good reason not to get taken alive, but that wasn't an option anymore. They were taking me to a cell, and I'd be sitting there until they shipped me out, and I doubted they'd leave me so much as a shoelace that I could use to do away with myself. I don't know if I could have done it, anyway. Going out in a blaze of glory was one thing, but killing myself felt too much like giving up, even though I knew I might live to regret that.

But I couldn't die until I found out what had happened to Laranna. Chuck and Laranna weren't here, which meant they'd either been killed or had gotten away, and I had to believe the latter. Maybe if I found out she hadn't made it, I wouldn't be so idealistic about committing suicide. For the moment, I walked. And watched.

The passage narrowed as we turned, and I tried to keep track of the lefts and rights, though it was difficult with the pounding in my head, but finally, I had to give up on it. Two descents, one climb, past what looked like living quarters for the troops, two different armories, and a lot of pissed off Krin and Anguilar. I felt their stares even of the ones with helmets, right through the visors.

Through all that and a few more storage areas, and then we came to a thick, solid door guarded by four troopers, two sitting at a table with their visors up, the other two standing on either side of it. The detention area. My new home, temporarily, however long it took them to arrange for my transport back to the Anguilar homeworld.

"Open it up," the guard in charge of me ordered curtly, and one of the troopers standing beside the door tapped a code into the security panel. I squinted at it but couldn't make out the combination, though it was the worst sort of wishful thinking that it would have mattered if I could.

The doors slid aside, and if I thought the hallways were narrow here, they went down to less than four feet across now that we were in among the cells. Bare metal doors, featureless, lacking even a slit to slide food through, and I wondered if they bothered to feed them. If any lived long enough to get hungry.

"In here," the head jailer grunted, pushing me up against the door, my cheek slamming into the metal hard enough for the impact to resonate through my sinuses.

He slapped a palm against the control beside the door, and the cold metal moved aside with a grinding of ancient motors. A shove against my back sent me stumbling a few steps inside before rough hands seized me by the shoulders and held me in place as one of them removed the restraints. Another shove, and the door closed.

It was dark inside the cell, the only light provided by a narrow strip of fluorescent material over the door, so it took me a long few seconds to figure out that I wasn't alone. The first thing I noticed was the toilet, of course, because it was the first thing I looked for. It was surprisingly similar to the human version, though I suppose it shouldn't have been a shock given that we all shared similar plumbing. It was at the center of the back wall and on either side of it were two cots.

The one on the right side was empty, but sitting cross-legged on the left was a shadowy figure, slim and wiry, head down, hands resting on his knees.

"You're an idiot for coming here," he said quietly, and I knew the voice immediately. "Just like I was."

I leaned against the wall for a second, catching my breath, before I could bring myself to look back at him.

"Hi, Gib," I said. "Long time, no see."

"This whole thing was a trap from the word go," Giblet said bitterly, still sitting with his chin buried against his chest. "This Zan-Tar may be an asshole, but he's a damned *smart* asshole."

"I think I remember us saying something like that a few weeks ago," I reminded him, slumping into the cot opposite Gib. Maybe playing I-told-you-so wasn't such a great idea given the circumstances, but Laranna and Chuck were at least wounded, maybe dead, and I was sitting in a cell getting ready to be sent for execution, so I didn't feel too bad about it.

"Then why the hell did *you* come here?" Gib demanded, legs unfolding as he put his feet flat on the floor and leaned closer to me. His face was bruised, dried blood matted at the edge of his scalp. "I mean, at least I have the excuse of being too screwed up about Dani to think straight. What's yours?" He waved his hands dismissively at me. "I told you not to come after me. You should have stayed home."

"Yeah, I should have stayed home while my best friend flew off to avenge the woman he loved who I got killed," I said, not trying to conceal the bitterness in my voice. "I would have been just fine with that because some computer says I'm supposed to be the leader."

"If you're such a badass leader," Gib countered, louder now as if the suggestion had made him angry, "then why did you let Zan-Tar bait you in? I'm a Varnell, you idiot…I'm supposed to do stupid shit and piss people off. You're supposed to be smarter. You're the one who was supposed to make all this worth it, to make everyone believe that we could win this fight." He stood and poked a finger into my chest in accusation. "You don't *get* to be normal and have weaknesses like the rest of us. When everyone else says to do the wrong thing, *you* have to be the one who stands in the way and says *no*! That's the price of the job!"

That was enough, the straw that broke the camel's back. I jumped to my feet and pushed him back, sending him toppling back onto the cot.

"Go to hell!" I snapped. "I never asked for any of this! I

was walking in the woods trying to figure out my life, minding my own Goddamned business! I never wanted to be some cult figure, I just wanted to be an infantry officer! I wanted to marry my girlfriend and have a normal job and normal friends…"

Gib grinned lopsidedly.

"And you wish none of this had ever happened then? You wish you could go back to the way things were?"

I sighed and settled onto my cot heavily, the springs inside it creaking beneath my weight.

"Of course I don't," I admitted. "I'm doing exactly what I was meant to do. Lenny was right."

"Lenny's always right," Gib agreed. "He lies, omits important things, misleads us, but when he's straight with us, he's always right."

"It doesn't matter," I insisted, shaking my head stubbornly. "You're my best friend, and there's no way in hell I was going to sit back and let you die. Wrong or not, stupid or not, it's what I had to do."

Giblet sighed, reached out and offered his hand, and I took it.

"And that's why we'd all follow you into hell, Charlie. Because we know you never give up on your friends."

The door slid aside with a juddering *clunk-clunk-clunk*, and General Zan-Tar stepped into the cell, flanked by an armed and armored escort of Anguilar soldiers.

"This is so sweet," he declared with a sardonic grin, "that I think I might throw up."

"What are you doing here?" I asked him, not standing up,

determined to avoid deferring to the Anguilar officer. "Taking me back to the Emperor already?"

"No," he said, walking between us with casual recklessness, as if he didn't believe I would take a chance at getting killed just to throttle him with my bare hands. Granted, if Gib hadn't been there, I might have, but he was right. "I don't believe in reporting to the Emperor unless I have something useful for him." He looked down his aquiline nose at me. "Your capture is significant, but it's not useful. Neither is your execution."

"In that case," I told him, brightening with false enthusiasm, "why don't we just call all this a big misunderstanding, and I'll be on my way?"

Zan-Tar shook his head, seeming genuinely amused.

"Look at you, Charlie Travers," he said, hands clasped behind his back as he paced between us. "I knew you'd come, yet still you managed to surprise us, nearly managed to assassinate me and free your friend here, simply because you consistently choose the least likely approach possible, the way that no one would believe you'd come, the way no *sane* soldier would choose."

"Well, there's a reason for that," Gib commented, rolling his eyes at me. "Here's a hint: it has to do with the sane part."

Zan-Tar ignored the crack, eyes still fixed on me.

"No, Charlie Travers, I would only take you to the Emperor if I could bring with you the news that Sanctuary had been razed, the resistance crushed permanently." His expression was genial, and I got the sense that this was the most fun he'd had in a long time. "You're going to give me the coordinates for that system before we leave this planet."

Ah. That's it, then. That's the reason I'm still alive.

"I hate to disappoint you, General," I told him, keeping my hands at my side, careful to meet his eyes and not glance away, "but I don't *know* the location of the Sanctuary system. None of us do. Only Lenny and the other versions of Lenny on the Liberty ships have the coordinates. Only Liberty ships can go there on their own. Our Vanguards have to dock with one of them to go there, and anyone else who needs to travel there has to go to a prearranged meeting place to rendezvous with a Liberty ship and be escorted in."

I'd rehearsed the spiel many times. We all had because it had to sound convincing. The only problem was, I'd never been a very good liar, and, looking at Zan-Tar, I couldn't tell if he believed me.

"I don't believe you," he declared, settling the matter, but then he shrugged. "But it wouldn't matter if I did. I'd be remiss in my duties if I simply accepted your statement without applying pressure to determine the truth."

Pressure. That didn't sound good, and I had an urge to curl into a fetal position. Torture was an ugly word, and probably even uglier considering the technology the Anguilar commanded. They could probably keep me alive for a long time, well past the point where I'd be begging them to let me die. And I didn't know how long I'd be able to resist. Luckily, I'd been telling pretty much the truth. Sort of. *I* didn't know the coordinates, but not because *no one* did. It was more because I couldn't memorize coordinates that long and didn't try because none of us were *supposed* to go there alone.

The way I'd told it sounded better. I'd been so caught up in imagining what *pressure* might entail that I'd missed the fact that Zan-Tar was still talking.

"I *could* lie to you, you know," he said, arms crossed, again affecting a lack of concern at any threat I might pose to him. "I could tell you that we'd captured your friends, that I'd kill them if you didn't cooperate. I know one of them is your life mate, and knowing you as well as I do, I'm also confident you'd reveal anything to save her." He sniffed, as if the concept of caring about my wife was a weakness that he didn't share. "But I respect you too much to think you'd believe it without being shown them, which I couldn't do. They were both wounded, we saw that much on the security tapes, but they escaped through the hatchway in the storage area."

His eyebrow quirked upward.

"Which we didn't even know existed previously, so thanks for revealing that to us, by the way. We haven't burned through the metal yet—those Gan-Shi built well, give them their due. But we will, and once we do, then we'll roll up the entire network of the Gan-Shi underground, and your compatriots with them. But that will take time, and now that I have you, I find I lack the patience to wait for that."

Oh, goody, at least I wouldn't have to wait for the torture to start.

I must not have been quite as good at hiding my fear as I'd hoped I was because Zan-Tar laughed.

"I know what you're thinking, Travers. You're imagining the horrible tortures I have in store for you to try to sweat the information out of you. And yes, if my predecessor were still in command, that might be the case. But I have enough experience in these matters to be aware of the shortcomings of using mere physical duress as an interrogation technique." He made a dismissive gesture. "Of course, everyone has a breaking point, and if I apply enough pain, you'll tell me whatever I want to hear." He cocked his head to the side. "But. Will it be the truth? That takes time. I'd have to check on the information you gave, then double-check, then interrogate you further, and by the time we'd confirmed everything you said, days may have passed. Perhaps enough time for your friends to escape or warn others, enough time for the resistance to evacuate Sanctuary." He stepped over to Gib and laid a hand on his shoulder. Gib tried to shrug it off, but Zan-Tar tightened the grip, and from the discomfort in Gib's eyes, Zan-Tar was pretty damned strong. "I could always take advantage of your weakness for your friends and focus my interrogation techniques on the Varnell. Force you to watch us carve him up, starting with that vile, deceitful tongue of his. But that runs into another issue. You see, people will spill their secrets as long as hope remains. If we hurt the Varnell *too* badly, you'll close down emotionally, consider him as good as dead, and seal your conscience off from any further pain we inflict."

He shook his head, letting go of Gib's shoulder. Gib worked the joint as if the hold had been painful, though he didn't rub it, probably not wanting to give Zan-Tar the satisfaction.

"What are you gonna do, then?" Gib mocked. "Pluck me like a chicken?"

"No," Zan-Tar said, shaking his head as a thin, cruel smile spread across his face. "*We're* not going to hurt you at all."

I suppose I should have been relieved at Zan-Tar's declaration that they weren't going to torture Gib, but the way he said it made it clear that whatever he meant, it would be so much worse. Zan-Tar nodded to the guards.

"Put them in restraints," he ordered, "and bring them with us. We're taking a little trip, Charlie…to the arena."

24

WHEN I'D RETURNED to Earth the third time, after the brief visit to the pizza parlor in Brandon and the longer one to the Snake Mound in Ohio, I'd finally had time to catch up on what I'd missed since 1987. One of the things that intrigued me was Mixed Martial Arts. I'd been a big fan of the PKA—the Professional Kickboxers' Association—back in the eighties, and MMA was a step beyond that, a veritable Bruce Lee ideal of combining all the martial arts into one competition. The fact that it had turned out that the most effective combination of martial arts had been boxing, Thai boxing, and Brazilian JuJiitsu hurt my feelings a little since I'd sunk so many years of my youth into Taekwondo, but it was all very similar to what I'd picked up from the Strada.

The coolest part of MMA was the octagon, the padded cage where two men entered to fight and only one emerged victorious.

The arena, I discovered on the long descent through the endless rows of stands, was a larger version of the octagon except with ten or possibly twelve sides instead of eight. The walls were higher by maybe a foot, and they were transparent rather than padded.

I tried to imagine the whole place packed with bloodthirsty aliens, cheering on their favorites as they tried to bash each other's brains in, the crowd chanting, fists pumping, spittle flying. No crowd today, no spectators other than a handful of Anguilar soldiers, General Zan-Tar…and us.

I tried to follow Gib into the ring when they took him, but one of the guards grabbed me by the collar and pulled me up short. Gib didn't resist as he was led through the gate into the ring, just waited patiently until his restraints were removed, then rubbed at his wrists and looked around. I did too, finally noticing the lone figure approaching from a door on the other side of the arena. He was Kamerian, tall, and powerful, with skin tinted a deeper gold than the most-tanned Australian surfer boy. Just like Tamura…he could have been the pilot's cousin, though that was likely just a function of my own unfamiliarity with the species.

He wore a singlet rather than a flight suit, dressed like an Olympic gymnast but muscled more like a weightlifter. Barefoot, no weapons, but no gloves, either. Gib stared at him with utter hatred, and I imagined he was picturing Tamura with Dani, bottling the frustration and fury I knew he'd felt when the two of them were together. But the Kamerian had him by a head and thirty pounds, and I couldn't see any way he'd be able to run with him.

"Hey, shithead," Gib called to the Kamerian as the taller man entered the ring, "how the hell did one of you gold-skinned assholes wind up fighting in the arena? You sleep with some Anguilar general's wife?"

Gib leered back at Zan-Tar, cackled a raunchy laugh. Zan-Tar didn't react the way Gib had likely hoped though, didn't seem to be angry. The Anguilar general merely chuckled, anticipation evident in his expression, like he was looking forward to Giblet being smashed into a thin, fine paste on the flexible floor of the ring.

Gib bounced on the balls of his feet, shaking his shoulders to loosen them, his head bobbing side to side like a professional fighter getting ready for a bout. The Kamerian wasted no time on any such frivolities, making a beeline across the ring straight toward Gib. My hands were clenched into fists behind my back where the restraint cuffs held them, my teeth grinding in anticipation of the punishment Gib was about to take.

The Kamerian swung at Giblet's head with a broad roundhouse, widely telegraphed, and Gib avoided it with a sliding sidestep, hands still up in the defense, feet moving just as he'd been taught by Laranna, Chuck, me, and every other unarmed combat instructor we'd had.

"What?" Gib taunted, spreading his hands for a moment before bringing them back to the defense. "You use that sloppy shit to beat up on peasants who never learned how to fight? I can't imagine you've ever fought anyone worth a damn because you look like a complete idiot."

I'd heard Gib use his vocal talents to cajole and woo and

convince, but I'd never witnessed him trying to intentionally infuriate someone. It pissed me off just listening to it, and I *knew* what he was trying to do. The Kamerian's eyes flared, and he lunged for Gib's legs in a takedown attempt, but Giblet hopped out of the tackle and slammed a heel into the back of the other fighter's neck.

The kick smashed the Kamerian's face into the canvas, where it bounced off with a spray of blood from the man's nose, and I thought Gib might linger to aim a kick at his opponent while he was down. Instead, he danced away, a sneer across his face.

"Come on, you miserable, oversized bastard! Get off the floor and actually try to hit me!"

What the Kamerian should have done at that point was to slow down, reassess, re-evaluate, and come in cautiously, try to pin Giblet into a corner where he could pound him without the chance the Varnell could get away. But he was far too pissed off for that. His lips split into an enraged scowl as he wiped the blood off his face and slung it away to spatter across the mat like the aftermath of a shooting in one of those mystery TV shows.

"I'll rip you to pieces, Varnell filth!" he said, speaking for the first time since he'd entered the ring, just a sign of how well Gib's taunting had worked on him.

Another wild lunge, but this time, Giblet ducked to the side and lashed out with a heel kick into the big man's knee. The crunch from the joint disintegrating was perhaps the most sickening sound I'd ever heard, though the scream that followed was a close second. The Kamerian collapsed, clutching at his knee, and this time, Gib didn't stand back and watch. I'd never seen him this vicious, ruthless. Blows rained down, but not wild aimed at wherever he could hit. They were targeted carefully at vital spots—the joints, the throat, the temples. Kicks, punches, knees, and after the first few, the Kamerian couldn't even put up a defense.

In ten seconds, he was motionless. In twenty, he wasn't breathing. Only then did Gib step away, sneering down at the dead Kamerian before aiming the same look at Zan-Tar.

"Is that the best you can do?"

"Of course not," Zan-Tar told him, agreeable as always. "If we'd started with the best, it wouldn't be much fun, would it?"

A cold lump formed in my stomach as I realized that the Anguilar general was enjoying this. Two Anguilar troopers filed through the swinging door and carried out the body of the Kamerian by his feet and shoulders. Before they'd cleared the ring, a door opened on the opposite side of the arena, and the Krin who emerged through it was just as big as the Kamerian, which made him a giant among his people. His fangs glinted in the spotlights, his talons sharp and flashing.

"Come to me, little Varnell," he hissed, entering the ring. "Let's have some fun."

AN ARMORED HAND pressed against my chest to halt my surge forward, and I wanted to look away from the blood oozing from the cuts across Gib's chest as my friend staggered back from the massive Krin, clutching at his wound. Red droplets fell from the

Krin's claws, and the snake-like alien grinned toothily, advancing.

"Not so talkative now, are you, Varnell?" the Krin wondered. Another swipe, and Gib barely ducked away from it, stumbling to the side, more blood dripping as he went. "Maybe you should have concentrated more on fighting and less on running your mouth."

"Maybe you're right," Gib admitted breathlessly, and I don't know if anyone but me would have noticed the barely discernable smooth tone in his voice. "Maybe I got a little too cocky."

The next swing came close, but it lacked the velocity of the last one, and Gib dodged it easier. I took a breath and sagged backward, sensing the difference.

"After all," Gib went on, "he was *just* a Kamerian. He wouldn't have stood a chance against a Krin, like you. You're twice the fighter he was, and I should have known better."

The Krin's chest puffed up as if he were a peacock displaying for a hen, and he seemed to forget about the goal of killing Giblet for a moment.

"You're damned right you should have. The reward for killing you is three thousand tradenotes, and that's enough to get me off this rock. Back to Krin where my people await me. Enough to afford a position on the reproductive advisory group…enough to ensure that I have a place fertilizing the eggs of the next generation!"

Which was *so* much more than I wanted to know about Krin breeding habits, but there you go. Gib kept moving, still obviously in pain but more confident now.

"And you should be," he agreed. "Genes such as yours would obviously be advantageous for the progression of your entire species. You should be fertilizing every egg in the clutch."

"I told them that before I left," the Krin said, shaking his head, his claws lowering, eyes staring at something light-years away. "They banished me for my attempt to seize the power that was rightfully mine, left me with a reputation so badly scarred that not even the Anguilar would accept me as one of their soldiers. Left me with nothing to do but fight in the arena here. But I'll show them…"

He'd launched into a full tirade, not noticing Giblet circling behind him until it was far too late. Gib tried the same attack that I'd used on the Krin when Chuck, Laranna, and I had entered the city, not because he was imitating me—he hadn't been around to see it—but because it was the safest way to attack a Krin, particularly one as large as this guy.

The Krin grunted and flailed but couldn't shake Gib loose of him, and panic twisted his expression into something much more relatable for a human. Heading under, the Krin still had the strength left for one final gambit. He reached back over his shoulder and sank his claws into Gib's flesh, just to the side of his neck, and ripped.

Giblet screamed but he didn't let go, squeezing even harder, and the Krin slumped backward, then fell on top of him. Gib still wouldn't let go, holding the hooks in until the Krin stopped breathing. This time, the Anguilar didn't even wait until Gib had managed to push the dead weight off the Krin off himself before stepping inside to haul the body away. Gib panted heavily as the load came off his chest, then moaned and pressed a hand against the back of his shoulder, trying to staunch the flow of blood.

"The Varnell has done well for himself," Zan-Tar commented casually, as if he were watching a fight on Saturday night at the auditorium. "I wouldn't have expected him to live through the first opponent, much less the Krin. But I fear this next one will be his last."

"Please!" I yelled, falling on my knees before him, lacking the breath and the strength to do more, not caring that I was surrendering my dignity, not caring about anything except keeping Gib alive. "Don't do it! I'm not lying to you! Other people might know the coordinates…we try not to let them find out, but they might figure it from looking at their instruments. But not me. I make sure I *don't* know. I can't tell you what I don't know!"

"Yet that is exactly what you'd say even if you *did* know, isn't it?" Zan-Tar pointed out, shrugging the pleas away. "The answer is not satisfactory."

My jaw firmed, teeth clenched, and I rose to my feet.

"Then send me in with him. I'd rather die beside him, fighting, than be paraded around in front of your emperor. You're not getting the coordinates out of me even if I ever knew them. Just put me in the ring and let me die with honor."

I didn't think he'd do it. Zan-Tar wasn't a stereotypical space nazi, not like Mok-La. Still ruthless, he wasn't stupid about it, didn't revel in cruelty. He was doing his duty as he saw it. That didn't make him a good man, but it did mean he wouldn't automatically do the most evil thing possible. However, this was a question of his duty, of finding the coordinates too the headquarters system of his enemy, and while I couldn't help him, there was no way he could know that.

Zan-Tar didn't answer immediately, regarding me with a careful, analytical stare.

"My peers," he finally said, "would consider you a fool. Not simply for your wish to die with your friend but for your decision to pursue him here at risk to your life. You've sacrificed long-term advantage for sentiment, for emotion."

"There are things," I told him, "worth sacrificing everything for. Even if there's no hope, there are things you can't give up on."

"I have considered," he admitted, "that a public execution of a figure such as yourself would not accomplish our goal. That it would turn you into a martyr, inspire others to take your place. However, if the entire galaxy were to witness you beaten to death in the arena, defeated in combat, the effect might be more in line with our aims to demoralize the resistance."

"Then you'll let me fight for him?" I asked, pushing down the sure of hope before it revealed itself in my expression.

"Yes." His eyebrow tilted toward me. "But not just now. For this...we're going to need a much larger audience."

25

"Damn you, Travers," Gib murmured, grunting in pain as I pulled the makeshift bandage tighter around his shoulder.

"Sorry," I told him, knotting the ragged, torn edges of what had been my T-shirt until a couple minutes ago. I wasn't looking forward to putting the Anguilar uniform tunic back on my bare skin. It had felt like sandpaper where it had touched my exposed skin before, and now there'd be nothing between me and it. It was warm inside the arena, and I considered just leaving the tunic off. "I need to make sure the bleeding is stopped."

"Not *that*, you idiot," he snapped, glaring at me. "It was bad enough you came here in the first place. This"—he motioned at the blood-spattered canvas with his good hand—"was a *good* thing. It gave Laranna and Chuck more time to get out of here, maybe go for help. The longer I kept this going, the better chance for you to escape. Instead, you have to go *beg* Zan-Tar to let you get in the ring with me, just to make sure this whole fiasco couldn't get any freaking worse."

I laughed softly, though there wasn't anything even remotely funny about the situation.

"What?" he demanded.

"I was just thinking," I said, taking the second strip I'd ripped off of my t-shirt and wrapping it around his chest, "that this is probably the way we were both destined to go out. I mean, you're a damned good pilot, and I'm not bad, but I couldn't imagine either of us dying in some big space battle, could you? This… back to back, one enemy after another trying to kill us…it feels right."

"Speak for yourself, you hairless monkey," he groused, wincing at the second bandage. "I would have been damned happy to die in bed, surrounded by beautiful women."

"Well, it looks like you're at least going to die famous," I said, nodding at the crowds streaming into the arena's grandstands by the thousands. "That crafty little Anguilar bastard."

Zan-Tar hadn't been kidding when he said he wanted a bigger audience. It had taken close to an hour, but he'd managed to rouse the Krin management of this place and get them to send out the word and bring in an audience. That part had probably been easy. The draw of a couple of political prisoners being executed by mortal combat was pretty high, and the crowd seemed excited to watch.

"When they come," I said quietly, "let me fight them. Don't jump in unless you can get a hit without being hurt. You get injured any more, you'll be useless."

"Oh, you think you'll be that much better than me, monkey boy?" he challenged. "I'll bet you don't take out your guy faster than I took out mine."

"I don't have the benefit of your winning personality," I reminded him. I finished tying off the last of the bandages and patted him on the arm. "There. That's the best I can do."

"Don't give up your day job, kid," he said, working his shoulders. "I feel like I'm back in restraints."

"Good," I told him, hopping to my feet. "You stay restrained, and I'll take care of this next guy."

"Ladies and gentlemen!" the announcer's voice boomed through the entire arena, painful in my ears. "Welcome to this very special edition of arena combat! Brought to you by our wonderful hosts among the Anguilar Empire, led by General Zan-Tar!"

The crowd cheered dutifully, though with an edge of genuine excitement.

"Our gracious commander has brought to us today two nefarious criminals of the terrorist resistance to the rightful domain of the Anguilar Empire, the slime-tongued Varnell con artist, Giblet Dennai'a, last of the Grana Varnell tribe!"

A chorus of boo's went from one side of the auditorium to the other, people leaping to their feet and making obscene gestures at Giblet, who returned them with one of his own.

"And with him, the leader of the resistance, the renegade Earthling criminal, Charlie Travers!"

Less of a reaction this time because none of them had ever heard of Earth, and most probably hadn't heard of me, either.

Just a general disapproving rumble, and I suppose that was the best I could hope for under the circumstances.

"And for the first time ever, this personal combat will be seen not just by the inhabitants and workers of Wraith Anchorage, it will also be broadcast live to all worlds in range, including directly into the Anguilar Empire!" More cheers. I looked up automatically and found the glint of the lenses of the cameras suspended high above us.

"The first opponents facing these infamous scoundrels, coming to us from the correctional facilities after convictions for inciting a riot and assault on a security guard, are Ferrous Polyposis and Yanna Glorian!"

Shit. Two of them. I should have known that Zan-Tar wouldn't make this easy. They were some species I'd never seen before, among the many humanoid types that the Creators had spawned from Earth DNA hundreds of thousands of years ago. If I had to guess their lineage, I would have said canine from the thick hair growing down to their brows and along their cheeks, the pointed teeth, and the high set of their ears. Wolf, coyote, whatever. Human enough except for the hair and teeth and hardened points of their nails.

They weren't that tall or massive, for which I gave thanks to God for small favors. Under six feet, maybe a 150 pounds each, though their muscles were twisted cords of metal. They said nothing as they entered the ring, the only sound a low growl.

"Get back," I told Gib over my shoulder, not taking my eyes off the two. "Don't interfere unless you think I'm about to get killed."

"Then I can start now," he cracked but did as I said, retreating to the transparent wall at the far of the enclosure.

"Hey, guys," I said to the two of them. "Ferrous and Yanna, right?" I raised an eyebrow questioningly. "You two related? Cousins maybe?"

They split up, trying to flank me, and I circled, not allowing it.

"There's no reason we can't all be friends," I told them. "I'm sure you guys have no love for the Anguilar, right? I mean, who does? They had to have taken over you guys' planet too. Why would you want to help them out by killing us?"

"Because killing you comes with a full pardon, you blathering yobbo!" one of them snapped, though I couldn't tell if it was Ferrous or Yanna. "Now, if you both hold still, we'll promise to make it as painless as possible."

As tempting an offer as that was, I wasn't about to take them up on it. Instead, I did what was probably the last thing they expected and attacked. One of them—I decided it was Ferrous just for convenience's sake—darted away when I lunged inward, but Yanna didn't react as fast. Claws swiped at me but missed by a foot, and then I was inside his guard, his entire body a target-rich environment.

No time for subtlety. Hammer fist to the 'nads that bent him over into the backfist to the snout and the breath left him in a wheeze, blood flowing from his nose and mouth, then a spin into a ridge-hand to the throat. Not gentle, like I'd done with the Air Force SP back at Andrews. This one was full force, and the trachea collapsed under the blow. Yanna stumbled away, gasping for air that wouldn't come, but I'd spent too much time on him, and Ferrous made me pay for it.

I should have put a shirt on, because maybe that would have cushioned the slash across my side. Claws dug into my flesh, and warm wetness soaked me just above the hip. A savage, burning pain spun me around away from Yanna as the dog-man collapsed, hands going to his throat. Before I could recover from the flare of pain and try to mount a defense, Ferrous struck again, this time a kick that swept my legs out from beneath me.

I didn't realize what had happened until my shoulders smacked against the mat and banished the wind from me in a gush of escaping breath. I'd spread the impact as much as I could by slapping to either side, but there was no way I'd be able to roll out of the position in time, and Ferrous's ravening fangs were bared in a lunge for my throat.

Gib slammed into him from behind, a flurry of blows that staggered the dog-man, though not enough to knock him down. Ferrous whirled into a backhand blow that caught Gib across the face and sent him sprawling backward, but the distraction had given me enough time to roll onto my feet. My side throbbed, and so did my ankle where the canine had kicked me, but I didn't let the pain slow me down because hesitation would have gotten Giblet killed.

This time, I didn't try for a choke, even though his back was to me. Instead, I hopped a step and came down with my heel into the back of Ferrous's knee. Had his legs been arranged like a human's, with the knee bending plantigrade, the blow would have hurt but wouldn't have been debilitating. But these two had knees that bent digitigrade, like a dog's, and when I smashed into the back of his, it shattered.

The canine howled in pain and tried to claw at me, but when he spun, the leg collapsed under him. Then I was on him, and even if I didn't have fangs, that didn't keep me from killing him. It was all instinct, the blows precise and measured and long practiced, and I tried not to dwell on them because there were some memories I just didn't want to have.

When it was done, I rolled off him and swore at the twinge in my ankle when I stood. The crowd roared, though I couldn't tell if it was with displeasure, bloodlust or enthusiasm. I didn't have time to think about it. I had to check on Gib.

"Are you all right?" I asked him, offering a hand up. He took it, moving his jaw as if making sure it wasn't broken while I hauled him to his feet.

"Just one more thing that hurts," he moaned, then nodded at my side, which was still bleeding freely. "How about you?"

The Anguilar guards came in, warning the two of us off with their weapons before they grabbed Ferrous and Yanna and dragged them both out the ring entrance. The spring-loaded door swung shut behind them. I found the remains of my t-shirt, wrapped it around my waist, and knotted it as tight as I could stand. It soaked through with red, but the flow stopped after a moment. I flexed, twisted, and swore again at the pain when I did.

"This sucks," I told him, "but I'll live."

"Wanna bet?" he laughed hoarsely.

I wanted to be mad at him for being fatalistic, but I couldn't. Despite the pain and the impending death, I laughed, too. It hurt.

"Wonder what's next?" I asked as the laughter faded.

It didn't really matter. They'd keep sending one opponent after another until we were too beat up to fight. We were both going to die, and the only hope I had was that Laranna and Chuck had gotten away. Maybe they were already in the transport, in hyperspace, heading back to Earth. Chuck could take over the training of the troops there while Laranna took over the resistance. I knew she didn't *want* the job, but I also knew she'd do it, and do it well. I just hoped she wouldn't let this drag her down, keep her from ever being happy again.

And me? Maybe I'd be a story they told kids at bedtime on Strada or Sanctuary, the stranger who'd led the resistance for a while before he bit off more than he could chew trying to save a friend. A cautionary tale about putting personal attachments above duty. Maybe they'd learn something useful from it.

The door on the opposite end of the arena opened again, and this time, only one figure emerged from it. But it only needed to be one. Seven feet tall, 300 pounds of muscle and bone, and a hint of horns at his brow, it was obvious what we were facing. And inevitable, I suppose. A Gan-Shi. They were built for the arena, or perhaps it had been built for them. There was no chance of surprise here, no hope that the two of us together could slow the thing down.

This was it.

The crowd cheered, chanted, and roared like a feral animal.

Ready for more blood, ours this time. They'd had a good show, and now the show was about to end.

"Any ideas?" Gib asked me as the Gan-Shi strode purposefully across to the ring.

"I guess hit him low," I said with a shrug. "Because we sure as hell aren't going to be hitting him high."

"I guess not," he agreed, then paused for a moment before putting a hand on my shoulder. "Thanks for coming back for me, Charlie."

"I knew you'd do the same for me," was all I could say.

The Gan-Shi's steps thundered as he stepped through.

There was something about the build of the bull-man, the set of his jaw, something familiar…and I fought to keep my mouth from dropping open.

The Gan-Shi smacked a fist against his chest and stepped into the middle of the ring to meet us, snorting and pawing at the floor.

"Make it look good," he whispered as he got closer, winking.

It was Shindo.

26

Gib circled around the Gan-Shi, not realizing who Shindo was, not knowing he was an ally…and I couldn't tell him. Not in front of the Anguilar and their cameras. Instead, I imitated Gib's movements, circling in the opposite direction, making it look as if we were trying to keep the Gan-Shi confused, trying to make sure it didn't know which of us to go for.

Shindo lurched toward me, waving a massive fist, and I barely stepped aside in time, finding out the hard way what the Gan-Shi had meant when he said to make it look good. Giblet didn't hesitate. When he saw Shindo commit, he did as well, rushing in and aiming a kick at the back of the Gan-Shi's leg. Shindo showed no reaction except to spin into a backswing at Gib's head, and the Varnell desperately hopped backward out of the way, limping from the kick as if he'd slammed his shin into solid concrete.

I had to do my part, and when Shindo took the backward

swing, I slammed my heel into his thigh…and only managed to push myself backward, the impact traveling up the muscles of my lower back like I'd jumped out a second-story window.

Cheering and taunting echoed off the arena walls, the crowd seeing our helplessness in the face of the Gan-Shi and loving it. As if fueled by their enthusiasm, Shindo took the offensive, charging straight into me. I retreated to the door into the ring, guessing where this was going…or hoping anyway, because the alternative was going to be painful.

Bracing myself, I held my hands up in a defensive posture, but Shindo didn't even bother throwing a punch, just grabbed me around the waist and slammed into the door with my shoulder, pushed it open, and took me through it. Outside. The glare of the spotlights disappeared into shadow as I came off his shoulder, struggling to stay on my feet.

"How's this going to work?" I asked, looking back for Giblet, who raced after us, confusion warring with determination on his face. The Anguilar were frozen in place for a moment, as if they couldn't believe we'd actually left the arena, and even from a hundred yards away, I could make out General Zan-Tar barking orders, telling his troops to get us back into the ring.

"This way," Shindo said. No explanation, no extraneous words at all, he just expected us to follow him.

I did, of course, because what choice did I have? Giblet gawked at me without understanding, but all I had time to do was motion for him to follow and hope he picked up the thread. An itch between my shoulder blades warned me that I was seconds from an Anguilar pulse round slicing right through my chest, that they wouldn't let us run for long. Their confusion was matched by the crowd's, their roaring and cheering transformed into restless murmuring, but that murmuring itself morphing into alarmed yells and shouts as I ran, and I turned to see what caused the change.

The audience entrances were about a quarter of a mile away, up a set of narrow-set stairs, and I could barely see it from here near the ring, but that was where all their attention had shifted. And so had Zan-Tar's and the guards'. I wondered for a long moment what could distract them from us, but then I saw...and heard.

Being from Ohio and having spent the last few years before my abduction in central Florida, I'd never experienced a stampede, and never thought I would. I certainly hadn't thought that my first one would be several hundred bipedal bovine humanoids storming a sports arena. Gan-Shi males poured down the steps, their bellowing roars eerily hollow in the vast arena, which was unopposed because no one in the audience was stupid enough to stand in their way, even the Anguilar troops.

Zan-Tar screamed orders at the troops, but none of them moved, his commands lost in the cacophony...or at least, I imagined, they had the plausible deniability of that excuse. Until Zan-Tar sprinted toward us, trying to get to Gib and me before we could make it to the exit, bringing the platoon of troopers who were his personal bodyguard with him. There were arena seats between them and us, civilians if not particularly innocent, and it should have restrained them from firing, but it didn't.

The scream of pulse fire nearly drowned out the screams of

the civilians, and I would have felt worse for them if they hadn't come here in the first place to see us beaten to death. Shindo yanked open the door the fighters had come through and waved us toward it, but before we could get through, the platoon cleared the intervening, living obstacles, and crimson fire splashed against the wall just to the side of the exit. I threw myself to the side, and Shindo ducked around the corner of the doorway, but the bursts were walking toward us, and as certain as I knew anything, I knew that we weren't going to make it out of there.

Except for all those Gan-Shi…

Under the hail of gunfire, I'd lost track of the stampeding herd, but they hadn't lost track of us. They slammed into the platoon, taking at least a dozen casualties as the guns swung their way but not stopping them in their rampage. The Gan-Shi trampled the Anguilar troopers under their feet, then paused to rip them out of their armor with their bare hands. Not Zan-Tar, though. He saw the herd coming and got the hell out of the way, retreating back up to the other entrance to the arena, the area where the rest of the Imperial troops were gathered.

I didn't wait around to see what his next move would be since it could well be finding a way to seal off this arena and us with it. Instead, I scrambled to my feet, grabbed Gib on the way, and pulled him to his feet and through the door. I expected Shindo to slam the door shut, but he didn't, just waited for us to get to cover, still watching the way we'd come.

I spared a glance behind us at the broad hallway and the doors to either side that I assumed were training areas for the fighters. People stepped through them in ones and twos, peering curiously at the commotion for a moment before they retreated into their rooms, surprisingly timid for people who made their living fighting to the death. No danger from them, but down at the end of the hallway, motion caught my eye, far away enough and deep in the shadows that I couldn't make out more than a blur.

The blurs solidified in another second. Krin, dozens of them. The Syndicate.

"Shit," I murmured, slapped Shindo on the arm. "We got trouble, man."

He took a look back at the Krin enforcers advancing at a quick jog, hands filled with clubs and knives, but just grunted and turned his attention back to the arena. I followed his gaze to the galloping herd of Gan-Shi, who hadn't stopped, hadn't charged into the remnants of the Anguilar troops, just changed course to head straight for us.

Gib and I backed out of the way, making room for the herd to squeeze through the entrance, and I expected them to keep moving, but they slowed as they came inside, and at the head of their column was Warrin, his teeth bared, snot bubbles coming out of his elongated nostrils.

"Greetings, human," he rumbled, shoving an Anguilar pulse rifle at me.

I grabbed it, and the mere feel of the weapon brought a broad smile to my face.

"Nice seeing you again, Warrin," I told him as another of the Gan-Shi handed a rifle to Giblet. "If we're going that way" —I pointed down the hallway toward the Krin—"we might want to think about clearing the tunnel of all those damned snakes."

Warrin snorted a laugh and tossed his head.

"It will be my pleasure." He turned back to the others, now packed into the corridor shoulder-to-shoulder. "Do not stop until they are jelly."

Watching the herd charge through the arena had been impressive, but watching them gather momentum again in the enclosed tunnel pounded through my skull like the drum solo from "In-A-Gadda-Da-Vida." The Krin must have been just as impressed as I was because their jog slowed to a walk, and from the hesitation in the front ranks, if they could have gotten the entire crew moving the other direction, they would have.

It wasn't happening. Warrin and his group looked as if they'd been waiting for this opportunity for their whole lives and weren't about to let it go to waste. Finally, the Krin at the front of the crowd managed to get it through to the ones in back that they had to go back the way they'd come, but it wasn't going to happen in time. The herd smashed into the Krin like waves washing over a beach, and this time, the cries of the injured and dying were loud enough to penetrate the drumbeat of the feet against the stone floor.

"Who the hell *are* these guys?" Giblet yelled into my ear.

"These are the Gan-Shi," I told him, "and this is Shindo. They're apparently on our side."

"We are on our own side," Shindo corrected me. "But for now, our sides run parallel. Come with me. There is someone you must see."

Following him wasn't easy, not when the floor had turned into a morass of mushed and shattered Krin, some of them still alive, though barely. Especially not when I had to back through some of it, keeping an eye on the other entrance into the arena to make sure the Anguilar didn't follow us through. I didn't believe they would…Zan-Tar was aggressive but not stupid, certainly not foolish enough to rush into the unknown with an enemy he'd never encountered before.

"They would have come with us," Shindo added, uncharacteristically loquacious as we picked our way through the carnage and the bodies. Well, Gib and I did. Shindo wasn't tentative at all about stepping on the Krin, be they dead or alive. "But my part required subterfuge, and they couldn't have matched either the speed or power of the herd."

I expected the rest of the Gan-Shi to be heading for one of the secret hatches down into the Below, retreating from sight again, but they'd slowed to a fast walk through to the other side of the dressing rooms, then waited for us. And emerging from the last of those rooms, tiny and insignificant compared to the towering Gan-Shi but entirely momentous for me, were Chuck and Laranna.

Both of them looked like they'd been through the wringer, their stolen Anguilar uniforms ripped, burned, and stained with dried blood, a bandage wrapped around Chuck's upper arm, another taped to the side of Laranna's head, but to me, they were the most beautiful sight in the world. Wordlessly, I ran to her and nearly dropped the rifle as I pulled her into my arms and kissed her. She returned it with equal passion, and the only reason we broke it as quickly as we did was the all-too-real possibility of the enemy finding us there and shooting us in a compromising position.

"I thought you were dead."

The words came from both of us at once, antiphonal only by a fraction of a second, and we both laughed.

"I guess I should have known better," she said, grinning churlishly. "I see you found a way to justify taking your shirt off." The concern in her eyes undercut the humor in her voice as she looked at the blood-stained rags wrapped around my hip.

"Are you okay?" I asked, touching the bandage at the side of her head gently.

"I have the mother of all headaches," she confessed, "but Shindo carried me all the way back to the Below, and the Mothers treated my wound and Chuck's. I can move and I can fight, and that's all that counts now."

"I'm fine, too," Chuck noted drily, pursing his lips as if waiting for a kiss, and I would have shot him a bird if I'd had a free hand.

"And how about me?" Gib wondered, spreading his arms. "I mean, I'm glad you two didn't get killed, but I *have* been a POW here for weeks!"

Laranna glared at him, clutching the handgun she still retained from the original battle.

"Yes," she agreed, "and if you hadn't been stupid enough to go running off into the first trap the Anguilar set for us, maybe we wouldn't have had to sacrifice our alliance with the Americans and nearly gotten all three of us killed trying to rescue you, you idiot."

Giblet winced, clutching at the red-stained bandage on his chest as if the words had opened the wounds again.

"Ouch! I suppose I deserved that, but couldn't the recriminations wait for our ingenious getaway?" He looked around. "Which, by the way, how is that supposed to work again? I mean, I assume you brought a ship with you, but now that you guys were blown and Charlie got himself captured, I assume they've locked down the docking bay."

"It wouldn't matter if they hadn't," I said, shaking my head, eyeing Shindo sidelong. "The Gan-Shi risked their lives, not just of their males but of their entire species on Wraith Anchorage, women and children, to get us out of the hands of the Anguilar. We're not abandoning them here to be hunted down once Zan-Tar gets his shit together."

"We're not?" Chuck asked, blinking as if in surprise before he shook his head. "I mean, no, of course we're not!"

"So, where are we going, then?" Gib demanded, wincing at the pain his instinctive shrug caused his shoulder. "I mean, the Anguilar have cruisers…they could stand off and reduce this entire city to ashes in an hour."

"The enemy has cruisers," I agreed, smiling thinly. "And I know a place where we can get one, too."

27

"Do we have a plan?" Giblet asked, shuffling along at my elbow. "Or is this our usual make-shit-up-as-we-go-along MO?"

"What do *you* think?" I asked, cocking an eyebrow at him without looking away from the corridor.

"Making shit up as we go along it is," he sighed. "Why do I bother to ask?"

"Could you possibly stop talking?" Laranna hissed, glaring back at him.

I had to agree, but I was grateful she'd said it instead of me. The train tunnels creeped me out. I'd been on the trains and had a fair idea of how fast they got up to in these tunnels, and all it would take was one of them interrupting our trip, and there'd be nothing left of the four of us or the Gan-Shi herd except a red mist. Maybe some of us could escape that fate if we were lucky enough to be able to crowd into one of the maintenance alcoves, but those were spaced out every half-mile or so and weren't nearly big enough to fit us all.

I tried not to look down the tunnel, at the vanishing point where the distant, dim glow of the light strips disappeared into darkness. Instead, I kept my eyes down on the cracked and worn surface of the maintenance walkway or on the massive, rippling muscles of the back of the Gan-Shi, even though the bastards made me feel entirely inadequate.

I'd asked Shindo why we couldn't use the Below to get around without detection, but his reply had been terse and to the point.

"Shipyards were built after the city was completed. Trains reach it. Our tunnels don't."

And that had been about all I'd been able to get out of him. Laranna hadn't been much more talkative, pleading a nasty head injury and lack of coherence until well after the plans had already been made, so I'd decided to try Chuck.

He hung back at the rear of our formation, nearly twenty yards behind the last of the Gan-Shi, doing the right thing, turning to check our six every few seconds.

"What's the story?" I asked him quietly. "How did you get the old cow to agree to come rescue us?"

"*I* didn't," he informed me, laughing softly. "*He* did." Chuck pointed at Shindo, in the rear rank of the Gan-Shi formation—though it was more of a movie queue than a tactical formation. "While the Mothers were patching Laranna and me up, he really laid into them, told them that if they were going to let us die fighting their enemies, he'd take as many of the males who would follow and go after us himself. The Elder was *pissed*." Chuck shaped a silent whistle and shook his head. "Damn, I thought they were going to lock horns, if you'll pardon the expression, like right in front of everybody, and I wouldn't have been willing to give odds who'd win that one. But the nasty older bull, Warrin, he came in on Shindo's side and told the Elder Mother that he'd go with him anyway even if she didn't order it. Surprised the hell out of me, and Shindo, too, I think."

I grunted noncommittally, not sure how to take that. I didn't know either of them well enough to make a judgment, but I sure wouldn't have expected Warrin to warm up to Shindo after the way he'd acted around him before.

"Thank God for small favors," I said, then motioned ahead. "I assume there's some plan to keep us from becoming bug splatter if one of those damned trains comes through? Or to keep the Anguilar from just sucking the air out of here and letting us all choke to death?"

"They have people who do grunt work on the maintenance crews for the trains," Chuck explained. "They're supposed to have them all shut down, trapped between stations. He shrugged. "That's taking a lot on faith, but the alternative was doing nothing, so…"

I nodded, then sucked in a breath and wiped sweat off my forehead. It wasn't hot down here, but it was just as stuffy as the Below, maybe even more so, and I was suddenly keenly aware of how much everything hurt, from my head right down to my feet but particularly the parallel gouges at my hip.

"This place is like twenty-five miles long," I reminded him. "How long is this hike gonna be?"

"Not much longer," he assured me, then shrugged. "I mean, I'm estimating because the maps they had of this place were scratched out on a wall with a piece of chalk, but the arena isn't that far away from the shipyards. The problem is, once we get out of this tunnel, there's gonna be an Anguilar security checkpoint."

"And did Shindo have any ideas about *that*?" I asked, eyes going wide.

"Diversions." Chuck snorted his skepticism. "They're going to have their people stage attacks in other parts of the station, try to make Zan-Tar think that's where we're hitting. Theoretically, there're no security cameras in here, mostly because the Anguilar didn't particularly care if any of the locals got themselves killed wandering out onto the tracks."

"Saying shit like that just makes me feel *so* confident about being out here," I told him, wincing. "I hope those diversions work, because we have about twenty rifles between the three hundred of us."

"Well, that's the other thing that's on the other side of the security checkpoint, apparently," Chuck said, grinning. "An armory."

Something ahead drew my eyes forward, a glint of light at the end of the tunnel, one that I dearly hoped wasn't an oncoming train, and the entire column of Gan-Shi stomped to a halt. Shindo turned, waiting for me with a look of impatience that silently asked why I wasn't up with him already. Jogging wasn't easy, not after the last couple days of abuse, but I did my best.

"The next train station is the closest to the shipyards," he told me when I'd come close enough for him to make the announcement without raising his voice. "We'll stop here and send a scouting force ahead." His head cocked to the side as if he were testing me. "We can't simply bash through the security checkpoint as we did at the arena. There are emergency seals there that can be brought down in seconds, and if they're lowered, not a million Gan-Shi could break through them."

I nodded curtly.

"Us four and you," I told him. "We could get away with pretending to have a single Gan-Shi worker with us, but not more than that."

"And you will not attract attention," he wondered, eyeing me up and down, "looking like you've just been through a war?"

"Given that they had to have heard what's going on here on the station," I replied, shrugging, "I think that will work just fine."

"Help!" I croaked, Chuck supporting me under one arm, Shindo half-dragging me by the other. The limp was affected but just barely, my hip spasming and cramping with each step. "We need help!"

A half a dozen armored Imperial soldiers advanced cautiously from the security checkpoint, their uniformed officer trailing behind. Even the officer lagging behind them, as if he was afraid to leave the desk behind its transparent blast shield, wasn't Anguilar by species, not out here on an armpit posting like this. Another Krin. Zan-Tar might be a bigshot, but before he'd brought his mission to Wraith Anchorage, it hadn't even been important enough for me to know it existed. All the ships we'd seen outside had begun construction in the last few months, just since the Anguilar defeat on Earth.

"What the hell is going on out there?" the Krin officer demanded, hand on his holstered sidearm as he approached behind the screen of armored infantry. "We had most of our troops called out for disturbances all over the station, and now we haven't heard anything in nearly half an hour!"

"It's the resistance!" Chuck told him, the desperate fear in his voice worthy of an Oscar. He pointed back the way we'd come. "They're hitting the city everywhere! They've shut down the trains and killed everyone in the arena!"

"Comms are down," I added, inserting a pained wince that wasn't acting. At least comms were down to this section because the Gan-Shi had smashed the relay module between here and the arena. With their hands. "General Zan-Tar sent us out to tell you to close the emergency seals and get ready to withdraw all troops to the completed cruiser to clear the base and prepare for dust-off so we can bombard the captured portions of the station."

The words flowed out like verbal diarrhea, off the cuff and straight out of my ass, but while they tumbled free, my eyes wandered independently of my mouth, scanning the scene behind the group. There *should* have been dozens of troops at the checkpoint, at least if the reports from Mayak and Shindo were accurate, but all I could see was this handful. Beyond the shielded security station, with its controls to lower the massive wedge of metal that was the emergency seal, there was nothing but open space right up to a dead end with three metal portals, each heavily armored and secured like a bank vault.

To the left, the armory. To the right, what I assumed was a storehouse of vital parts for the ships under construction—power cells, proton cannons, and hyperdrive coils, if I had to guess. And straight ahead, beckoning like the Holy Grail, the airlock to a tender, an orbital transfer shuttle meant to take personnel and troops out to the spaceships under construction.

"What's this *thing* doing here?" the Krin asked, sneering at Shindo as if he'd just noticed him, though how he could have missed a seven-foot-tall minotaur was a mystery.

"He's loyal to us," I assured him. "We ordered him to help carry me after I was wounded so my subordinates could keep watch with their rifles."

I still had mine, of course, slung across my back, and I took my arm off of Chuck's shoulder and patted the stock, then kept it there, just one sharp move away from pulling it to the front.

The Krin's eyes narrowed as if he'd suddenly developed a working brain, and I knew that was a bad sign.

"If you want," I said, taking a limping step away from the silent, statue-like Shindo, "I can send him away now that we've arrived." I nodded to the Gan-Shi. "You may go."

I'd never know if the Krin would have accepted that and let us through because Shindo had been waiting for the word *go*. It's amazing how fast something as bulky and ponderous as the Gan-Shi could move when he wanted to. I didn't even see the punch that connected with the Krin until it was on the backswing and the officer had already flown six feet through the air, his head at a *wrong* angle when he landed with a heavy thud.

That was the trigger for the rest of us, and I didn't waste time making sure the others noticed it, trusting them as I always had. Just a push on the buttstock of my rifle and the weapon swung around under my arm, the muzzle coming upward until it came even with the chest of one of the armored troopers, and I pulled the trigger with my left hand, awkward but faster than trying to move my right into position from the stock.

The long burst at nearly point-blank range blasted right through the trooper's chest plate before he or any of the others could react to the death of their officer, and flashes of actinic lightning from either side of me told the tale of Laranna, Chuck, and Giblet, which I had to think meant four of six down. I shifted my hands into a proper grip on the rifle, hunted for the last two, and found one of them just as he brought the yawning muzzle of his pulse weapon in line with Shindo.

I wasn't the only one who shot the trooper, three crimson threads of scalar energy intersecting on his torso and ripping him to pieces in a shower of sparks and a wave of heat. But that left one of them still standing. Over the last couple years, I'd developed, if not quite a spidey-sense, at least a sort of mental image of each battlefield I was on, a general picture of where every combatant was located. And I had the sudden, sickening realization that the last remaining Imperial armored trooper was on the other side of our line, blocked from all of our lines of fire by Shindo.

We could either shoot through the Gan-Shi or let him be

shot, and probably a couple of us hit as well, and looking at things from a purely tactical point of view, we should have done it. *I* should have done it. I didn't, even knowing it could mean our deaths, because I'd developed another sense in the last couple years, one even more useful. Who I could and couldn't trust.

Shindo didn't let me down, and he didn't stand there and let the Imperial soldier shoot him, either. I didn't know what species was inside the visored helmet, but the trooper had to weigh at least 250 with the armor, yet Shindo lifted him three feet into the air with one hand gripping his neck and the other pushing the receiver of the Anguilar rifle into his armored chest.

The trooper blasted a spray of rounds into the far wall, kicking his legs like an infant throwing a fit, before Shindo slammed him headfirst into the floor. The metal of the helmet rang on impact with the stone, and maybe the armor was protection enough to keep the blow from killing the Imperial soldier, but sufficient concussion passed through for gloved hands to go slack, and he dropped his rifle.

Shindo pulled the soldier into a bear hug, then twisted his head until the helmet stared backward and the armor went limp, dragging down limbs with no power to resist. I took a step toward the security station, but Laranna was faster, sprinting the thirty yards like she was in a high-school track meet. Her hands flew over the controls, and the armory door slid aside with the annoying musical accompaniment of warning buzzers, and Chuck jogged over and ducked into the armory. I gritted my teeth at the possibility that some fail-safe system could trap him inside, but there was nothing we could do about it.

I'd expected Shindo to run back the half-mile or so to the train station and let the others know it was safe to come out, but instead, he put his head back and bellowed a warbling, basso-profundo roar that could have been heard back in DC, I was sure. Before the echo had died, another roar answered.

"They're coming," he told me.

"Go get yourself a gun," I said, nodding toward the armory. He frowned, and I figured he had to be thinking about the beliefs he'd followed till now, the ways of the Mothers. Pacifist, unwilling to touch a weapon even if that somehow meant they could kill the shit out of each other with their bare hands in ritualized fighting.

Finally, though, he nodded, a motion that seemed somehow final, a verdict handed down by a hanging judge.

"I think we all will."

28

"Do you think they know we're coming?" Chuck whispered, hanging over my shoulder in the tiny cockpit of the tender.

Looking back at him, I rolled my eyes.

"Even if they do, they're not listening in on us."

He shrugged but didn't look embarrassed. Just nervous. I couldn't fault that. The tender was barely larger than a lander except most of this ship was cargo and troop space, with precious little for the drives. In fact, calling the glorified maneuvering thrusters that were all the engines the thing had *drives* was a gross exaggeration. If the cruisers orbiting Wraith Anchorage launched a single fighter, we wouldn't be able to run from it for more than a minute before it blew us out of space. And forget fighting. The only way to make the little tin can into a fighter would be to open the airlock and fire a pulse gun out the door. Which would have been problematic since we weren't wearing spacesuits.

Hell, I didn't even have a *shirt*.

"Getting cold?" Laranna asked from the pilot's seat, the corner of her mouth quirking up as if she'd read my thoughts.

"How can you tell?" I asked. "Do I have goosebumps?"

"You have something," she smirked, looking at my chest, and I covered my nipples demurely.

"I don't know how you guys can be so casual about this shit," Chuck admitted as the distant, gleaming spider-web-in-the-dew of the construction yard grew into the hundred-yard-wide network of superstrong tubes connecting the hulks of Anguilar cruisers, more intimidating with each second of forward travel. "I mean, we left Shindo and his people there on the station, and sure they have guns but none of them have any experience with the things. But we're counting on them to keep Zan-Tar occupied while we *somehow* take this cruiser."

He motioned broadly at the warship, which was nearly complete and less connected to the construction web than the others, as if the thing were less a spiderweb to capture errant flyers and more a series of cocoons turning caterpillars into butterflies.

"And even then, even if we can commandeer the thing, even if it's operational, there are only the four of us to fly it in combat against *two* other Anguilar cruisers! And that's not even considering the concept that maybe the Anguilar have gotten tired of you stealing their cruisers and, I don't know, maybe installing biometric security or something."

"The Anguilar *have* been too full of themselves to bother with that kind of thing," I told him. "But yeah, you're right, with Zan-

Tar in charge, I don't know we can count on that kind of sloppiness anymore."

Chuck made an interrogative face.

"And if they did? If we can't just sit down at the controls and fly the thing?"

"Then we'll figure something out," Giblet told him from where he searched through a utility locker in the back of the tender. "Haven't you got that yet? It's what we do. Not saying I'm crazy about it, but that's what we do."

"Oh, yeah?" Chuck snapped, turning on the Varnell. "Is *that* your style? Because it seems to me like *your* style is doing whatever you think is right and the hell with the rest of us."

Giblet paused in his search through the locker and scowled at the Ranger officer.

"Yeah, I screwed up," he admitted, though there was nothing apologetic about his tone. "I was stupid, thinking with my heart and not my head, doing exactly what the Anguilar wanted me to do. And you guys should have stayed home and let me die for being an idiot. But that's not what we do, is it?"

"When I screwed up," Laranna put in quietly, no looking away from the controls and the fast-approaching bulk of the cruiser, "and got myself captured by the Anguilar on Strada, Gib and Charlie and Brazzo and Lenny all came back for me, even though they could have been killed." She glanced back and smiled at me. "That was because Charlie was in love with me, but the others came along without question."

"That's all good," Chuck said, "and I can appreciate not leaving your buddies behind, but if you want to win this war, at some point, you're going to have to start acting like an army, not the damned Scooby Doo gang."

"The what?" Giblet asked.

"Never mind. It just means you need to start thinking about more with your head than your heart."

"Maybe you're right," I admitted, reaching over to cover Laranna's hand with mine, "but I don't know if that's the kind of leadership this kind of army would follow."

"Here you go, fearless leader," Giblet said, tossing something at me. I caught it by instinct, a bunched up wad of fabric, and unfolded it to find some kind of sleeveless T-shirt that looked as if it were designed to be worn under the combat armor. "Looking at all that hairless monkey skin is turning my stomach."

I pulled the garment on over my head, gaining a little in the way of psychological comfort, the slightest relief against the chill on the little ship and not much protection other than that.

"Thanks, Gib," I said, nodding to him. "Is there anything else back there we can use?"

"No battle armor or plasma guns, if that's what you mean," Giblet replied with a shrug. "There're some space suits, though. Not sure what we're gonna do with them…"

I looked from Laranna to Giblet, the most obvious enemies of the Anguilar state, the ones who'd be recognized by their species the easiest.

"I do."

THE AIRLOCK OPENED with a metallic clunk, and on the other side was an Anguilar officer. Not a Krin, not a Copperell, nor any of the other subject peoples, because they didn't allow anyone but pure-blood Anguilar as officers on board their star cruisers. The disdain in his face when he saw Chuck and me standing in the cruiser's utility lock was evident, the normal look-down-the-nose superiority of the Anguilar when met with any other species. He probably felt as if he could afford to be disdainful with the four armored troopers as his escort. At least that part was good thinking when investigating an unexpected ship, maybe a result of Zan-Tar trying to hammer tactical thinking into his people.

"What the hell are you two doing here?" he demanded. "We have no scheduled deliveries until tomorrow!" Keen eyes looked us up and down. "And why do the two of you look like you've been rooting around in garbage like a pair of scavengers?"

"Pardon our appearance, sir," I said, using my best bowing-and-scraping attitude, copied from what I'd seen of the Copperell serving in the Imperial military. "But have you not received warning from the main station about what's happening there?"

Chuck glanced at me sidelong, eyes narrowing as if in critique of my acting abilities, but I ignored him.

"There's some problem with the comms," the Anguilar said with a shrug. "No surprise on this ancient junkpile. Why? What have you heard?"

"We were sent here by General Zan-Tar," I told him, nearly sighing in gratitude that the communications sabotage had worked. "There's been a resistance attack, and they've recruited the Gan-Shi to their side. Things are bad, sir." I shook my head, spreading my hands as if to show my various cuts and contusions. "General Zan-Tar is evacuating to his cruiser, and he wants to make sure that this ship is away from the construction web and safe before the resistance can get their hands on it." I cast my eyes downward, trying to demonstrate the desperation and fear I sold him. "It may be necessary to fire on the city."

Come on, I urged silently. *Let us in. Don't we look beat-up enough for this?*

The officer's scowl turned into a thoughtful frown, and I could see the wheels turning behind his cold eyes. He couldn't contact the city, couldn't get orders from his commander, and if I'd been dealing with the Krin or the Copperell, that might have been enough to make them hesitate, to wait and see if someone else would take charge. But he was Anguilar, and every one of these cocky sons of bitches thought they should be emperor.

"You say the general may be trapped in the city, eh?" he asked, a glint of avarice and naked ambition in his eyes. "Then we shall be forced to come to his rescue, no?" He motioned at us with the sort of dismissive wave that a French chef might make when telling his waiters to clear away food that had fallen to the kitchen floor. "You lot, get yourself to the troop quarters, clean yourselves up, and put on presentable uniforms. And I don't want to see you looking like this again for as long as you're under *my* command. I don't care if it's the end of the Empire."

"Yes, sir!" I agreed readily. "Thank the gods that this ship is ready to launch!"

"Ready to do more than launch," the Anguilar harrumphed,

pausing as he'd been about to turn away. "Fully armed and more than able to lay waste to this garbage dump on our own!"

And that was all I needed to know, but I wasn't yet ready for the conversation to end, because I had to keep their attention on us and away from the auxiliary airlock across the compartment... and the flashing yellow warning that the outer door had opened.

"Sir," I said, raising a hand as he was about to turn away again, gesturing at my wound and Chuck's, "may we have your permission to go to the medics and have our injuries treated?"

The Anguilar's reply was a sneer.

"We have no medical crew on board, of course. We barely have a complete bridge crew and only half our allotment of engineers! Go see to your own wounds and make yourselves useful... we have only the one squad of soldiers for security, and we'll need you both in armor, whether you've trained at it or not."

The light turned green, and a cheerful tone chimed as the inner lock door opened, a sound I couldn't distract them from. Gun barrels that had been pointed in our general direction turned along with visored helmets, and if the last one to react was the officer, that wasn't a shock, but it also meant he was the only one to see Chuck and me pull out our handguns.

He opened his mouth to shout a warning, hand going to his own holstered sidearm, but both were interrupted by a burst from my pistol. His ambition died with him, and Chuck and I might have, too, if Gib and Laranna hadn't flown out of the airlock, spraying pulse fire from their rifles. I dragged Chuck to the ground with a hand at his collar just ahead of the shower of sparks and debris from the armor spalling away under the withering barrage of rifle fire. By the time I disengaged myself from him and got my pistol around, all four of the troopers were already toppling like trees in a hurricane.

"Check fire!" I yelled, jumping up before the last hollow thump of metal as the armored corpses fell to the deck.

Rifles littered the floor, and I availed myself of one rather than retrieving the other two spares Gib and Laranna had carried with them outside on the hull of the cruiser once they'd slipped out of our airlock during the docking procedure. The Empire-issue space suits looked like burlap bags wrapped by belts in some Depression-era child's Halloween idea of Buck Rogers. Built one-size-fits-all and cinched down with adjustment straps, the only things that weren't outsized and misshapen were the helmets, adjustable on the inside.

Visors popped up, revealing the faces of my wife and best friend.

"Laranna, you and Gib get to engineering!" I ordered, jogging past them, seconds ticking down in my head. "Chuck, we're going to the bridge! I figure we got about two minutes before they're both locked down, so move!"

29

I should have been more worried.

Not that I *wasn't*, but I should have been more. This was a desperation move, no sugar-coating it, something we'd done before but with more people, with support, with something resembling a plan. I'd come to Wraith Anchorage with no thought other than to free my friend, certainly hadn't intended on fomenting a revolution, and now I felt like one of the fellowship in that first Lord of the Rings movie, running from one collapsing section of the Stairs of Moria to the other just ahead of the inescapable claws of the Balrog.

They'd only made their escape through sacrifice, and I was deathly afraid that the sacrifice was gonna be one of us. We'd already come inches from it, not for the first time, and there were only so many times you could roll the dice before they came up snake eyes. If it was me, I wouldn't mind it—that is, I wouldn't mind it if it meant the others got away. That wasn't my fear, it was that I'd lose someone else.

It was a constant background hum, like working next to a transformer, the entire time Laranna and I had been together, sometimes louder than others, and right now, it should have been the scream of a passenger jet on takeoff, but it was still that background hum.

Empty corridors blurred by with one open door after another, giving testimony to the accuracy of the Anguilar officer's account of his personnel, and hope of everything going smoothly built momentum with each section we cleared.

Barely a full bridge crew. Half an engineering crew. No other troops. It calmed my breathing despite the outright sprint, kept my heart rate at closer to normal when I had no reason to be that confident. Everything going well meant that there was an inevitable bottomless pit looming ahead. Or maybe it was just a function of how freaking crazy the last couple years had been that in a situation where even if we took this ship, we still had to face down not one, but *two* other cruisers with a crew of four, I still thought things were going too well.

We hit the intersection that split between the fore and aft sections of the ship and didn't spare a word for the parting. I wanted to look back, to get one final memory of Laranna just in case, but the clock inside my head was one of those movie bomb timers with big, red letters counting down. There wouldn't be functional security on this ship yet, not with the skeleton crew, which meant there'd be no one watching the spy cams from the utility bay, but when the officer in charge of the construction—

their equivalent of a major, if I'd read the markings on his uniform correctly before I shot him—went to check on an unscheduled docking and didn't radio back within two or three minutes, some bright boy would start using their head and get the idea to seal things up and shut things down until they found out what was happening.

Most of the ship lingered in a dolorous, dingy half-light, about one section in three illuminated from the overhead panels, maybe because all the power hookups weren't complete yet or maybe in some sort of energy-saving mode. The shadow reinforced the ghost-town atmosphere in the ship, and it wasn't until Chuck and I reached near enough for the harsh light of the bridge to take its place as the last beacon in the chain that I thought about how we'd handle the bridge crew.

That is, I knew what I *should* do, but I hadn't actually forced myself to face it until that moment. *Shit*. I guess if you wanted a clear conscience, you shouldn't fight a war.

The bridge crew didn't look at all what I expected, because I suppose I'd expected a conventional contingent as I'd seen on the rest of the Anguilar cruisers I'd boarded. The cutting edge of the Anguilar military, simply because they couldn't risk untrustworthy or disloyal troops on the bridge of a weapon this powerful. That must not have applied to the teams they left on ships under construction.

Five crewmembers, four of them enlisted techs—Copperell—and only one Anguilar officer, the helmsman. He was also the only one armed. I saw them a long time before they noticed me, close enough for me to give the techs nicknames in my head.

Porky, the one with his head halfway into an exposed panel and his gut straining his uniform tunic. Bugs, the one holding the wall up, supervising Porky, his sobriquet forming because of ears that made his face look like a taxicab with the doors left open. Daffy, just because his cynical laugh was the last thing I heard at twenty yards away, right before one of them turned and saw us. Smurfette because she was the first female I'd seen in the Imperial service, even if she was deep amber instead of blue.

Then there was the Anguilar helm officer, who I didn't bother to call any name other than Anguilar because the hell with humanizing these guys. He'd been in the middle of a tirade against Smurfette when Chuck and I entered the collar passage to the bridge, the narrow tunnel that could be sealed off in an emergency, and the female Copperell's eyes went wide as she looked past him at the two humans rushing them.

"Why aren't you looking at me when I correct you, you ignorant breeder?" the Anguilar snapped in the instant before his gaze automatically turned to catch what had distracted Smurfette.

He went for his gun even in the face of two rifles, suicide, yet I didn't believe it was because the Anguilar were determined to go down fighting. I already had proof that wasn't so. No, I think it was because they were such vain, self-important assholes that they didn't believe any inferior species could actually get the drop on them. Given another moment to reflect on the situation, he might have made a different choice, but time wasn't a luxury we had.

Chuck and I fired at the same time, and either one of us would have been enough to put an unarmored Anguilar down.

Together, we blasted bits of him across the main view screen, and Smurfette screeched as she wiped flash-cooked Anguilar off her face. The rest of the Copperell gawked at the two of us, the smoking muzzles of our pulse rifles, and their hands went up, their faces, whether pudgy or homely or duck-lipped, went from deep tan to something much paler.

"Please don't hurt us!" Porky begged, dropping a wiring tool from his hands, then waving them to show they were empty. "We give up!"

And they meant it, even Smurfette, who'd recovered from her shock remarkably quick and dropped out of her chair and onto her knees, pleading for her life.

"You're him, aren't you?" she asked me, hands spread out on the floor in front of her, eyes wide as she stared up at me. "You're Charlie Travers."

"You're with the resistance," Bugs added, and the way he said it made it seem less an accusation than a prayer. "They've tried to keep what's happening a secret, but the rumors are all up and down the fleet." His hand shook as it went from a straight-up-and-down surrender to a gesture my way. "You're the one who blew up the *Nova Eclipse*."

"You killed Seraph Nix," Daffy put in, a manic snort that was the closest he could come to a laugh punctuating the words. "And you took back Strada. Everyone knows it."

"We want to surrender," Smurfette reiterated, standing, hands held high. "We want to defect." She shook her head. "Almost every Copperell I know who's in the Imperial military would defect if they could get away with it."

Chuck and I exchanged a look. Was this for real, or was it just some new strategy to get our guard down before one of them tried to kill us?

"Watch them," I instructed Chuck, then hunted on the comm panel for the intercom link to engineering. Finding it, I touched the button to open a line. "Laranna, Gib, this is Charlie. We have the bridge secured. What's your status?"

"Um, Charlie," Laranna replied after a beat, with a hesitance in her words I was unaccustomed to hearing from her, "we've got a situation here. There are three Copperell engineering techs in engineering who say they want to defect. I can't be sure, but I think they're telling the truth."

"Yeah, we got four of them up here, too," I informed her. "And I don't know what the hell to do with them because we don't have enough spare people to keep an eye on them and don't know the ship well enough to try locking them up somewhere."

"We could put them on the tender," she suggested. "Deactivate the engines and lock them in."

"Don't lock us out!" Smurfette insisted. "We can help you. You're taking this ship, right? We can help you operate it."

"We want to join you," Porky said with a stutter ironically appropriate for his sobriquet. "Let us prove ourselves."

I wanted to say no, a reflex as natural as breathing and just as sensible. We didn't know these guys, and putting them in charge of systems during combat was a particularly stupid form of suicide, and yet…

There were four of us. Chuck at weapons, me at helm,

Laranna and Gib in Engineering, making sure nothing shut down power to the drives or the weapons. No one to work the comms, no one to monitor damage control, no backup at all, and if it was theoretically possible to run a ship this size with four people, it certainly wasn't dealer recommended. I closed my eyes, knowing my time was limited. It wouldn't take forever for Zan-Tar to figure out where we went and that we weren't still on the station, and if those cruisers hit us before we were out of the web, we were dead.

"All right," I said, "this is how it's going to work. Laranna, you have the main controls in your station and deactivate the rest. Gib holds the gun and mans the door, the others monitor the systems, and if there's a problem, they tell you. Anyone makes a break for the door or tries to take control of engineering back from you, they get shot. Clear?"

"Clear. Good luck up there." If Laranna disapproved of my decision, her voice didn't betray the feeling, and I had the sense that she trusted my judgment without question, which both comforted me and yet also made me intensely uncomfortable.

"What about us?" Smurfette asked, the hopeful expression on her face contrasting sharply with the blood spatter from the dead Anguilar on her uniform tunic.

"Chuck," I said, "you remember how to operate the weapons on one of these things?"

He'd been one of the first people we taught, because it was my policy to have as many of our leadership positions as possible filled with personnel who were cross-trained in basically everything we might do, so they could teach it to others. But that had been weeks ago, months even, and it wasn't as if the intervening days had been uneventful.

"Yeah," he confirmed, sliding into the seat at the tactical control station and pulling on his restraints. He set his rifle against the bulkhead, tucked into a nook formed by the juncture of two different stations, and drew his handgun, then set it on the control panel beside his right hand. He nodded to me. "Ready when you are."

I scanned the faces of the others, searching for duplicity, deceit, bad intention, but not finding it. If any of these four were spies, they were *good* spies, excellent liars, and I just didn't see how Zan-Tar would have been able to predict any of this enough to get a crew full of well-disciplined Copperell operatives on this boat.

"Any of you know how to fly this thing?" I asked them. "Because if I have to fly it, then you're all getting locked up in the tender. The only way this works is if someone else mans the helm and I watch everyone."

"I've been cross-trained at helm," Bugs said, his expression twisted in disgust, "but do I have to"—he motioned at the remains of the Anguilar officer draped over the helm station— "*touch* him?"

I rolled my eyes at the Copperell, grabbed the Anguilar by the shoulder, and hauled his corpse away from the control panel, then dragged it out to the bridge entrance and tossed it aside. It wasn't a dignified or respectful way to handle the dead, but if I hadn't had any use for the Anguilar when he was living, I had even less concern for him now that he was a sack of burned meat.

I mean, no group of people is one hundred percent bad, but when you self-select the most ruthless, ambitious, self-important pricks from a society of intergalactic pirates, every single one of them males trying to make sure they got to breed and have their bloodline in the ruling class, well…it's a little easier to dehumanize an enemy like that. I didn't recall Poppa Chuck crying too much about the Luftwaffe pilots he shot down or the bombs his plane dropped on Germany during the war.

Bugs pulled off his tunic and did his best to wipe blood and other nasty bits off the chair and the control panel, and Porky went to help, cleaning hologram projectors with his sleeve. I cleared my throat and made a hurry-up gesture, and Bugs finally settled into the seat, then tapped the controls to life before looking back at me.

"I need someone to release us from the construction web," he said, pointing to a duty station across the bridge. "Tono can do it." He nodded to Porky, and the chubby man looked to me for permission.

"Yeah, go ahead," I told him, then I turned to Smurfette and Daffy while he took up a position in the vacant seat. "What about you two? You good for anything, or should I just have you go for coffee?"

"I'm trained in damage control and life support, Charlie Travers," Smurfette volunteered.

"Just *Charlie* is fine," I assured her. "Go ahead."

A questioning look to Daffy got a nervous chuckle and a shrug of helplessness.

"I'm just a power-feed repair tech," he admitted. "I don't

know how to operate any of this stuff. I was just up here trying to get the security cameras in the docking bay working. That's uh… that's why Major Eddo had to go in person and check out the tender's arrival."

Daffy flushed at the words, probably realizing what that meant.

"Well, thank God for you being bad at your job." I pointed to the communications panel. "Go ahead and sit there, assuming you can figure out how to open up the intercom connection to engineering."

He nodded and fell into the seat quickly, as if he was grateful to be out of range of my attention. Just what kind of reputation did I have among these people? Maybe I didn't want to know.

"I'm disengaging the magnetic grapples," Porky—*Tono*—announced, tapping a series of controls. "Then we should be able to use maneuvering thrusters to get out of the construction web as long as…"

"Attention cruiser G-45781," a nasally Anguilar voice echoed off the bridge bulkheads, and Daffy started, would have jumped right out of his chair if he hadn't been strapped in. "You are not cleared to power up your reactors, and you will not be allowed to disengage from the web. Shut down your power feeds and prepare to be boarded."

"They've overridden the locks," Tono warned, a plaintive whine in his voice, as if he expected me to blame him for the failure. "We're not going to be able to pull away…"

"Not with maneuvering thrusters," I agreed, then bared my

teeth in a grin. "You, Bugs," I said, pointing at our helmsman, "full power to the plasma drives. Blast us right out of this shit."

"But that could burn right through the hull if it conducts with the web," he blurted. "And my name is Quorra, not Bugs!"

"Your name is Bugs," I told him, jabbing my finger his way, "until you get us the hell out of this web!"

"Yes, sir," he said, gulping. "Full power to the drives, sir."

"Daffy," I said to our impromptu communications officer, "get me engineering."

"Daffy?" he repeated, but did as he was told and nodded to me. "You're on with them."

"Laranna," I said, "the bastards are onto us, and they've locked us in."

"What are you going to do?" she asked me, nothing but certainty in her voice, like she knew I'd already made a decision.

"Kick the door open. Everyone down there should strap in and get ready for a jolt."

"Oh, Travers," Gib moaned in the background as if he understood completely what I meant. "You're not going to do what I *think* you're gonna do, are you?"

"Most likely."

"Hey, Travers," Chuck said, then shook his head. "I mean, *sir*. I think those Anguilar cruisers are heading our way."

I checked the sensor readout and saw the avatars that I knew the Anguilar used for friendly ships curving around the other side of the collection of white polygons that represented Wraith Anchorage. On an intercept course.

"Bugs," I said, a hard edge to the words, "full power. Now."

30

I REALIZED a moment too late that I hadn't bothered to strap in and only had time to grab at the back of the nearest acceleration couch before the gigantic ship bellowed her defiance and threw herself against the golden chains restraining her. Some ancient god shut within a mountain tomb for thousands of years, finally awakening and bent on vengeance.

The poetic imagery did nothing to make the ride any smoother, and the ship did her dead-level best to shake herself to pieces as the stern view of the construction web disappeared in an eruption of white sunfire.

"Damage control?" I yelled over the crescendo of the roar. When Smurfette didn't reply, I yanked myself close enough to smack on the shoulder, her head snapping around in alarm. "Damage report!"

She nodded and squinted at the readouts, and I wondered if

she'd be able to focus on them with the vibration of the superstructure.

"The shields are holding," she told me. "But not for much longer…"

Something broke. At first, I would have been willing to bet it was the hull cracking in half, overstressed by the tug of war between the drives and the magnetic anchors of the construction web, but a sudden lurch forward overcame the limitations of the inertial dampeners and tossed me forward hard enough that my grip on the seat nearly pulled my arm out of its socket.

"We're free!" Bugs exulted, and the view on the forward screens confirmed his boast as the main body of Wraith Anchorage leapt toward us, along with the two Anguilar warships.

"I can see that! Hard to port! Thirty degrees and take us down to half power."

The ship groaned at the maneuver, as if she'd spent her strength breaking her bonds and had little left for gallivanting around on another quixotic mission.

"I'm getting feedback from the sublight drives," Smurfette reported, brow knitted in a frown. "I think they may have taken some damage during the burn. Deflection off the magnetic anchors."

"Is there anything we can do about it?" I asked her, but she was already shaking her head.

"Not without putting back in at another drydock," she said. "But if the drives are misaligned, we could rip the hull apart under heavy boost. We should think about jumping to hyperspace and getting out of here."

"Duly noted."

"They're hailing us!" Daffy squealed. "It's General Zan-Tar!"

Because of course it was. Instead of being stuck on the station, safely insulated from all the decision-making and out of my hair, the tricky bastard had managed to catch a shuttle to one of the cruisers.

"Put him on the main screen," I instructed. "Chuck, arm the main guns and target whichever one of those ships the transmission comes from."

"And how the hell am I supposed to know *that?*" he wondered, though he still went through the motions of feeding power to the particle cannons.

"Daffy, which ship is the hail originating from?" I asked. The Copperell scowled at me, apparently no fonder of his nickname than the others were of theirs.

"I'm not a communications tech," he reminded me. "How the hell would I know? Do you want the message on the screen now?"

Damn, these guys were copping an attitude already, and they'd just defected a few minutes ago.

"Bring it up," I told him. "Chuck, get ready to aim the main guns at the ship on the right." Not because I knew Zan-Tar was in that one, but we had to make a choice, and we'd be in firing range in less than a minute, if I was reading the sensors right.

Zan-Tar didn't look any prettier projected larger than life on the screen than he had face-to-face in the cell, but I preferred him far away.

"You're full of surprises, aren't you, Mr. Travers?"

I'd expected anger, maybe even outrage. After all, I'd not just screwed up his little plan to deliver me to the Emperor, but I'd done it after convincing him to let me die in the ring defending Gib, and that had to sting. But instead, there was amusement in his expression, maybe even admiration.

"Not my surprise this time, General," I told him, counting off the seconds until weapons range in my head. "It helps to have friends."

"I wasn't speaking of your jailbreak," he corrected me. "That was a simple matter of recruiting allies, and you've shown a true talent for that." Zan-Tar grinned almost in genuine good humor. "Almost as much of a talent as my people have for making enemies. No, what I refer to is your decision to stand and fight rather than making the sensible decision to flee while you could." He shrugged. "Not that I didn't expect you to come after your friend, of course, though that was, like this, a suicidal gesture. But once you had him, against all odds and all reason, I would have thought you'd count your luck on your way back to your homeworld."

"That's the thing about recruiting allies, though," I reminded him. Thirty seconds until firing range. "You can't just make promises and then skip out on them. Maybe that's why you guys have so many problems making friends."

"Oh, you mean the Gan-Shi?" he asked, his smile broadening and taking on a savage edge. "I'm sure they're having a wonderful time slaughtering the Krin Syndicate…and more power to them. The only reason we tolerated the Syndicate at all was that they kept the food moving. With them cleared out and the Gan-Shi having revealed themselves as treasonous, our way forward is fairly clear. We'll slaughter the stupid cows and replace them with workers from Copperell. There are too many of the useless bastards on our headquarters world as it is, just mouths to feed who never lift a finger. Here, they can grow our food and supply the shipyards for our inevitable attack on Earth." I didn't think it was possible for an expression to grow that cruel and still technically qualify as a smile. "Of course, the city won't need to be nearly as big for that. I suppose we can start reducing costs by blasting the Below with a particle barrage…"

I wanted to tell Daffy to cut the transmission, but I didn't trust him to find the control quickly enough, so I lunged over and did it myself.

"Helm, cut forward thrust, spin this ship one hundred and eighty degrees just as fast as you can, and half power ahead!"

I'll give Bugs credit, he didn't question me, didn't point out how big of an idiot I was being, just carried out his order wordlessly. Though that might have been because he was scared of being noticed by Zan-Tar, and at least I was turning us around.

This time, I grabbed the restraints of the command chair and pulled myself into it against the angular momentum. I didn't know how the inertial dampeners worked, but whatever gravitic magic they commanded had its own weakness—angular momentum. It leaked through every time, trying to pitch me across the bridge, and only the safety harness held me in place.

"What the hell are we doing?" Chuck demanded. "What happened to targeting the cruisers?"

"Change in plans," I snapped, brain running a few miles an hour faster than my mouth, and both of them suffering under the strain of the rollercoaster-ride swing as the ship turned on its axis. "We can't take both of them on, not with this crew. What we *can* do is make sure they don't use this shipyard for anything but recycling scrap."

"Won't that, you know, let them shoot us in the ass?" he wanted to know.

"Not if Bugs here can keep that web between us and them." I eyed the man curiously. "*Can* you do that?"

"You might have asked me that a few seconds ago," Bugs complained tautly.

"The Anguilar are coming after us full-throttle," Chuck told me. I really had to have the computer graphics on this thing changed if we intended to fly in it much longer. The translator goo in my head transformed the alien scribblings into English, but it couldn't do anything about the garish colors and twisted, nonsensical patterns they used for their sensor avatars. It took me two seconds to figure out what Chuck had seen, that the cruisers had increased speed and would be in firing range in thirty seconds. And we were at least a minute of flight time from the edge of the vast construction web.

"Can't go around, have to go through," I murmured. "Bugs, cut thrust to a quarter power, ninety degrees to port, and helm control to tactical. Chuck, you see that cruiser under construction right there?" I pointed to the skeleton of an Anguilar warship, still deep in the grasp of the shipyard's cross-hatch structure.

"Yeah?" He nodded.

"Make it go away."

His chest-deep grunt might have been his answer or it might have been an instinctive reaction to the thundering drumbeat of the steering rockets. My fingers curled in the safety harness of the command chair, the other hand clasping the rifle to my chest. I'd nearly forgotten about my determination to be the watchdog for our new Copperell recruits, not because I'd grown to trust them implicitly in the last few minutes but mostly because there'd just been too much else to think about.

If one of them wanted to betray us, now was as good a time as any, with the ship slewing sideways, pushing the others into their seats and nearly throwing me off my feet. The targeting reticle for the particle cannons drifted sideways across the main screen and finally reached the edge of the ship under construction, and I was about to yell at Chuck to fire. The man was multi-talented, though, a competent tactical officer besides being a doorkicker, and he waited until the glowing lavender triangle that the Anguilar somehow thought looked like a badass crosshairs for a big gun had centered itself on the target.

"Firing," Chuck announced.

Twin spears of unbridled atomic fury reached out and smashed through the spine of the fetal warship and through the construction web. Vaporized metal blew a clear path through the wreckage, and Bugs, bless his heart, steered us right into the center of it.

Gritting my teeth and squinting as if I were biking through a Florida lovebug swarm, anticipating the impact of the debris. Distant thumps teased me, promising something larger, something fatal, but then we were through the hole and through the debris cloud and I could breathe again.

But not relax. If we could make it through that hole, they could, too.

"Bugs, ninety degree turn to port," I snapped. "Get our nose pointed back the way we came."

The cruisers didn't follow, probably because Zan-Tar had more experience commanding a warship than I did and knew it was a trap, but their cannon fire did. What remained of the partially constructed cruiser disintegrated under the barrage from the two warships, jets of flaming plasma seeking us out, and I had my mouth open to order evasive maneuvers, but Bugs beat me to it, veering off to starboard.

"Bugs, ninety degrees starboard, and make for the next ship in the web. Comms," I said to Daffy, "patch me through to the Anguilar."

The knocking on the hull from the maneuvering rockets nearly drowned out Daffy's confirmation that we had Zan-Tar on the line, but the general's face taking up the middle third of the main screen spoke for itself.

"You don't want to come over to the other side and throw down?" I asked him, spreading my hands. "Fine. You keep talking about your fleet coming to Earth, but I'll tell you what—by the time I get done with this shipyard, there won't be much ship or much yard left of it."

There, the next one hovered in the reticle, more complete than the first, though still missing its drives.

"Fire!"

Not quite as spectacular as the first one, but still satisfying, the drive housings blew apart all the way up to the reactor core. No power cells in that one yet, but they'd have to start from scratch on the outer hull, though I couldn't have told it from Zan-Tar's reaction, as equanimous as if he'd been a circa-1987 Tampa Bay Buccaneers fan watching yet another loss.

"Oh, Charlie," he said, shaking his head, "that's the difference between us. Every ship, every resource, every outpost your resistance gains, you have to negotiate for, reach agreements with the locals, pay workers, arrange for their support. If we want to rebuild the construction web and the partial hulls you've destroyed, we'll order our slaves in the mines to produce more minerals, order our so-called *allies* to do the actual construction work, and if need be, we'll conquer some new *allies*. As I said, loyalty is often a problem in the long-term, but force works wonders in the short-term."

One of the Anguilar ships boosted our way, the other hanging back, and I didn't need Chuck's warning when it came, interrupting it with an order to Bugs.

"Full thrust, ten degrees starboard, ten degrees down!"

That was the tricky part about commanding a ship, the thing that made it even harder than learning to fly a Vanguard. In a fighter, all I had to do was react, steer the thing whichever way I wanted it to go, and after a while, it was like driving a car...it came naturally. Being the captain of a warship meant translating the instincts that told me which way to turn and how fast to run into quick and concise orders that could be followed by a helm officer who might or might not be as good steering the boat as I was.

Bugs was…pretty good. We cleared the blast zone before the cruiser fired again, and the cascade of molten metal from the construction web spun off past us, propelled by its own destruction.

"You want to keep playing Whac-A-Mole, Zan-Tar?" I asked him, realizing I hadn't bothered to end the connection and neither had Daffy. "We can do this all day, or at least until I have to go to the bathroom."

And now that I'd said it, I *did* have to go, and I cursed softly.

"Oh, no, Mr. Travers," Zan-Tar assured me, "I'll leave it to Colonel Mala-Thon to keep you occupied. I have better things to do. As I said, you have a talent for finding new friends, and that's more worrisome than your talent for stealing my ships. I can't have yet another supply of manpower, another port your ships can call on safely to cut through our territory. I'm afraid if we can't have Wraith Anchorage, then no one can."

31

THE TRANSMISSION ENDED, the full screen filled with the crosshatch of the web, at least where it hadn't been torn apart by particle cannon shots, and on the other side of it, the gleaming mountains that were the Anguilar warships. Not their actual images because battles were rarely that close in space, where point-blank range was still a hundred miles, but a simulation based on the optical cameras and the sensors. Close enough to see Zan-Tar's ship turning, boosting back toward the main body of Wraith Anchorage.

"Bugs, Chuck," I ordered tersely, pointing ahead of us as I clambered into the command chair, "full thrust ten seconds that way, then braking burn and turn us into the web for a shot that'll give us space to fly through. Clear?"

"That Anguilar bastard is going to be right on top of us," Chuck warned.

"Then you'd better get ready to take him out," I shot back, pulling on my harness, "because there are tens of thousands of innocent Gan-Shi on that station, and I'm not sitting here and watching them get killed. I asked if we're clear?"

"Yeah, we're clear." Chuck scowled. "But if we get killed, my last words are going to be 'I told you so.'"

"Duly noted. Bugs, execute."

The boost felt like nothing, wouldn't have spilled a full mug of coffee if I'd been lucky enough to have one, but the next part wouldn't be so easy.

"Enemy ship is turning to pursue," Chuck informed me, getting a head start on the whole I-told-you-so thing.

"Turn and burn, Bugs," I said as we reached the ten-count in my head.

And there was the part that overtaxed the dampeners and would surely have thrown me right across the bridge if I hadn't decided to buckle up for safety. Not as bad as it would have been without the gravity-resist technology, of course. I wasn't sure about the exact boost, but it had to be somewhere north of a hundred gravities, enough to break every bone in my body without a little alien magic thrown in to cushion things.

The bad part about that fancy, stop-on-a-dime braking, though, was just how fast the pursuing cruiser caught up with us. Chuck didn't warn me about it because he was too busy working the cannons and taking helm control over from Bugs, but I didn't need him to, not with the enemy cruiser slicing through space like a dart aimed straight at us.

The particle cannons punched through a thick filament of the shipyard facility, this time close enough that I could make out debris blasting out into the vacuum from both splintered ends of the massive cylinder. And maybe a few humanoid figures, though that could have been my imagination. Bugs took back control, shoving open the throttle and bursting through the newly opened gap in the web just as the Anguilar cruiser opened fire on us.

My gut clenched up at the flare of lightning, and the entire ship shuddered as the defense shields shed energy, but he'd jumped the gun, just outside the effective range of the weapons. Zan-Tar wouldn't have, and I suppose I should have been grateful that he'd delegated the job to this Mala-Thon dude.

"Keep the pedal to the metal," I told Bugs, my eyes fixed on Mala-Thon's ship. She'd blown past us and was in the middle of her own turnaround. My instinct was to spin us back into her, take her out, and if I'd had a full resistance crew, or maybe even a US Space Force one, I might have done it. "Take us over the top of Wraith Anchorage, around the north pole docking cylinder."

I couldn't see Zan-Tar's ship, not with optics or the sensors, which meant he was on the other side of the station, and if we didn't get to him quick enough…

"We got a thermal bloom on the other side of Wraith Anchorage," Chuck announced. It was little more than a red glow at the edges of the station's lower structures, nothing I could see on optical, but I knew what it meant before he told me. "I think they're bombarding the city."

"No shit," I ground the words out, furious at Zan-Tar but angrier at myself. Despite the fact that the Mothers had basically extorted me into the agreement, I'd still made it, still given my word that I'd free them from the Anguilar. "Get us over there, Bugs!"

"My name is *not* Bugs!" he insisted, and I would have dismissed the objection if he hadn't chosen that moment to spin us around for our braking burn.

"Chuck..." I began, about to tell him to target the trailing ship during the deceleration.

"Way ahead of you," he assured me, eyes fixed on the tactical screen.

We swung around yet again, the second hand of the galaxy's biggest clock face, turning every minute, or so it felt. With every pendulum swing of this ship, the view changed, slices of reality like riding a Tilt-A-Whirl at the State Fair. The ragged edges of the tattered construction web, the glowing bits of debris still tumbling through space from the destroyed ships, the gleaming white domes and spires of Wraith Anchorage...and the ship gaining on us. She sliced through space like a great white intent on gobbling up Robert Shaw and Roy Scheider, and all I wanted was a giant-sized SCUBA tank to stuff down her throat. What I had was Chuck Barnaby.

"Smile, you son of a bitch," I murmured as he pulled the trigger.

She was right on the edge of effective range, too far away for a surefire kill shot but too close for her shields to shrug it off the way ours had on her last attempt. Her shields flared into a sphere of blazing white, a street light coming on as dusk dropped the world into shadow. For the space of a heartbeat, I dared think we might have taken her out of the fight, overloaded her power feeds. That hope died when her drive glowed even brighter than her shields, outpacing us as we decelerated, off on a course that would take her minutes to reverse.

We'd bought time, and that was much as I could have hoped for. Another turn of the clock, another spin, maneuvering thrusters drumming their familiar song into my head, and as we arched over the north pole docking cylinders of Wraith Anchorage, my worst nightmare came into focus.

Zan-Tar's cruiser hovered in station keeping orbit about fifty miles off the ventral bulge of Wraith Anchorage, just above the south pole docking bays, pouring blast after blast of particle cannon fire into the outer shell. The city was thickly armored, enough to hold up against a meteor strike or a solar flare, but it wasn't shielded against particle cannons. Shields took hyperdrives, and no one was going to waste hyperdrives and power cells on a city too large to travel anywhere, not when a few feet of rock should have been sufficient.

It wasn't, not against point-blank shots from an Anguilar cruiser, and clouds of vaporized rock and metal floated around the cruiser, billowing into a nebula of orange and white. Worse than that, burning oxygen blossomed in short-lived flames as emergency seals were breached, and the next ones in line came down. The gap in the side of the station seemed tiny compared to the vast bulk of the thing, but it had to be over a mile across and God alone knew how deep.

Inside that section of the city, carved out of the walls, was the Below...and the Gan-Shi.

"Fire, Goddammit!" I snarled, not caring about the range, just needing to distract Zan-Tar.

"Tactical has helm control," Chuck said, and the cruiser shifted under the hammering of the steering rockets. "Firing!"

Too damned far away. The cruiser's shields lit up for barely a second, maybe enough to shake Zan-Tar's command chair, not enough to do any damage. If we'd kept our acceleration coming over the top of the city, we might have reached effective range before she had the chance to maneuver, but that would have meant sailing right by, and the entire purpose of this maneuver was to save the city, not ourselves.

"She's turning," Chuck said, "but she's not running."

That was bad news because our cannons had a few seconds before their capacitors recharged and theirs didn't.

"Helm, evasive," I snapped.

Bugs, to his credit, didn't need to be told twice and reacted with instincts that would have done any of our experienced ship crews proud. The dorsal maneuvering thrusters put their shoulders into the side of our ship and *pushed*, skidding our cruiser sideways as fast as physics would allow. Not quite fast enough.

God grabbed us by the throat and *squeezed*. The viewscreens flickered and went out, plunging the bridge into darkness, but I couldn't be sure for a few seconds if it was the lights that had failed or my eyes, because my head seemed to be as battered as the ship. Emergency lights colored the bridge a dull red before the screens lit up again, dimmer, duller, and much less informative. Optical cameras only, the main sensors down, but they told an ugly enough story.

Zan-Tar's cruiser advanced slowly, inexorably, ready to finish us off, and it took that sight to shake loose the fog over my thoughts.

"Engineering!" I rasped after wasting another second hunting for the intercom control. "Laranna, we need power now!"

"We've lost the main power trunk, Charlie. It'll take a couple minutes to rig a bypass."

And that was that. The main trunk took the feed from the power cells to the drives and weapons, and without the hyperdrives, we had no shields. A couple minutes was more than any of us had to live.

"Auxiliary power is coming up now," Laranna added almost apologetically, as if she realized what her announcement had meant and wanted to make up for it.

At least the lights coming back on made the bridge a little more cheery. Except for Porky holding his head in his hands, moaning softly, while Daffy lolled in his chair, barely conscious. The rest seemed unhurt, though it was a temporary reprieve. The return of the sensors made that clear.

Zan-Tar's cruiser was seconds away from their next shot, the one that would blow us to floating debris, and if she happened to miss, Mala-Thon's ship had managed to get herself turned around and was only thirty seconds or so from weapons' range.

A beep and a flashing light on the armrest of my command chair told me a transmission was coming in, though Daffy wouldn't be relaying it or anything else for a few minutes. I stabbed the control to pull it up, not on the main screen but the smaller one built into the armrest. It was, of course, Zan-Tar.

"I won't insult your intelligence by claiming I'd allow you to surrender," he said, tilting an eyebrow toward me. "I know you have no incentive, and as you made very clear to me, you'd rather die fighting. However, I *would* like that ship back intact, so if there's any deal to be made, you should tell me now."

"You can have this ship back in pieces," I sighed, sitting back in my chair. "Preferably about the size of atoms, since that'll hurt less. And if I have any regrets, it's only that I'm nursing a concussion and can't come up with anything pithier to say for my last words."

"It would be wasted on me," he said, spreading his hands. "I have a terrible sense of humor."

Chuck caught my attention, wiping a trickle of blood off his nose and motioning to the main screen, his expression reminiscent of a student who hadn't studied for the exam and had just found out it would be postponed. The long-range sensors had just come back online, fuzzing in and out as they built a more coherent picture of the space around us. Whatever they showed, whatever had gotten Chuck so worked up, I had the sense it would be better if I didn't give it away to Zan-Tar, and I tried to glance inconspicuously out of the corner of my eye. A pair of glowing sensor avatars teased at my peripheral vision, though what they were or where they came from wasn't clear.

Whatever they were, Chuck thought they were a good thing, which meant that I had to stall.

"It's okay," I told Zan-Tar, "no one laughs at my jokes anyway. For example, you ever hear about the Kamerian who was arguing with a bunch of Strada in a bar who the toughest of them was?" The general blinked, staring at me in confusion. "No? Well, this big Kamerian bruiser was in a bar out in the pirate sectors, and he runs into a group of Krin, and they start going back and forth about who's the toughest, the Kamerian or the Krin, and finally, the Kamerian says, 'I'll show you who the toughest is!' He runs out and comes back with a big snapping turtle, big amphibian with a shell, that once it bites down, it's hard as hell to get it to let go."

Now the entire bridge stared at me, even Chuck, who presumably knew why I was doing this, but I persisted.

"The Kamerian, he pulls down his pants and lets this big-ass snapping turtle bite right down on his unit. It just really digs in hard, and the Kamerian is obviously in agony, but he leaves it there and whips it around, smashing it into the bar, breaking glasses, knocking over chairs…then finally, after a couple minutes of this, with the Kamerian roaring in pain, he slams the snapping turtle down on the tabletop in front of the Krin and gouges its eyes out with his fingers to get it to let go of his dong. Then, he stands there in front of the Krin, fists on his hips, blood dripping from his Johnson, and says 'Can any of you wimps do that?' And the Krin are really quiet for a second until one of them near the back raises his hand and says, 'I *think* I can, as long as you promise not to gouge my eyes out afterward.'"

Zan-Tar was expressionless for a long moment, but then his face cracked and he chuckled, the laugh growing into an uncontrollable guffaw, and even the Copperell on the bridge joined in, Daffy's chortle the loudest of them. I pretended to laugh as well, but the humor didn't reach past my face, and I used the camouflage of a chuckle to duck my head and check the tactical screen. The two sensor avatars had been identified by the ship's Identification-Friend-or-Foe system as Anguilar cruisers, but also noted they'd been flagged as missing in action...and I knew exactly where.

Zan-Tar looked aside, his good humor fading as he snapped an interrogative at someone out of view of the camera, and I figured his crew had finally seen it, though I hoped not in time. The transmission ended, and I braced for the shot I figured he'd trigger now, just to make sure I didn't get away no matter what else happened.

The shot came, but it wasn't from Zan-Tar, and it didn't hit *us*. Four coruscating lances of atomic energy converged on Zan-Tar's cruiser, fired from too distant a range for any of them to be fatal, but the combined firepower of two warships unleashing their full wrath at once couldn't be shrugged off. The Anguilar ship transformed into a Christmas-tree ornament of pure white, and I hoped the converging shots had blown her up, but the glowing orb drifted away from the station, now clearly a defense shield taxed to its limits, transforming nuclear energy into kinetic.

"Colonel Travers, I assume that's you in there?" The voice came over the command chair speaker, small and tinny, yet I still recognized it.

"You're damned right it is, Colonel Voight," I sighed. "And I'm very glad to see you, though I wonder how the hell you happened to be here right now."

"We'll get into it when we're done with this, Colonel. Things to do, people to see, ships to blow up."

Zan-Tar might have heard the exchange, as fast as his cruiser boosted out of the area, but apparently, Mala-Thon on the second cruiser wasn't quite as convinced that discretion was the better part of valor because he didn't vacate the area. Instead, he charged straight into the *Victory* and the *Endeavor*, guns blazing in a headlong boost straight toward the side of Wraith Anchorage.

The American starships split up with matching starbursts of steering jets, and the particle blasts passed between them. It was the only shot Mala-Thon was going to get. This time, the range was close enough that the Anguilar cruiser had no chance of surviving the fusillade, and there was no expanding globe of a defense shield, just a static discharge as it failed. The rear half of the cruiser separated in a wash of fusion plasma and gravitic force and tumbled backward from her original course, but the nose kept its original course into the side of Wraith Anchorage.

I cursed reflexively, leaning forward in my seat as if I could pull the wreckage away from the station with my bare hands, but nothing I could do would stop it. The naked rock beneath the skin of the station's underbelly, superheated and cracked to its core by the bombardment of Zan-Tar's cruiser, shattered and peeled away, exposing a gaping cutaway of the interior corridors and compartments.

A hint of green tinted the shower of outgoing flotsam, and all it could be was the station's hydroponic farms venting into space, the source not only of food but atmospheric maintenance. The lifeblood of the entire city spewed out into the vacuum, and somewhere in the cloud of detritus had to be hundreds, perhaps thousands of dead. Krin, certainly, probably Copperell and other patrons of the Anchorage, but all I could think of were the Gan-Shi.

And Zan-Tar. His ship was nothing but a bright star of fusion plasma, burning away from Wraith Anchorage at full throttle until she reached the minimum safe jump distance and a rip in the fabric of space swallowed her up.

Gone. Leaving death and destruction behind, and it would have been easy to blame this on him, but the truth was, he was inevitable. I'd spent the last two years leading the Anguilar Empire around by the nose while I kicked them in the ass, and instead of congratulating myself, I should have been getting ready for the backlash. Zan-Tar was the shape it had taken, but the Anguilar weren't going to go down without a fight.

"Bugs," I said quietly, into the silence of a mortuary, "do we have the sublight engines back up?"

"Yes…yes, sir," he told me, the stricken look on his long face evidence that he knew what had happened and it had bothered him as much as it had me.

"Take us to the south pole docking cylinder. Chuck, tell Colonel Voight to meet us there with a squad of Rangers." He blinked, uncomprehending.

"Why me?" he wondered. "Why not the comms guy?" He gestured at Daffy.

"Because you set this up," I told him with not quite a glare but something close. "Don't bother denying it. Just get them to the dock. We have to go see if there's anyone on this station left to save."

32

"I did it for my father," Chuck told me.

I didn't turn to look at him, not from anger but because the armored space suit had shit for peripheral vision, and I had to watch every entrance in the broad corridors of the lower section of the Anchorage to make sure we weren't swamped by Krin Syndicate thugs looking for vengeance.

Well, I didn't *have* to watch, since we had a full platoon of Rangers under Colonel Chapman's personal command with us rather than the squad I'd requested, not to mention Laranna and Giblet, but it was best to set an example. I suppose we didn't strictly need the suits, since the emergency seals had cut off the parts of the city that were open to space, but the place had also taken one hell of a battering, and that was a chance I wasn't willing to take. The damage was evident even here, where the seals hadn't failed, visible in the yawning cracks in the walls, piles of debris where parts of the ceiling had crumbled.

The walkways down here were broader than the tourist areas, meant for hauling cargo, supplies in, food out, broad enough for the Rangers to walk in a classic wedge formation, which I'm sure made Chapman happy but made me more nervous since more room meant more places for bad guys to hide.

But we hadn't seen anyone, either victim or innocent, dead or alive, and I guessed it was because this section was mostly utility areas and workers' quarters, and either they'd been killed during the bombardment or they'd taken the hint and gotten the hell out to the northern half of the city. That was a relief in some ways, because we weren't equipped to render aid to the entire population, but it also meant we hadn't seen any of the Gan-Shi. Maybe because there were none to be seen.

Chuck had made the comment over the private, suit-to-suit line, though *how* private the connection actually was, I wasn't sure. Chapman struck me as enough of a micromanager that he might listen in on it, and as the battalion commander of the Rangers, he even had the authority to do it. Then again, what the hell did I care?

"George?" I asked. "What does George have to do with this?"

"He heard about the transmission from General Zan-Tar."

"Oh, yeah?" I barked a laugh. "I wonder who he heard *that* from!"

"It wasn't me," Chuck insisted, outrage bringing his voice up an octave. I turned my head to look aside at him, and the anger in his tone was matched by the look in his eyes. "I'm an Army officer. And Dad still has a lot of connections."

"Okay," I told him, making a soothing gesture. "I believe you." That seemed to pacify him, and he went on.

"He called me. Said he knew you and that you weren't going to abandon your friend. He told me I had to save you from yourself, that you were too damned stubborn to ask for help."

"And the President just signed off on this?" I asked, turning again, this time in disbelief.

"I'm not an idiot. I didn't go to the President first…or even second. Colonel Voight owed you one, so I went to her first. Then to General Gavin. He didn't approve, but he also didn't want to lose you as an asset. His words."

I grunted. That, at least, sounded like Gavin. It was honest, which indicated he was telling the truth.

"He told me to go with you, that he'd work on the President to see if he could send the cruisers after you ASAP."

I nodded, even though he couldn't see it. The rest, I'd gotten from Voight while I waited for the shuttles to meet us at the docking cylinder. The cruisers had entered the system as far out as possible and drifted in under minimum possible thrust, then waited in the cover of one of the larger asteroids. How long they would have waited there for something significant to happen wasn't clear, but as things had turned out, it had been less than two days before we'd stolen the cruiser and kicked the whole thing off.

I don't know why I was irritated by the whole thing. George, Chuck, Gavin, and Voight had saved my life, saved *all* of our lives, and done it in a way that proved I wasn't nearly as smart as I thought I was.

Okay, yeah, *that* was definitely why I was irritated, and if it was stupid, I could only plead youth. Odin had sacrificed an eye for wisdom. If all I had to sacrifice was a little ego, it was a small price to pay.

"How the hell are we gonna find them?" Giblet asked, and it took me a second to figure out he'd done it over the open frequency rather than the private one Chuck had used. "I mean, if there are any of them to find. The last we saw of the males, they were arming up to take on the Syndicate. They could be anywhere, and you saw what happened to the Below…"

He sounded truly concerned, which surprised me for a second, given that he'd barely had any interaction with the Gan-Shi. I winced as the answer became clear. Gib was concerned for the same reason I was. He blamed himself. If he hadn't come after Zan-Tar, we'd never have had to rescue him, and the Gan-Shi would never have been involved.

"We can't stay down here forever," Colonel Chapman warned. "Colonel Voight wants reports every hour, and there're no comms in here."

"If you need to go back," I told him without hesitation, "go ahead. I'd rather have the Rangers along, but I'll find the Gan-Shi on my own if I have to."

And that ended that. If Chapman thought I was going to be deferential to him because Voight and Whistler had pulled my fat out of the fire, he was sorely mistaken. I wasn't always right, but as far as he was concerned, I *was* always in command.

"If Shindo is around," I went on, answering Giblet more than Chapman, "he'll find *us*. What we need to do is find the nearest hatch to the Below. If there's anything left of it."

"Before we headed to the arena to bust out you and Gib," Laranna said, "the Mothers showed us a map of the access tunnels, just in case we had to retreat back to the Below. There should be a hatch right at the edge of the hydroponic farms." She turned and offered an expressive shrug, exaggerated enough to make it through the armored suit. "If it wasn't buried during the attack."

That seemed more and more likely as we moved through corridors increasingly choked with debris. I cursed under my breath at the legs sticking out from the edge of a couple tons of rockfall, knowing there had to be more that we hadn't seen. My teeth ground against each other at the mental image of the Gan-Shi kid we'd talked to buried under debris, and I wondered if I really wanted to find them, wanted to see the results with my own eyes.

The entrance to the hydroponic farms seemed to confirm my worst fears. The double doors had been warped and crushed when the ceiling above them collapsed, and the rubble had cut off the entire section and everything in it. The air went out of me like I'd been kicked in the gut, but Laranna grabbed my arm and pointed off to the side of the wreckage.

"There. It's still intact."

The hatch had once been concealed behind a façade, but the thin rock of the false wall had collapsed along with nearly everything else in this section, revealing the bare metal. And that big-ass locking wheel.

"Colonel Chapman," I said, "get me a couple Rangers turning that thing counterclockwise. Strong ones."

The colonel, of course, gave that order to the platoon leader, who passed it on to the platoon sergeant, who passed it on to one of the squad leaders, and finally, with typical Army efficiency, two of the bulkier Rangers in first squad slung their rifles and took positions on either side of the locking wheel. They might have grunted with effort, but their sealed helmets kept the sound effects private, their work as silent as if a couple of Lenny's construction bots had opened the door instead.

The hinges made enough noise to make up for the silence of the soldiers, though, squealing in protest as they pulled the ancient entrance open. I touched a control on the wrist of my suit, and a headlamp affixed to the center of my helmet snapped on, filling the entrance with harsh, white light.

No debris choked this tunnel, just a fine layer of dust that seemed to cover every surface, most of it still hanging in a cloud that shifted with the breath of the ventilation system. I looked back at the others.

"We don't need the whole platoon down here," I decided. "Chuck, you're with me."

He hesitated a moment as if my decision surprised him but then followed me down the stairwell. I picked my way carefully, the confines of the helmet keeping me from seeing my feet or looking at the steps as we descended. The armor of the suit and the padding inside it would probably keep me from breaking my neck if I did fall, but it wouldn't protect my dignity, and that was almost as bruised as my hip and head. I'd grabbed some ibuprofen from one of the Rangers when we were suiting up, and the handful of Vitamin-I had at least dulled the pain of my injured hip enough to allow me to get into the suit, but the stairs taxed the capacity of the medicine, and I wasn't sure how long I could keep this up.

Any of this.

It was a good ten minutes of descent before we reached the first hatchway, the uppermost of the Below levels, and I wondered if we should just go all the way to the bottom and work our way up…or as close to the bottom as we could travel, given that at least half of it was open to space. Deciding I didn't have the patience to wait that long to find out, I waved Chuck toward the locking wheel and put my back into turning it.

My back didn't like that much, and warmth trickled down my leg from where the wound in my hip reopened, but there was nothing to be done about it. Carbon dioxide built up inside my helmet, not enough to restrict my breathing but enough to cause helmet panic. By this time, I knew what it was and that it wouldn't hurt me, but it bugged me that the American-issue space helmets lacked the ability for me to unlock and lift the visor to get a breath of fresh air.

The wheel broke free, and Chuck stumbled back while I had to stomp a foot down to keep from lurching forward. Regaining our footing, we yanked the portal open, and the faint illumination from the strip lighting of the stairwell gave way to utter darkness, broken only by the glow of our headlamps.

Standing in that glow was Shindo.

He raised a pulse rifle toward us, and I held my hands up, palms out, and yelled over my suit's external speakers.

"Wait! It's me, Charlie!" When he paused, I worked the latch for my helmet and twisted it off, the air down here even stuffier than I remembered, the ventilation system finally shut down after all these centuries. "I'm glad you're still alive," I told him. "The Anguilar are gone, but we couldn't stop them in time…"

I couldn't finish the sentence, helpless in the silence we shared.

"How did you get here?" Chuck asked him. "We left you and Warrin and the other males at the Anguilar construction docks."

The question was enough to get Shindo talking when my expressions of regret had not been.

"We slaughtered the Krin Syndicate enforcers who came to oppose us and were on our way to the fortresses of their masters when the word came of the attack by the Anguilar. Warrin led most of the others into battle while I returned to the herd."

"Did…" My mouth went dry, and I had to swallow and try again. "Did you make it in time?"

By way of answer, Shindo stepped aside, and when I moved farther into the doorway to follow, my headlamp shown across a chamber much smaller than the veritable city I'd seen lower into the Below. Reinforced with thick bands of the same type of alloy used in starship hulls, it was maybe a hundred yards across and just as deep.

Packed shoulder to shoulder, wall to wall in the shelter, were what had to be well over 20,000 Gan-Shi, females and children mostly. The previous antipathy was gone, and in their cow-like eyes, I saw only fear and desperation.

"The Elder Mother stayed at the rear," Shindo said in a low rumble. "Until the others had cleared the area. She was struck by debris and killed, along with several hundred of the older females of the herd. They are near panic."

"It's all right," I said, yelling the words to carry. "It's gonna be okay! The Anguilar are gone, and we're going to take care of you! I promise!"

"And how," Shindo wondered, "are you going to do that?"

That was a damned good question. I hoped I could come up with a damned good answer.

"No," Warrin said. "We will not stay here."

We'd found him and the rest of the males—the ones who'd survived—resting in the arboretum outside the smoldering, blackened remains of what had been the Syndicate estates. The idea of a suburban subdivision crossed with a 19th-century Spanish fort and plopped down in a gigantic space station was counterintuitive, but the Krin were making the most of their position, and apparently their idea of comfort wasn't too different from ours.

Or hadn't been when they were still alive. Krin bodies littered the ground, most of them still smoldering from the pulse rifle bursts that had killed them, but others with their limbs and often heads askew. Carnage, and if I didn't feel sorry for a bunch of Krin gangsters who'd made their living forcing otherwise peaceful

Gan-Shi into a position where they had to fight to the death just to keep from starving, neither was I jumping for joy at having been the instigator of the slaughter.

Had the conquerors been human or Kamerian, they might have been lounging languidly inside the palatial mansions of their newly defeated enemies, but Gan-Shi weren't big on living under a roof, I'd noticed. Some of the males *were* sitting or lying down, though I would have been willing to bet those were the injured.

The rest stared at our Rangers with dull distrust, probably thinking we looked too much like Anguilar troopers in our armored spacesuits. Shindo had the same sort of expression as he met Warrin's gaze.

"Warrin, that decision is up to the Council of the Mothers and the"—he tripped over the words, emotional for perhaps the first time since I'd met him—"whoever the new Elder is."

The corridors behind us were crammed with Gan-Shi women and children, gawking like tourists at the luxurious housing of the upper floors of the station, seemingly not bothered by the carnage left over from the battle with the Krin. Here and there, a few of the older children would duck into doorways and emerge with armfuls of food in small kitchen containers or water jugs to be passed around.

"No, it's not." Warrin's jaw was set in stubborn, unyielding insistence, and I sighed, wondering what Chapman thought about arguing with a bunch of cow people.

"Look around," I told the old bull, waving at the mass of the herd, and the empty areas the Krin had once ruled. "The Syndicate is done. The Krin and their gangs are either dead or in hiding, or they took off at the first sign of the Anguilar attack. The entire station is yours. You can make it what your people once dreamed of, the Convergence, a place where you can affect change."

I was leaving out the part about the Anguilar coming back to finish the job, but I hoped we could do something about that.

"Our people have lived too long without a real sun over our heads," Warrin insisted, "without real grass beneath our feet. But that is not the reason." He shifted his rifle to his left hand and pointed into the Krin fortress with his right. "Inside there is a monitoring center for this station." He shrugged. "Not the main control center, just an auxiliary, but it shows the readings from the main one. Which is now destroyed, thanks to the Anguilar."

"What is it, Warrin?" Shindo asked, stepping nose to nose with his elder in a challenging gesture that was met by a snort from the other bull. Shindo backed up a half-step, and Warrin relaxed. "What did you find out?"

"This place was never in a stable orbit around the system's sun," Warrin told him, though he looked around at the rest of us as he spoke. "Its position is constantly corrected by steering jets running at low yield almost constantly. Those thrusters were disabled or destroyed during the attack by the Anguilar. It will take months, but this entire city will burn up in the sun, and there's no way to reverse it in time."

"Well...*shit!*" Chuck swore, staring at the Gan-Shi open-mouthed. He'd taken off his helmet once we were out of the southern regions and away from the heaviest damage, and Laranna and Gib had done the same, which I suppose was a result of my poor example, but I figured with the size of the city, we'd have plenty of warning of a catastrophic atmosphere venting. "What the hell are we gonna do now?"

"We get them all out of here," I said. Every eye turned toward me, and I sighed. "It's the only answer. And we owe it to them."

"But, Charlie," Gib said, eyes wide, "there are like twenty thousand of them!"

"The Liberators," Laranna said, and I nodded.

"We have to send out the call, get all five of them out here. It'll still be a tight squeeze, and God knows, they're all going to have to be hosed out pretty good afterward, but we can manage it in time."

Just, but I didn't say that part. These people needed hope, not something else to worry about.

"And take them where?" Chuck asked, shaking his head. "I mean, as much as I think America's open-minded about taking in political refugees, these guys aren't going to want low-rent apartments in Minneapolis."

"Maybe Strada?" Gib suggested, eyeing Laranna. "There's plenty of open space there."

"And plenty of predators that would make a quick snack of Gan-Shi children," she reminded him. I thought of my first night on Strada after bailing out from a crashing Starblade, and nodded.

"There's only one place we can take them," I said. "Sanctuary. Open spaces, no really dangerous wildlife, and plenty of farmland to support them."

"I have heard of your Sanctuary," Warrin said, his expression thoughtful. "Neither the Krin nor the Anguilar would find us there. I say this is where we should go." He looked at Shindo. "What say you, brother?"

Shindo regarded him silently and took a moment to look out at the gathered ranks of his people before turning to me.

"This Sanctuary," he said. "What is it like?"

"Only a small portion is settled," I told him, smiling in memory of the place. It felt like forever since I'd been there. "Most of the continent where we have our farms and training grounds is uninhabited plain, rolling grasslands where only the wind makes a sound."

Shindo nodded.

"Then I would see my people have a home under the sun and the sky. But for me…and, I think, for many of the younger bulls, our fight isn't over. You work to free those such as us. We fought with you for liberty or death. I am not dead yet, and like your Harriet Tubman, I would still see those like me taste liberty."

I offered Shindo a hand, not knowing if his people had the tradition of shaking or not, and he took it.

"Welcome to the war, my friend."

33

"You caused me no end of trouble, you know that, Charlie?"

I stared out General Gavin's window at the Potomac River, wondering how many years it had taken the man to earn this view. It was majestic, a fitting reward for a lifetime of service, yet I didn't envy it. Offices like this and the rank that went with them were as much a prison as the cell I'd endured on Wraith Anchorage.

"I know, sir," I told him. "But I also know you sent Colonel Voight after me."

Gavin shrugged as he joined me in the window, a shot glass in his hand. It was mid-afternoon, but I suppose it was five o'clock somewhere.

"Care for a little Grey Goose?" he asked, lifting the glass in salute.

"Thank you, sir, but no," I said. "My body clock is all messed up, and I had what I guess you could call breakfast about an hour ago."

Gavin nodded understanding and downed the shot anyway, then sighed with contentment.

"It's gotta be a weird life, bouncing around between the stars. I wouldn't mind taking a ride in one of those ships myself. If I could ever convince the President to let me take the trip." He eyed me sidelong, the corner of his mouth turning up. "Of course, now, we'll have one extra cruiser for me to choose from when the time comes."

"Maybe," I countered, meeting his glare when it came.

"I pulled your ass out of the wolf trap, son," he reminded me.

"You did," I acknowledged. "And I'm grateful." I turned away from the view and paced back across the office. "But I think we've been getting some things bassackward, General. When I came here, it wasn't so I could keep stealing cruisers for the USA until you didn't have to worry about an Anguilar attack anymore. You'd never get there, not if I hijacked another dozen of them. The Anguilar lost a shipyard at Wraith Anchorage, but they have others, and I can't touch them yet, not from here."

"Then why *did* you come?" Gavin asked, setting the glass back on his desk.

The words would have sounded more natural if spoken in anger, yet the tone behind them was more curious than furious. Maybe the vodka had chilled him out enough to deal with my insubordinate ass. Was it against regs for him to be drinking here?

Was there anyone short of the president who could give him grief for it?

"I came here because the resistance needed an ally," I reminded him. "Because you're the only planet around with this big a population that hasn't already been taken over by the Anguilar. We need your help hitting them where they live. I want an entire combined arms division ready and under my command in six months or I'll resign my commission and pull everyone out. No more training, no more fabricators, no more fusion reactors."

That got a rise out of the man, and he turned on me, anger sparking behind that controlled expression.

"I could have you court-martialed for disobeying orders, stealing government property, kidnapping Major Barnaby, and assault on that Air Force SP."

"You could," I acknowledged readily. "And then I'd resign my commission and pull everyone out, and if you tried to have me arrested, my wife, a full wing of Vanguards, and a few platoons of Strada would break me out and kill anyone who tried to stop them. You'd have two cruisers, a couple wings of Starblade fighters, a few hundred pulse rifles, and no way to make any more." I cocked an eyebrow at him. "I've been gone a few weeks. Is the fusion reactor completed? The fabricators? Can you finish them without the Peboktan helping?"

Gavin shook his head, though it was clear he didn't want to admit it.

"The Liberators are going to be busy for a few months ferrying Gan-Shi back to Sanctuary from Wraith Anchorage," I said, sitting down in a chair across from his desk, not caring if that was some kind of breech of protocol since he still stood. "Until then, we've had to send the Vanguards back to watch over Strada and the other resistance worlds. I won't do anything until the Liberators are back in place and we have the Vanguards at our disposal. Worst-case scenario, you have *three* cruisers, the Starblades and a couple complete fusion reactors, half a dozen fabricators, and the ability to make a lot of your own weapons. Best case…" I shrugged. "Best case, the United States is the leader of the planet in an optimal position to be a major player in interstellar politics."

Gavin sat on a corner of his desk, tapping a finger against its mahogany surface, staring back out the window but at nothing in particular.

"I can sell that," he granted. "Not easily, but the new cruiser helps. I'll have to run it by the President…and explain exactly why I allowed you to run off after your friend and sent our only two starships after you, but winning cures all ills."

It did, even if I hadn't strictly won this battle on my own.

"Details, Travers," Gavin pressed. "I'm going to need details. Where are you taking my people, and why? Who's in command, and how much say do our officers get in the planning? These are all things President Louis is going to need to know, not to mention the Senate." He snorted a humorless laugh. "At least this time, we don't have to worry about any of the sloppy bastards leaking it to the press, not unless the Anguilar have managed to plant spies on Earth."

"A combined arms division," I reiterated. "And that's going to be the entire Ranger battalion, the new armored battalions, Marines, special ops, the works. The ground commanders will have input to their use, and I swear to you that I *will* listen to them, but final say has to be mine." He opened his mouth to object, but I cut him off. "Whatever you may think of my military experience, sir, we both know I don't waste people's lives, whether they're human, Strada, or anyone else."

Gavin nodded reluctant assent, and I went on.

"We start training in a month, ship out in six months, deploy for at least another six, maybe more unless you can train and equip their replacements in time."

The chairman of the joint chiefs grunted like I'd kicked him in the stomach, and I knew he had to be imagining the costs of doing just that.

"And the cruisers stay here?" he reiterated. "The fighters, too?"

"Yes, sir. Unless I find out the Anguilar are targeting you and you need to deploy forward to stop it. The cruisers stay in this system."

Gavin nodded, blowing out a long breath as if surrendering to the inevitable.

"And where exactly are *my* troops going, Colonel Travers?"

"Copperell, General." I caught a glimpse of my reflection in the framed West Point diploma on Gavin's "I-love-me" wall, and the face staring back at me bore little resemblance to the disaffected college kid I'd once been, or even the Army officer I'd wanted to be. "The Anguilar Imperial headquarters. We're taking down their Empire, and it starts on Copperell."

"Fine." Gavin's expression hardened, all the give suddenly gone. "But no more personal vendettas, Travers. If you're serious about fighting a war, then we fight it like professionals, not some damned hill tribe in the Middle East settling old scores. That's non-negotiable, and I don't care how many cruisers you pull out of your ass. Try anything like this again, we'll pull out and take our chances against the Anguilar on our own."

"No more vendettas," I promised, briefly offering him a three-fingered Boy Scout salute. "I have Giblet's word. He learned his lesson." I cocked my eyebrow toward him. "But I can't promise there won't be any more rescue missions. Just like the Rangers, General, and just like *you*...we don't leave our people behind."

Gavin made a face but then allowed it to relax into a thin smile.

"I suppose that's the best I can hope for." He sighed. "At least this one was far enough away that we can spin it however we want. That's the advantage of an interstellar war—most of the fighting will be so far away, there won't even be cell phone videos on the internet." The scowl emerged again. "Though we might have to include some embedded reporters."

"Oh, wonderful," I moaned, covering my eyes. "Because there's nothing that makes a military campaign run smoother than a bunch of reporters. It worked so well in Vietnam."

"Then let's do better than Vietnam," Gavin suggested. "Let's do better than we have in any war since then. I'm giving you the division, Charlie, but you and I both know they're only going to mean something if you fight this war to win. I know your grandfather was in World War Two. Did he tell you what we had to do to win that war?"

"He did," I acknowledged, controlling the wince that wanted to break through the stone face I affected. Poppa Chuck had told me all about bombing German cities, about making deals with the Soviets despite what we knew they were going to do. About the refugees they couldn't help because they had to keep moving. "I'm hoping it doesn't come to that. The Axis in World War Two didn't have anywhere to run. The Anguilar do…they're nomads by nature. If we make things too hard for them to keep hold of here, I believe they'll pack up their shit and vacate this galaxy."

"And if they don't?" he pressed, rising from his desk and standing over me, though I didn't believe he was trying to intimidate me so much as get the measure of me. I stood up from the chair and met his steady stare.

"You're a young man with a relatively clean conscience, Travers," Gavin went on. "No one wins a war with a clean conscience. I need to know if you're willing to do what's necessary."

Images passed across my memory. Jax, dying for his people. Brazzo, dying for his friends. Dani, dying for no reason at all. And Zan-Tar laughing at that stupid joke like it was the funniest damned thing in the world just after killing hundreds of people.

"Yes, sir. I'll do whatever I have to."

I owed too much to too many to do anything else.

Amazon won't always tell you about the next release. To stay updated on this series, be sure to sign up for our spam-free email list at jnchaney.com.

Charlie and the rest of the crew return in Sanctuary's End, available on Amazon.

CONNECT WITH J.N. CHANEY

Don't miss out on these exclusive perks:

- Instant access to free short stories from series like *Backyard Starship*, *Sentenced to War*, and more.
- Receive email updates for new releases and other news.
- Get notified when we run special deals on books and audiobooks.

So, what are you waiting for? Enter your email address at the link below to stay in the loop.

https://www.jnchaney.com/taken-to-the-stars-subscribe

CONNECT WITH RICK PARTLOW

Check out his website
https://rickpartlow.com

Connect on Facebook
https://www.facebook.com/DutyHonorPlanet

Follow him on Amazon
https://www.amazon.com/Rick-Partlow/e/B00B1GNL4E/

ABOUT THE AUTHORS

J. N. Chaney is a USA Today Bestselling author and has a Master's of Fine Arts in Creative Writing. He fancies himself quite the Super Mario Bros. fan. When he isn't writing or gaming, you can find him online at **jnchaney.com**.

He migrates often, but was last seen in Las Vegas, NV. Any sightings should be reported, as they are rare.

Rick Partlow is that rarest of species, a native Floridian. Born in Tampa, he attended Florida Southern College and graduated with a degree in History and a commission in the US Army as an Infantry officer.

He has written over 40 books in a dozen different series, and his short stories have been included in twelve different anthologies. Visit his website at **rickpartlow.com** for more.

Printed in Great Britain
by Amazon